WITHDRAWN

REVOLT
AGAINST
ROME

REVOLT
AGAINST
ROME

MARK RICHARDS

ISBN Paperback: 978-0-578-69668-3

Printed in the United States of America

Book Cover and Interior Design: Creative Publishing Book Design

For my grandchildren, Ian, James, Kara,
Owen, and Mera.

PROLOGUE
WINTER AD 26
The Territory of Germania Inferior

Gerfrid clamped his jaws shut to stop his teeth from chattering and pulled his ragged wool cloak tightly around him. It did him little good on this brutal evening fit neither for man nor beast. He peered from the prow of the small skiff he had hired to take him across the Rhenus to the opposite shore, where the Roman fortress of Valkenberg awaited him. He could scarcely see on this moonless night as the sleet whipped about on the uninviting, frigid waters of the swollen river.

Ignoring the weather and his passenger, the boatman stroked his oars in stoic silence. The only sounds were that of the creaking oars punctuated by an occasional grunt, followed by tiny splashes. The wind blew hard against them, inhibiting the progress of the small vessel. This was the widest part of the Rhenus just before it debouched into the *Mare Germanicum*. No doubt the rower was fatigued and laboring hard, but since he was getting triple his normal fare for this evening's work, he did not complain.

Gerfrid had traveled several days across the lands of the Frisii: first, south on the Vecht River to where it intersected the Rhenus and then west along the river toward the sea. This crossing was the final leg of his journey. He had news—no, urgent news—that he needed to convey to his Roman handler, for he was an informer. In exchange for coins—on occasion a generous sum—he provided information to his master, Quintus Sorvinius, a Roman official stationed at Valkenberg. Gerfrid was a member of the Frisii, a powerful German tribe that dominated large swathes of lands in the northwestern section of Germania, which bordered the sea to the west and extended inland. He kept Rome informed on the doings of the Frisii for, even though they were a staunch ally, Rome was always eager to learn of the activities of the German tribes—friend or foe.

But why had he—a native Frisian—ended up a spy? This story traced back to his birth. When he was born with a withered right arm, the tribe pronounced that he would be useless in most endeavors. He could not be a warrior or farmer, could not harvest timber or raise cattle—the principal economic activities of the Frisii. He was shunned by his village, and there was not a woman suitable for him. But Gerfrid discovered his niche: what he lacked in terms of physical prowess, he made up for in mental acuity. He was quick of wit and a survivor. He curried favor with the Romans and reported his observations of the Frisii's activities and, in exchange, was compensated well for his services. He did all of this in secret, of course, for if his people discovered or even suspected his duplicity, he would be executed in a most painful manner. He did not view his actions as traitorous for, in his mind, he owed no loyalty to those who had disdained and rejected him. He was not worried about anyone being alarmed by his absence from the village. The cruel truth was that no one really cared if he was missing.

The boat continued making plodding progress as the weather turned even uglier, if that were possible. The northern wind picked up and blew sleet sideways. At last, he spied in the gloom the flickering torches from the watchtowers of the fortress at Valkenberg. "Almost there. I'll bet Sorvinius rewards me well for the information I bring him tonight. Wait till he hears this.

The boat glided into the shallows and thrust itself upon the shore with a gravelly crunch. Gerfrid was a cautious man. He had requested that he be dropped off some distance above the quay so that no prying eyes would spot him—his life depended on it. On meticulously counting out the agreed-upon sum of Roman coins and handing them to the boatman, he nimbly leaped upon solid ground. Without a word, the boatman turned about and rowed back into the waterway. Gerfrid looked around to get his bearings and then headed downriver. The shoreline was barren except for the looming silhouette of the massive fortress up ahead. Upon arriving at the gates, which were closed as usual at this time of night, he cupped his hands around his mouth and shouted in guttural Latin at the guard high up in the nearest watchtower, "I am Gerfrid and have urgent news for Quintus Sorvinius."

A bored Roman legionnaire peered from above and replied gruffly, "Wait, someone will be with you shortly." After a brief delay, the gate edged open. An *optio*, the commander of the guard on this unpleasant evening, appeared. He was heavily armored and kept his right hand near his sheathed *gladius*—the small, notorious Roman stabbing sword that had carved out an entire empire. He repeated his reason for requesting entrance. In response, the optio grunted and motioned him to enter and follow him. Gerfrid trod down the wide avenue through the freezing slush, which further numbed his already frozen feet. They passed barracks, workshops, and supply buildings, now silent and shuttered. He stumbled on in the darkness before arriving at the headquarters of his Roman benefactor.

* * *

Quintus Sorvinius worked by an oil lamp. He had finished his evening meal some time ago and since he was not sleepy, and there was little else to do on this winter night, he continued with his tasks. The *Saturnalia* festival had been celebrated weeks ago and the month of *Decembris* had passed by them. They were now entering the coldest period of the year. Various dispatches were piled on his worktable, waiting to be recorded and sent to Rome. Quintus's job was to log all communications and correspondences bound for Rome and the other parts of the empire and ensure that they were sent in a timely manner through the various ships docked in the harbor of the *Mare Germanicum*. He knew that the Governor and the various legates of Germania, who commanded the military fortresses along the Rhenus, found it irksome that all letters and official correspondence had to go through him. However, that was the way it had been mandated by the all-powerful rulers of Rome.

Sorvinius was a retired centurion. He had served faithfully in the Roman legions, mostly in Germania, including a span of ten years under the leadership of Tiberius Claudius Nero, now Emperor Tiberius, the most powerful figure in the western world. Quintus owed his present position to the Emperor. The imperator trusted him implicitly and knew he was a loyal subject. And because he was trustworthy, he had unofficial duties as well. He was an informant;

he supplied reports to Tiberius on not only the Germanic tribes but the Roman occupiers as well, and for good reason. Germania had seven legions—the highest concentration of legions among all the territories of the empire. Tiberius wanted to ensure that the legions along the Rhenus remained loyal to him. It was prudent to keep a wary eye on the military commanders as one of the legates might decide he would make a better emperor and march his troops on Rome. Then, there were the Germans. The border of Germania was considered the most volatile in the empire, an area simmering with revolt. The lands along the Rhenus had remained calm for the last fifteen years but that was no guarantee that the peace would endure, though Tiberius desired it.

Quintus paused his work to draw his cloak more closely around him, and he rubbed his hands together to warm them. The several glowing braziers in his room generated meager heat on this glacial night. He could never get used to the deep cold that gripped the land at this time of year. It was not that he was complaining. How could he after the turn his life had taken once he'd retired from the legions: the most powerful man in the world, Tiberius Caesar, called him a friend, he had a military pension from his years of service with the eagles, and he was paid handsomely in his current position. What was not to like? It was quite an improvement for a dirt-poor farm boy raised in the mountainous regions far north of Rome.

His musings were interrupted by a knock at the door. His Greek freedman, Chelos, entered. "Sir, there is a German named Gerfrid here to see you. He says he has urgent news."

It was late, and it was cold. How impudent of the man to show up at this hour. His first instinct was to send him back out into the night and tell him to wait until morning, but then, he thought better of it. Why would Gerfrid want to see him at this late hour and in such dreadful weather? If the man had traveled in weather such as this, it must be something important. He had brought him valuable information in the past too. Sorvinius sighed. "Very well, Chelos, send him in."

Gerfrid entered the room, stomping his feet to get the feeling back in them.

Sorvinius examined the wretched figure before him. Crusted ice clung to his heavy cloak, his hair was drenched, and his teeth chattered. Yet, despite this, his eyes burned with a glowing intensity. Sorvinius's senses heightened and his stomach churned. He had a feeling there was something gravely amiss in the land of the Germans.

"Gerfrid, what brings you out at such a late and gloomy hour as this? Perhaps you have news of significance for me?"

Gerfrid responded in broken Latin, "My apologies for the late hour, but I bring important news that, I believe, you would want to hear immediately."

Sorvinius nodded. "Out with it then. You know I value these tidbits you pass along."

Gerfrid coughed and wiped his mouth on his sleeve before he began. "Two days ago, the various tribes of the Frisii gathered in Eadric's village. You know of Eadric. He is one of the most respected chieftains of the Frisii clan. That is why they chose his settlement to meet. They discussed the tax levies imposed on them by the new Governor. There was a general—what do you call it—oh yes, a consensus, among the tribal chieftains. They believed it would be impossible to pay the taxes without selling their lands and indenturing their families into servitude." He glanced upward at Sorvinius to gauge his reaction.

Sorvinius sighed impatiently. "Go on. Out with it."

"The tribal leaders agreed that they would continue to plead their case with the Governor. But if they are unsuccessful, they will revolt against Rome. They are beginning to prepare for war."

Sorvinius attempted to maintain a neutral expression as he contemplated his informant's words. This could just be a rumor unsupported by any facts. "I see. And you came by this information...how?" he asked sharply.

Gerfrid didn't shrink from the question. He replied boldly, "I was at that meeting. I volunteered to make sure there was enough ale to go around. I listened to every word."

Sorvinius fingered a small sack of coins and tossed it to his informer. "You have done well, Gerfrid. Keep me apprised of any future developments." As the Frisian turned to leave, Sorvinius interjected, "Oh, and as usual we will keep this information and our little meeting to ourselves. Understood?"

Gerfrid nodded and departed.

Spurred by the news, Sorvinius pushed aside all the other documents littering his table and immediately began composing a letter to the Emperor, detailing what he had just heard. Upon completion, he eyed the parchment one more time. He was about to add it to the pile of other dispatches going out, but he paused. He knew that all official correspondences were reviewed and vetted by Tiberius's praetorian prefect, Lucius Aelius Sejanus. He neither liked nor trusted the praetorian chief. In his opinion, the man was a ruthless snake who would not hesitate to slit a throat to achieve his ambitions. He fingered the document. No, not this one. This was for Tiberius' eyes only. The information was too important and required the Emperor's immediate attention. Besides, it would enhance his reputation when Tiberius received this critical intelligence directly from him.

He was no stranger to the intrigues of the empire. He knew of a back door through which he could circumvent Sejanus and get this information straight to Tiberius Caesar. One of his former commanders, Lucius Appolanius, was a military advisor to Tiberius. Appolanius would ensure that this personal correspondence was received directly by its intended recipient. He hastily scribbled the instructions to Appolanius, asking him to personally deliver the information to the Emperor.

He leaned back in his chair, scratching his chin. What in Hades was Julius Frontinius Gallus, the new Governor of Germania, up to? No doubt he was lining his pockets with the heavy taxes, but driving the Frisii into open rebellion, that was pure recklessness. Many of the appointed governors of the Roman provinces were rapacious. That was a fact of life. But this sounded disastrous. He put the document and his instructions for Appolanius in the dispatch pouch for a ship that would leave the next morning.

Night oozed into a chilly cold dawn. Nothing seemed to have changed in the physical world of northern Germania from the previous day, but on that cold night the fates of many had been altered irreversibly. Whether this was the gods' intervention or simply the course of human history—who was to say? Little did Quintus Sorvinius know that his letter to Tiberius would unleash a series of events over the coming months that would tragically impact thousands of lives in the territory of Germania.

SPRING AD 26

Roman Territory of Germania Inferior
Town of Oppidum Ubiorum
(Modern Day Cologne)

The fallow field was bathed in slanting rays of sunlight. Birds chirped and insects trilled, heralding the new season. On the far left, the Rhenus, turgid with spring snowmelt, flowed swiftly by. The trees lining the bank uncovered their first green buds. Off in the distance, a straw archery target was mounted upon a wooden tripod, standing in an empty field.

Two figures stood on the barren turf. Both were clad in tunics and long woolen cloaks that whipped about them in the wind. At first glance, the two men appeared nondescript. The older one had a bit of girth to him and streaks of gray lacing his hair and short beard. The younger of the two could almost be described as slender. His countenance had been softened by the years, but he was still a handsome figure with his angular cheekbones and aristocratic nose. There was little doubt that he was a member of the equestrian class—he looked the part.

The two men were stark contrasts to each other: Marcellus, the heavier, older one was a commoner and had risen through the ranks of the legions to that of a centurion. On the other hand, Valerius, the younger one, was a former tribune and hailed from a rich and privileged family. Despite the vast social gulf between them, they had become steadfast friends—a bond forged in blood and bravery on the battlefields of Germania.

To an observer, these were just two regular men perfecting their archery skills. However, they were far from ordinary. If one were to gaze at their faces and into their eyes, one would quickly surmise that these were hard men, ones who had seen and experienced much in their lives and were not to be trifled with. Their stares were unwavering and as stony as flint. The second extraordinary thing about them was their weapons. Their bows were large and, by comparison, dwarfed all others. Their arrows were as thick as a man's index finger and longer than an arm.

Though they had long since left behind military service in the legions—fifteen years now—they continued this martial exercise of shooting their giant war bows. Valerius drew the bow so that the fletching of the arrow rested near his cheek. He let out half a breath and centered the arrow on the target, aiming slightly higher to account for the breeze that blew into his face. Now, he had the sight picture he desired. Exhaling slightly, he released the sinewy cord. The arrow streaked across the field in a blur and struck the target in an explosion of straw. He did not pause to admire his aim; there would be time to evaluate his proficiency later, and besides, when one fired a bow in a hostile situation, admiring the accuracy of a shot could have fatal consequences. He methodically retrieved another arrow from his quiver and sighted the next missile.

To his right, his fellow archer, friend, officer, and confidant mimicked his movements. With a sudden *twang*, Marcellus released his arrow. He withdrew his last shaft from the quiver and swiftly sent the arrow hurtling toward the target. When finished, he looked over at Valerius shooting his final arrow. Marcellus then gestured toward the target. "Shall we go assess the damage?"

"By all means," replied Valerius. As the two men walked toward the target, the former tribune angled his face so that the sunlight warmed his skin. He inhaled deeply, savoring the warm spring air. It had been a long winter replete with snow, ice, and howling winds. The cold here in Germania was fiercer than he'd experienced in Rome, where he had spent his first twenty-plus years, but if asked, he would respectfully say that he preferred Germania to Rome. This was his home now. He was content here. He had a loving wife, four beautiful children, and a prosperous business. He smiled inwardly. The gods had been kind to him. He could not fathom why but his life had been truly blessed. He had avoided almost certain death in the German hinterlands several times, only to emerge intact and move forward with his life.

There were several reasons Valerius favored the German territory. All roads may lead to Rome, but this proved to be both a blessing and a curse. Yes, it was the center of the empire and reflected the epitome of cosmopolitan living and culture, but the city was overcrowded, prone to plagues, and ridden with crime. The urban metropolis was a hotbed of political intrigue ruled by ruthless men. One had to tread carefully among the various factions or risk losing one's head. On the other hand, life was simple out here on the German frontier. It had its risks, like most places, but one had more control over one's destiny. Further, the air was crisp and clean, and the threat of violence from bandits and thieves was less likely.

As they strode toward the target, there was silence between them. Valerius thought this strange as Marcellus was usually of an ebullient disposition. It wasn't that the pair needed to converse; they were such good friends that their lack of dialogue posed no awkwardness. It was simply uncharacteristic of Marcellus. Valerius stole a sidelong glance at his companion. Despite being in his fifties, the centurion's frame was still erect and his gait steady. He had chosen to remain mostly clean-shaven even after his military service had ended, except for a short beard adorning his chin, which was now mostly gray.

Valerius felt extremely lucky to have met this man seventeen years earlier. It had been his first assignment as a tribune, and he had been stationed on the German frontier with the army of Publius Quinctilius Varus. It had been a massive army of three legions, almost seventeen thousand men. It had been the best Rome had—*had* being the descriptive word for they were gone now, all gone. Massacred by an alliance of rebellious German tribes under the leadership of the duplicitous Cherusci Chieftain, Arminius. Valerius and Marcellus were the only two Roman officers who had escaped the carnage.

They had fought their way out of the Teutoburg Forest along with a few others and managed to warn the garrison of Vetera, located on the Rhenus, of the revolt. But that had been just the beginning of their tribulations. The two men had been urgently dispatched to Rome to inform Caesar Augustus of the massive defeat. Valerius shuddered briefly as he remembered that fateful evening. He had interrupted a social gathering of the imperial family. After nearly two weeks of hard travel by horse, he looked disgusting. The Emperor had taken great offense to his appearance and grown apoplectic at the news of the terrible destruction of three legions. Germanicus, the adopted grandson and a rising prince in the imperial family, had admired his pluck and saved him from the Emperor's wrath.

A year later, under the command of Germanicus Caesar, Valerius and Marcellus had participated in a massive reprisal against the German population on the other side of the Rhenus. The resultant slaughter of the German tribes had been horrific. Yet, several times, the Roman legions had almost been trapped again in the German forests, barely managing to escape. Valerius had been captured but evaded death once more and returned to the legionary camp a year later.

The two men continued walking toward the straw target. Finally, Valerius could stand it no more. "I give up. Why so pensive?"

"Oh, you know, melancholy thoughts."

Valerius wasn't letting him off that easy. "Let me guess. You were thinking about the Teutoburg, weren't you?"

Marcellus stopped abruptly and turned toward his companion. "You guessed it, Tribune."

He had continued to address Valerius in this manner even though they were the best of friends and their military careers had ended many years ago. It was purely out of habit, for Marcellus had been in the legions for many years, and after all, Tribune Valerius had been his senior officer. Old habits truly did die hard.

"Marcellus, do you miss it? I mean the legions, your life as a centurion?"

At first, he thought his companion hadn't heard him. But upon closer observation, he could see that he was forming a response. Marcellus pursed his lips. "I have never been happier in my life than

I am now. I adore my wife, Brida, and my daughter, Claudia. Family life agrees with me. I have more money than I ever thought possible, and I have a great friend in you. I live a leisurely life; the rigors of the legions are long past."

He paused, contemplating his next words. "Now, you asked me if I miss it. The answer is a resounding no. Am I proud of my service in the legions? Yes, damn right I am. I served Rome well and cared for the men under my command. I like to think I was a good officer." He abruptly stopped and stared off in the distance.

Valerius waited for a bit and then spoke, "But—"

"But nothing, Tribune," he exclaimed. "The Teutoburg still sticks in my craw. I get angry just thinking about it. All those fine troops annihilated because our leaders had their heads far up their collective arses. And then that campaign in Germania. The slaughter of innocent civilians. It just sickened me. I do my best to not think about it. Ruins my whole day, my outlook on life. Know what I mean, Tribune?"

"I do, Marcellus. Like you, I sometimes recall those days. I prefer not to, although I still have nightmares. But enough of these morose thoughts. Come, let's see the results of our efforts."

The target bristled with arrows; an impressive feat as they had shot at a distance of about two hundred paces, around twice the distance of a normal archery target.

Marcellus silently counted the arrows in the target, pointing with his finger. "Fifteen in the target, Tribune. Now, let's see who the odd man out is. He began plucking his arrows out, which were identifiable by a dab of red paint around the shaft. "I have eight arrows, Tribune, which means you only have seven. Looks like you're buying the wine…again, I might add," he smirked, "and you get to retrieve the failures." He pointed out past the target.

"It must be my bad luck, or perhaps the wind. How about the best of three volleys? Are you game?"

"You are a glutton for punishment. Of course, I accept the challenge. Besides, we need the practice after the long winter sojourn."

Valerius recovered the arrows beyond the target and rejoined Marcellus. The former centurion appeared to have regained some of his normal joviality. "When you first asked me to join this business venture of trading with the Germans, I was a little cynical. At the time, I had no great love for anything German. But you know what? I enjoy doing business with them. Your wife, Hereca, being German, certainly helped ease me into this situation. And I find the Germans to be straightforward in their dealings, not a slippery bunch of eels like some others I know."

"Slippery eels," chuckled Valerius. "Now who might you be referring to?"

Marcellus scowled. "I believe you know exactly who I'm referring to. Those scheming aristocratic bastards in Rome, that's who."

They'd reached their original starting point, which was clearly marked by a line of stones. They took their positions, ready to fire another barrage of lethal arrows downrange. However, the clatter of a horse's hooves sounded behind them, and they turned in unison. Valerius shaded his eyes against the glare of the sun. He observed a mounted figure. As the horse cantered toward them, a dull glint caught his eye—a metallic helmet. This was most certainly a military man. The pair stood in silence, watching the man approach.

Marcellus broke the stillness. "I wonder what this arsehole wants. The black cloak and the sign of the scorpion on his breastplate—he's a bloody Praetorian."

Valerius's heart plummeted, a sense of dread seizing him. Why was a Praetorian officer seeking them out? There was no one else in the vicinity and he didn't appear lost, so they must be at the receiving end of whatever the man had to say. He grimaced. Valerius had interacted with Praetorians many years ago, back in Rome. It hadn't been a good experience. As a rule, they were an arrogant and boorish bunch, believing they were privileged because of their close association with the Emperor.

The Praetorian dismounted. His helmet, which was set horizontally upon his crown, identified him as a centurion. He stopped just short of the two men. His expression severe, he produced a scroll from within his cloak, and without acknowledging them, began to read.

"Tribune Valerius Maximus and Centurion Marcellus Veronus, you are commanded—"

Marcellus gave the officer a confused glance and interrupted, "Wait, I retired from the legions years ago and Valerius Maximus resigned his commission. We are both civilians."

The Praetorian glanced at the pair, his expression contemptuous. He began once again. "Tribune Valerius Maximus and Centurion Marcellus Veronus, you are commanded to report without delay to the Emperor, Tiberius Claudius Nero Caesar, at the imperial palace in Rome." The Praetorian looked up from the scroll and said nothing more.

Valerius waited a few moments, letting the silence hang. "Is there anything else?"

The Praetorian shook his head. "No, there is not."

Marcellus stepped closer to the Praetorian. "No, there is not, *sir*."

The Praetorian appeared flustered, unsure of what to say. He was used to intimidating others, not vice versa.

Marcellus growled, "Come on. It's not that difficult a concept.

You addressed us by our military titles; thus he," pointing at Valerius, "is your superior officer. Please observe standard military courtesy. Out with it."

Anger welled up on the face of the Praetorian. His hand edged lower toward the handle of his sword—this did not go unnoticed by Marcellus.

Marcellus moved so close to the Praetorian that he invaded his personal space, standing face-to-face with the officer.

"If you move your hand one bit more, I'm going to rip you apart. Try and draw that piece of iron and see what happens. Again, please observe proper military protocol and address your superior officer with the respect he deserves."

The Praetorian noted Marcellus's steely gaze and intimidating bulk. He gritted his teeth. "Sir, the scroll holds no other content." He handed the document to Valerius.

The tribune examined the text, noting the imperial seal of the Emperor. There was no doubt it was an official summons. Valerius looked up from the document and spoke in a laconic tone, "You have discharged your duty, Centurion. Now, leave us before my companion sends one of his arrows up your arse."

The Praetorian took one look at the large arrows protruding from Marcellus's quiver, turned about, leaped upon his horse, and swiftly rode away.

The pair gazed at the retreating figure. Valerius tapped the scroll against his leg and turned toward Marcellus. "I see you have mellowed with age," he said in a sardonic tone.

The centurion sneered. "Never liked those impudent Praetorian fucks. I remember you dealing with them back in Rome. As I recall, you have no love for them either."

"I most certainly don't. But enough of that Praetorian arsehole. What concerns me is the terse wording in this scroll. Why are we addressed by our military titles, which we both had forfeited ages ago, and why have we been summoned to Rome to meet with Tiberius? The Emperor hardly knows me, and what he knows of me, he doesn't like. No love lost there. He was present that fateful night seventeen years ago, and there was great anger directed at me. He wanted me exiled or perhaps even executed for reporting the Teutoburg disaster to Augustus. On top of that, I was subsequently decorated for valor by Germanicus for my part in the reprisal campaign against the Germans. You know Tiberius was extremely jealous of his nephew about that victory over the Germans. So again, why is he summoning the two of us and what's with the military titles?"

"Why indeed, Tribune, and we no longer have Germanicus—may the gods watch over him—to protect us. You'd told me he was the one who spoke your praise to both Augustus and Tiberius. I'm as puzzled as you are, Tribune, and I don't like this one bit. You are more familiar with the machinations of the empire than me. What do you suggest we do?"

Valerius paused in thought, mulling over his options. "There is no doubt we must go to Rome, but before we do that, perhaps I should visit the legate, Gaius Labenius. He commands the Twentieth Legion stationed here at the fortress in Oppidum Ubiorum. I have mentioned to you that I went through tribune schooling with him back in Rome. I consider him a friend. Maybe he can shed some light on this bizarre summons. Come on, we need to get home."

"Sounds like a good idea," agreed Marcellus. "I'm afraid I'm not much help here. A bit out of my element with the higher politics of Rome."

▲

After an unexpectedly eventful day, Valerius returned to his magnificent home on the outskirts of the town. It was a brick and wood structure with a red tiled roof. The dwelling had running water, heated floors, a small garden in the peristylium, and all the other comforts of the fine homes of Rome without the headache of living in a large city.

Valerius entered through the large wooden main door. Hereca, his wife, was arranging a vase full of early blooming spring flowers on a low table. She was a tall woman with broad shoulders but carried herself with a feminine grace. She had piercing blue eyes that were sharp and intelligent. She looked up and gave him a radiant smile, her glowing face framed by her short ginger hair. She then frowned. "You look anxious."

"That would be an understatement."

"Would it have anything to do with a sinister-looking character, a legionnaire, who stopped here seeking you? He was clad in black. I didn't like the looks of him."

Valerius was about to respond when his four children came bounding into the room to greet him. Leading the charge was Aulus, the oldest at twelve, followed by Juliana, ten; Calvus, eight; and Paulina, seven. They all had Roman names, much to the disappointment of his German wife. Valerius hadn't insisted they have proper Roman names simply because he was a Roman; he had done it because they lived in a Roman society. Many cultures had been infused into the empire, adding much flavor and variety to the Roman ways, but underneath it all, it was still a Roman world. He was just being practical. They would have a better chance of succeeding in life if they adopted Roman customs. This did not stop

Hereca, though, for she had her own German pet names for each of the children. Valerius didn't mind this; in fact, he liked the guttural names she called them.

"Father," cried Aulus, "you're back early today from your archery with Uncle Marcellus. When are you going to take me?"

"And me too!" shouted Calvus.

"You're too young," admonished Aulus. "Look at you. Your arms are like twigs!"

'I'm almost as big as you!"

Valerius grinned. "I will take both of you soon enough. I think the bows are a bit too much for you now, but soon. By the gods, you're getting bigger every day!"

"What about the girls?" Juliana queried. At ten, she was already a flaxen-haired beauty. "We want to do things with you also."

Valerius laughed. "I don't believe archery is appropriate for young ladies, although I wouldn't rule it out. Perhaps we can take a sailboat out on the river when the weather is warmer. That would be fun, don't you think?"

Aulus jumped in. "Sailing for boys too!"

"No," countered Paulina, "it is not. You have your archery."

Valerius threw his hands up, looking beseechingly at his wife. "Children, listen, we will figure something out. But right now, I need to speak with your mother alone. Go out and play for a while. It's a beautiful day."

Hereca shooed them away. Both parents watched the pack, who were arguing among themselves, retreat down the hallway. When they were alone, Hereca glanced in trepidation at her husband. "As you were saying…"

"That *sinister* figure, as you described him, was a Praetorian officer. Praetorians are an arrogant bunch and report only to the Emperor. He gave me this." He held up the scroll.

Hereca quickly scanned the parchment, looking baffled. "I don't understand. You have not worn the uniform in fifteen years. Why would the Emperor want to see you?"

"Why indeed! I don't mean to alarm you, but the Emperor is not exactly fond of me. There is no way I can ignore this."

She looked at him with a troubled expression and quickly threw her arms around him. "This makes no sense to me," she said anxiously. Their private moment was interrupted by a knock at the front entrance. The door was answered by one of the servants. Valerius looked up from his wife's embrace to see his elderly parents, Sentius and Vispania.

His mother and father were surprisingly spry despite their advancing years. Fifteen years ago, when Valerius returned to Rome after the campaign of retribution against the German tribes following the Teutoburg disaster, his parents had been appalled that he had brought home a German wife, a barbarian princess, with him. Despite her lack of insight into the Roman culture and manners, Hereca had won his parents over with her tenacity and intelligence. She had quickly absorbed the language and customs of the Romans and yet maintained her identity. Valerius and Hereca had returned to Germania to set up a fledgling trade business. They periodically returned to Rome with the children in tow to have them visit their grandparents.

But Valerius had told his parents that they belonged in Germania with him. He had reasoned that they would be near their grandchildren and life was more tranquil there. They hadn't needed much convincing. While Germania didn't offer the majesty or sophistication of Rome, they concluded that they would be better off close to their son, his wife, and their grandchildren. His father had retired so there were no impediments or economic ties on that front. Though they had been lifelong residents of Rome, in no time, his parents had relocated to the German frontier—a decision they'd never looked back upon.

Sentius cleared his throat and said, "I hope we are not interrupting anything."

Valerius grinned weakly. "Not really, Father, but I could use some advice. Come, let's go into the *tablinium*. I need to discuss something with you both."

He led his parents into the formal study and waited for them to take their seats. "Wine, Father, Mother?"

Sentius nodded. Vispania gave her husband a disapproving glance. She was always harping on about her husband's liberal consumption of the grape, which he purposely ignored.

Valerius disregarded his mother's glare and poured some wine for his father out of an elaborate silver carafe.

With Hereca standing by his side, Valerius began, "I was at the archery field with Marcellus today when a Praetorian officer delivered me this summons." He handed the document to his father. "I am to journey to Rome along with Marcellus and report directly to the imperator, Tiberius. The Praetorian addressed Marcellus and me by our military titles."

Valerius observed his father's face turn pale at his words. "What is it, Father? I saw your expression change as if someone kicked you in the gut. Come on, out with it."

Sentius looked at his daughter-in-law and then his wife, unsure of what to say in their presence. He nervously cleared his throat and stammered, "As–as…you know," he stopped speaking and glanced again at his audience, who stared at him, waiting for him to continue. Sentius pursed his lips resolutely and began again. "As you know, I keep in close correspondence with some of my colleagues in Rome." He picked up his cup of wine and sipped it, aware that everyone was hanging on his words. "They inform me of the ebb and flow of political events in the city. And, according to them, to be summoned by Tiberius is not a good thing."

"How so, Father?"

"When Tiberius succeeded Augustus—what twelve, thirteen years ago? At first, everything appeared to go smoothly. The empire went about its business—no violence, no bloodshed. Oh, Tiberius was no Augustus. He was never popular and his disposition was taciturn. But commerce flowed, elections were held, and people got rich. However, over the past several years, there have been whispers of prominent citizens disappearing or committing suicide. Those that were lucky received trials in the forum, but they were rigged and the outcomes the same. It seems those who have opposed or offended the imperator in any small way have been severely punished. Some say it is the doing of the Praetorian Prefect, Sejanus."

Sentius paused and shakily wiped his mouth with his sleeve. "My correspondence with my friends, which had previously featured barbed and witty commentary on the politics of Rome, has all but dried up. They hinted to me that it would be unwise to mention anything that would be considered offensive to or a criticism of our imperator."

"Father, surely you are not implying that someone is going through the correspondences of a few old men?"

"That is exactly what I am saying," he said fervently.

Valerius held his hands up in a placating gesture. "All right, Father. I believe you." He paused for a moment and then spoke decisively. "This is what I am going to do." He snatched his wax tablet from a nearby table and began composing a missive, carefully etching a message in the wax with his stylus. "I'm going to send a message to my friend and colleague, Gaius Sepulchius Labenius. I already mentioned this to Marcellus, and he agreed it might be a good idea. As you will recall, Labenius and I grew up together. We partook our tribunal training in the same class on the Field of Mars many years ago."

"I remember him," responded Sentius. "Good family. His father later became a senator."

"Indeed," replied Valerius. "Gaius was fortunate in that he was posted with the legions in Hispania, not Germania, and thus escaped the Teutoburg disaster. His legions were recalled from the province to Germania to fortify the Rhine after the Roman defeat in the Teutoburg. He has been here ever since. I served with him under Germanicus when the legions invaded the lands across the Rhenus in retaliation for the Teutoburg affair. He is a good officer."

He examined his writing and nodded in satisfaction. "I'm requesting an urgent meeting with Gaius for dinner tonight. I know he is a busy man, but we have maintained our friendship over the years. Hopefully, he will accommodate my request. Maybe he can offer clarity about this situation."

▲

His request for a dinner meeting was quickly confirmed within an hour of his messenger's departure. Valerius absently rifled through his closet for something suitable to wear for his appointment. Certainly not a toga; no one wore them out here on the frontier. He wanted something not too dressy yet possessing some degree of formality. His options were limited as his apparel was sadly lacking because he required little in the way of fancy clothes to conduct his business. Most of the time, he wore a plain tunic, and if the weather was cold, leggings.

He finally settled on a cream-colored tunic of fine weave, one that Hereca had purchased for him. She had complained to him on several occasions that he need not look so ragged, and despite his objections, she selected clothing for him. Thank Jupiter and Mars that she had. With his attire decided upon, he sat on the bed. His mind raced at the implications of the imperial summons and what his future courses of action might be. He took a deep breath to calm himself—he had been through more difficult periods. The fact that he had survived the Teutoburg disaster and, several years later, capture by the Germans on the battlefield attested to his survivability. If he could persist through those events, he could handle just about anything the Goddess Fortuna threw at him, including this meeting with Tiberius.

He rose and began to get dressed. He reminded himself not to forget the new wine he had bought from Gaul. It was delicious and he knew Gaius would love it.

Valerius arrived early at the legionary fort for his dinner with the legate. It was only a short walk of half a mile, or a bit more, from his house. He was admitted through the massive gates that were flanked by wooden towers. The encampment—bustling with activity even at this late hour in the afternoon—evoked powerful memories. Legionnaires moved about in formation to the loud commands of their centurions. He heard the familiar clang of the hammer and anvil as weapons were forged. He could smell the aroma of baked bread in the legionary kitchens.

Taking it all in, he strode down the *via principia,* the main avenue of the garrison, carrying a small jug of wine. He entered the commander's house, the *praetorium,* and was quickly ushered into the legate's dining room. He was the first to arrive. He looked about, admiring the tasteful decorations. The living conditions of a legionary encampment were austere, yet Gaius had transformed the dining area into a setting that was elegant and unpretentious. The stone floors were graced with beautiful woven rugs of wool, thick and with striking colors. Small statues of marble and bronze were placed in niches across the room, and the hanging tapestries gave it a feeling of warmth. The long dining table of polished wood gleamed in the light of the various oil lamps placed strategically throughout the premises.

Gaius appeared from a second entrance. "Valerius, my good friend, how are you?"

Valerius proffered a wide smile. He gave the legate a quick once-over. The man looked like a military leader. He was trim and his legionary cuirass fit his muscular form well. His hair was cut short, now greying at the edges. While his face was youthful, there were signs of weariness etched upon his features. The demands and responsibilities placed upon a legate were a heavy burden.

"Gaius, how are you? I have brought a gift from the gods." He extended the small amphora of wine in his arms. "This is a special vintage from Gaul. It is the best I have discovered, better than what one can procure in Rome, I would opine. I hope you like it."

The legate eagerly accepted the amphora and grinned. "Then we shall sample it tonight. Come, sit down. Dinner should be served shortly." With that, he nodded to the servant standing in the shadows, and the two men sat at the table. A parade of servers materialized with trays of steaming food, including venison and braised fish in olive oil, garnished with spring greens, and a variety of boiled vegetables. Gaius made a show of unstopping the seal on the amphora and poured the scarlet liquid into silver goblets. Both men raised their chalices in a silent toast and sipped their wine. "By the gods, this is good stuff," exclaimed Gaius. "You must tell me the source of this wine." He held the jug out in front of him and read the stamped label. "J&L imports. That doesn't say much, does it?"

Valerius grinned. "I'm glad you like it. As you are aware, I transport a variety of goods between the provinces in Gaul and the German territories. One of the side benefits is that I get to sample some of the new and rare vintages. This happens to be one of them. I am told the grapes from this vineyard grow along the banks of the Rhodanum (Rhone). I don't know anything about the importer or, worse yet, how to procure more of the wine. Hence, I have a limited supply. But, as you proclaimed, it is excellent stuff."

Gaius grinned. "Who would have thought it—Valerius Maximus, a wine snob. After all that swill you consumed during our training days, you're now a purveyor of fine wine."

Valerius chuckled. "Wine snob, hardly, but one must know a good quality vintage when it comes along. My livelihood depends on it."

The pair discussed their respective families, the state of civil unrest across the Rhenus, and the spring weather. Both men then began sampling the cuisine. Between bites, Gaius paused to dab his lips. "Tell me, Valerius, why the urgent need to dine with me this evening? Let me guess, you wish to rejoin the legions."

In return, Valerius offered a tight-lipped frown. After a few moments of silence, he spoke in a hushed tone. "Ironically, you are not far from the truth. After a long winter of being indoors, this morning, Marcellus and I ventured out to practice with our bows when a Praetorian officer interrupted our exercise. He handed me this." Valerius thrust the parchment bearing the Emperor's seal toward Gaius.

Gaius quickly perused the document and then deliberately scanned it again. He gazed at Valerius, a look of consternation crossing his features. Then, he rose from his chair, dismissed the servants, and shut the two doors that led to the dining room.

Valerius sat there, a feeling of foreboding coming over him. The wine felt sour in his stomach and the rich food lodged in his throat.

Gaius finally sat down, edged closer to Valerius, and spoke sotto voce. "Valerius, have you done something to offend the imperator? Are you involved in politics or have you criticized our great leader, Tiberius?"

Valerius let out a nervous chuckle. "Me, political? No, nothing at all. I run my business and pay my fair share of taxes. I don't know how I might have offended—"

Gaius interrupted, "Do you maintain correspondence with anyone in Rome?"

"No, Rome is foreign to me now. All my family and friends are here in Germania. Why do you ask?"

Gaius looked about furtively, ensuring they had complete privacy. "Listen to me, Valerius, and listen well. Things are different now. People who criticize Tiberius or cross him politically end up committing suicide or simply disappearing. Those more fortunate are banished."

Valerius sighed. "My father hinted at the same thing. He keeps in touch with some of his old colleagues in Rome. He spoke of arrests. He believes they even read his mail."

"Your father is correct, and it is more sinister than just reading mail. I suspect there are imperial spies everywhere, including here on my base. That is why, every few months, I have my officers and legions swear an oath of fealty to Tiberius."

Valerius contemplated these words. "What has happened to make the imperator so suspicious of everyone? Have there been plots against his life?"

The General shrugged. "Who knows?" One change that has occurred is the appointment of Lucius Aelius Sejanus as the Praetorian prefect. You remember him. We served with him on the campaign in Germania. He was attached to the staff of Germanicus. In my opinion, he is an oily, ambitious snake who is not to be trusted."

Valerius frowned as he tried to recall the man. "Ah, I remember him now. The tall guy with a slightly hooked nose, right? Didn't know him well, but what I knew of him, I didn't like. He was always lurking about, listening to what everyone was saying."

"He is to be avoided at all costs. He has begun his own private reign of terror because Tiberius trusts him implicitly. He runs the government and screens who Tiberius meets with and the correspondence he views."

Valerius chuckled softly.

Gaius appeared puzzled. "What?"

"Oh, I was just thinking of what Marcellus would say about Sejanus."

The General looked at him expectantly.

"Marcellus would use one of his old expressions from his years in the legions—you can't polish a turd."

Gaius spluttered with laughter. "Yes, I could see him saying that. How is the old warrior, by the way?"

"He is fine. He is as puzzled as I am about this…difficulty."

"He is a good man. Rome owes men like him a great debt. Centurions like him are the backbone of the legions."

Valerius heaved a sigh. "Yes, they are." He stared at the wall opposite, lost in thought, but then shook himself out of his reverie. "Getting back to the matter at hand, what would you suggest I do?"

Gaius answered without a pause. "You have to go to Rome to see what Tiberius wants. There is no way you can evade the long reach of Rome, even out here on the frontier. My intuition tells me that he wants you to do something for him—but what? I have no idea. If he wanted you eliminated, why would he summon you all the way to Rome? Do you have any idea what he might demand of you?"

"I'm as puzzled as you about this summons. He has never favored me. In fact, he has been downright hostile. He was in attendance the night I delivered the news of the Teutoburg disaster to Augustus, and he has never forgiven me for it. Thankfully, Germanicus intervened on my behalf and made me part of his staff. I have kept a low profile these past fifteen years, concentrating on running my trading business. Surely he can't hold a grudge for this long a time."

The legate muttered a curse. "And Germanicus is no longer with us." He paused, letting his words sink in. "Listen, Valerius, be very careful when you speak with Tiberius. As I said, it appears he wants you to perform some service for him, but I believe he wouldn't hesitate to dispose of you and Marcellus if you displease him in any way. Don't give him an excuse to do so. I know you, and if you don't mind me saying so, at times, you can be quite insolent. You have an obvious disdain for authority. I had witnessed some of the exchanges between you and Germanicus, who, I remind you, was the commanding general and second-in-line to succeed Augustus. I don't know how you got away with your effrontery, but you did. Germanicus overlooked your imperfections; Tiberius will not."

Valerius stroked his jaw in thought. "I know I was a bit disrespectful, but I would do so again. Germanicus, for all his brilliance and leadership, underestimated the Germans and their leader, Arminius. Varus did the same thing, which resulted in a devastating defeat, and I didn't want to see that happen again. I'm sure you're aware how close Germanicus and the legions came to falling into a Teutoburg trap again when we invaded the lands across the Rhenus in retaliation for Rome's defeat. But thank you for your advice, Gaius. I'm fortunate to have a friend such as you. Tomorrow, I will seek transportation to Rome by sea. But for now, let us enjoy the feast you have prepared for us. We have barely touched our dinner!"

The two men dug in and began eating in earnest, liberally sampling the wine. Labenius studied Valerius. "When you return—note that I said when and not if—I would be most appreciative if you would share with me what mission he wants you to undertake. I strongly suspect it involves affairs here in Germania and may have strategic implications for the entire territory."

"Of course, Gaius. As soon as I return, I will let you know."

▲

Valerius returned home that night and walked into the small foyer to find Hereca impatiently pacing the floor, an anxious expression marking her countenance. She looked up at him expectantly, hoping for some good news. Valerius wasted no time in getting to the point. "Gaius confirmed what my father had said. An element of fear has been fostered throughout the empire by the actions of Tiberius and his prefect, Sejanus. Gaius stated there were imperial spies everywhere reporting the activities of citizens, including in his own legionary fortress."

"But what are we to do?" Hereca asked anxiously.

Valerius held up his hand to calm her down. "Gaius thinks the Emperor needs me for something—he has some endeavor he wants me to complete. Listen, I know Tiberius does not favor me, well, perhaps in more realistic terms, he doesn't like me. But if he wanted to eliminate me, why summon me all the way to Rome? That's good news. Although, for the life of me, I can't think of what help I might be able to render him. I'm out of touch with Rome and I'm not active in politics. All I do is run our lucrative trading company and make sure I pay every single denarius that is owed in taxes."

Valerius pondered his words for a moment. "If I had to speculate, it must have something to do with Germania, although I'm not sure what. Certainly, he doesn't care for my military expertise. Marcellus and I will need to leave within a day or two at the latest. I will seek passage on a boat down the Rhenus to the port at Valkenberg and then on to Rome."

Sighing, Hereca moved toward him and placed her head on his shoulder. "We are far away from Rome, why can't they leave us alone? Surely after all these years of being absent from the city and out of the public eye, there must be someone else who can serve the Emperor?"

Valerius offered a stiff smile. "One would think so. I mean, how does he even remember me, an obscure tribune? I expect I'll find out soon enough. Come, let us go to bed. I expect tomorrow will be a busy day."

CHAPTER II
DEPARTURE

The day after—for one did not want to keep the Emperor waiting—Marcellus appeared in the foyer wearing a knee-length tunic and a light cloak to ward off the chill. He carried a small bag containing his personal belongings and in the other hand was the soft deer-skin satchel with his large war bow. In addition, strapped to his side was his *gladius*, a worn but well-cared-for stabbing sword from his days in the legions.

Valerius gave him a quizzical look. "I thought we were going to Rome, not to make war on some belligerent barbarians."

Marcellus frowned. "Well, Tribune, you should know by now that the empire is a dangerous place. We are traveling downriver to the mouth of the Rhenus and then embarking on a lengthy journey by sea. We will be open to attack. In such an event, I intend to defend myself."

"But, Marcellus, Rome rules the seas. There are no rival sea powers. Those days are long gone and besides—"

"Listen, Tribune, I feel safer carrying my weapons. If nothing happens, which I sincerely hope is the case, then I have hefted this extra baggage for naught. But if danger is to strike and we don't have our bows and swords, the result will be most undesirable. I have no intention of letting that happen. To me, the choice is obvious."

Valerius pondered his remarks and sighed. "I suppose you're right."

Hereca, who had been standing off to the side, spoke, "I wholeheartedly agree with Marcellus. I would feel better if you took your weapons along with you."

"Alright, alright." He walked down the hall to an adjacent room and opened the door to a small alcove: a storage closet. He peered into its recesses. Hanging from various hooks were his armor and weapons, all neatly organized and ready to be used. He grabbed the leather harness and belt to which was attached his sword and scabbard. Grasping the hilt, he slowly withdrew the blade. Well oiled, it slid out smoothly with a slightly metallic hiss. He examined the weapon. The sword, a *spatha*—longer than the standard Roman gladius—was razor-sharp and without a speck of rust. Satisfied, he rammed the blade back in.

Next, he gathered the satchel containing his war bow and a large quiver full of arrows. Last, he collected his *pugio*, a wickedly sharp dagger. He gathered up his weapons, shut the door, and ventured back into the hallway.

His wife, children, and parents had all assembled in the atrium to see Marcellus and him off. The children, openly weeping, stood huddled together, their eyes downcast. Next to them stood Hereca, her eyes brimming with tears. This was unusual, for his wife was a tough woman and was seldom moved to tears. Valerius silently cursed the Emperor and Goddess Fortuna for interfering with his tranquil life. He asked himself for the hundredth time why he had been cast into such a fate—couldn't they just let him be?

Valerius's parents and Marcellus discretely turned about and moved away as Valerius embraced Hereca and then each of his children. He had never been physically separated from them for more than a few weeks, and this stint would last about two months, assuming things went well. He put on a brave face and attempted to speak with conviction. "No need to be sorrowful. I shall be back sooner than you expect and return with magnificent presents for everyone."

His words were met with silence, but he didn't know what else to say. Frowning at his lack of success, he moved toward his parents. He spoke softly so that Hereca and his children couldn't hear. "Please look after them in my absence. I'm sure Hereca would welcome your assistance."

His parents returned his gaze with lugubrious expressions. Valerius continued, "Look, there is nothing to worry about. I am trusting in the legate's words that Tiberius wants me to perform a service for Rome. Hopefully, it is something I can do." He proffered a slight grin. "Perhaps I can even be in his good graces once again. You never know."

Sentius nodded. "Yes, I hope so," he said as both parents embraced him. Valerius broke away and approached Marcellus. The centurion looked at him expectantly. Valerius nodded. "We need to get going." With that, he hefted his belongings, turned, and waved one final goodbye before walking out the door. They were off to Rome.

* * *

Three weeks had passed and they were nearing the end of their voyage. The pair stood by the ship's railing, under an achingly blue

35

sky. The squat transport was in full sail and making good progress with a steady breeze. The waters parted smoothly as the prow of the ship knifed through the waters of the *Mare Nostrum*. The voyage had been uneventful thus far: After floating downstream in a small barge to the mouth of the Rhenus at the port of Valkenberg, they had boarded a merchant ship named Neptune's Blessing. Favorable winds and calm seas had facilitated their journey south along the coast of Germania, past Gaul and then to Hispania. Making good time, they had sailed through the rocky promontories known as the Pillars of Hercules yesterday.

Last year, Valerius would have sailed on one of his own ships. Their trading company had owned several transports such as this one under the command of Captain Sabinus, one of the partners in their business venture. Sabinus was an old hand from the imperial Roman navy and had retired to join the thriving business. Unfortunately, he had died unexpectedly from one of the plagues that had swept across the land. Having no expertise in nautical matters, Valerius and Marcellus had decided to sell the ships and concentrate their trading in the Rhine, with the occasional excursion to Gaul for wine. The raw goods received from the Germans were sold to willing traders along the Rhenus and, from there, shipped to ports of call throughout the empire.

It had been a boring voyage thus far, but given the fickle nature of the seas, *boring* was good. The ship, a merchant transport with squat lines and a crew of fifteen, was in good repair and made excellent headway toward their destination, the port of Ostia at the mouth of the Tiber. The hold was filled with hides and freshly cut hardwood—already trimmed and ready for use for the expanding construction of the city of Rome.

From his position near the prow, Valerius gazed across the length of the boat. He estimated it to be about one hundred feet long, which was the average size of a merchant ship, although he had seen some as long as a hundred and fifty feet. The single mast had a huge square sail, which was now swollen with the wind, and the hull was double planked to support the weight of the cargo. The ropes and lines creaked and groaned as the transport advanced ploddingly, heavily laden with cargo. Glancing at the rear, he saw one of the crew manning the tiller.

The captain of the vessel, a man named Artimus, was a heavy-set individual with a full beard. His weathered face was the texture of leather from years at sea. He was also a taciturn man. Valerius and Marcellus, who were the only passengers, had sporadically attempted to engage the master of the vessel in conversation but had received only laconic replies, barely bordering on politeness. On the other hand, the man appeared to know his business and brooked no nonsense from the crew. The men of the ship were constantly in motion, always attending to the needs of the ship. There was no slouching about with Artimus at the helm.

Marcellus and Valerius basked in the warm sun and savored the refreshing breeze as they leaned against the ship's railing. Suddenly, Artimus appeared next to them, proffering a wide grin. This was the first time he had actively sought conversation with them. Perhaps he was finally warming up to them. "You two must come on my ship more often. This is some of the best weather I've ever seen on my voyages from Germania. I anticipate the seas to remain calm. We should reach the port of Ostia in a few days."

"Good luck! Good luck!" bellowed one of the crew members. He pointed toward the port side where a pod of dolphins had materialized, frolicking in the wake of the ship. The entire crew lined along the ship's railing, reveling in the sight of the majestic creatures. The dolphins put on a spectacular show, their fins slicing through the water as they soared above the foamy wake of the ship and dove into the water once more. The seamen cheered this spectacle, for these sea creatures meant good sailing.

"Aye," replied Marcellus, "this has been one of my better voyages. Not that I'm an experienced sailor, but some of my passages have not been as pleasant. Know what I mean, Captain?"

Artimus chuckled. "The sea can be quite fickle at times. Damn near lost my ship on several occasions. Had waves breaking over the bow of my boat. Thought my arse was done in by Neptune for sure. But here I am, sailing along in calm seas. I should make a nice profit on my cargo this time."

Valerius smiled. "I'm glad this will be a prosperous voyage for you, Captain. By any chance, did you happen to know a colleague of mine, a Captain Sabinus?"

"Know him?" he exclaimed. "He was a legend in the sea trade! I was sorry as Hades to hear of his passing. May I inquire how you were acquainted with him?"

"We go way back, Sabinus and me, to when I was a young tribune. Saved my arse once. Then, more recently, we were business partners in our trading venture on the Rhenus," replied Valerius.

Artimus gave him an incredulous look. "Wait, you mean to say you're the former Roman officers he teamed up with?"

"Indeed, we are," chimed in Marcellus.

"I've heard stories of your service in the legions. If even half of what he told me is true, you are luminaries in your own right. One night, in a tavern at a seaport in Gaul, Sabinus spoke to a bunch of us sea dogs about your survival in the Teutoburg and subsequent campaign against the Germans. Proud as a peacock he was to have you two as business partners."

Valerius nodded. "Sabinus was a skilled navigator and what's more, a savvy businessman. Marcellus and I had complete faith in him to carry our goods down the Rhenus to the various ports in the empire. I miss his crusty wit. He took cursing to a whole new plane. I had never heard such invective as he spewed forth."

The captain chuckled in agreement. "Aye, that was Sabinus. And you are correct; he was a skilled pilot who could sail a ship on dry land if need be. I remember on one occasion—"

"Sail off the starboard bow!" cried the lookout from mid-deck.

Artimus frowned. "Sorry, I'll need to attend to matters. We shall continue our discussions later."

Marcellus gazed at the blue seas, mesmerized by its gentle swells and the sunlight glinting off the water. He sighed. "As much as I admire the serene beauty of the sea, it would be nice to plant my feet on *terra firma* once again. But I'm thankful for the tranquil seas over our journey. Thank you, fucking Neptune."

Valerius snorted. "I see you are as reverent as ever to the gods. Before you start, I know, despite your odious pronouncements, you and the gods have an understanding."

"Well, it's true, Tribune. Look at me. I'm living proof. I mean, if the gods were displeased with me, surely they would have never let me survive the Teutoburg disaster and the subsequent incursion into Germania."

"Yes, I've heard that refrain before, oh favored one. Once we arrive in Ostia, we should travel on one of the barges going up the Tiber to Rome and find an agreeable place to stay. I remember a few of the luxury inns near the imperial palace. They will be hideously expensive, but what the Hades, we can afford it." He grinned in smug satisfaction.

Valerius and Marcellus continued their idle chatter for the better part of an hour, oblivious to the captain's hushed discussions with the crew. Moments later, Artimus sauntered over to them, his face grim. "I don't know how to break the news to you, but we have a problem."

"What is it, Captain?" Valerius asked.

"That sail my lookout spotted has been shadowing us. I've even altered our course, but it continues to follow. Worse luck, the sail is not that of a merchant; I believe it to be a pirate vessel."

Valerius remained calm, although his stomach churned. "Captain, surely you are mistaken. I haven't heard word of pirates in years."

"No mistake, Tribune. I would wager they are Cilicians. Evil scum."

"How can that be, Captain? I thought Pompey Magnus eradicated them some eighty years ago. He slaughtered those who opposed his fleet on the seas and granted clemency to those who surrendered and vowed to no longer partake in piracy."

"That he did, but there are always some rogues who continue to ply the trade. These bastards are clever. Their raids are infrequent and in the grand scheme of things, are only considered a nuisance by the imperial navy and thus, not worthy of any further action. I have no doubt they are after us."

"Will they catch us?" Valerius asked.

Artimus let out an audible sigh. "Easily. We are weighed down with cargo and this is a heavy ship. Their vessel is sleek and light timbered."

"Can we fend them off? How many men do they carry and are they well trained?"

The captain shrugged. "I would guess that they outnumber us. The pirates are more cutthroats than warriors, but my crew are not exactly trained fighters."

"Well, we are," Marcellus reassured him. "The tribune and I will give them some discouragement. We've brought our weapons along. These bastards are going to rue the day they fucked with this transport. They may not be deserving of the imperial navy's wrath but they are of mine. Come on, Tribune, let's get our weapons. Hades is waiting for them; they just don't know it yet."

A short while later, the two officers emerged from their quarters near the stern of the ship with their bows strung, quivers full of arrows, and swords strapped to their sides.

The captain's eyes nearly popped out. "Jupiter's arse, where did you get those bows?"

Marcellus offered a sardonic smile. "We have deployed these weapons on a number of occasions, much to the chagrin of our adversaries, I might add. These arrows can go through a man at close range and are accurate at long distances. Now, why don't you get your crew ready to repel the boarders and tell us where our best vantage point is here."

Artimus replied, his tone bitter. "I believe their ship will attempt to maneuver close to ours, and they will throw their grappling hooks to wed the ships together. Once they do, they'll swarm in through the sides. And if they succeed in defeating us, it's more than likely that they'll toss the survivors into the sea."

Valerius pondered the captain's words. "That is cruel. How are pirate ships armed? Do they have bolt throwers and catapults?"

"Nah, none of that. Besides, they don't want to damage the ship or its cargo—that is what they are after. We need to wait and see how they'll approach us. My ship can't outrun them, laden with cargo as she is. They have more maneuverability, so for the time being, stay amidships. That would be the best place."

"Then Marcellus and I will station ourselves amidships. Captain, go organize your crew."

Once Artimus was out of earshot, Valerius turned to Marcellus. "How do you think we should defend the ship? I have little experience in naval conflict."

"As do I, Tribune." Marcellus looked at the approaching vessel, still some distance away, and bowed his head in concentration. "Let me ask you a question. What did they teach you during your military training? What is key to defeating an enemy?"

"Well, a lot of things. But I remember our instructors telling us to concentrate on the foe's weak point, but somehow, I don't think that is relevant here. Let me see, exercise command and control, but again, not applicable here."

"You got closer with the latter point, Tribune. Almost there. Go on."

"Let me think," he muttered. "Command and control. Not much I can do on this ship. Their command and control... Hah, I got it! We attack their command and control."

"Precisely, Tribune. That pirate vessel will not be expecting our barrage of arrows. When they are within range, we'll first go after the man at the tiller. That will fuck up their approach. Once we take him out, we'll identify their captain and focus on him. I sense that their crew will not know what to do without a leader."

Valerius grinned. "I like the plan. What happens in the event they have a second-in-command who is willing to lead them?"

"Then we fill his arse with arrows as well."

The pair glanced at Artimus and his crew, now gathered near the stern. The men had an assortment of weapons ranging from swords and daggers to thick wooden clubs. However, they were sorely lacking in armor and spears. It was hardly an impressive display of force and certainly not one to match heavily armed pirates.

Valerius returned his gaze to the enemy ship, still distant but getting closer by the minute. He could now observe their crew eagerly lining the rails, waiting for the opportunity to board what they believed to be a defenseless merchant ship. As the afternoon wore on, the pirate vessel moved nearer. Sunlight glinted off the swords and pikes of the pirate throng. Valerius could now distinguish the individual features of the pirates. They held their weapons up high and snarled curses, which were carried by the wind. They were a scurrilous looking bunch. But he noted an absence of armor. He guessed few, if any, had any military experience. They looked like a mob of untrained fighters who expected easy pickings. But they were in for a rude awakening, and it was approaching soon.

Just as Artimus predicted, the enemy ship maneuvered parallel to the transport. Around thirty of the pirate crew lined the railing, and they were almost within bow range. "Ready?" roared Marcellus. The two men pulled their bowstrings taut, all the way back to their cheeks. There was a twang as both released their deadly missiles. Inopportunely, the moment the deadly projectiles were shot, a swell lifted the ship higher. The arrows soared high, missing their intended target. Valerius muttered a silent curse and deftly withdrew another arrow from his quiver. Marcellus did the same. Two more arrows were delivered to the enemy ship. This time, both arrows struck with such force that the unfortunate pirate manning the tiller was swept off his feet by the impact. The rudderless pirate ship veered away at a slight angle as the tiller swung free.

Before the pirate crew could react, another volley thudded into two more men. While smoothly notching the next arrow, Marcellus growled, "I don't see their leader yet. Just keep shooting into them." With that, he released the arrow, which pierced through an unfortunate pirate's skull. The pair launched several volleys, slaughtering more of the enemy.

By now, most of the crew of the pirate ship were cowering behind whatever they could find. Another pirate rushed over and manned the tiller. He crouched behind a shelter used for foul weather so that they could no longer target him. One individual, a large man with a full beard, stood apart, exhorting the men to take their positions and prepare to board. He waved a sword to spur them on. Marcellus pointed with the tip of his bow. "I think we've found our man. Let's take him down and end this."

Calmly and deliberately, the two men took aim. They released their arrows simultaneously. The pirate captain went down hard, both arrows piercing his torso. Marcellus pointed at the figure manning the tiller. He had shifted his position and was partially exposed. "Let's go after him again. He'll be a hard target, but we'll give it a try."

The pair unleashed arrows at the man. To evade them, the man ducked and leaped to the left, and as he did so, yanked at the tiller. He was unscathed, but his evasive actions had an unintended consequence—the pirate ship veered directly toward the merchant vessel. With a tremendous crash, the bow of the pirate vessel collided into the side of the merchant ship. The ugly sound of shattering timber filled the air. The crews of both ships were hurled to their decks by the force of the impact. Marcellus and Valerius lay sprawled on their backs. Marcellus grunted heavily as he lifted his bulky form off the wooden surface. "Pluto's cock, I didn't expect that."

A tall figure with long dark hair picked himself off the deck of the pirate ship and threw a grappling hook. The line arced toward the merchant ship and struck the deck. The hook embedded itself into the railing of Neptune's Blessing and the line was yanked taut. Several more grappling hooks were flung, drawing the merchant ship into the pirate vessel's deadly embrace. The two ships crashed into each other yet again, but less violently than before. The tall man, now the new pirate captain, nimbly leaped to the deck of the merchant ship, near the stern. "Follow me," he shouted, motioning for the crew to move forward. "Let's get these b—ARGH." A gladius skewered his chest, cutting off his last words. The man collapsed in a heap in front of Marcellus, who breathed heavily at the exertion of sprinting forward. More pirates leaped over the railing of the ship but were savagely swarmed by the crew of the merchant ship. The few surviving pirates that had boarded the merchant lost heart at the death of their second-in-command and the bloody end of their unfortunate comrades. They scrambled back as the ropes attached to the grappling hooks were severed by the merchant crew.

The enemy ship veered away, listing slightly to one side—the pirate crew frozen in fear at the devastation that had been wreaked upon them. As quickly as the threat to the merchant ship had arrived, it dissipated. Everything abruptly became still except for the transport plowing through the calm seas. The merchant crew cheered at their victory.

A relieved Artimus emerged from below decks where he had run to inspect his vessel for any damage. "Thanks to my double planked hull, there is minimal damage below." He eyed his two passengers. "I don't believe I've ever seen anything like that. Serves those bastards right. Too bad you didn't kill them all. But now I understand what Sabinus said about you. My thanks and that of my crew to both of you."

"Glad we could be of service," said Marcellus. "Too bad they got away. They belong at the bottom of the sea."

"Maybe they are headed for the bottom after all," said Artimus. "They may have sustained considerable damage below the main deck of their thin planked vessel. I hope Neptune sends their craven hearts to Hades."

The crew approached them in small groups or individually and offered their thanks, no doubt bewildered at the display of archery and the swift death that had rained upon the Cilician vessel. After a while, the excited chatter died down and the ship resumed its course toward the port of Ostia.

⚓

Valerius stood alone against the railing of the ship as it heaved slightly in gentle swells, waiting its turn to enter the harbor. Marcellus was off telling war stories and other tall tales to the crew. The sail had been furled as preparations were being made to dock. In the distance, Valerius could see the quay of the busy port of Ostia. Many ships with tall masts occupied the artificially constructed harbor. Large warehouses rose from the water's edge, eager to receive a vast amount of goods to supply the city of Rome. Positioned at the front of the harbor was a magnificent edifice with stone pillars that rose above all else: a temple dedicated to the Roman sea god Neptune.

Valerius gazed at the water, which glinted like diamonds in the sunlight. Sea birds squawked and flitted about. Once again, he contemplated why he was here. He could not fathom what assignment—if indeed that was the reason he had been summoned—Tiberius had in mind for him. He had no connection to Rome anymore. As far as he was concerned, he was out of sight and out of the minds of those who called this city their home. All his family and friends were back in German territory on the banks of the Rhenus. Furthermore, he did not miss Rome at all and had no desire to return here—this was in no way a homecoming. The ship slowly edged closer toward land. From Ostia, it was only a ten-mile trip to Rome. His unknown fate awaited him there.

CHAPTER III

ROME

After they arrived in Rome late in the morning, Valerius dispatched a messenger from the inn where he was staying to the imperial palace. The written note politely asked if the following day was suitable for an audience with the imperator and, if not, when. The messenger returned without delay, stating that his presence along with that of Centurion Marcellus Veronus was requested at the third hour the next morning. Valerius was a bit surprised he had been granted an audience so quickly, and he was heartened by the timely response. It further strengthened the hypothesis that Tiberius was anxious to speak with him on a matter of some urgency. He had expected to wait several days or even a week. With that business taken care of, he turned to more hedonistic pursuits. He and Marcellus went to the baths to eradicate four weeks of salt spray and sweat. Rome had the best baths in the empire. And since meeting the Emperor while smelling like a goat wouldn't improve his already rocky relationship with Tiberius, off they went.

The bath they visited did not disappoint. It was located in the forum area, near the temple of Jupiter Optimus Maximus. The building was elaborate and beautifully designed, bordering on decadent. In the *tepidarium*, the oblong hall that housed the swimming pool, the adornments were the epitome of elegance. A giant dome covered the pool, allowing filtered light to illuminate a floor of brightly colored mosaics. The bathing pools, lined with marble tiles, were filled with crystal clear water warmed to just the right temperature. While the pools were soothing, in Valerius's opinion, relaxing in the steam room was, by far, the best part. He could have stayed there all day. He was scraped and massaged into a languorous state. He had to admit that if there was one thing he missed about Rome, it was the baths. Oh, there were baths in Germania and throughout the empire alright, but they were nothing compared to the luxuriousness and grandeur of those in Rome.

Now back at his accommodation, relaxed and refreshed, Valerius sighed in contentment. He lay supine upon his soft bed at the Inn of the Dove, a stylish place not far from the Roman forum and the imperial palace. It was a far better lodging than his cramped and uncomfortable quarters onboard the ship. Since it was mid-afternoon, he decided a short snooze would enhance his feeling of contentment. He had just put his hands behind his head when he heard a slight rustle. Looking at the room's entrance, he spied a small piece of parchment being slid beneath his door.

Curious, Valerius rose from his bed and picked up the note. It read *I will meet you in your room tonight after the dinner hour.* And it was signed, *A*. Who in Hades was A, and why would she—he deduced it was a she based on the penmanship—want to meet with him? Who knew he was in the city besides Tiberius? He hurried out into the hallway, but it was empty.

Valerius knocked at the door of the room next to his. Marcellus opened the door. "I thought you were going to take a quick nap?"

Valerius merely brushed past his friend, entered the room, and handed Marcellus the note. The latter squinted at the parchment and then looked up at Valerius. "This looks like it was written by a woman. I won't tell Hereca if that's what you're worried about."

"Your humor isn't appreciated now. One, I have no idea who 'A' might be, and second, who knows I'm in the city except for Tiberius and his advisors? This cryptic note is a bit unsettling."

Marcellus frowned in thought. "No old girlfriends with a name beginning with A?"

"No!" Valerius exclaimed. "And even if I did have one, how would she know I was in the city?" He fretted, struggling to make a decision. "This is what we're going to do. We'll have an early dinner and then come back to my room and wait for our mystery guest. Have your sword ready. I don't trust whoever sent this. It could be some form of entrapment by the Emperor or his minions. Perhaps this is some convoluted plot hatched by Sejanus. We will be prepared for whatever comes our way."

"Sounds like a plan, Tribune," said Marcellus. "I must admit, it is a bit confounding. We have only been in the city, what, a few hours, and already the intrigue has begun."

Later that evening, after a hurried meal of broiled fish and vegetables at a nearby establishment, the two men returned to Valerius's room. Their swords were within arm's reach, to be used at a moment's notice. They waited as dusk fell and darkness slowly descended on the city. They lit several oil lamps, which cast a dim glow on the walls. More time passed but still no visitor. Valerius began to think the whole thing was a ruse. Perhaps the note had been slipped under the wrong door. It was certainly a possibility as the note had not been addressed to him. The oil lamps continued to burn with no trace of their visitor.

Valerius and Marcellus sat in silence, each lost in their own thoughts, when there was a barely perceptible tapping at the door. Valerius nodded at Marcellus and rose from his chair, gripping his long sword. With a heave, he yanked the door open. In front of him stood a woman in a light green stola—of exceptional quality, by the look of it—and a thin veil obscuring her face. He reached behind the woman and grabbed her, forcing her into the room with his free hand. She gasped in protest at her rough reception. Valerius then quickly kicked the door shut without loosening his hold on the woman. Marcellus menacingly leveled his sword at the mystery figure.

"Unhand me," said the clandestine visitor.

"Who are you?" Valerius demanded.

The woman in front of him slowly uncovered her face. Valerius gasped in recognition. Despite the years, her face remained youthful, framed by vibrant, cascading brown tresses. "Lady Agrippina, forgive my rudeness. I knew not it was you who sent me the note."

The woman grinned at his discomfiture. "Is that the way an officer and a gentleman greets a woman of the imperial family, the widow of the late Germanicus Caesar?"

Valerius could feel the blush rising on his face. "My ap…apologies," he stuttered. "Please pardon my manners. I knew not who you were." Recovering somewhat, he continued. "Let me introduce you to my old friend and comrade, Centurion Marcellus Veronus. Marcellus, this is the Lady Agrippina, the widow of Germanicus."

Her face brightened. "Ah, I've heard that name before. My husband spoke fondly of you, Marcellus. Now, let's skip this "lady" stuff and call me Agrippina."

Valerius, still in a state of bewilderment, spoke. "Of course, Agrippina, but why are you here? I could have come to your residence if—"

Agrippina held up her hand. "Shush. I came in secrecy. It is best no one knows I am here, especially Tiberius. Listen to me, Valerius. You are in grave danger. I'm firmly convinced that Tiberius had my husband poisoned. Anyone who was friends or associated with my husband and I are being persecuted by Tiberius and that worm, Sejanus. They believe we are part of a conspiracy to take the throne."

"Agrippina, I don't understand any of this, and how did you even know I was in Rome?"

She adopted a vulpine expression. "I have my sources."

Valerius appeared perplexed. "As a statement of fact, I have been out of the army for over fifteen years. I run a thriving business on the German frontier and have no ties to Rome except to pay my taxes. Why would I be considered a threat?"

She grimaced and her voice became husky with emotion. "You assume these are rational people. They are not. My entire family is under suspicion, even my sons and daughters. The only one Tiberius seems to favor is my son, Gaius—whom everyone knows as Caligula—and he is only in his teens."

She wiped away a solitary tear streaking down her face. "Listen to me. My husband thought a great deal of you, Valerius. He said Rome needed more men like you who are dedicated to their home, their family, and their nation. Marcellus, he said the same about you."

"Thank you for those kind words, my Lady—I mean—Agrippina. But I still don't understand. Tiberius wants something from me. He couldn't have summoned me to Rome just to dispose of me."

Agrippina stared at him. "You are correct on that account. But if you displease him in any manner, he will not hesitate to have you executed and your family sold into slavery. He is a ruthless, vindictive old man who has no compassion for anyone. I could supply you with a list of people who have offended him in some major or even petty way who are no longer with us."

"My father expressed similar sentiments," said Valerius. "He was concerned about my recall to Rome."

She leaned closer to the two men and lowered her voice. "But there is more to this story. Listen carefully, this is what I know. Weeks ago, Tiberius received a dispatch from Germania warning him of a possible German uprising against Rome. Sejanus dismissed the news as gossip, but this didn't dissuade Tiberius. The Emperor and the Germans have a long history, most of which is unpleasant. Tiberius is always fearful that there will be another revolt and slaughter of his legions. Now, this is where it gets murky. From what I've heard, Sejanus is the one who recommended Gallus, the current Governor of Germania, for the position. Those two are thick as thieves. Sejanus and Gallus must be up to something, and Sejanus is covering for his friend. Somehow, your name was brought up as someone who might investigate what is going on in Germania concerning a rebellion. I'm not sure who bought your name up; it might have been Tiberius himself. But you must be extremely cautious. Either Sejanus or Tiberius could eliminate you."

Valerius stroked his chin in thought. "I know there is no love lost between Tiberius and me, but I don't recall ever being at cross-purposes with Sejanus back in the German campaign. We hardly ever spoke."

"Envy," opined Marcellus. "He doesn't like you because you were decorated a hero of Rome, and you were Germanicus's favorite. It's as simple as that. The General listened to you. At least, that's my take on this."

Agrippina gave them both an imploring look and addressed Valerius. "Please be careful. You were a loyal supporter of my husband, and I would hate to see anything happen to you. I must go now. The longer I linger, the better the chance that my absence being discovered." She grasped Valerius's hand with both of hers. "Good fortune, Valerius. Once again, be careful. If I can be of any assistance in this matter, please contact me. Farewell." She abruptly turned around and departed without further ado.

Valerius sat across from Marcellus and frowned. "Agrippina's words haven't instilled a great deal of comfort—not that I was confident of a friendly reception tomorrow. We must appear eager to do anything Tiberius demands of us. Our manner must be punctilious."

"What in Hades is 'punctilious'?"

"You can guess. No missteps. We must be painstakingly obedient to please. If he says jump, we ask 'how high?' Got it?"

"I believe I get the gist of what you said, Tribune. Punctilious it is."

The next morning, Valerius, along with Marcellus, stood in the cramped antechamber of the imperial palace on the Palatine. There were no seats. Two imposing, stern-faced Praetorian guards—their steely gaze directed straight ahead, faces empty—stood outside the massive doors of the imperial audience hall where Tiberius sat in judgment. Several other suppliants also awaited their turn. One paced back and forth, while another stood in a corner and stared at the floor, anxiously wringing his hands.

Valerius wore his best toga, a cream-colored garment of the finest weave. Marcellus, on the other hand, refused to wear a toga no matter the circumstances. He was a centurion, and centurions, in his eyes, didn't wear togas. That was reserved for the nobility. Instead, he wore a plain knee-length tunic. It was clean and had been freshly pressed this morning. Valerius didn't even attempt to convince him otherwise. He knew it was something Marcellus wouldn't do, despite the scheduled audience with the most powerful man in the empire.

The large wooden doors to the audience chamber were thrust open. Two Praetorians appeared, dragging away a despondent man, who was sniffling in despair. Just as quickly, the doors were shut from the inside. Marcellus turned to Valerius and spoke quietly, "I've never met with an Emperor before. I hope I survive the experience."

Valerius frowned. "Just remember what we spoke of earlier back at the inn. Emperors put their marching boots on one at a time, just like you and me. The difference is that they believe the sun rises in the east out of their arse. So indulge him. Don't speak unless you are addressed directly by Tiberius. It is me he dislikes, so let me bear the brunt of his words. I will do the speaking for both of us. In the event he decides to do away with me, there is a chance you may be spared. Let's see what he wants from us and pray that the Lady Agrippina has mistaken Tiberius's disposition."

With that, the doors opened. The chamberlain appeared and gave the pair a supercilious glance. "Tribune Valerius Maximus, Centurion Marcellus Veronus, you are next. Please follow me. Stop where I do—about ten paces from the imperator—and wait to be addressed." He turned about and began walking. The two men followed and strode down a wide aisle, flanked on both sides by empty wooden benches. The capacious chamber had a high-vaulted ceiling. As they approached, Valerius noted several advisors and a scribe, who would record the entire conversation, to the right on the audience floor. Sitting in an elaborately fashioned curule chair, which was resting on a dais raised about four feet above the audience floor, was Tiberius. On the imperator's left stood Sejanus in his Praetorian uniform, replete with gleaming armor and the sign of the scorpion affixed to his breastplate. His appearance was impeccable, his hair finely barbered. The entire configuration of the room and the placement of Tiberius and his lieutenant had but one purpose: to intimidate.

Valerius approached Tiberius and stopped at the requisite ten paces away. He had not seen the Emperor in over fifteen years, and his haggard appearance shocked him. His face was lined and what little remained of his hair was gray. He was in his sixties and had not aged well.

Tiberius glared at the two men, his gaze mostly directed at Valerius. He then spoke. "Tribune Valerius Maximus, hero of Rome." His tone was anything but friendly, dripping with sarcasm. He continued glowering at the two Roman officers. "You are out of uniform."

Although Valerius had not expected a warm reception, the sudden verbal attack unnerved him. The Emperor's remarks were unequivocally hostile and biting. He searched quickly for an appropriate response. After a brief period of silence, he responded, "My apologies, Imperator. The fault was mine. Please forgive my indiscretion."

Standing at the side, Sejanus smirked, knowing that Valerius was squirming inside. "Did my Praetorian officer not inform you that you were recalled to active duty? What do you have to say for yourself, Tribune?" He emphasized the word *tribune* to make his displeasure clear.

"Yes, an oversight on my part. Again, my sincerest apologies. Please tell me how I may serve Rome once again," said Valerius.

Tiberius remained silent, continuing to scowl, no doubt knowing he was making his subjects uncomfortable. At last, he spoke. "As you are probably aware, I have seven legions along the Rhenus, which is more than anywhere else in the empire. But this region continues to be a troublesome spot." He paused, waiting to see if Valerius would add to the subject.

Valerius decided to remain silent. He would let Tiberius do the talking.

Tiberius continued, "Rome cannot afford, nor will she tolerate, any rebellion from the Germanic tribes. The treasury is stretched thin. Other areas of our rule to the south and east require our attention. Now, this is where you enter. I want you to keep me apprised of the doings of these devilish tribes along the Rhenus. They are always fomenting rebellion."

Valerius was relieved. He now understood the purpose of his summons. Agrippina's assessment had been correct. This was the duty Tiberius wanted him to perform. He cleared his throat, all the while glibly forming a diplomatic response. "Sire, of course, I'll do what I can. I am but a modest merchant, trading goods in Germania. Although I am curious, sire, as to why would you select me and my former centurion for this mission."

A look of annoyance crossed Tiberius's countenance. "Don't give me that. You're a lot more than some unassuming merchant. The tax records suggest you are quite profitable. My sources tell me that you have much influence among the German tribes. Your trade is primarily with them. Even your wife is a German, although why you could not marry a proper Roman matron is beyond me. Your trading venture permits you to interact with the German clans. Furthermore, you have extensive experience in military matters with these German barbarians."

Valerius silently crowed, for the Emperor had just admitted that he needed Valerius and Marcellus for their expertise on German affairs. In all probability, it was Tiberius who had thought of them for this mission. The tribune offered a silent prayer of thanks that he had been scrupulously honest and paid every single denarius owed to Rome for his business transactions must have been under considerable scrutiny.

"It is true, sire, that I have some influence among the various tribes along the Rhenus. I trade quite freely. My wife is instrumental in the negotiations. While I speak the language well, she understands them better than I do."

"You do more than trade along the Rhenus," Tiberius sneered. "I have been informed that you trade with the tribes in the interior of that accursed territory. Now, as I recall, Tribune, that is illegal. What do you say to that?"

Valerius shrugged. He knew there was an edict against trading with the hostile tribes in the interior of Germania, far away from the Roman presence on the Rhenus. He also knew that his trading company had occasionally violated this decree. "We trade principally with the tribes along the Rhenus. This is where our trading vessels can access goods. We do not seek trade with those other tribes in the interior as they are bellicose and not to be trusted. If we have traded with these folks, I'm sure it wasn't by design."

Tiberius was having none of it, his voice rising once again. "Rubbish, Tribune. Did you really think I would accept that pathetic explanation? I cannot believe you are spinning that tale. You may have been able to get away with that kind of nonsense with Germanicus but not me. And he is no longer here to protect you. You are insolent."

Valerius shuddered internally at the verbal assault. *Insolent.* It was the same word Gaius Labenius had used to describe him. He needed to return to the subject of what he could do for Tiberius. "Sire, please tell me how I can be of service with respect to the Germanic tribes. Tell me what you need me to do."

"Alright, let's get to the heart of it. I've been getting unconfirmed reports—rumors, if you will—that an insurrection is once again brewing in that infernal territory."

"Might I inquire as to who is plotting the revolt, sire? As you are well aware, there are many tribes and factions."

"It was reported to me that the Frisii are actively planning an uprising against Rome."

"The Frisii, sire? They have been staunch allies of Rome in the past. They greatly assisted Germanicus in the invasion many years ago."

"I don't need a history lesson!" shouted Tiberius. "Tribune, my sources tell me it is the Frisii."

"Yes, sire, of course, the Frisii. I haven't dealt with them, but I can probe into the situation."

"Good, Tribune. I want you to keep me informed of what is transpiring there in the north. So, you understand, your mission is twofold. First, you will use your connections to keep an eye on the Frisii and any other German tribes contemplating rebellion. Any intelligence you gather is to be reported to the Governor and me. Second, in the event that there is an armed insurrection against Rome, you will assist and provide counsel to the proper military commanders on how to defeat the Germans. You have more experience than most in fighting these barbarians."

"Sire, I am curious as to why you have sought Marcellus and me for this mission. Isn't this something Governor Gallus should be handling?"

A trace of a grimace crossed the Emperor's face. "I have my reasons, Tribune. You possess knowledge of and skills with the German peoples that Governor Gallus does not. I will dispatch a message to Governor Gallus informing him that you will be acting as my agent concerning the affairs of the Frisii. Of course, you will need to meet with Gallus and keep him informed of what transpires. Understood?"

"Yes, sire. What is the best way to communicate with you and your advisors?"

"You may use the imperial dispatches arranged through the legionary fortresses along the Rhenus. You seem to be on good terms with Gaius Sepulchius Labenius, the legate at Oppidum Ubiorum. Speak to him about it."

Valerius cringed. *Gaius had been spot on about spies in his own encampment. The fact that Tiberius knows about our meeting is proof of that.* "I will return immediately to Germania, investigate this potential rebellion by the Frisii, and keep you apprised of what I hear."

Tiberius stood, eyeing the two Roman officers. "Don't disappoint me, Tribune, and that goes for you as well, Centurion. You are tasked with the same mission as the tribune. The two of you are in this together. Is that understood, Centurion?"

Marcellus stared straight ahead and dutifully replied. "Yes, sire. You can count on us."

"Very well. You are both dismissed. My chamberlain will hand you a letter of introduction to Governor Gallus on the way out."

They exited the imperial audience chamber, the door closing behind them. Valerius whispered through the corner of his mouth, "Not a word until we are clear of the palace. Understood?"

Marcellus grunted in reply. The two officers walked down the hallway. Praetorian guards stood positioned along their route, paying no attention to them. They made a sharp right and strode down another corridor before reaching the exit. They continued walking along the avenue, which merged with one of the main thoroughfares of Rome. The crowds had thickened since they had entered, and the noise level had swelled.

Marcellus turned to Valerius. "That was my first time meeting an Emperor, and I never want to experience that again. By Venus's magnificent tits, that was one Hades of an ass-chewing. You were correct, Tribune. He really doesn't like you. No matter what you said, he went after you." He chuckled. "So much for your *punctilious* decorum."

Valerius grimaced. "I had kind of expected such a reception, but the ferocity of his anger surprised me. That arsehole Sejanus was reveling in my misery. He stood there smirking the entire time." He stopped walking and faced Marcellus. "On the bright side, we still have our heads attached to our shoulders. We need to get back home directly and begin our mission—our lives hang in the balance. We will seek passage on the next ship sailing north to Germania. The sooner we can depart this city of vipers, the better."

"Should we contact Lady Agrippina and inform her of our discussion with the Emperor?"

Valerius paused. "No. Tiberius might find out about it. Better not to take the chance. Let's get going."

Marcellus offered a wry smile. "And this time, no arsehole pirates to fuck up our voyage."

Valerius grinned. "Agreed."

CHAPTER IV

THE TERRITORY OF THE FRISII

Chieftains representing the various clans of the Frisii had gathered once again. They assembled in the main lodge house of the village. It was a warm spring day, and many had discarded their cloaks, preferring their woolen tunics. Murmured conversation filled the air, punctuated by the occasional laugh. Eadric, the chieftain of the village, rose from his wooden bench. He was not the leader of the Frisii nation—no one possessed that title—but he was the leader of the largest clan, and they were the hosts this day. Moreover, though not the proclaimed chieftain of the Frisii, he was the closest thing to it. He was an imposing individual with a sizeable physique and was old enough to have acquired the wisdom that years impart. He glanced around the room and held up his arms for silence. The conversation quickly ceased.

"Welcome all. I hope you are all enjoying the hospitality of my village." He paused with this remark, his expression turning solemn. "We all met over the winter concerning the vexing issue of the increased taxes imposed on us by Rome. The levies demanded of us this year in terms of hides are nearly double that of the previous year. We recognized that it would be impossible for us to meet the quota even under the best of circumstances. The alternative was to sell our land and our children into servitude to meet the tax payment."

He paused to survey his audience and then continued. "Waging war against Rome is not a matter to be taken lightly. We have all witnessed the disastrous results suffered by other Germanic peoples who revolted years ago. Tragically, some of those tribes no longer exist."

Angry shouts filled the lodge. Eadric held up his arms once again for silence. He began again. "Let me summarize where we are: our entreaties to the Roman tax official, the *quaestor*, were rebuffed. Our quotas remain the same—no exceptions or remedies. All of us agreed when we met previously that we would revolt against Rome—an armed insurrection—rather than sell our land and surrender our children to servitude. However, we decided to continue to pursue this worrisome tax discussion with the Roman officials."

Eadric turned to his left. "I would like to have Birgir discuss his latest face-to-face meeting with Cornelius Quadratus, the Roman quaestor. As you will recall, we had designated Birgir to be our envoy as he is well-versed in Latin and possesses excellent negotiating skills. Birgir, come up here."

Birgir, a middle-aged man of small stature and studious appearance, walked to the front of the assembly. He peered at the audience for a moment before beginning. "Last week, I ventured up the Vecht, where it intersects the Rhenus, and then upstream to Noviomagus to meet with the quaestor, Cornelius Quadratus, for a second time. After waiting most of the day outside his office, he finally agreed to see me." Birgir paused, disappointment etched across his face. "I explained to him that the Frisii can't possibly pay the new taxes imposed on us as they are almost double the amount of the previous year. My manner was polite and restrained but Quadratus had little sympathy for our plight. He angrily denounced our tribe, calling us a bunch of whiners, and said that if we had any common sense, we would pay the new levies."

Birgir frowned as he remembered the conversation. "I tried to keep my tone civil and asked him what authority the Romans had to double our taxes. The man laughed in my face and said that it was because they could do whatever they chose. I again implored him to reconsider, stating that we would need to sell our wives and children into servitude to meet the new levies. The man greeted my remarks with scorn. He replied that if it was so, then that is what we should do. Then, he turned his back on me and told me to leave as he had another appointment."

There was silence. Eadric walked up to the front of the assembly and clapped his hand on Birgir's shoulder. "You tried your best, Birgir. No need to be ashamed."

Eadric gazed at the mustered chieftains. "You have now heard of our exchange with the Romans. They appear to be unyielding. Nothing has changed about our situation. Our strategy, which we had decided upon months ago, was to prepare for armed conflict."

He continued in a desultory tone, "I will join Birgir and attempt to gain an audience with the Governor of the territory one more time, but I'm not optimistic that this will bear fruit. Our problems began when this new Governor, Gallus, took over the reins a year

ago. Quadratus, his quaestor, is just following his directives. We must exhaust all other possibilities before resorting to armed conflict. Does anyone have anything they wish to contribute at this time?" His query was met with silence—no fractious debate, just a solidarity of purpose. "Good, then we are all in agreement."

Eadric and the other chieftains would have been shocked if they had known that Emperor Tiberius was already aware of their conversations earlier that winter. He had his spies everywhere—which was the reason Valerius and Marcellus had been summoned to Rome. If the Frisii were planning a surprise revolt, that ship had already sailed.

If the same scenario had presented itself to the other German tribes, there would be angry exclamatory outbursts and thumping of chests with cries to kill the accursed Romans. There was none of that here: just grim determination and cold, calculated fury, which made it all the more ominous. Was war coming to the German territory once again?

CHAPTER V

RETURN TO GERMANIA

Valerius and Hereca sat with Marcellus in their *peristylium,* the garden area of their home. It was an unusually warm spring evening made even more pleasant by a variety of colorful flowers in full bloom, which filled the air with their fragrance. Several oil lamps illuminated the surroundings, providing a warm glow to the idyllic atmosphere. It had been a joyous homecoming that afternoon as the children and Hereca had swarmed over Valerius, smothering him with hugs and kisses, thankful for his safe return.

Now, the children had been put to bed, and by prior agreement, Marcellus had arrived at Valerius's house to discuss what they were going to do about the task delegated to them by Tiberius. Perhaps *delegated* was too kind a word and *commanded* more appropriate. Either way, one thing was clear: their lives depended upon their success. Hereca was a necessary participant for, although she was not an officer in the legions, she knew the German tribes and their ways better than anyone.

While Valerius spoke the language quite fluently as a result of his service under Germanicus, he was often flummoxed by the behavior of the Germans. They were a prickly bunch and didn't think as he did or trust him. This is where Hereca would be indispensable. The success of their trading company was, in no small part, due to her savvy. The Germans could be crafty—bordering on duplicitous—but seldom did they get the better of Hereca, and if they did, she would cut off any future dealings with them.

Valerius patiently recounted to Hereca what Tiberius had demanded of them and the purpose of their reinstatement in the legions. Their dual role was to be military advisors in the event of armed conflict and to be civilian spies posing as traders. He then mentioned the Frisii tribe, which, according to Tiberius's sources, was planning an insurrection. Hopefully, they would engage in a mission of peace and the decision to revolt had not already been made.

A puzzled expression settled on Hereca's face and she pursed her lips in thought. The two men looked at her in silence, waiting for her to speak. Finally, she began. "From what I know of the Frisii, they are a proud people and not given to rash decisions. They are deliberate in their thoughts and action and not prone to impetuous behavior like some of the other German tribes. Their dominion encompasses a large swathe of land at the western edge of Germania and extends to the sea. They are farmers, fishermen, and traders. Of all the tribes, they would be at the bottom of my list of potential rioters. After we meet with Governor Gallus, we should go visit the Frisii and talk to their leaders under the guise of having goods to trade with them. Let's feel them out—see what they are thinking."

Marcellus replied, "Hereca, are you sure it's a good idea for you to accompany us to meet with Governor Gallus? Tiberius tasked us with this duty as officers of the legions." Although Marcellus's comment was well-intentioned, it made Hereca furious. German women were not raised to be subservient like Roman matrons. They were wildly independent, often accompanying their husbands in battle. By the light of the oil lamp, Valerius recognized that all too familiar glint in her eyes which he knew from experience was not a good thing.

Hereca responded, her tone laconic, "Oh, so I'm expected to be the good wife and watch you two march off on this suicidal mission. By sweet Minerva's arse, that would be a debacle!" She had picked up some colorful swear words in Latin over the years from the Roman-ized settlement in which she lived. "Although the Frisii are not my tribe, I do understand them better than the two of you combined. I am going with you to meet with the Governor and will not brook any dissension from you or my husband. Your lives are at stake, and you'll have a better chance of succeeding with my help."

Marcellus was too stunned to offer a response. But Valerius deftly stepped into the conversation. "Hereca, of course we could use your help with this mission. You are indispensable; you know that. I believe Marcellus was only speaking from the perspective of the legions, and it would serve no purpose for you to become involved in matters concerning the military aspect of our mission. Isn't that right, Marcellus?"

The discomfited Marcellus breathed a sigh of relief while attempting to avoid Hereca's withering glare. "Y-yes, yes," he stuttered. "Hereca, I'm aware of how much you've contributed to our venture and your skillful handling of these Germans, who are sometimes hostile to us. Forgive me. In no way did I mean to diminish your role."

Ignoring his wife's severe stare and lifting his arms in a placating gesture, Valerius continued, "Now, Hereca, let's look at this rationally.

First, Marcellus and I will need to meet the Governor with our letter of introduction from Tiberius. The letter does not mention you—only Marcellus and me. And we will be in uniform. Now, the Governor isn't going to like this one bit. He'll think we are interfering in his affairs. I would feel the same if I were him. This is a military issue, and Marcellus is correct, you shouldn't be part of that process. The intervention of a German female in the military matters of the state wouldn't be welcomed. You understand that, don't you? It would make a delicate situation worse."

Before she could protest, he hurriedly moved on. "But the way I see this, we need to move on two distinct paths here. One, formally through the Governor as dictated by Tiberius's letter of introduction, and second, through discussions with the Germans. This is where you will be most helpful. Perhaps, as you suggested, you could initiate a dialogue with the Frisii."

Not appeased at all, Hereca scowled at her husband and then Marcellus. She stood up abruptly and stormed out of the room without saying a word.

Valerius stared at her retreating form and shrugged. He offered a rueful smile. "She gets like that sometimes, and there is nothing one can do or say that will mollify her." Valerius remained silent for a few moments and then continued, "Now, back to the issue at hand. Our first order of business is to visit the Governor, Julius Frontinius Gallus. He has established his headquarters and residence at Noviomagus, which, conveniently for us, is downriver in the same direction of the territory of the Frisii. We can take one of the river barges downstream from here. Do you know anything about our esteemed Governor?"

Marcellus shook his head. "Only what is common knowledge. He is newly appointed, last year, in fact. If he is like many other governors, he is out to fill his own coffers. If I had to speculate, it is no coincidence that there is talk of rebellion among the Germans after the selection of a fresh governor."

"Aye, I believe you are spot on with your observation," responded Valerius. "What I don't understand is this: if there is trouble brewing, why doesn't Tiberius go directly to Gallus? Why are we involved? Tiberius squirmed a bit when I asked him that very same question. He almost choked on his words when he said that we had expertise in German affairs. There are dynamics surrounding the Governor and Sejanus that I do not fully understand."

Marcellus stroked his chin in thought. "I'm certainly not knowledgeable about political intrigue, although I did see a fair share of backstabbing in my years of service in the legions. But I would surmise the following: first, and this is most important, Tiberius needs us. He recognizes that we know this territory as well as anyone. Second, we are expendable. If we fail, he can wash his hands of us. As much as I admire the Lady Agrippina, I don't buy that Tiberius holds any special grudge against us. He might not like us, but that is neither here nor there. I don't doubt there is real animosity between Agrippina's family and that of Tiberius, but we are not part of that. He wants us to succeed. Although Tiberius didn't come out and say this, I don't believe he has full confidence in the abilities of Gallus, considering what is at stake."

"By Jove, Marcellus," exclaimed Valerius, "well stated! Astute observations. He does need us. Before we departed for Rome, we speculated that if he wanted us dead, he wouldn't have summoned us all the way to Rome. Despite his harsh words, and as much as he dislikes us, above all, he does not want a German revolt on the Rhenus boundary. The Emperor works in mysterious ways."

As Valerius paused, Sentius walked into the room. "Anyone know where I could get a good glass of wine?"

"Ah, Father, I was hoping you might show up. We could use your counsel."

"Not intruding on anything important, am I?"

"No. As a matter of fact, we were just discussing our meeting with Tiberius." Valerius poured wine from a silver chalice. "Here, try this. I imported this vintage from Gaul. Hope you like it," he said, his mouth curving into a confident smile.

Sentius sipped the wine and smacked his lips. "By Jove, this stuff is delicious! Where did you get this wine?"

Valerius grinned. "I picked up a limited quantity a while ago. I knew you'd like it. It's from a distributor in Gaul called J&L. We plan on taking some along with us to help lubricate our endeavors with the Frisii."

"I hope you can get more of it. Superb flavor. Very mellow on the palate. By the way, where is Hereca?"

Valerius and Marcellus exchanged knowing glances. "She is indisposed, Father. We can speak without her present."

"I see. Well, how can I help? You looked like you were having a serious discussion."

"We were, Father, we were. In fact, Marcellus and I were attempting to formulate a plan on how to proceed with the mission tasked to us by Tiberius. What can you tell us about Governor Gallus? You are better connected to the politics of Rome than either of us, and you have moved in the same circles as Gallus."

Sentius scowled. "Oh, him." He paused, pursing his lips and carefully choosing his words before continuing. "Gallus is a very ambitious man. His family is filthy rich. He has always toadied up to Tiberius, but from what I hear, it was Sejanus who got him appointed."

"That's what Agrippina said," voiced Valerius. "She believed Sejanus is involved in this somehow."

"You saw Agrippina?" inquired Sentius.

"Yes, Father, we did. She has her own opinions about this. We may need her help if things head south."

"Well, I believe she is correct. I would conjecture that Sejanus and Gallus are in this together. I have encountered Gallus several times over the course of my career. In my opinion, he isn't overly intelligent, but what he lacks in smarts, he makes up for in cunning and ruthlessness. People who have opposed him have met dreadful ends. I have always tried to steer clear of the man and not get ensnared in any of his schemes. His cupidity knows no bounds. More recently, I heard his son, Tigranus, has been helping him govern the province. The son is in his early twenties, and from the rumors I hear, somewhat of a brute. He and his young cronies do what they please, brutalizing the local population with impunity and raping women." He let out a small sigh. "I wish I had better news to give you."

Marcellus and Valerius exchanged glances. "Father, how should we approach the Governor? What do you suggest?"

"First, be circumspect. Try to convince him you are on his side and just want to help as directed by Tiberius. I sense that Tiberius selected you two because of your military experience against the German tribes—no one can argue that point—plus your status as merchants in the German lands who speak their language. Whatever you do, don't confront him. Remember, he has vast powers as the Governor of this territory. He wouldn't have you formally executed because you are Tiberius's envoy, but it would not be beyond the realm of possibility to have you murdered by brigands. He could blame it on the local Germans. As I said, the man has a ruthless streak, and as for his son, stay clear of that depraved creature."

"Thank you, Father. You've been a great help. Before we depart, I need to speak with Gaius Labenius. I promised to keep him apprised of developments. Perhaps he can offer advice on how to proceed. In fact, I am going there shortly."

* * *

Later that day, Valerius entered the offices of General Labenius. The legate flashed him a warm smile. "You are back. Sit down and have a glass of wine. I trust you had a satisfactory meeting with our Emperor?"

"I'm not sure *satisfactory* is an appropriate word. It was hardly a pleasant discussion, but you were correct in your assessment at our last meeting: he needs me for something."

"And what may that be, Valerius?"

"It was a bit surprising. Tiberius has received word that the Frisii are about to rebel against Rome, and he wants Marcellus and me to investigate this through our role as traders with the German peoples. Oh, and this plan will include Hereca as well."

Labenius steepled his hands in thought. "That is rather strange. The Frisii have long been our ally."

"I said the same thing and was chastised to no end for stating the obvious. We are off tomorrow to Noviomagus to meet with Governor Gallus. Tiberius commanded us to coordinate our efforts through Gallus. What do you know of him?"

Gaius shrugged. "I've only met him once since he arrived at Noviomagus. I am surprised that he has not scheduled an inspection of our fortress and state of readiness; at least, that is what I would've done if I were governor. I've heard ugly rumors about his conduct in Rome, but I can't confirm or deny these reports. My advice is to be extremely cautious around him."

"Thank you. My father said the same thing."

"Is there anything I can do to be of assistance?"

"I'm not really sure, Gaius. The whole thing is rather confounding. Why couldn't the Governor handle this matter? The politics of this eludes me, but I believe this will be a mess of snakes. I'll let you know if there's any support you might be able to provide. Thank you for your time and help."

"Please don't hesitate to request help from me. Not to overstate the obvious, but you are treading dangerous waters."

CHAPTER VI

FORTRESS OF NOVIOMAGUS ON THE RHENUS RIVER

Tigranus urged his mount forward as he and his followers approached the towering gates of the Roman fortress of Noviomagus. The military complex was a sprawling affair that dominated the landscape. The massive fifteen-foot timber walls were perched upon a slight bluff overlooking the river and numerous ships were anchored at the quay below.

The gates were wide open at the *porta praetorian,* the main entrance, facilitating the stream of people and wagons flowing into the fortress. He passed through the opening, nodding at the legionary sentries as he and his posse of six trotted their horses toward the stables.

Tigranus scowled. His head pounded from his copious consumption of wine. His ill-temper was further heightened by their unsuccessful hunt. They had crossed over the Rhenus in search of deer and wild boar. It had never occurred to him that their abortive search of game was a direct result of their inept bumbling—plied with wine as they were—around the woods and fields. Every sensible beast had long fled by the time he and his men had arrived.

Tigranus knew he was late for the discussions with the representatives of the Frisii nation. His father had said that it was an important meeting and he was not to miss it. He knew he would be furious with him for being late: he was in for a first-class ass-chewing. This further fueled his disagreeable disposition.

A stable boy approached to take the reins of the horse. Tigranus tossed the leather straps at the young lad, who fumbled with them. Angered, Tigranus lashed out at him with his quirt, leaving an ugly welt on the side of the boy's face. The boy let out a whelp and scurried away in fear. Tigranus strode toward the Governor's residence.

He barged into the audience chamber like he owned the place. He saw his father frown in disappointment. He was late—so what? He knew he looked slovenly: dirt streaked his face, his clothes and boots were caked in mud, and a wine-fueled glaze inhabited his eyes. In Tigranus's mind, a meeting with the German nationals was not important.

As Tigranus quickly surveyed the room, he noted the seated figure to the left of the Governor, the quaestor, Cornelius Quadratus. As the legate's Fifth Alaudae Legion was stationed here at Noviomagus, the military commander, Cethegus Labeo, was also in attendance.

Tigranus observed who he assumed were the two representatives of the Frisian nation. His father had patiently explained to him yesterday who they would be meeting with and why he should be there. The towering man was most likely the chieftain and the other, a slight, unassuming figure, must be the negotiator. The two Frisii turned as Tigranus stepped toward the front of the audience chamber.

"Ah, at last!" exclaimed the Governor. "This is my son, Tigranus. Please forgive his tardiness. Tigranus, these are the representatives of the Frisii, Eadrad and Bigid." Gallus looked at the two men questioningly to make sure he had got their names right.

Eadric smiled. "Honored Governor, I am Eadric and this is Birgir." Eadric seethed with rage. *How could this fool not even remember our simple names?*

"My apologies to you both," responded Gallus. He turned toward his son. "Please come up here, Tigranus. We are discussing a tax matter with our Frisian ally." He returned his gaze to the two Frisii as if nothing was amiss. "Now, where were we? Oh, yes, you believe the new tax levy is too high."

Gallus stroked his chin in thought for a moment before continuing. "I believe I understand your position; after all, the levies have increased significantly."

Eadric responded in a calm tone, "Yes, nearly double, honored Governor."

Gallus responded, "You must realize that the cost of administering the empire is high. The expense of maintaining the forts, roads, and the towns along the Rhenus is hideously exorbitant. No doubt you have benefited from enhanced trade as a result of the Roman pacification and establishment of markets. Now, don't deny it, Eadric. Prosperity is abundant in the lands of the Frisii. Furthermore, the Frisii live in peace. Your potential enemies understand that an attack against the Frisii is an attack against Rome."

Birgir nodded in agreement and replied in a mellow tone. "Governor, of course we understand the costs are high, and the

Frisii are grateful for the protection that Rome affords us. As we have stated in the past, we are willing to pay our fair share for the security that Rome provides us. Perhaps we didn't articulate our position very well—my Latin is not that good, and I have trouble expressing my thoughts sometimes. We appreciate all the beneficence that Rome bestows upon us. We are willing to pay what we remunerated last year, even a bit more, if necessary, but what you currently demand is too high—almost twice the current levies. It will break our people and force them into servitude to satisfy our debt."

The Governor quickly retorted, "Oh, come now. Your settlements and villages are thriving. Surely you are embellishing your story. I must say though, it is a good negotiating posture. You Germans are a sly bunch. I had heard about your cunning before I arrived. Now, I'm beginning to understand why."

Gallus paused for a moment and then pronounced his final decision. "Our position is firm. The tax amount stands. No reduction."

Birgir opened his mouth to speak but realized the futility of further conversation. He discerned that any angry outburst or threat would serve no useful purpose. Searching for the right words, he finally replied, "Thank you for your time, Governor Gallus." In deference, he nodded at the other Romans present. With that, the two Frisians turned about and departed. The chamber doors were opened for them by a pair of servants. As the doors closed behind them, they heard boisterous laughter from the Romans seated inside and words to the effect that they were a bunch of sheep. The two men strode away, their faces purple with anger.

* * *

Valerius, Marcellus, and Hereca sailed on a small ship down the Rhenus as it flowed northwest from their home at Oppidum

Ubiorum. Valerius had insisted that they bring a supply of the J&L wine to assist them in whatever negotiations were required, but Marcellus had demurred, noting that it was bulky to transport. He also noted that giving such good quality wine on the Germans, who had notoriously poor wine palates, was a waste. Valerius agreed that it would be burdensome but stated that they would use porters wherever they traveled to carry the precious commodity, and in the end, it would be worth the effort and trouble to take the wine with them.

At midday they glided past the legionary fortress at Novaesium and continued downriver. Later in the afternoon, the ship sailed in view of Vetera. The sight of the towering walls of the imposing military fortress gave Valerius chills. *Was it really seventeen years ago when I stumbled out of the German forests with Marcellus and a few others, pursued by a posse of bloodthirsty barbarians intent on not letting me inform the garrison of the horrific disaster suffered by Varus and his three legions? Me and my small force were the only survivors of the vicious ambush by Arminius and the German coalition of tribes. The commander of the fortress, General Saturnius, had dispatched me to Rome to inform the Emperor, Caesar Augustus, of the massive defeat. We had ridden non-stop to Rome for almost two solid weeks to convey the urgent news.*

Valerius briefly ruminated on those days. He wondered what had happened to his friends Lucius and Julia, who had survived the experience with him. Lucius had been a young legionnaire in his first posting and Julia the daughter of the legions' veterinarian. The last he heard, the couple had settled in Gaul, but he had lost touch with them and hadn't heard from them in years. He hoped they were alright.

Valerius glanced at Marcellus. He appeared to be equally struck by the appearance of the fortress, his gaze distant. No doubt he was having similar thoughts.

The captain of the vessel interrupted their reverie. "Would you care to stop here and refresh yourselves?"

Valerius glanced at Marcellus, who shook his head. Valerius felt the same way. "No, thank you, Captain. Perhaps at the next garrison."

Early that evening, they finally arrived at their destination—the port of Noviomagus with its sprawling military complex. Valerius was certain he would be refused lodging at the Governor's opulent residence, so they rented rooms in the civilian town outside the walls, a place named the Quayside. As accommodations went, it was a far cry from luxurious, but the pickings were slim. He sent a polite note to Governor Gallus along with the letter of introduction from the Emperor, letting him know he had arrived and was prepared to meet with him when the Governor was available.

Three days later, they finally received a reply. Evidently, the Governor thought little of his note and the letter of introduction from Tiberius . It was petty behavior on Gallus's part, but Valerius had anticipated it. They were to meet the next day at the fifth hour.

Valerius checked his uniform and armor from head to toe to ensure that everything was in place. He had assiduously polished his breastplate and helmet in anticipation of his meeting with the Governor. This was the first time he had donned his tunic and armor in many years. He turned toward his wife. "Hereca, what do you think? Do I look like a proper Roman officer—a tribune in the Roman Imperial Army?"

Hereca appraised him and smiled. "You do, and a handsome one at that."

Valerius was about to reply when there was a pounding at the door.

Answering the door, they saw Marcellus with a scowl on his face as he held his body armor—a series of metal plates to cover his torso and shoulders attached to a leather jerkin—up. "I can't get this bloody thing to fit me no matter what I do. I'm all thumbs. Can you help me?"

Valerius gestured with his arm. "Put it on. Let me see what the problem is."

Using both arms, Marcellus hefted the armored vest over his head and then attempted to slide it around his torso, which was already covered in a padded undergarment known as a *subarmalis*. The armor stopped short of encircling his chest and torso.

"I didn't know iron could shrink!" Valerius exclaimed. Hereca burst out laughing at his barbed humor.

Marcellus's scowl deepened. "Go ahead and mock me. So I've added some girth over the years. Let's see what you look like when you get to my age."

Hereca's giggling stopped abruptly. "Oh, Marcellus, stop being a curmudgeon. Valerius's quip was quite funny. It was just at your expense. Now, off with the armor and let me look at it."

Marcellus lifted the heavy armor off and handed it to Hereca. She carried it over to the single wooden table in their room and placed it on the surface. She examined the armored jacket and turned it over. "Here," she said, "are the leather straps connecting the back and front of the armor. They just need to be adjusted, and quite a bit from what I can see." She chuckled again, ignoring Marcellus's dark looks.

She painstakingly undid several knots on the left and right and increased the slack to lengthen the leather straps. "Now try it."

Once again, Marcellus raised the armored garment over his head. To his delight, the armor fit him perfectly this time. Grinning sheepishly, he replied, "Thanks, Hereca."

"Now would be a good time to discuss our approach when the three of us meet with the Governor and his staff," reminded Valerius.

Hereca flashed a triumphant smile, for, in the end, she had prevailed and was accompanying her husband and Marcellus to Gallus. Back at home, after she had stalked off, she had continued to remonstrate unendingly against her lack of inclusion in the meeting with the Governor and stated that she would be an asset at the gathering because of her knowledge and understanding of the German tribes. Valerius had retorted that she wasn't included in Tiberius's letter and thus would be an uninvited guest. Hereca had countered by saying that although she hadn't been included in a formal sense, implicitly, she was because she was an integral part of the trading company, which was one of the reasons Tiberius had selected her husband and Marcellus for this duty. In the end, she had been victorious.

Valerius had finally concluded that it was worth the risk to take her along to the meeting rather than face her wrath over the ensuing period. He believed Gallus might take issue with her presence, but the benefits of having her involved in the process were worth it.

Valerius began, "As my father indicated, this Gallus fellow is a ruthless bastard who will resort to any means necessary to get his way and make himself rich. Furthermore, he is the Governor of the territory and has absolute authority and dominion over all people, including us. The only standing we have in this spectacle is Tiberius's note to the Governor that we help him with any potential crisis of a diplomatic or military nature with the Frisii."

"So, what do you propose?" inquired Marcellus.

"We should be deferential but not to the point of being obsequious. Show no weakness. We weren't selected by accident but rather for our experience and knowledge. We didn't volunteer for this—we were chosen by Tiberius. We are experienced military officers and have good connections with the German tribes. We need to convey to Gallus that we are here to help him and not to interfere with his governance of the province."

Hereca frowned. "I don't like this at all. There will be great anger directed at us. Gallus will not appreciate the fact that he is being forced to accept our assistance."

"Correct," Valerius said. "And we must not openly confront him on anything he says, no matter how insulting his remarks. That includes you too, Hereca, and don't give me that injured look. I know how you can be at times. Marcellus received a dose of your waspish tongue back home. All of us need to contain our emotions. Above all, we need to succeed on this mission or we will be in serious trouble with the Emperor."

There was a brief silence among them. "Well," said Marcellus, "then I think we should all be deferential toward the Governor and his staff, and hopefully, he will let us get on with the mission assigned to us by Tiberius. I have a question. What happened to punctilious?"

Valerius grinned at Marcellus's banter. "No. This arsehole doesn't warrant punctilious, only the Emperor does."

That afternoon, the trio entered through the open gates of the fortress and walked past the barracks blocks, the quartermaster stores, the bakeries, and the armory. They headed toward the middle of the encampment, walking down the *via principalis*. Normally, legionary fortresses were grim affairs with bleak surroundings, but here at the intersection of the two main roads was a magnificent colonnaded structure with a courtyard and a basilica cross-hall surrounded by many offices.

They entered a reception area bustling with activity. Valerius walked up to an officious-looking clerk seated at a table. "Tribune

Valerius Maximus, Centurion Marcellus Veronus, and my wife, Hereca. I have an appointment with Governor Gallus."

The clerk nodded and pointed to the left. "Go down the main hallway. When you reach the intersection, there will be a large doorway with two guards. Announce your presence to them."

Valerius gestured for Marcellus and Hereca to follow him. He immediately began walking down the main corridor. After a short distance, they came to an intersection with another hallway. Two strapping guards stood in front of a double door leading to the Governor's audience hall. Valerius announced himself to the guards and then turned back to join Marcellus and Hereca. One of the guards entered the chamber, closing the door behind him. He quickly returned. "The Governor is expecting you. Please enter."

Valerius led the way, Marcellus and Hereca following close behind. Seated on an elaborately carved curule chair was a swarthy middle-aged figure. He had a small, pointed, dark beard, which added a certain nuance of cruelty to his features. This person, he assumed, was Governor Gallus. He noted several other figures off to the side. He approached, his hob-nailed boots clacking on the paving tiles, and came to a halt about ten paces away. Dispelling his nervousness, he offered a slight bow. "Tribune Valerius Maximus at your service, sir. With me are Centurion Marcellus Veronus and my wife, Hereca."

Gallus rose from his seated position, his tone incredulous. "Is this a prank? This is what our beloved Emperor sends to assist me in my governance of this territory—a tribune who looks to be in his mid to late thirties. Most military officers your age are legates by now."

He turned his gaze toward Marcellus. "And you. Most centurions your age have long been put out to pasture." He didn't bother to address Hereca and turned back to the tribune.

Valerius decided to remain silent and not be apologetic. *Let him vent his spleen, then I will speak.*

Gallus shifted, uncomfortable that he had received no reply. His desire was to put them on the defensive, but the tables had been turned. "Well, what do you have to say for yourself?"

Valerius offered a disarming smile. "What you say is true, honored Governor. Centurion Marcellus and I have been retired from our military ranks for over fifteen years. Our beloved Emperor Tiberius recalled us to active service to assist Rome and you here in Germania."

"For what purpose?" Gallus growled. "I didn't request any support. I'm unaware of any crisis."

"Governor, earlier this spring, Marcellus and I were summoned to Rome from our homes upriver in Oppidum Ubiorum. Apparently, Tiberius received word that there was a nascent rebellion brewing. He reinstated us to our former ranks and charged us with the duty of assisting you and your staff. We were ordered to—"

"Who is plotting rebellion?" thundered the Governor.

"Tiberius mentioned the Frisii, sir."

A young man leaped from his seat and sneered, "The Frisii? Surely you are joking! They are a bunch of sheep."

Valerius directed his gaze toward the outraged individual. He guessed this person was the Governor's son, the one he had been warned about by his father. Upon looking at him, he felt an instant, visceral dislike for the man. His dark hair, unlike that of most Roman men, was long with oily curls. He had a beaked nose and protruding lips, which gave his countenance a permanent leer.

"And you are?"

"I'm Tigranus, the Governor's son," he said proudly, puffing out his chest.

Gallus interrupted, "Forgive me for not making introductions. Yes, this is my son. Over here to the left is my quaestor, Cornelius Quadratus, and to my right," he gestured with his arm, "is the military commander of the Fifth Legion, Cethegus Labeo."

Gallus continued, "Your assistance is for naught. I'm aware of no rebellion by the Frisii. In fact, I just met with their representative not too long ago. We have a minor tax dispute with them, that is all. I would hardly characterize that as a revolt."

Valerius nodded in agreement, but he caught the knowing glances of the others in the room. Something was afoot here. "Governor, I'm also unaware of any rebellion by the Frisii, but Tiberius summoned Centurion Marcellus and me all the way to Rome. If I might paraphrase his words, he said that Rome couldn't afford and wouldn't tolerate another German rebellion. He stated that the empire was stretched thin. He ordered Marcellus and me to offer our assistance and resources to you, and I stress the word *ordered*—we didn't volunteer for this."

Gallus was silent. "And what qualities do you bring to us? Your name is vaguely familiar, but your notoriety eludes me."

Valerius was shocked that Gallus had not inquired of his background earlier. That would have been his first action had he been in the Governor's position. "Marcellus and I are experienced legionary officers in the campaigns against the Germans. Both of us—"

The legate, Cethegus Labeo interrupted, "Experienced how?"

Valerius looked toward the General, a tall thin man with a haughty expression. "Marcellus and I were the only two officers who survived the Teutoburg disaster. Furthermore, we personally assisted Germanicus Caesar with the training of the troops and the tactics for the invasion of the German interior fifteen years ago. I was personally decorated with the honor of Hero of Rome."

There was a stunned silence in the room. Finally, Gallus sputtered, "As you said, that was fifteen years ago. Things have changed along the border. We are at peace now. How is that relevant today?"

"Good question, Governor Gallus. Over that period, we have been operating a trading business with the German tribes along the Rhenus. I speak the language fluently."

"What about the woman?" inquired Tigranus. He leered at Hereca, undressing her with his eyes.

Valerius struggled to mask his contempt for Tigranus. Composing himself, he began. "My wife, Hereca, is a member of the Dolgubni tribe. She understands the Germans better than I do. As I'm sure you know, Governor, the behavior of the Germans can be unpredictable and baffling at times. As I have witnessed, their capacity for ferocity is unrivaled."

Tigranus snorted. "They are not a threat anymore."

Ignoring the jibe, Valerius continued, struggling to hold his emotions in check and forcing a mellow tone, "Governor Gallus, if you wish us to depart and do nothing, that is certainly your prerogative. We can't force you to accept our service, but I would remind you that we are the personal envoys of Tiberius Caesar. He commanded us to see you."

Gallus paused in thought, turning the alternatives over in his mind. He didn't appreciate having these people foisted upon him by the Emperor no matter their experience and qualifications. At last, he spoke, his tone anything but polite, "What do you suggest, Tribune?"

"This is what I propose. Marcellus, Hereca, and I should meet with some of the Frisii elders under the guise of seeking trade with them. After all, they might have heard of our reputation as merchants from our various commercial dealings with the other tribes. We will travel downriver and sail down the Vecht northward to the fort at Flevum in the Frisii territory. Once we arrive there, we will seek out the Frisian leaders in their main villages. We will try to ascertain their true intentions and get back to you. If they are hostile, perhaps we can persuade them to change their minds."

Gallus studied the three and then nodded in acquiescence. "Very well. It seems like a reasonable course of action, but I want you to let me know where, when, and who you are meeting with. Understood?"

"Of course, sir. We would do that out of courtesy to you. In fact, Tiberius insisted that we coordinate all of our efforts with you."

Gallus cleared his throat and then picked up a quill and dipped it into an inkwell. "Since you are going to Flevum, which is our only major Roman fortress in the Frisian territory, I will give you a letter of introduction to the commanding officer. He looked toward Labeo. "General, what is the name of the garrison commander at Flevum?"

"That would be Tribune Florus," replied Labeo.

Gallus penned a brief message. He waited until the ink was dry, folded the document, and sealed it using his signet ring on hot wax. He then looked up, holding the parchment. "This document identifies you and your mission to Tribune Florus. I have instructed him to cooperate with whatever you need."

Tigranus couldn't contain himself any longer. He stood up and angrily exclaimed, "Father, how can you let them do this? They are usurping your authority."

Gallus gave his son an angry scowl. "Enough, Tigranus."

Valerius shifted his gaze from son to father, then back to the son again. He noted the knowing glances exchanged between the quaestor, the legate, and the Governor. Something was going on there and he didn't like it at all. He directed his attention back to

Gallus. "Thank you for your understanding on this matter, Governor Gallus. I believe we have taken up enough of your valuable time. I will try to establish contact with the Frisii and arrange a meeting. I will report the results of our discussions back to you and await further instructions."

CHAPTER VII

RECRUITMENT

H is eyes glinting with hatred, Gallus watched the three departing figures. In the past, he had dealt with more formidable opponents and had always prevailed in the end. This would be no different. Once the doors had closed behind them, he stormed over to where his son was standing and delivered a backhand blow to his face. "Never contradict or second guess me in front of others. Understand?"

Seething with anger, Tigranus wiped away the trickle of blood escaping his lips. He met his father's livid gaze for a moment before breaking eye contact. "Yes, Father," he replied.

He patted his son on the back. "Good." He walked over to a small table. "Now, everyone, gather around me." Quadratus, Labeo, and Tigranus stood around the table. "We cannot have these outsiders interfering in our business matters and reporting back to Tiberius in Rome. They are a nuisance that needs to be disposed of."

Quadratus, who had long been Gallus's associate in many business and political ventures, spoke in a worried tone. "I agree, Governor, but they have that letter from Tiberius. They are his envoys. Does that not offer them protection?"

Gallus snarled, "They are an impediment, nothing more. Once we find out who they are meeting among the Frisii and when, we will have them ambushed and killed. Even better, we will make it look like the Frisii did it."

The three men beamed their silent approval.

▲

Valerius, Marcellus, and Hereca returned to their lodging outside the fortress. They had said little on their way for fear of being over-heard. Valerius spoke first. "Well, what do you think of our esteemed Governor and his little band of thugs?"

"As I'm sure Hereca would agree, they wouldn't make very good traders," said Marcellus. "Did you see the way they all exchanged anxious glances when they mentioned the only issue with the Frisii was a minor tax matter? *Minor*, my arse. I think there is some serious disagreement with respect to the taxes imposed upon the Frisii. If I had to guess, they have substantially increased the tax levies, hoping to line their own pockets."

Hereca chuckled. "It was obvious that they were lying. What a bumbling bunch they were."

"No, Hereca, not bumbling," said Valerius. "They just lack finesse. My father described Gallus as a ruthless individual. Don't forget that. We shouldn't underestimate him. At the end of the meeting, remember when Gallus asked us to inform him of where and when we are meeting with the Frisii? Why does he need to know that? I will tell you why: It's likely he intends to murder us in the land of the Frisii. He can then claim to Tiberius that we were waylaid by brigands or killed by the Frisii."

"What if we clandestinely make our exit from here and travel downriver? We could ignore his instructions," suggested Marcellus.

"That was my first thought," said Valerius, "but they will have us watched. As we speak, I'll wager that there are men posted surreptitiously outside this inn, tracking our movements. Besides, Tiberius instructed us to keep Gallus as well as himself informed of our progress. Keeping the Governor out of the loop isn't an option as much as I would like to."

Hereca looked confounded. "What do we do—just let them ambush us?"

Valerius proffered a wan smile. "Not quite, Hereca. I think, between Marcellus and me, we can muster a force of mercenaries to accompany us. It will be more than a match for anything the Governor can throw at us. What do you say, Marcellus?"

Marcellus had a gleam in his eye. "Oh, I'm up for that, Tribune. I think we can get all of the help we'll need here in Noviomagus. We can start our recruiting at the taverns tomorrow or, better yet, maybe even tonight. In fact, I would suggest tonight. No time like the present."

Valerius acquiesced. "Tonight, it is."

⚐

Clad in civilian garb, knee-length tunics, and light cloaks, Marcellus and Valerius ventured out into the streets of the town that evening. *Town* was a kind word to describe the collection of taverns, eating establishments, and brothels that had sprung up over time in the shadow of the military stronghold. Valerius had questioned Marcellus's decision to visit the taverns at night given that this would only add to the danger, to which Marcellus had responded that the evening hours were the best to find the type of men they were looking for. In the fading twilight, the pair walked down the muddy avenue. There were no paved thoroughfares in this collection of hovels—only dirt roads that turned to glop at the first sight of rain. Given the unsavory places they would visit this evening, both men concealed their swords beneath their cloaks. Finally, they ventured down a narrow lane.

"Now, Tribune, you let me do the talking. No offense, but I have a bit more experience with these types of establishments. Know what I mean?"

"I understand, Marcellus. But are you sure you remember what these places are like? After all, you haven't graced these dens of inequity for some time now that you're married and have settled down."

Marcellus laughed. "Correct, Tribune. No, I haven't, but I understand these places from years of experience, and I know what kind of man I'm looking for. So, let me take the lead. All right with you?"

"Sure, Marcellus. Lead the way."

The first establishment they encountered was a tavern named the River Rat. An aged and lopsided wooden sign above the entrance proclaimed fine food and wine. It was a ramshackle-looking building with one of the walls sagging to the left. On either side were other dilapidated buildings with the same look of weary decay. Marcellus shook his head. "Doesn't appear promising, but we'll give it a try."

Marcellus pushed the door open and peered into the dim interior. An assortment of ragged individuals sat in front of a large wooden plank that served as a bar. A few others were seated at scattered tables. The hum of conversation abruptly ceased. All eyes turned toward the newcomers. The smell in the room was revolting—a mixture of unwashed bodies, vomit, and piss. Marcellus wrinkled his nose at the stench. "This place is vile. No self-respecting mercenary would visit this tavern. Let's move on."

Before they could turn about and leave, a large individual with a bald head and a craggy face rose from a table at the far end and approached them. "Look at this, we've some fine gentlemen visiting the Rat. Not to your liking, eh? Not good enough for you?" Following the actions of their leader, the three other men at the table stood up menacingly.

Marcellus acted swiftly. He strode toward the advancing figure and smashed his fist into his face, sending him sprawling to the floor. He lay there unmoving. "No, it is not good enough for my colleague and I. Now, go back to your drinking, all of you." For effect, he brushed aside his cloak to reveal his sword. The pair turned and departed.

Valerius chuckled. "That was quite a debut. I see you've mellowed with age. The tavern was as despicable as its namesake. I hope the other places we visit are better than that."

"They'd better be, or we will find no recruits. Let's keep moving quickly. I don't believe we will have anyone from the River Rat come after us, but it's prudent to be watchful."

Striding down the dirt avenue, they encountered the next establishment, a place named the Sword and Shield. It was a spacious wooden structure with a slanted red tile roof. The heavy oak door was massive and shut snugly, preventing any noise from escaping the tavern. Marcellus smiled. "This place is more to my liking. Looks promising. Let's see what we find here."

They pushed the large door inward, which swung smoothly on well-oiled hinges. As they stood in the alcove, they noticed that the place was well lit with numerous oil lamps placed strategically at the tables and on the bar. The pine floorboards were scrubbed clean with no residue of spilled wine or food. Several men briefly looked their way and then turned their attention back to what they were doing. Games were in progress, and the clatter of dice filled the room.

"C'mon," said Marcellus. "I'm thirsty." He walked up to the bar like he owned the place and squinted at the amphorae behind the bar, which had signs describing the vintage and the prices. He nodded to the proprietor and pointed to the amphora on the far right. "Get me two of that."

Marcellus handed a mug to Valerius and turned his back to the bar to survey the room. He sipped his wine. He didn't wince at the taste; it was surprisingly above average for a tavern on the outskirts of a legionary fort.

Valerius followed Marcellus's actions. He surveyed the individuals in attendance, but he had no idea what he was looking for. He would let Marcellus do that.

Marcellus's eyes roved the room, first to the left, then the right, and back to the left again. He settled his gaze on a middle-aged man sitting at a table accompanied by a comely tavern wench with an overflowing bodice. He had his hand on her thigh, his expression reflecting a state of mild inebriation. *This one has potential*, thought Marcellus. Even in the dim light, he saw a menacing, thin whitish scar down his jawline. Definitely not a shaving cut. The man was slim but muscular. Overall, he appeared fit. No paunch despite the wisps of grey on the fringes of his short hair.

Marcellus turned toward Valerius. He nodded in the direction of the man and the wench. "We need to talk to him." With that, the two sauntered over to the table and stood over him. Marcellus eyed the individual. "By the looks of you, I would venture to say you are a retired legionnaire."

"Who the fuck wants to know?" he slurred.

"I'm Marcellus and this is Valerius." With that, Marcellus pulled up a chair and sat; Valerius did the same. "How long ago did you retire?"

"What business is it of yours, and did I invite you to sit here?"

Marcellus ignored the question and jumped in. "Ah, my assumption is correct. You are or once were a legionnaire. I would also presume that you're bored out of your mind."

"What if I am?" he replied in a laconic tone. "How does that concern you?"

"Just thought you might be interested in a business proposition from one retired legionnaire to another. Want to hear more?"

The man sighed and shooed away the girl, who gave the interlopers an irritated glance. "Name's Rufus Placidus. Recent optio of the Fifth Legion, fourth cohort, second century. Now retired."

Marcellus extended his arm. "Retired Centurion Marcellus, and to my left, former Tribune Valerius Maximus." Catching sight of the innkeeper, Marcellus raised his arm and gestured for another round. He turned back toward Rufus. "Why did you retire?"

Rufus sat up straighter, knowing that he was facing two superior officers, and let out a sigh. "I realized I was getting too old for soldiering. Legionary life is hard on a man—you understand that. Plus, I knew the prospect of getting promoted to centurion was unlikely. I was stuck in rank as an optio. Put in twenty years. Paid the price. I fought with Germanicus on the campaign against the Germans sixteen or more years ago. Almost lost my life on several occasions during those festivities."

Marcellus smiled. "The tribune and I were there. We served on Germanicus's staff. Really got in the thick of it on numerous occasions. We retired shortly after that."

"What kind of business proposition do you have in mind?" Rufus inquired.

"We are looking to recruit a small mercenary force. The tribune and I are on the Emperor's business and need to travel into the lands of the Frisii. I will be blunt. This could be dangerous, but we pay well."

"How much?"

"How does—let's say—one hundred sesterces sound from start to finish?"

Rufus's eyes bulged. That was an enormous sum. He quickly responded, "I could use the coin. My retirement pay only covers the necessities. I might be willing to be in your employ. Tell me more."

"Excellent!" exclaimed Valerius. "We could use a man like you. Now, listen up. As Marcellus stated, this venture could be perilous, but then again, nothing might happen. We are on a mission into the land of the Frisii. To be perfectly clear, it's not a military endeavor. We will all be in civilian garb but heavily armed. We believe there are elements who might not approve of our undertaking. But I will not elaborate any further on that right now. You still interested?"

Rufus nodded. "I'm no stranger to threats."

"Good. Know of anyone else who might be handy with a sword and is looking to earn some honest coin? We would be willing to reward you with a finder's fee for each man you can refer to us."

Rufus smiled. "I have a few friends and acquaintances who might be interested in your offer. When do you need them?"

"Well, it is nighttime now, so tomorrow would be good. We need to assemble our little force as quickly as possible. Why don't we meet here tomorrow afternoon? We will interview any prospective recruits you might find."

"Short notice, but I think I can find a few good men. I will see you here tomorrow."

Marcellus clapped his hand on Rufus's shoulder. "Nice to make your acquaintance, Rufus. Look forward to working with you."

The two officers ventured out into the night in search of the next tavern. Not far down the muddied path and close to the water, they found the next establishment. A sign next to the entrance proclaimed the place to be the River's Edge. They entered through a battered wooden door. The gloomy interior was crowded with patrons and a few women of the night. Raucous shouts from several gaming tables punctuated the air as the pair wandered up to the bar. Again, Marcellus pointed to the wine he wanted and ordered two glasses. Holding their mugs, they turned and faced the center of the room, appraising the patrons for those who might fit the needs of their mercenary force. It was a disappointing mix, not much in terms of the talent they were seeking. Most of the men appeared scrawny. A few others appeared physically fit, but they looked washed out from too much wine over a long period.

Suddenly, a commotion erupted at one of the gambling tables. Chairs scattered everywhere. "You cheats," roared a large man with a wide girth. He drew a long, wicked dagger and pointed it threateningly at two ragged men. "I'm going to cut you both up," he slurred.

The two figures were not cowed by the knife. They, in turn, drew their own daggers. From the backroom behind the bar, a massive individual with a shaved head emerged. "Bloody Hades!" he yelled. "What's going on here?"

Without waiting for an answer, he leaped toward the pair of ragged men, smashing his massive arms into theirs. The daggers clattered to the floor. Without hesitation, he seized both men by the scruff and tossed them out the door, into the night.

Then, he came back to the table to confront the instigator of the fracas. He glared at the man across the table. "Drop the knife now, Brutus. I will not ask you a second time."

The man snarled. "I'm not afraid of you, Ox. Fuck you. Try and take it from me."

The man named Ox lifted the table and upended it on the defiant knife-wielder, knocking the ruffian to the floor. Moving nimbly for a big man, he advanced quickly toward the fallen figure, but the man was not finished just yet. He jabbed his dagger up from his prone position. Ox snarled and punched the man in the face, ending all his efforts. He then picked him up by the shirt and threw him outside. He returned, dabbing at the blood on his arm with a linen rag.

Marcellus and Valerius turned toward each other and exchanged knowing glances. Marcellus gestured for the man known as "Ox" to join them. He ordered another mug of wine and handed it to the hulking individual. Ox nodded his thanks. "You own this place?" Marcellus inquired.

"Nah. I'm just hired help," he said with a guttural German accent. He extended his hand. "My name is Cedric, but everyone calls me Ox."

"Alright, Ox. I'm Marcellus and this is Valerius. Do you have any military experience?"

"No. I was born a slave, but I became a bodyguard because of my size. Now I'm in this dump. I know how to use a sword and shield if that's what you're asking. I'm not ashamed to admit I was a slave so, if my past troubles you, that's your problem."

Marcellus proffered a wide smile. "Interested in listening to a business proposition?"

Ox returned the grin. "I might be. What is it?"

"We're putting together a small mercenary force for security purposes. It's not a bunch of brigands if that's what you're thinking. It's a legitimate venture, not a lawless scheme. We are on the Emperor's business in the land of the Frisii. It could be risky. We aren't sure what we might encounter in the way of hostile forces. The pay is a hundred sesterces, start to finish."

The massive figure dabbed the cut on his arm, seemingly in thought. "You think it isn't dangerous here?" He displayed his bleeding arm, which was crisscrossed with scar tissue. "I hate this place. When do I start?"

Marcellus shook his hand. "Soon, my friend. As early as tomorrow. We need to recruit a few others. Where can I contact you?"

Ox gestured with his thumb. "Right here in the back. I have a room there. And Marcellus, Valerius, thank you for taking a chance on me. You won't be disappointed."

The two Roman officers exited and moved onward in search of the next tavern.

CHAPTER VIII

FLEVUM

The next day, Hereca, Marcellus, and Valerius sat huddled in their lodgings outside Noviomagus, reviewing the things that needed to be done. They had recruited fifteen men for their armed band, many of whom had been recommended by the retired optio, Rufus Placidus. Valerius examined the names scrawled on a wax tablet. "Here they are. I have reservations about some of these men, but we don't have time to expand our search for more individuals. Marcellus and I agreed that the former optio, Rufus, would make a good leader. We will appoint him our second-in-command. Furthermore, I want Ox assigned as our personal bodyguard. Just his presence should be enough to scare most men off."

Marcellus snorted. "Indeed, Tribune. He has a formidable figure. I have met few men as powerful as him—a good find. The next thing we need to do is arrange transportation downriver to Flevum and stock up on rations. We have mouths to feed besides our own."

"I have reserved a ship," said Valerius. "Hereca will look to purchase rations this afternoon. Marcellus, while Hereca is organizing things, why don't we inform the men that we'll gather down at the quay tomorrow morning for transport downriver."

"Good idea. This is going to cost us a bloody fortune, but in my humble opinion, it is money well spent. We are as good as dead without our small force. Maybe we can ask the Emperor for recompense." The centurion chortled.

"Perhaps we could ask him for palaces for each of us while we are at it, Marcellus. But for now, let's get going. We have much to do."

⁂

Hereca strode along the quay, pleased with herself. She had visited several vendors and purchased quantities of diluted wine, biscuits, flour, salted fish, and dried fruit. She had inspected the provisions and was satisfied with the quality of the food and drink.

Walking past the quay, she decided to visit the shops to see what merchandise might be for sale. She was looking for nothing of importance but thought it would be a welcome respite, especially given the perilous undertaking on the horizon. She inhaled the warm air, savoring the beautiful day and thoroughly enjoying her small shopping trip. She stopped at a small enclave that featured a variety of gaily colored scarves. She fingered the material, noting the tightness of the weave. She was about to examine a scarlet wrap when she was startled by a voice behind her.

"Well, look who is here frequenting our little town. The German wife of the tribune hero."

She quickly turned about to see the leering faces of Tigranus and two of his cronies. Hereca stared at them. She then quickly glanced about and was alarmed at how few people were about. The shopkeeper, sensing trouble, had disappeared. This wasn't good, and she didn't like the looks she was receiving. She gave Tigranus a stern glare, hoping to throw him off balance.

"Not speaking, pretty one? Are the likes of us not good enough for you, a German, no less?"

Hereca silently cursed. Her lack of a response had been a mistake and had only emboldened Tigranus and his friends. "I'm doing some shopping in preparation for our journey to the land of the Frisii—the expedition your father ordered us on. Now, if you'll excuse me, I must be on my way." She turned about to walk away but the man on the left shifted, blocking her path.

"In my experience," said Tigranus, "German women are not nearly as passionate in bed as Roman maids. How about you and I test this hypothesis?"

Hereca was furious. She needed to respond to this rogue in terms he would understand. "Tigranus, the only thing smaller than your dick is your brain. The answer to your invitation is no."

The two men accompanying Tigranus chuckled at her crude wit, which only served to infuriate Tigranus. His faced mottled in anger. He attempted to grab her arm but she quickly moved to the side, evading his effort.

The three antagonists had made a grave error in judgment. They assumed they were dealing with a woman who was like the timid wenches inhabiting the vicinity of Noviomagus. They could not be more mistaken. Hereca was the proud daughter—the only child—of a Dolgubni chieftain. She had been raised to participate in the same combatant training as the young men—in short, she was a warrior princess. She could throw a javelin as far as many of the men in her clan, and she could fight alongside them with spear and shield if necessary. She had the beauty of a German princess but the heart of a fighter who would not hesitate to unleash violence.

Hereca considered her options. There would be no reasoning with this group. She needed to act. There were three of them and they had obviously been drinking. Given their relaxed posture, they weren't expecting any resistance. In a heartbeat, she knew what needed to be done. She insouciantly slipped her right hand inside her light cloak, grasping the bone knife handle hidden there, and fitted it snugly into her palm. Suddenly, she shifted swiftly to her left, kneeing the figure blocking her path squarely in the groin. The man collapsed with a groan. In the same motion, she withdrew the slim blade concealed in her cloak and moved towards Tigranus, lightning-fast, slicing open his ear lobe. The third man wisely backed away.

Tigranus uttered a curse, grasping his ear. His hand came back covered in blood. "You bitch," he screamed, "look what you've done! You cut me!"

"I suggest you move away from me now," said Hereca, "and consider yourself fortunate that I didn't hurt you as I could have. Move now," she hissed, "or I will gut you like a fish." For effect, she held the glistening blade at belly level, the knife steadfast in her hand.

"This isn't over," snapped Tigranus.

"Yes, it is," said Hereca. "Now be on your way."

The three figures quickly departed. Tigranus clutched his ear while trying to support the man with the injured groin.

She hurried back to her room, anxiously looking over her shoulder to see if she was being followed. She arrived and found Valerius and Marcellus deep in discussion over their mercenary force. They both looked up as she appeared in the entranceway.

Valerius knew his wife well and from the expression on her face, he knew something was amiss. "What's wrong, Hereca?"

"I was accosted on the street by that piece of shit, Tigranus, and two of his cronies. I sent them packing."

Valerius was relieved but, at the same time, dreaded what she might say next. "Sent them packing...how?"

"I kneed one of his friends in the stones. I assume he will recover."

"And...?" he prompted.

"I nicked Tigranus's ear with my knife—just enough to draw blood. Nothing serious. I wanted to gut him but I exercised restraint."

Valerius heaved a sigh of relief. "I'm glad you're alright, and it appears you've taught them a lesson. Tigranus will probably be reluctant to go to his father about this. What can he say—a woman overpowered three men on the streets and injured two of them? I think not, but we have certainly made a strong enemy in Tigranus."

Marcellus snorted. "Hereca, please never get mad at me. I treasure my stones and have enough scars on my face as it is."

Hereca chuckled. "Marcellus, I may give you extra leeway but not you, dear husband." She directed a mock glare at Valerius. For effect, she produced the knife from deep within the folds of her cloak.

"Ouch," Valerius winced. "In all seriousness, you'd best not be on the streets by yourself anymore. That lout Tigranus might lurk about with even more men. The outcome next time might not be as fortunate."

The next day, fully provisioned, their journey was finally underway, and they glided downriver toward their destination, Flevum. The ship resembled an oversized barge with a single sail and a small bank of oars. The vessel was primarily used to transport troops and supplies up and down the river network, which made it the perfect size for their needs.

The journey was about fifty miles. The first part of their voyage would take them down the Rhenus about twenty miles west; then, where the river split into two, they would head north on the Vecht for thirty miles, directly into the heart of Frisii territory.

Valerius, Hereca, and Marcellus stood near the prow, enjoying the refreshing breeze on their faces. Their recently recruited force was assembled aft under a large awning. The men were in various stages of repose: a few were engaged in conversation while a solitary game of dice had broken out, interrupted by shouts of glee and disappointment.

"I wonder what the Goddess Fortuna has in store for us," mused Valerius. "It's not the enemy that worries me, it's who the enemy is. That is our conundrum."

"Agreed," said Marcellus. "But if we survived the Teutoburg and Germanicus's ambitious campaign, surely we can persevere now. We are pitted against an unscrupulous governor and a single German tribe, and what's more, the Frisii may not be actively revolting yet. And I put a definite emphasis on the word *may*."

"A great risk, as I see it, is if we are caught between the Governor's forces and the Germans. This would put us in dire straits—a no-win scenario. If this turns out to be the case, not even a Greek mathematician could calculate our odds of success," said Valerius.

Hereca and Marcellus exchanged quizzical looks. "Greek mathematicians?" inquired Hereca.

"You know," said Valerius, "Pythagoras, Euclid to name a few."

"Who are they?" asked Marcellus. "Greek general who use mathematics in their strategies?"

Valerius heaved a sigh of frustration, realizing his hyperbole was way off the mark. "Never mind, just a figure of speech."

"My husband," intoned Hereca, "you speak strangely sometimes. Better to get right to the point."

"Aye," said Marcellus. "Speak like a centurion."

"Marcellus, I know how you centurions speak, and it is laced with strong profanity. Forget what I said about the Greeks. Will the Governor and his minions ignore the immunity bestowed upon us by Tiberius and attack us despite the little army that we have assembled? Are the Frisii really going to revolt or is that just tavern gossip? If the Frisii decides to take military action against Rome, when will that happen, and will it put us in the middle of the two forces?"

Hereca stepped forward. "Leave it to me. I will find out what is going on with the Frisii. The Frisii men will underestimate me because I'm a woman, believing me incapable of deciphering their intentions. I have my ways. Someone will let something slip—you watch. To Hades with your Greek mathematicians and their odds. What do they know?"

Marcellus chuckled. "I don't believe the Frisii have a chance."

Later that day, Marcellus stood amidships, ready to address the mercenary force. He was to explain to them in simple terms what their mission would be. He gazed at the assembled men. He had done this countless times as a centurion. The men gazed back at him expectantly. He examined the small band—*not a bad lot*. They all looked like tough men. He knew that a few probably had unsavory pasts. But that was not his concern. He needed men who could fight if the circumstances demanded it.

He offered a thin smile to the group. "Welcome to our expedition into the land of the Frisii. The destination of this ship is Flevum.

We'll sail down the Rhenus until the river joins the Vecht. From there, it's northward up the Vecht for about thirty miles. We'll disembark at the Roman fortress at Flevum, and from there, we venture inland. We are entering into trade discussions with a few of the Frisian leaders."

He paused, pacing the deck. "Now, most of you are wondering why my trading partners," he motioned with his arm at Valerius and Hereca, who were standing off to the side, "require an armed escort to discuss trade agreements with a peaceful German tribe. That's a good question. The politics of this is complicated. In truth, we really are traders, but our real purpose is to uncover the intentions of the Frisii. Are they going to revolt against Rome? There is a possibility that others might attempt to stop us from reaching the Frisii or perhaps, the Frisii might not be so welcoming. The Germans are an unknown factor at this point. Now, nothing may happen at all, in which case it will be the easiest coin you've ever earned. But there is the real possibility that we may engage hostile forces. From this point forward in our journey, you will speak to no one outside of this group about our trade venture. The fewer people who know, the better. And besides, you will have no free time. We will all be together until the conclusion of our journey. I will now ask my business partner, Valerius Maximus, to say a few words."

Valerius stepped before the men. "My friend and comrade, Marcellus, is a former centurion. I'm a former tribune. We both know a bit about fighting. We have chosen a second-in-command from among you. Rufus, would you please come up here?"

The man stepped forward. "Rufus is a recently retired optio with extensive combat experience. We will all be wearing civilian garb, but make no mistake about it, we will run this as if it is a military operation. You will do as ordered. If you don't, you will be discharged without pay. Furthermore, once we are in Frisian territory, each man will be placed at a precise position in a formation for maximum security in case of an attack. You aren't an unruly mob walking into danger. Listen to your leader, and the odds of us surviving this and you getting a generous payment of coin will be higher. Nothing would make me happier than to dispense your coin to you without encountering hostilities. Let us hope this is the case."

* * *

Meanwhile, back in Noviomagus, the Governor had convened his small council, which included Tigranus, Cornelius Quadratus, and Cethegus Labeo. Gallus fumed. "It seems our Tiberius-appointed emissaries are a cunning bunch. My spies have reported to me that they have amassed a small force as protection. It will make it that much more difficult to dispose of them."

"How many men have they assembled?" inquired Quadratus.

"Not exactly sure, perhaps a dozen, maybe more."

Quadratus snorted. "Not a problem, Governor. I have recruited a much larger force of reprobates. They will take care of our problem."

"Are you sure you have enlisted enough men on such short notice?"

Quadratus beamed. "Most definitely, Governor."

"You are using Lupus?"

"Yes. He recruited the men we needed."

"Excellent, Cornelius. And where will you attack them?"

Quadratus didn't hesitate. "In the land of the Frisii on their way to the meeting with the tribal leaders. As I recall, you told them that they are to report to the commander at Flevum, Tribune whatever…"

Gallus replied, "I did order them to report to Tribune Florus. That will delay them by at least a day or two. Is that sufficient time?"

"Yes, everything is set. I have several informers in Flevum who will alert our forces. Lupus's men will disembark upriver from Flevum, out of sight of any inquiring eyes. We will ambush them on their journey from Flevum to the villages of the Frisii. It is around a twenty-mile journey from the river to the main village in the Frisian lands, and the road passes through rather rugged terrain. We will attack them there."

"Excellent, Quadratus."

Tigranus jumped to his feet. "Can I join them, Father? I don't like that tribune, and I covet his wife. She would be a pleasure to bed."

Gallus glanced at his son as if noticing him for the first time. "What happened to your ear?"

"Things got a little out of hand at one of the taverns. It's but a scratch."

The Governor scowled. "I don't know if it would be wise for you to accompany this expedition." He looked toward Quadratus for his opinion, who, in turn, nodded in acquiescence.

"Go ahead. You may join them. Make sure you eliminate them to the last man...and woman."

⚊⚊⚊

Valerius stood outside the walls of Flevum with Marcellus. They were both in uniform again. It seemed appropriate given the circumstances—visiting a legionary fortress with a letter of introduction from the Governor. Valerius examined the piece of parchment bearing the Governor's seal. Was this supposed to be a courtesy call to the commander of Flevum or something else? Gallus was hardly one to stand on politeness, especially if it involved someone else. If he had to guess, this was probably just a delay tactic so that he could plot their demise.

⚊⚊⚊

Valerius and Marcellus began walking toward the gate of the fortress. In their absence, the tribune had directed Rufus to train the men on how to deploy and position themselves in a tactical sense. Hereca was not upset that she had been excluded from the visit to Flevum—there was no useful purpose for her to enter the stronghold. Her task was to find a messenger, hopefully a Frisian, to send as an envoy to the large village about twenty miles away. This was to be done as a courtesy to let the Frisii know of their visit and its purpose.

▲

Marcellus spoke. "Do you know anything about this Tribune Aulus Florus?"

"About as much as you," replied Valerius. "Look at this as an educational opportunity. We get to observe the state of readiness of the legionnaires manning this garrison and the walls of the fortress. If hostilities do erupt as Tiberius fears, we'll get to see how well protected we might be."

Marcellus snorted. "Why am I cynical about what we are about to see? I'm trying to be optimistic but based on the meeting with the Governor and his legate; I fear we'll be disappointed."

Valerius continued walking, deep in thought. After a bit, he replied, "I'm not sure. It was hard for me to read the legate, Labeo, when we spoke to the Governor. He didn't say much. Personalities aside, the complete dismissal of the Frisii as a threat is concerning. One thing we have both learned is to never underestimate one's enemy. I have a feeling there is a sense of complacency with respect to any German threat. But maybe we will be pleasantly surprised at the fortress's state of preparedness."

The two men passed through the gates and were escorted by two burly legionnaires to the *principia*, where the headquarters was located.

Along the way, they passed the barracks, bathhouse, stables, granaries, and workshops. There were a series of guard posts at various strategic points manned by legionnaires. Valerius glanced at Marcellus, who was intensely scrutinizing the surroundings and the legionnaires on guard duty. Valerius noted the beginning of a scowl forming on the centurion's face. Something was displeasing Marcellus and Valerius intuitively understood the reason—it was the citadel. The place was a mess: the guards' uniforms were slovenly, the streets were strewn with trash, and there was a general atmosphere of malaise. Even the legionnaires' postures were lacking, most of them slouching at their posts.

At last, they entered the headquarters of the commander. There, they saw a thin young man with an aquiline nose—presumably Tribune Florus. The escorting legionnaires departed, shutting the door behind them. Marcellus analyzed the man before him. *The tribune could not have been more than twenty-one. This had to be his first posting.*

The officer nervously cleared his throat. "Welcome, I'm Tribune Aulus Florus, commander of this fortress. The Governor sent word that you would be stopping by."

Valerius offered a brief smile. "*Salve*, Tribune. I'm Tribune Valerius Maximus, and this is Centurion Marcellus Veronus." He handed the sealed parchment to the officer.

The tribune broke the seal and read the contents. He looked up and offered a smile. "How may I be of service?"

"Did Governor Gallus's messenger inform you about the purpose of our visit to the land of the Frisii?" Valerius inquired.

"Ah, not really," he spluttered. "But this document notes that the two of you are to pose as traders to discern if there is any cause for concern regarding a potential rebellion by the Frisii. Did I get that correct?"

Valerius answered, "Yes, but we *are* traders. Centurion Marcellus and I retired from military service many years ago. The Emperor requested that we investigate reports of a possible uprising among the Frisii. Since you are the only major Roman outpost in the Frisian lands, have you noticed anything? Unrest or an increase in robberies or murders?"

The tribune shook his head. "Everything has been peaceful, from what I have observed. Are you sure your intelligence about an uprising is correct?"

"What about patrols? Have they noted anything unusual?" Marcellus asked. "After all, the Frisii are clients of Rome and under her governance. We are supposed to be guaranteeing their security and ensuring that commerce flows throughout their territory."

Florus looked confounded. "Patrols? No, we don't venture out of the fortress. We focus almost all our attention on the shipping on the river. This is a major commercial port. There have been no regularly scheduled patrols since I've been here."

Marcellus sighed. "Let me ask you a question, Tribune. How long have you been here?"

"About six months," Florus replied nervously.

Marcellus pressed on. "Who is the senior centurion responsible for the security of the fortress?"

"We don't have one. Centurion Marinius died shortly before I arrived. I inquired with headquarters about a replacement and they said they would be sending a new centurion, but no one has arrived yet. I have repeated my request several times, and they keep repeating that they'll send someone."

"How did this Centurion Marinius die?" inquired Valerius.

Florus hesitated. "I'm not sure. I heard he had a drinking problem."

Valerius and Marcellus exchanged knowing glances. Valerius adopted a stern expression. "I'm to assume you have been in command here since you arrived from Rome and that this is your first assignment?"

"That would be correct," replied Florus.

Valerius spoke. "Listen, Tribune, I'm not here to tell you how to do your job. I understand that this is your first command. I remember when I was in your situation. Centurion Marcellus can attest to that. He was my centurion." Valerius and Marcellus traded grins. Valerius then proffered Florus a reassuring smile. "If it were me, I would have mounted patrols out into the land of the Frisii, letting them know who is in charge and that they are under the protection of Rome's legions. Did General Labeo back at Noviomagus not provide you any guidance on what to do?"

The tribune fidgeted with his military belt. "I've received no assistance from General Labeo. We are at the arse-end of the empire here. Nobody visits or cares about us. The troops know it, and they feel abandoned here. The morale is quite low."

Marcellus spoke harshly. "Doesn't General Labeo ever come here for an inspection? It's not that far a boat journey from Noviomagus, maybe a day or two."

Florus replied, his voice trembling. "No, he has never come here. My orders and instructions come by way of dispatches. Would you like a tour of the fortress?"

"By all means, Tribune. Marcellus and I would appreciate that. Lead on."

The three men headed down the *via principals*, which connected the main gate at the front of the fortress and the rear gate. The stronghold was rectangular in shape, with the longer sides featuring the front gate and the rear gate, the latter of which was located at the quay. It had all been laid out meticulously by the legions' engineers. The side bordering the river featured an extra-wide wooden gate to accommodate the flow of goods from the docks. The walls of the fortress were twelve feet tall and made of earth, except for the one bordering the river, which was a wooden palisade tower of perhaps fourteen feet.

Near the front gate, the three men climbed the ramp to the turf wall. Atop the wall stood a crenulated wooden breastwork about chest high. The front wall—one of the longer sides of the rectangle— boasted a commanding view of the wide plain below. Surrounding the wall were a series of three wide ditches, each about nine feet deep. The trio began walking along the rampart. They arrived at the first of the heavily framed wooden artillery pieces. The weapon was about four feet wide and reinforced with iron. Incorporated into the frame was a long wooden slot used to fit the large bolts. The timber palisade was cut lower to allow the artillery piece to discharge its bolts against anyone foolish enough to assault the fortress.

Marcellus rubbed his hand over the frame of the contraption. "Let me ask you a question, Tribune Florus. What is the range of this bolt thrower?"

"I don't really know," he responded sheepishly. "I have never seen them in action."

Marcellus was silent. The tribune squirmed in discomfort, knowing he was about to be rebuked for the fortress's lack of preparedness.

"So you have no way of knowing if these bolt throwers do work. I assume no one has inspected the torsion ropes to ensure they won't snap upon use. You know they are supposed to be replaced often as the hemp tends to rot."

The mortified tribune replied, "I didn't know that."

Marcellus continued, "In addition, these are crew-served weapons, usually by three men. It requires coordination to reload the weapon and fire it accurately. I assume you have no idea as to the proficiency of the crews?"

Florus shook his head. "No, I don't," he said diffidently.

"Drill," emphasized Marcellus. "These crews must be drilled over and over. They should be able to operate this weapon in their sleep. They should know this piece of equipment like it's their woman. Fine-tune it. Fire it rapidly and accurately."

"How many men do you have in this garrison?" asked Valerius.

"There are two understrength cohorts plus a vexillation of slingers we agreed to take on. Nobody at legionnaire headquarters knew what to do with them so I decided we might be able to use them."

"Smart decision, Tribune. At last, positive news," said Marcellus. "What is your total strength?"

"As of yesterday's report, we have a little less than a thousand men."

The three continued walking, passing more of the artillery pieces. They reached the intersection of the walls and made a right turn. Florus motioned with his arm. "This is the breadth of our rectangular fortress. If you look ahead, you can see where the walls were lengthened to enlarge the fortress. This was completed about a year ago before I came here." They moved on to where the rampart was extended.

Marcellus halted and gesticulated with his arm. "Let me ask you something, Tribune Florus. Surely during your training period as a tribune, they taught you about legionary fortresses?"

Florus nodded.

"What is the standard number of ditches to be employed at the front of a turf berm?"

"I know there are supposed to be three, but the engineers only placed two ditches where the walls were extended. They were supposed to come back and oversee the completion of the third ditch but they never did."

"And have you ever requested that they come back and finish the project?" inquired Marcellus.

"No," responded the tribune meekly.

"Rule number one of the legions," said Marcellus. "You don't ask, you don't get."

"I suppose you're correct. Shall we continue our tour?" said Florus, anxious to move on.

Marcellus frowned in disapproval. "I think I have seen quite enough. What about you, Tribune Maximus?"

"Oh, I agree. I have seen more than enough."

Marcellus turned to the young man. "Listen to me, Tribune Florus. The defenses of this fortress are vulnerable. Not only are there just two ditches, but the rains have eroded the existing trenches. They are no longer formidable obstacles capable of deterring an assaulting force. Furthermore, the state of readiness I observed leaves something to be desired. Putting it more bluntly, the capabilities of the legionnaires of this citadel to repel an attack are shit. If an attack occurred today, you would be overrun in a heartbeat."

"But we are at peace and are allies with the Frisii. Surely no one would attack Flevum!" exclaimed Florus.

"That may not be the case anymore. Our relationship with the Frisii is under duress. They are an angry people," said Valerius.

Tribune Florus cast a morose look, clearly overwhelmed by the harsh criticism and knowledge of the danger his fortress now faced. "But what am I to do?"

Valerius responded. "Call an assembly, a *consilia*, of the centurions of the two cohorts and let Centurion Marcellus and I speak to them. There is much to be done here in what may be a very short amount of time. Make no mistake, you are in charge here, but let us tell them what needs to be done. Your lives may be at risk depending upon how well you can prepare your troops. Your centurions will seize the opportunity, I know they will. Let's get started."

Florus offered a weak smile. An experienced officer would have been offended by the criticism offered by Marcellus and Valerius, but given his lack of familiarity with the defense a fortress required, he welcomed their suggestions, especially since there was a real possibility of an assault upon his citadel. "I appreciate your help. I will call an assembly of the centurions right away."

CHAPTER IX

PREPARATIONS

The twelve centurions of the two cohorts—six centurions from each cohort—gathered in the headquarters, restless to hear the subject of the hastily called meeting. In addition, they were joined by the optio commanding the auxiliary detachment of slingers. The officers were veterans, a few having over twenty years of experience. Their faces were weathered from years of exposure to the elements. Their demeanor was calm, yet underlying their placidity was a hint of anxiety. Rumor had it that the subject of the gathering concerned the tribune and centurion who had appeared this morning and toured the fortress with Tribune Florus.

The room was small, perhaps fifteen by twenty-five feet, and surfaced with worn wooden plank floors. Two small windows allowed angled sunlight to brighten the space, where five wooden benches were arranged one behind the other. There was a murmur when Marcellus, Valerius, and Florus entered the room. The men dutifully rose to attention at the appearance of their commanding officer.

Florus stood in front of the centurions. "Gentlemen, please take your seats. Thank you for coming on such short notice. I have with me today Tribune Valerius Maximus and Centurion Marcellus Veronus. They are here at the behest of Governor Gallus with urgent news. Tribune Valerius, I believe you would like to address the officers present."

"Indeed. Thank you, Tribune Florus. Centurions, I will get to the point directly and not mince words. Centurion Marcellus and I were informed in Rome of a possible revolt by the Frisii. Just to give you some background, the centurion and I are long retired from military service. Both of us are experienced in battle with the Germans. We were part of the invasion under Germanicus Caesar fifteen years ago. Presently, we engage in trade as civilians with the various German peoples. But we have been recalled to active duty and our previous ranks have been restored. Our mission is to venture into the land of the Frisii in civilian garb and, as experienced traders with the Germans, ascertain the intent of the clan, to see whether they are planning an uprising."

One of the centurions—who appeared to be senior to most of the others—stood. He was a large man and bulky in appearance. "Sir, Centurion Glaucus at your service. Sorry to interrupt you, but doesn't this alleged plot appear to be a bit far-fetched? I mean, the Frisii have always been friends to Rome. We have observed no indication of any planned hostilities. Perhaps this is just a bit of wine-fueled tavern gossip. Might I enquire about the source of your information in Rome?"

Valerius glared at the centurion. "Of course you may, Centurion. Over two months ago, Marcellus and I were summoned to Rome to meet with an individual you may have heard of. His name is Tiberius Caesar."

Centurion Glaucus blanched and sat down amid a few sniggers from the audience. Valerius continued, "Gentlemen, now, listen carefully. It could be that this is all just some wine-fueled tavern gossip as Centurion Glaucus suggested or perhaps even a ludicrous rumor. We understand how information gets distorted or amplified, and I fervently hope that this is the case. But if it is not a tall tale and there really is a revolt brewing, this citadel is the only Roman fortress in Frisian territory and would appear the most likely target. Centurion Marcellus and I were given a tour of this citadel by Tribune Florus and frankly, it is our consensus that this place would fall—and fall quickly—in the event of an all-out assault by the Frisii. We believe much needs to be done in a very short time to improve the defenses of this fortress. Now, Centurion Marcellus has many years of experience in the legions and knows how to defend a place such as this. I will turn the floor over to him."

"Thank you, Tribune Maximus. The first thing we both noticed was the absence of a third ditch on the newer portion of this bastion. Furthermore, all the ditches are in disrepair as a result of the spring rains. There is not much we can do about that in the short amount of time available to us as it would take months to repair them; thus, we will concentrate on what we can fix."

Marcellus paused, eyeing the assembled centurions. "There are a number of things you can do to enhance your chances of survival, and make no mistake about it gentlemen, that is what we are talking about—survival. Some of these steps are easy, some not. First, I would suggest mounted patrols out beyond the walls. I was told this is not something you're currently doing. The patrols will provide early warning in the event of an attack. Second, all gates should remain shut and barred at all hours of the day and night unless someone is being admitted into the fortress. I realize this will disrupt the flow of commerce, but this is a necessary precaution. Along with the secured gates, I would suggest that the guards be doubled. From what I saw when I entered this fortress, the entire Frisian nation could have walked through the gates without an alarm being sounded."

Some of the centurions shifted uncomfortably in their seats, knowing what Marcellus said was true. "Now, for the tough part. If the warning of an attack were given at this instant, I would dare say that most of the men would have no clue where their places on the wall are. You need to start drilling so that everyone knows where to go and quickly. Begin drawing up sectors of the wall by unit. You will need a mobile reserve force in case of a breach."

"What about the crew-served weapons on the wall?" queried one of the centurions.

"Ah," said Marcellus, "how prescient. That is my next point. On my tour of the ramparts, I was informed by Tribune Florus that there has been no practice with the artillery. Furthermore, based upon my inspection of the bolt throwers, I have doubts whether even half of them are capable of working. These artillery engines are vital for the defense of this fortress. They require constant maintenance. My suggestion would be to get those crews up to their pieces, perform the required maintenance and repairs, and then start practicing. Oh, and I saw no ammunition on the ramparts—no bolts up there. How can you fire them if there are no bolts? Likewise, all the stockpiles of spears and arrows should be opened up now. Get them out of the supply rooms and workshops and up on the ramparts."

"Centurion Marcellus, how soon might the Frisii attack us?" a voice was heard from the audience.

Marcellus shrugged. "Who knows? Not to alarm you, but the Frisii could very well be marshaling their forces just a few miles from here at this very moment."

Marcellus saw the gathered centurions hanging their heads. He knew his criticism had stung. It was time to create some enthusiasm. "Listen, I know I have been harsh, but the lack of discipline and lax security in this citadel is disquieting. I understand it is difficult to enforce regulations when you believe you are in a secure place at the arse-end of the empire. But look at it this way—you have a second chance. No one has attacked yet. If the Frisians do come after our asses, you are going to be ready. You're good legionnaires; otherwise, you wouldn't have been promoted to your current positions. Are you with me on this?"

Centurion Glaucus stood once more. "Speaking for all of us, I think a strong kick in the arse is always good motivation, and I believe you are correct; the men in this room are good officers." He turned toward his seated companions for affirmation. "Am I correct?" The men all stood as one. "I think we're ready to get to work."

Marcellus flashed a pleased grin. "Good. I know it is late in the day, but what I suggest is this: we immediately gather the crews to fire the weapons. It is urgent that the ballista gets tested and is made ready in the event of an attack. That would be my highest priority among the things that need to be done. Then, I would propose that we all get together for dinner. Tribune Florus, I'm sure you could arrange for an evening meal to be shared by all the officers under your command."

Florus replied. "Of course, Centurion. Perhaps the cooks can prepare something special in honor of our guests."

Marcellus nodded in approval. "Tribune Valerius has several amphorae of a new vintage of wine from Gaul that he believes to be the best in the empire. Of course, he will need your opinion on this."

The centurions all cheered in agreement.

Valerius stood off to a side, admiring Marcellus's performance. He was a Roman officer who knew how to lead. In a short period, he had the centurions eating out of his hand—their display of enthusiasm was remarkable.

Valerius also realized that he would need to get word to Hereca, who was staying outside the walls of Flevum with the rest of the mercenary force, that he would be probably spending the night at the fort.

Dusk was nearing. Valerius, Marcellus, and Florus stood on the ramparts near one of the ballistae. Centurion Reginus, the officer responsible for this section of the rampart, nodded to the crew. The weapon had two large wooden levers that were used to ratchet the torsion ropes on the artillery piece. Two legionnaires began furiously cranking the levers. A third man loaded a four-foot-long wooden shaft upon which was affixed a fearsome pyramidal iron head. He placed the bolt in a wooden slot and notched it to the firing mechanism. The two legionnaires who had cranked the machine stepped back slightly. The loader stepped behind the artillery piece, sighted the weapon, and pulled the release mechanism.

With a loud twang, the ballista released the bolt. It shot out in a blur and arced far from the ramparts before smashing into the earth in the distance. Tribune Florus and Centurion Reginus grinned triumphantly.

"Good one," said Marcellus. "I would suggest you have the crew continue practicing with the little daylight we have left. Now, let's move to the next ballista."

The four officers walked along the ramparts to the next artillery piece and waiting crew. The three legionnaires looked toward Centurion Reginus for instruction.

"We don't have all day; load the weapon," ordered Centurion Reginus. The two legionnaires manning the large wooden levers began vigorously cranking them back and forth. They were close to maximum torsion when there was a sudden crash. The old and rotted hemp to the left of the ballista had torn under tremendous tension, breaking the torsion lever. The wooden knob struck an unfortunate legionnaire of the crew, the force of the release sending him sprawling. The man groaned in agony, his right arm now at a crooked angle.

Reginus and Florus looked on in horror, not quite believing what had just occurred. Marcellus was the first to react. He stooped over the injured legionnaire. "We need to get this man to a medicus. Tribune Florus, I would suggest, for safety's sake, that any future testing of these weapons should require less than full tension and the men should step away when ready to fire. Let's move on to the next ballista."

That evening, the officers' dinner progressed splendidly, fueled by the J&L wine that Valerius had transported from his supply cache in the town outside the fortress. The scarlet nectar was supposed to be a gift for the Frisii, but Valerius had decided to allocate some for this occasion. The cooks had done an admirable job of creating a delicious dinner on such short notice. There were several main dishes, including fresh river fish and a succulent roast goat. An assortment of breads, cheeses, and fruit accompanied the meat. The men ate and drank heartily and the atmosphere was almost festive.

Centurion Glaucus rose from his seat. He shouted for quiet and raised his goblet. "I would like to propose a toast to Tribune Valerius and Centurion Marcellus. From all of us, we wish you a successful mission and a speedy return to Flevum."

Everyone raised their goblets in unison. "A speedy return!" they shouted.

"And bring us more of this wine," cried a voice from a table. Everyone laughed and repeated the refrain, "And bring us more of this wine."

Centurion Glaucus remained standing. "Perhaps Tribune Valerius would like to tell us the story of how he met Centurion Marcellus."

"Yes, tell us," urged the men.

Valerius looked toward Marcellus for guidance but the centurion just shrugged. "Not much to tell. On my first assignment—some seventeen years ago—I was a very green tribune and had been assigned to the payroll records for three legions when I was introduced to a certain centurion named Marcellus. It was a difficult period because, in the space of a few short days, I had found myself in General Varus's bad graces."

"His shit list," exclaimed Marcellus amid muffled laughter.

"Precisely," said Valerius. "Varus despised me for political reasons and had me all but thrown out of his command tent."

There was a hushed silence at the mention of Varus's name. "You were with Varus's army?" Tribune Florus asked, awed.

Tribune Valerius nodded grimly. "Aye, we were."

"And you survived?" Glaucus asked.

Marcellus replied, "We were the only officers to survive the Teutoburg carnage. The two of us plus a handful of others fled through miles of German forest and bog while being pursued by a band of angry Germans. They didn't want any survivors to warn the

127

fortresses on the Rhenus. We ran and fought Germans for over a week. Finally, we managed to escape and reach the fortress at Vetera."

There was a collective gasp from the audience. Marcellus pointed at Valerius. "Not only did he survive, but you are also looking at the tribune who rode almost nonstop to Rome to tell Caesar Augustus of the defeat."

A barrage of questions was directed at the two officers, but Marcellus held up his hands for silence. "Tribune Maximus, tell them the story. It was your finest hour or perhaps, maybe your darkest."

Silence enveloped the room. Valerius grinned sheepishly. "Well, my specific order from the legate at Vetera, General Saturnius, was to ride at full speed to Rome and personally deliver the news of the Varus defeat to Caesar. I took the order literally. I arrived in Rome late in the evening after riding hard for almost two weeks with little rest. I smelled like a goat."

He paused to survey the room. The officers were transfixed by the tale, hanging on to every word. "So, I reported to the imperial palace covered in filth and appearing completely disheveled. I bluffed my way into the palace by clutching a piece of parchment that had nothing on it and saying I had urgent news that could only be delivered to Caesar. I interrupted a social gathering of the imperial family."

"Who was there?" shouted one of the centurions.

"Let me think. Augustus, of course; his wife, Livia; the current Emperor, Tiberius, and Germanicus. Their wives were also present."

"And you still have your head?" cried another.

Valerius smirked. "Yes, but only barely, thanks to Germanicus. There was great anger directed at me, but Germanicus took me aside and said he admired my pluck for appearing as I did. In the end, my tattered form may have saved me."

There was a hushed silence in the room. "There is more," said Marcellus. "We went on to serve with Germanicus in the reprisal campaign. Valerius was no longer a green tribune. He may have saved the legions from another Teutoburg disaster. Thank the gods Germanicus listened to him. We managed to survive and recapture two of the eagles lost in the Teutoburg."

The dinner lasted long into the night with much drinking and boisterous talk. Several times, Valerius contemplated leaving, but he knew intuitively that he had to stay until the end. It would not be good form to leave the banquet early; thus, he remained and drank wine with the other officers.

▲

The next morning, a bleary-eyed Valerius and Marcellus stood with Tribune Florus just outside the gate. They were going to meet their mercenary force in the town to make final preparations. Valerius glanced about and noted that the guards had already been doubled as Marcellus had suggested. Furthermore, the men on duty had paid attention to their appearance. Their uniforms were worn with care and their postures erect. "I see things have already started to improve."

The tribune beamed. "Yes, thank you for noticing. We have begun our metamorphosis. We took your suggestions seriously."

Valerius replied, "You have much to do. I wasn't exaggerating when I said your lives could depend on it. They very well might. Now, listen to me and listen well. If Marcellus and I don't return within five days, assume the worst and prepare for war. It's likely that the Frisii will have done away with us. There might be the possibility of another ambush by bandits, but the most probable scenario is that the Frisii are already in the midst of an insurrection. As I said, this fort at Flevum will be the first thing they attack. At the first sign of assault, get word to the Governor and the Fifth Legion. They will send reinforcements to relieve the siege. Got it?"

"I understand, Tribune Valerius. But for all of our sakes, I hope to see you return soon."

"I would like that as well," quipped Marcellus. "Just a little piece of advice to add to what Tribune Valerius said: take command but listen to your centurions. They are experienced officers and know what to do. Now, we need to begin our journey. We hope to be off early tomorrow morning. For all our sakes, may the Goddess Fortuna be with us."

CHAPTER X

LAND OF THE FRISII

Marcellus and Valerius sat huddled in conversation with Rufus in a small tavern outside the walls of Flevum. They had changed back into their civilian garb to avoid attracting any curious eyes. The former optio spoke. "We kept ourselves busy while you were away. First, I succeeded in getting shields for the men who didn't have any. I procured throwing spears too—German made. Not of the finest quality but effective."

"Not legionary shields, I hope," said Valerius. "We cannot look like a military force traveling into Frisian territory. Remember, we are traders with a protective security force. No hint of the legions."

"I was careful to not purchase anything resembling the legions' equipment," replied Rufus. "But I must admit, it came at the expense of quality. The shields we were able to procure aren't all that good, but I guess they will have to do."

"That is acceptable," replied Valerius. "I understand that we lack Roman armor and shields, but that is the price we must pay to maintain our subterfuge. What else?"

"Drill," replied Rufus. "We trained in our formations. I believe you told me that we would be traveling using the diamond formation—men on the front, back, and flanks. They all know their designated places and how far apart they should be. I was impressed by them. They picked it up right away. Some have done this sort of thing before, others not. I thought they might be indifferent, but they took it seriously. No joking or slacking. It was all business."

Marcellus turned to Valerius. "We got this guy at a bargain. We should probably have paid him more. Excellent work, Rufus. I thought we would be learning all this on the march, but you have taken care of it already."

"They could use more practice. No doubt about that. We can do a drill tomorrow while on the march. In the event of an ambush, we've rehearsed how to move to a consolidated position for defensive purposes. I would hardly call then well-trained troops, but they have an idea of what to do if we come under attack. They are back in their rooms sharpening their weapons now."

"We'll gather on the main road in front of the fortress tomorrow at first light," said Valerius. "Make sure all the men understand this. Now, I need to check with Hereca to see if the mules and supplies are ready to go." He rose from the table. "Thanks again, Rufus for your assistance."

Valerius returned to his room in the town. Hereca was laying on the bed, exhaustion etched on her face. "I hope you had a good time at the Roman fort because I have been slaving away non-stop since you departed. I procured the mules and the remainder of the supplies. This town doesn't have a lot to offer in terms of goods. I believe I purchased the last two mules available. Same with the remainder of the wine and food rations. I guess I'm spoiled since everything is available back home. Oh, and perhaps most importantly, I hired a guide to take us to the largest village near Flevum. His name is Hallr and seems trustworthy. He said it's a long day's march from here. He stated that the village chieftain, whose name is Eadric, is a powerful leader and spokesman for many of the tribes of the Frisii. He is our guy. If we want to talk trade and judge the state of the Frisii, this is who we should speak with. Oh, I also dispatched a messenger to this Eadric telling him we will be coming."

Valerius hugged his wife. "Thank you, Hereca. You would make an excellent quartermaster in the legions. If it makes you feel any better, my day wasn't great either. The small banquet we partook of last night was nice, but the state of the fortress was disheartening."

Hereca broke away from their embrace. "How so?"

"Where should I begin? Assuming we survive the discussions with the Frisii, which would be a big *if*, and we make it back here to the fortress, we wouldn't survive an attack by the Frisii on the fort."

Hereca looked at him questioningly. "And why not? It looks formidable."

"Because the fort is under the command of a raw tribune, and the men have slacked off to the point that the defenses are in poor shape. They are forgotten men. No one from higher command ever comes here to inspect. The outer ditches, the artillery pieces, the men, all of them need a lot of work. We better hope this Frisian insurrection is just a rumor."

Hereca frowned. "I was hoping for better news on that front. Even if we return here unscathed, there is a chance the fort will be overrun?"

"I'm afraid so," sighed Valerius.

MARK L. RICHARDS

▲

Their journey did not begin expeditiously. In fact, it was a debacle. They faced great difficulty in packing the mules with the provisions and gifts for the Frisii. The men were inexperienced on how to secure and distribute the weight of the goods, especially the wine, on the animals. As a result, the load began to slide off even before they reached the outskirts on the main road. Marcellus cursed and fumed, muttering to himself that they should abandon the mules and the wine altogether. After much delay, they finally began their excursion. The men had enough sense to avoid Marcellus. Hallr, the Frisian guide, smirked at the chaos.

Once their journey was underway, Valerius contemplated the state of the road upon which they were traveling. The initial portion outside the fort had been maintained well by the legionary force, but once they had progressed about a mile, the road morphed into a dirt path, though still passable. By comparison, he had trekked on far worse ground. He pondered once again the difficulties they might encounter. Would the Governor send a force to ambush them? This was the most likely outcome, although not a certainty. Had he read the Governor's intentions wrong? He thought back to what his father had said about Gallus. The man was nefarious and no stranger to the use of violence. An ambush of his contingent would be the perfect solution to rid himself of Valerius's meddling. Would their mercenary force act as a deterrent? *Maybe*, he thought, *but what is to stop the Governor from recruiting an even larger force? It will just be more challenging for Gallus to eliminate us but not impossible.*

He walked up beside Marcellus. "I've been considering the likelihood of Gallus attacking our little force. Don't you think it might be difficult to engage us in this type of terrain? Can he assemble a

134

force of men and move them to this vicinity in such a short amount of time? We met with them, what, five days ago?"

"Ah, Tribune, spoken like a true military man—thinking of logistics and the terrain that the enemy must travel. To answer your question, yes, it will be a challenge but not impossible. I sense that if Gallus plans on ambushing us, the assailants will not be well trained—they're more likely to be a bunch of ruffians. The legions will not be connected to this attack—nothing that could be traced back to the Governor. Word might get back to Rome about who attacked us otherwise. But I read this as you do. I believe he will send a collection of cutthroats to attack us and then blame it on the Frisii. After all, we are in Frisian lands. Who else would assault us in their territory?"

"In any event, we are prepared. I'm pleased with our force and our progress, except the late start. The men are in an efficient diamond formation—two men at the front, back, and flanks, while the remainder are in the center with us and the mules. Rufus knows his stuff."

The group continued plodding on in the early afternoon.

CHAPTER XI

INTO FRISII TERRITORY

They called him Lupus, wolf. No one knew if that was his given name, but it was the moniker he was known by. The name seemed appropriate for there was something savage and feral about him. He was not a big man but it wasn't his size that intimidated people but rather his countenance. His eyes were a grayish blue that blazed with a hate-filled intensity. To add to this, he had two enlarged incisors that gave him a wolf-like appearance. A high forehead covered with cascading greasy locks and thick simian eyebrows completed his cruel and minacious appearance.

Lupus was a thug without a speck of remorse. He had found his niche in this world as an enforcer for the Governor's tax collector, Quadratus. Most Roman officials frequently used the heavy arm of the legions to enforce tax collections but not this current administration.

Governor Gallus and his quaestor, Quadratus, preferred to use unofficial, less sanctioned means to collect their bounty and for good reason—it kept the tax collections completely private and out of the official records of the legions, where every denarius would need to be accounted for. They had found the perfect instrument in Lupus.

Lupus had caught the attention of the newly appointed Governor a little less than a year ago. There had been a dispute at the docks of Noviomagus between two warring factions of labor gangs. As a result, nothing was being loaded or unloaded from the dock, bringing commerce to a standstill. Lupus had approached the Governor's staff offering his services to resolve the disagreement. A frustrated Gallus had given him permission without a second thought. The next morning, the bloody and dismembered bodies of the leaders of the warring factions were found neatly arranged along the main wharf. The dispute ended immediately and Gallus found a new associate to help him establish order in the territory of Germania.

Now, Lupus and his army of ruffians were pursuing a small force that was seeking trade with the Frisii. Quadratus had given him explicit orders. He was to seek out this trade delegation and destroy it to the last man. Accompanying his group of thugs was the Governor's son, Tigranus, who wanted special revenge on a woman who was part of the group. Ordinarily, he would have been annoyed that such a person, whom he had no authority over, was foisted upon him, but there was something about the young man that he liked; they were almost kindred spirits. Lupus had heard stories about Tigranus and his less-than-wholesome activities and found them similar to his own lifestyle. Besides, it was another avenue for him to curry favor with the Governor. All in all, it was a good thing to have Tigranus accompanying him.

Lupus didn't bother to ask why these people needed to be killed. It was of no concern to him. Guilty or innocent, it didn't matter. He had been given short notice for his mission and had thus hastily assembled his horde of thugs. However, he didn't view it as a problem as he knew where to get the kind of men capable of carrying out this brutal task. He had recruited over forty men and was confident that this would be more than enough to kill the group of merchants who had offended the Governor. How hard could it be? His hand-picked men would make short work of the trade mission.

Upon being informed of his prey's departure from the Roman fortress, Lupus and his men had left their boats upriver above Flevum. From there, they had cut diagonally through brush and forest toward the main road entering Frisian territory. They had done this so that they would not be observed by any of the legionary forces manning the fortress. Once they had slaughtered their prey, they would exit the same way, leaving no trace of their presence. The deaths of the trade merchants would be blamed on the Frisii or bandits. It would have no connections with the Governor.

Lupus's chief tracker, a man with a weasel-like face, trotted up to him, nodding in deference to his leader. "They are perhaps an hour ahead of us. We should be able to catch up with them soon."

Lupus pondered the words of his scout for a bit and then waved for everyone to gather about him. The rabble congregated about Lupus. "Our target is only about an hour ahead of us. Now, I don't want to spend any more time than I must in Frisian land. We are going to move at double our normal pace. I want to end this quickly. We can get back to the river where the boats await us by tonight and then sail tomorrow morning for the taverns of Noviomagus."

The men whooped and hollered at the thought of returning to their familiar hangouts.

Lupus held up his hands for silence. "Once our adversary is in sight, we attack. There are only about a dozen of them. We will easily overwhelm them with our numbers and slaughter them. No survivors. None must escape."

"Except the woman," interjected Tigranus. "She is mine, and I want to give her some special attention as payback for her insolence. Her end will not be pretty."

Lupus nodded wearily. "Except for the woman. Let Tigranus have his fun. Now, let's get moving. We need to pursue them and then attack. Move. Move!"

▲

Valerius walked side by side with Marcellus and Hereca. He occasionally glanced to the rear to see if there was any threat from that direction. "Marcellus, so far so good. Even better, this road is navigable; not a Roman paved road, mind you, but it's more than passable. It looks as though it is well-traveled."

Marcellus rubbed his right leg, which had been wounded by a spear in a skirmish with the Germans long ago. "Maybe, but now I remember why I quit the legions. My fucking leg is killing me. After seventeen years, it still hurts."

Valerius gave him an inquiring look. "Do you want to stop for a bit and rest?" As soon as he spoke the words, he regretted them. He knew his friend was sensitive about his age and stamina. He was rewarded with a harsh glare from Marcellus.

"Listen, Tribune," he spat. "Just because I'm old doesn't mean I'm weak. I will out-march and out-fight every man—"

Hereca interrupted Marcellus's diatribe. "Oh, Marcellus, stop it. We all know what a great soldier you were—no, correction, are. My husband was not questioning your fortitude. He has told me on numerous occasions that you are a truly magnificent centurion, unmatched in the legions. Your exploits and bravery are renowned. He is simply concerned for your well-being. Whether you like it or not, you are getting along in years. I say we all rest right here for a while and we'll brook no nonsense from you or any other man here. Valerius, you are tired as well, are you not?" She gave him a wink that the centurion could not see.

"As a matter of fact, I was just going to suggest that we take a break. We have been pushing hard all morning."

Hereca turned toward Marcellus. "So that is that."

Valerius called out to the advance guard to halt. He clamped a hand on Marcellus's shoulder. "Look, I'm bushed, and I know you are feeling pain. Stop with the *I'm the toughest centurion here* routine. You need a break, I need a break, and the men are tired as well. Hereca is exhausted."

The bewildered Marcellus grunted and then sat down, knowing he had been bested by Hereca once again. He didn't like it, but he knew it would do no good to protest, so he remained silent.

* * *

The gang of thugs that Lupus had collected rushed forward along the wide dirt trail. They moved as a mob lacking discipline. Most had expected to catch up to their prey by now, but each bend in the road yielded nothing but an empty landscape. The rapid advance by the men over the last several miles had tired them out. Many gasped for breath and fell behind the vanguard, but nonetheless, the mob continued their pursuit, eager to dispense with their targets. The quicker they came upon their prey, the better.

⚤

Valerius gulped down water from his water-skin and then wiped his mouth on his sleeve. By the gods, the water tasted good even if it was lukewarm. There was murmured conversation among the men, and the mules munched contentedly on sweet grass. It had been chilly earlier this morning when they'd set out, but now, the full force of the afternoon sun beat down on them to the point where many had sought to rid themselves of some of their garments. Valerius gazed about to ensure that the men were upholding proper security—they were. Men were posted off to the flanks, front and rear, vigilant for any sign of an impending attack. He was about to ask Marcellus if he was ready to move when a shout from one of their band echoed from the rear. "Men approaching!"

Marcellus was up in a heartbeat. "Form a shield wall on me." Just as they had drilled, in a matter of moments, they had transformed themselves into a compact fighting force. Valerius and Marcellus had their bows ready in seconds. A mob of venomous looking men charged at them from about two hundred and fifty paces away. There was no doubt as to their intentions.

Both Marcellus and Valerius swiftly released their first volley, then another, followed by another. The results were devastating. The arrows were fired into a compact mass of charging men. They could not miss—the arrows all found their targets.

Tigranus had situated himself in the middle of the pack. He glanced in horror as several men ahead of him were knocked to the earth by a barrage of arrows. This was not supposed to happen; it was to be an easy triumph. He looked up to see the source of this danger.

In a blur, an arrow streaked toward him, cutting along the side of his neck. He screamed in pain, grabbing at his bloody wound.

The charge by the brigands faltered as more men were struck by the fierce blizzard of arrows. Lupus raced forward, screaming above the din of battle, waving his sword menacingly at his own men. He began marshaling his forces. "You lot attack the left flank, you lot, the right side. There are only two men with bows. Close in on the enemy. Attack now before we are all slaughtered."

The mob split into two sections—one to the left, the other to the right. They surged forward toward their prey.

Valerius and his men were in a line, forming a shield wall. Hereca, Hallr, Ox, and Marcellus stood behind the barrier of men, acting as a mobile reserve force in case there was a breach. Although the men comprising the shield wall were not trained Roman legionnaires, they comported themselves like experienced soldiers. As the mob approached, now within twenty yards, Rufus issued the command. "Spears ready! Release!" A shower of spears was hurled from the ranks, striking the charging band of ruffians. Men went down, pierced by the projectiles. The charge wavered once again.

Lupus advanced to the front of the pack, urging the men to attack the shield wall. He pointed his sword and screamed. The men then began to attack again. The rabble, now down to less than thirty, closed in on the shield wall. There was a huge crash as the two forces collided. Sword thrusts were exchanged amid screams in the once tranquil meadow. A half dozen of the cut-throat band were felled by Valerius's men, but they took a few of the defenders with them. The mob, with their greater numbers, enveloped the shield wall, threatening to flank both their right and left sides.

Valerius found himself facing a thick-set individual missing most of his teeth. The man wielded an ax and viciously swung it. Valerius blocked the blow at once, his shield absorbing the heavy thump of the weapon. His opponent swung the ax once again. This time, Valerius used the opportunity to thrust his shield forward, throwing his foe off balance. With a lightning-thrust, he pierced his antagonist's torso with his sword. The man crumpled to the ground. Suddenly, the man next to Valerius in the shield wall screamed in pain and fell to the ground—the victim of a wound to the shoulder. Ox deftly moved into the gap before it could be exploited, wielding a huge wooden club. He swung it in a high arc and slammed into one of the assailants. The man howled and fell back.

Hereca, positioned behind the wall of men, felt useless. Both Marcellus and Ox had plunged forward to plug the gaps as several of their men fell. She decided to take the initiative as well. She seized a spear that she had planted by her side. She raised the weapon to shoulder height, feeling its heft and grip. It was perfectly balanced. She had been renowned for her prowess with the javelin in her younger days as a German warrior princess. Although she had not hurled the javelin in many years, she trusted the strength of her arm. She singled out the man who appeared to be the leader of the attacking thugs, the one who was animatedly directing the assault. Without a second thought, she let out a shout and heaved the lance.

The missile sailed at her intended target, streaking through the short distance between them. But her aim was too high. It flew past her intended target, over his right shoulder, and struck another. If she had lowered her aim for center mass, it would have hit the bandit leader square in the torso. Hereca was angry and disappointed; she had failed.

Lupus grimaced at the near miss. He spied the thrower of the spear, a woman. His features contorted with anger and he let out a howl. He charged at the center of the enemy group, directly toward the woman in the rear rank. He recklessly threw his body at the shield wall, consumed by the thought of how he would gut her and watch her die slowly.

While engaged with one of the ruffians, Marcellus caught the movement out of the corner of his eye. A savage figure had hurled himself at the mercenary on his right, and the man had been pushed back by the force of the charge. Marcellus angled his shield toward the menacing cutthroat who had penetrated the shield wall—just in the nick of time, as a sword bounced off his shield. The centurion stood face to face with the wild figure, who now confronted him. A second swing smashed into his shield. Marcellus crouched low and viciously thrust his sword into the man's groin. The sword penetrated deeply, the centurion then withdrawing it quickly and twisting it for maximum damage. Lupus collapsed in a screaming heap, his life's blood pouring from a gaping wound. He died almost instantly.

Suddenly, a band of warriors charged out of the forest. Valerius recognized them as Germans immediately. They were in a wedge formation dressed in woolen tunics with no armor. Each man carried a long wooden spear affixed with an iron point and a small round shield. He assumed they were Frisii. They screamed their battle cries and slammed into the disorganized mob, that were attacking the beleaguered Romans. At the sight of the reinforcements, the now leaderless pack fled in panic back down the dirt road from whence they had come, pursued by the Frisians. The newfound German allies dispatched those too slow to make a getaway and returned to Valerius and his men. They stopped short of where the crew stood.

The leader of the Frisian warriors spoke in broken Latin. "Greetings, my name is Sigiberd. My chieftain, Eadric, said that a party of Roman traders would be departing Flevum and venturing into our lands to discuss possible trade with us. I believe you had dispatched a messenger from Flevum letting us know of your intentions. It appears that you have a trading rival. Dangerous business, trading. No?"

Valerius ignored the sarcasm about a trading rival and replied in German. "Thank you for your assistance, Sigiberd. We had been forewarned about a potential assault upon our persons. My name is Valerius, and this is my wife, Hereca."

"My husband and I don't normally travel with armed escorts," said Hereca, "but we heard a disturbing rumor that there was an element that didn't want us to meet with the Frisii. We are grateful for your assistance. Will you help us see to our wounded?"

Sigiberd rubbed his jaw in thought, thinking of what to say next. He had not anticipated the Roman to speak German proficiently or have a German wife. *Impressive*, he thought.

"Certainly. My men are at your disposal."

Valerius turned toward Rufus. "The men did exceedingly well. You trained them to fight like an experienced unit in a very short time. What are our casualties?"

"Our losses were kept to a minimum, although it would have been much worse if the Frisii had not come to our rescue. We lost one man, Brutus, to a stab wound in the throat. Hallr, our guide, was also slain. Three are wounded but are expected to recover."

"Make that four wounded men," said Ox as he wrapped a bandage around his left arm, the same one that had been injured in the tavern fight.

Marcellus snorted. "Again, Ox? You seem to attract these types of wounds. In the tavern or on the battlefield, blades have a way of finding you."

"Don't I know it. And my wound from last week was just about healed. But I'm not going to complain. As the Tribune said, the carnage could have been much worse had the Frisii not showed up. I'll take this scratch any day. Let's hope this is the end of this."

▲

The afternoon wore on. After treating the wounded, the Roman force followed the Frisii. They trekked onward for the remainder of the day and into early evening. Finally, they arrived at a large village with hundreds of dwellings, replete with large fields of crops and grazing oxen.

Marcellus, Hereca, and Valerius had been directed to one of the guest huts in the Frisian village. The others had been assigned two other dwellings. Valerius had been informed that they would be summoned to meet with the chieftain, Eadric, later that evening. When they were alone, Valerius spoke in a hushed tone, lest someone was listening outside the daub walls of the dwelling. "This is the way I think we should conduct our discussions with Eadric. He will be slightly suspicious given what occurred on our way here. An ambush of Roman traders by foreigners in his territory. Ha! It makes no sense. I will make the introductions and talk about what we do as traders. He might have heard of us and our reputation."

Valerius paused for a moment. "Here is where it gets a little delicate. I will hand off the dialogue to Hereca. She will discuss possible trading while at the same time, gently probe the Frisii as to what their intentions might be. Her inquiries will appear much more innocent and disarming than if I were to make them. I sense that this Eadric is a crafty fellow. We dare not engage in any deceitfulness. Look for changes in his facial expressions as clues to what he might be feeling."

"What about me? Marcellus inquired.

Valerius gazed at the centurion. "I'm sure the chieftain would prefer his native language. We will be speaking German. Pay attention and see if you can pick up anything from their body language. No doubt there will be other advisors there."

The three looked at each other in silence. "Are we agreed then on how to proceed?" Valerius asked.

They all nodded. Then, Hereca spoke, "There are a couple of things I should mention. During the attack upon us back on the road, I stood behind the shield wall. I observed the entire sequence of events unfold while you were engaged. I noticed that one of the attackers looked familiar. Even with a helmet, I recognized the face."

The two men looked at her quizzically. She stared back. "It was the Governor's son, Tigranus."

"Are you sure?" Valerius asked.

Hereca gave him a sharp glance. "Yes, it was him. Typical of the coward, he was in the rear. I believe an arrow wounded his neck, but I cannot be sure. I was hesitant to speak of this on the way here for fear that our Frisian escorts might overhear me."

"Well, that settles it," said Valerius. "The Governor will go to any extreme to stop us. He isn't finished with us yet. We will need to avoid him at all costs."

"There is more," said Hereca. "As we traveled through the village to this dwelling, I observed the size of this village and the inhabitants. There is something amiss."

"Go on," said Valerius. "I trust your instincts about these Germans. What's bothering you?"

"There are more males of warrior age than one would expect from a village this size. They greatly outnumber the women and children and that is just what I saw in the area we traveled through. Who knows how many other camps may be set up beyond the huts of the village?"

"So you believe the Frisii may be marshaling their forces close to this village to advance upon Flevum from here?"

"Yes. I cannot be certain, but it is the most likely scenario."

"Anything else?" Valerius asked.

"Yes, there is," replied Hereca. "I don't know if you picked up on it, but when we first arrived, the glances we received from the villagers weren't exactly warm and friendly. There is an air of hostility; yet, the Romans are supposed to be their allies."

"You are suggesting we are in extreme peril," said Valerius.

Hereca snorted. "What I mean is that your Greek mathematicians may be correct. The odds against us have risen."

Valerius, Hereca, and Marcellus faced Eadric and his small retinue of advisors in the spacious longhouse, the largest of the dwellings in the village. Proper introductions had been made for all those present in the lodging. Grass reeds carpeted the floor, and the doorways and windows were wide open, ushering in a welcoming breeze on this warm night. Valerius studied Eadric. The man was massive and robust-looking despite his years. He sensed that he was not just a renowned warrior who ruled by his physical presence; he was more than that. Many Romans dismissed Germans as simple barbarians who didn't have the mental acuity or cultural sophistication to succeed in the Roman world—this was a mistake. He knew from his dealings with the German leaders of various tribes that they were quite cunning and highly intelligent. The fact that they didn't speak Latin well or follow Roman customs was neither here nor there.

Valerius had brought several large amphorae of the J&L wine into the house as a gift for the Frisian chieftain. Goblets had materialized and everyone was poured a cup of the amphorae's ruby red contents. Eadric hoisted his chalice. "A toast to your safe arrival."

All those present drank deeply. Valerius decided to take the initiative. "I hope you enjoy this wine. I discovered this vintage in Gaul. I hope to trade this wonderful wine throughout Germania, including with the Frisii. It is good, is it not?"

Eadric smacked his lips. "Although I'm not an expert on wine, I must admit it has a pleasant flavor." He gestured for his guests to be seated. He then began in broken Latin. "I understand you had a bit of trouble on your way here from Flevum?"

"There's no need to speak in Latin. As you have no doubt heard, my wife and I speak your language," Valerius replied in German. "It will be easier to converse in your language. To answer your question, yes; we did have a spot of trouble with bandits. They were about to out-flank us when your men arrived. They need not have bothered. We had them right where we wanted them."

Eadric looked puzzled for a moment and then burst out laughing. "That's what I like—a Roman with a sense of humor. But, tell me, why were these people after you? Why attack a bunch of Roman traders who had no goods, except for, perhaps, this delicious wine? Strange, is it not?"

Valerius shuddered internally. Eadric was perceptive. Now, how was he going to explain this? He paused to gather his words. He needed to tread lightly here. "Yes, it is peculiar. Our trading company has no doubt made a few enemies in the course of conducting business—rival traders—but this attack upon us appears far beyond bad blood. Fortunately, before we embarked, we were given an anonymous warning that there might be violence perpetrated against us. As a result, I assembled a security force to accompany us. There were no survivors from among the wounded who attacked us—your men made sure of that. We thank them for rescuing us."

Eadric stroked his chin in thought, appearing to have bought Valerius's explanation. "Tell me about your trading company. I might have heard something about your enterprise, but tell me your story."

"I was a former tribune in the Roman imperial army. My friend and business partner," he said gesturing toward Marcellus, "was a former centurion. My wife, Hereca, is a member of the Dolgubni tribe. We met many years ago under very adverse circumstances. To make a long story short, we saved each other from certain death."

"I'm curious," said Eadric, "why you wore the uniforms of the legions when you arrived at the fortress at Flevum when you are traders."

Valerius had not anticipated this question. The messenger to the Frisii Hereca had dispatched must have seen them in their uniforms when they arrived at Flevum. Thinking quickly, he offered a glib reply, "When we spoke to Governor Gallus at Noviomagus to inform him that we were going to enter trade discussions with you, we reported in our old uniforms to make an impression on him, even though Centurion Marcellus and I have long left the legions, over fifteen years ago, in fact. Governor Gallus thought it might be a good idea to continue to wear our uniforms when we reported to the commander at Flevum."

Eadric adopted a puzzled expression. "Your wife does not wear the uniform of the legions, does she?"

Valerius gazed at Eadric, not sure whether it was an attempt at humor or if his remark served another purpose. Perhaps it was heavy sarcasm? "My wife, Hereca, is an equal partner in our venture and a large reason for our success, but no, she does not wear the uniform of the legions though she could. Hereca was raised as a warrior princess. Her father was the chieftain of her clan. You should see her wield a spear."

Eadric nodded in understanding. "I see."

"Now, back to our mercantile discussions. We trade mostly upriver on the Rhenus with Germanic tribes bordering the river and with a few in the interior. We have a solid reputation as fair traders. We barter, exchange, and trade in many different kinds of goods from all over the Roman empire: fabrics from the east, wine from Gaul and Italia, iron pots, saws, axes, mirrors, glass—you name it, we trade it. We thought it was time to expand our horizons to the land of the Frisii. Frankly, I vastly prefer trading with the Germanic tribes to fighting them."

Eadric smiled briefly. "You trade with the tribes of the interior? Some are not friendly with Rome, no?"

Valerius gave Hereca a quick glance. This was her prompt. Hereca proffered a warm grin. "Yes, Eadric, we trade with several of them. There are restrictions, you understand. We are prohibited by decree of the Emperor from trading iron weapons and ingots with all the German tribes. We bring goods from Rome in exchange for timber, hides, horses, and oxen. I like to think that the various Germanic tribes enjoy the luxury items we supply. Even the Cherusci and Chatti trade with us."

"Impressive. I didn't think those tribes would ever trade with Romans."

Hereca laughed. "We prefer to not think of ourselves as Romans. We live in Oppidum Ubiorum—that is our permanent home—and we speak German with our trading partners. I must admit, it was difficult to gain the acceptance of some of the tribes in the interior. That is another reason we decided to visit the Frisii. You have long been allies of Rome, and we thought you might welcome the trade."

Eadric narrowed his eyes. Something Hereca said had irked him. She spotted the change immediately and continued, "Of course, we met with Governor Gallus to get permission to speak with you. He gave us his blessing."

The Frisii all frowned in unison at the mention of Gallus's name. "And what do you think of this new Governor?" Eadric asked.

"Governor Gallus is the appointed governor of this territory. We have only met him one time. We hope he will be accommodating with respect to our trade ventures, especially with the Frisii," replied Valerius.

Hereca probed deeper, her tone innocent. "You know, my husband and I could speak with Governor Gallus about making an exception for the Frisii to trade iron ingots and spearheads. After all, the Frisii have long been allied with Rome. Would that be agreeable to you?"

Eadric's features darkened. "Even though we are allies of Rome, I don't believe Governor Gallus would be amenable to that." The chieftain appeared to gain some semblance of control. "I will consult with the other chieftains about your request to trade with the Frisii."

"Would you like us to be present to answer any questions?" Valerius asked.

"That will not be necessary. There is an internal disagreement at present due to some economic difficulties."

"We would be willing to meet with the Frisian leaders at any time—"

Eadric interrupted, his tone laconic, "I said that will not be necessary. Please return to your dwellings. Perhaps we can speak again of this tomorrow." Eadric rose, signaling that the meeting was over.

The three small huts the traders' party were housed in were all clustered together and located away from other dwellings. Darkness had descended and several imposing guards milled about, standing next to the doorways with their spears in hand. As the evening wore on, the level of celebratory noises increased. Shouts and raucous laughter filled the air while martial drumming and shrill flutes joined the clamor.

The three huddled together in whispered discussion. Hereca had that familiar stormy look about her as she glanced at the two men. "We must leave here tonight. I believe they intend to make war on all Romans, including us. We cannot wait to find out if I'm wrong."

Marcellus glanced at her. "What do you mean? We must make a stealthy escape?"

"Yes," replied Hereca gravely.

Valerius looked at his wife. "But they let us keep our weapons. That doesn't fit into your line of thought."

"Eadric probably figured there was no way we could fight our way out of the middle of a German village. We are not a threat, just an annoyance," said Hereca.

"How certain are you of their intentions?" Valerius asked.

"I believe they will attack Flevum soon. Perhaps as early as the day after tomorrow. If we hear and observe them feasting long into the night, we will know for sure. It is customary to have a large celebration the night before embarking on war. As we passed others on the way to our dwelling, I heard one woman say something about the *beserker* tonight, which is the warrior festivity before battle."

"All right. Marcellus and I will visit the other dwellings and warn them. We will abandon all baggage and travel as light as possible. A small amount of food, water, and our weapons."

Valerius turned toward Hereca. "How long can we expect the celebrations to continue?"

His wife shrugged. "Who knows, but this is just the beginning. If I am any judge of things, I'd expect the festivity to last quite a bit longer. Hopefully, the guards will join the celebration."

The three sat and listened to the racket in the village. Although they were weary after their long, exhausting day, they were on edge. The thought of sleeping did not even pass their minds. Outside, the celebration continued in full swing.

CHAPTER XII

FLIGHT

Well after midnight, the yelling and carousing ended. Hereca looked at her husband. "Now is the time. I am going outside. If I see anyone, I will tell them I am going to relieve myself. I will inform the others if it is safe."

Hereca returned a bit later with a smug look on her face. "No guards. They must have wandered off. The men are ready in the other huts. We have tied cloth around the mouths of the three wounded men so they will not cry out. Their legs are unscathed, so they can walk."

The small band quickly assembled outside their huts. Valerius motioned for Rufus to approach him and spoke softly. "I want you to take the lead. Move cautiously through the village. Once we get to the outskirts, we will begin running toward Flevum. Understood?"

Rufus nodded and then began walking past the longhouses and outbuildings of the village. The moon was partially obscured by low hanging clouds, masking the settlement in darkness. Along the way, they saw men and women passed out on the ground, some snoring, some deep in inebriated sleep. Off in the distance through the trees, a myriad of campfires burned in the night, proof that others had joined Eadric's clan. As they moved past a figure slumped against the tree, the man awoke. "Who are you?" he slurred.

Hereca stood in front of the man, obstructing his view of the others. "We are returning to our encampment for the night," she said in a hushed tone. "Now, go back to sleep before you disturb the others."

The man rubbed his eyes, grunted, and then rolled over on to the ground. The small group continued picking their way silently through the eerie encampment.

Once outside the village proper, the group slipped past the animal pens. Horses nickered and stomped nervously at the presence of the strangers, but that was all. Next was the oxen enclosure. A few of the beasts shuffled around but made no other noises. They continued onward and reached the fields, which were now laden with barley and oats. They could not detect any sentries and so they silently crept onward, leaf litter crunching softly beneath their feet.

They reached the edge of the last field and, finally, the beaten earth of the path back to Flevum. Valerius jogged up to Rufus, who was at the front of the ragged formation, and spoke in a muted whisper, "Set a pace that will not exhaust us yet move us steadily forward." Moving in unison, they began jogging.

They ran at a continuous pace for what seemed like hours—the only sounds were the pounding of their feet on the dirt track and their labored breathing. Valerius had been observing his group, especially the three wounded, from the middle of the pack. He was proud of them. No one had complained, but he sensed that the men were at the end of their endurance. They had been holding up, but for how much longer could they continue? He'd considered himself to be fit, but now, he felt as if he were ready to drop. His lungs ached and his legs felt like dead weights. He accelerated to reach Rufus and signaled him to halt. A collective sigh was let out by the group.

No words were spoken. They rested their hands on their bent knees, sucking in lungsful of precious air. The three wounded had fallen to their knees. Valerius circulated among the men, checking on them. He stopped in front of Marcellus and was about to ask him how he was holding up, but when he recalled the centurion's brief diatribe on the journey to the German village, he decided against it. It was a touchy subject—one he had no desire to revisit. He spoke in a hushed tone. "Well, my friend, we're in a familiar predicament. We're having the Germans chase our asses through forest and moor, just like the Teutoburg."

Marcellus grunted. "Familiar indeed. The flight from the Teutoburg was much longer, but all the same, this is a perilous situation, and we are fleeing for our lives. I keep looking over my shoulder, but why bother? All I see is darkness. As if I could really see the Frisii approaching from our rear."

Valerius clapped his hand on Marcellus's shoulder. "We shall escape, just like the Teutoburg."

Hereca sidled up to the pair and spoke in a low tone. "What are you two discussing?"

"Hereca, do you think they will come after us?" Valerius asked.

She paused in thought. "I have been contemplating this very same question all night. On one hand, we are not important to the Frisii—we're just a bunch of traders. Eadric certainly has more important things on his mind. But…"

"I knew there was a *but* in this. What is it?"

"We have defied them. Their pride demands that they come after us and dispense their form of justice, which means they will kill us. I believe Eadric is highly suspicious. You heard his tone when he addressed us. It was not exactly trusting. He didn't buy that bit about us being eager traders seeking to expand our business. More importantly, they might believe that we know of their intentions to attack Flevum; therefore, they will try to stop us from warning the garrison. I believe they will send men on horses as soon as it is discovered that we have bolted."

"That is exactly what I've been thinking, Hereca, and it is why we must make haste. Let us hope our disappearance is not discovered until well after dawn. It is going to take us all night to return to Flevum. Enough dawdling. We need to get moving again."

In response, Hereca let out a weary sigh. Valerius went over to Rufus and motioned with his arm that they were to begin again. "Let's get going and pick up the pace. Our only chance of survival is to get to Flevum before the German pursuers reach us."

Driven by desperation, they journeyed onward into the night, now moving at an even quicker pace. Valerius observed a few struggling to keep up. He was sympathetic to their limitations for he was not used to this grinding pace either. He understood that these were not trained and hardened legionnaires who were familiar with such physical demands, but the thought of the German cavalry running them down made him shiver. After all he had been through in the past with the Germans, he was determined not to meet such an ignominious end. His thoughts turned to his children. He had to return to them at all costs. His thoughts were interrupted as three men collapsed—a wounded man and the two who had volunteered to assist him. They were a tangle of arms and legs in the middle of the road.

Valerius seethed. He approached the jumble of men on the road. Now was not the time for kind words. "Get off your arses now," he hissed, "unless you fancy a German lance piercing your innards. If that is the case, we can leave your sorry arses here. It's your choice."

The three men gave him baleful glares but shakily rose and began jogging down the road once again. Onward the band of troops struggled, their pathway lit by a sliver of the moon. Spurring themselves forward, they conquered more miles. After a while, Valerius tapped Rufus on the shoulder, signaling him to halt. Despite his exhaustion, Valerius made a quick headcount to ensure they had not lost anyone. They were all here.

After catching his wind, Valerius addressed the men. "I know you are all drained. I'm as tired as you, but as I'd said previously, the harsh reality is that we must get to Flevum before the Germans catch up to us. Both Hereca and I agree that the Germans will pursue us. By my reckoning, we are about halfway there. Only ten more miles to go. This is going to be the toughest ten miles of your life, but we have a chance to survive. I know you can do this. Let's get moving. Just concentrate on putting one foot ahead of the other."

They crossed several small streams, passed through a stand of dense timber, and then moved through gently rolling hills covered more with brush than forest. After a while, they stopped for a short respite before pushing through again. Onward they trekked into the darkness for several more miles, their breaths reduced to ragged gasps. Valerius studied the night sky. He could tell from the position of the stars that dawn would shortly arrive and, with it, a force of German cavalry. He looked toward his men, who were now huddled in an exhausted heap. The breaks were becoming more frequent as the men were worn out, but they had to move again. He grimaced at the thought of it. He waded among the men and spoke in a quiet yet firm tone. "Everyone up. Come on. I know you are drained. So am I. Not much farther," he exhorted. "On your feet. Let's go."

With a collective groan, the band rose once more and began jogging into the darkness. Over the next hour, men tripped and fell several times. The group had to halt while the humbled figure picked himself off the ground and shakily rose to his feet to continue once more.

Dawn arrived. The dark silhouettes of the trees bordering the dirt road morphed into grey and then green. Valerius glanced over his shoulder anxiously, looking for any sign of the Frisian warriors. Like the others, he gasped for breath. By his reckoning, in a few more miles, they would reach Flevum. He moved next to Hereca. "We are close." He grabbed her arm to support and help her along.

She shrugged him off. "Husband, I can do this on my own. See to the others who are struggling." He ignored her and continued running next to her. They rounded a turn in the road, and far off in the distance across the open plain, he spied the dark silhouettes of the walls of the fortress. They were almost there.

The sight of Flevum galvanized the others. Together, they surged forward and picked up their pace. But their spurt of energy was short-lived. The rapidity of their stride diminished as fatigue set in. Over the sound of their labored gasps, Valerius heard the distinct whinny of horses. Looking over his shoulder, he spotted a mounted force of Frisii approaching. Valerius knew his group was in no shape to repel an attack, outnumbered as they were by a superior force of mounted cavalry, but surrender was not an option. "Halt," he managed. "Shield wall."

The men staggered into position, ready for battle. Valerius and Marcellus unstrung their bows. The Frisian cavalry thundered toward them, now only five hundred yards away. Valerius picked an arrow from his quiver and notched it. Out of the corner of his eye, he saw Marcellus do the same. They would quickly be within range. Valerius could now make out the features of the warriors charging at them. He was getting ready to draw the string on his bow when he heard shouts behind him. Turning about, he spied a *turma* of mounted Roman legionnaires advancing toward them. Facing forward again, he witnessed the Frisian riders come to a halt at the appearance of the Roman cavalry. To his relief, the Frisii quickly turned about and departed.

CHAPTER XIII

RETURN TO FLEVUM

Valerius, Marcellus, and Hereca strode toward the quarters of Tribune Florus, accompanied by the leader of the mounted patrol that had rescued them, Decurion Sylvestus. Florus was awaiting them in his cramped office. He smiled warmly at their arrival. "Welcome. I'm glad to see you make it back to Flevum."

"Yes, but just barely," replied Valerius. "Oh, by the way, this is my wife, Hereca, a German princess of the Dolgubni tribe. You will want to hear her thoughts on the Frisii's intentions."

"A pleasure to meet you, Hereca. I am anxious to hear what you have to report," answered Florus.

Valerius gestured toward the decurion. "First, thanks to the intervention of your mounted patrol under the direction of Decurion Sylvestus, we are alive and reporting back to you. We escaped the German village in the middle of the night and ran all the way back here. I firmly believe that the Frisii view us as an enemy. Just as we caught sight of Flevum, their cavalry appeared at our rear. Propitiously, your mounted patrol arrived. The Frisii elected not to engage in battle, turned about, and fled. Now, let me allow Hereca to recount our experiences in the Frisian village. She will offer you her observations."

Hereca began. "Tribune, as soon as we entered the Frisian village twenty miles from here, I knew things were amiss."

"How so?" Florus asked.

"First, the number of men of fighting age were disproportionately higher for the size of the village. I know these things from my own experiences growing up with the Dolgubni tribe. Second, the glances we received were overtly hostile. If the Frisii are supposed to be our allies, one would expect a friendlier or at least neutral reaction. Third, when we spoke with their chieftain, Eadric, and his advisors, every time we mentioned the Governor's name, their expressions darkened. I believe there is serious loathing there. Last, after we met with their chieftains, that evening, the village celebrated their *beserker* festivity, which is traditionally held the night before commencing hostilities with an enemy."

Florus gestured with his arms, his palms facing upward. "Still no actual hostilities. Where does that leave us?"

"Tribune," said Marcellus patiently, "we need to prepare for an assault. All the signs are evident. We do not doubt that the Frisii are intent on waging war against Rome. True, they have not attacked us yet and their horsemen turned about at the sight of our cavalry, but we are certain they are on a war footing. Their forces may be approaching Flevum as we speak. I would strongly suggest that the first thing you do is dispatch a vessel to the legate of the Fifth Legion, General Labeo, and tell him you are under attack. It will take a day for it to reach Noviomagus and perhaps another two days for a relief force to arrive."

"I will dispatch a ship right away."

"Excellent," said Valerius. "If you don't mind, let me help you draft the message to Governor Gallus and General Labeo. Then, you can update Marcellus and me as to your state of readiness. You will need to get the folks who are living outside the walls into the fortress. They are in peril."

Valerius looked over the Tribune's shoulder as he etched a message on a wax tablet. Florus finished and handed it to Valerius.

Governor Gallus,

Indications are that the Frisii intend to attack Flevum. Respectfully request reinforcements immediately.

Tribune Aulus Florus

Valerius examined the message. "Well, it is short and to the point, but not strong enough. Based on what you have written, Gallus might not send any assistance until he knows you are under siege. I would suggest you change the wording. First, instead of writing *indications,* I would state that a large force of armed Frisii is marching upon Flevum and are ravaging the countryside. Then, state that we will not be able to withstand a prolonged siege given the estimated number of warriors. This makes the message strong and clear. Gallus will need to act."

"But we don't know the number of warriors and, as of yet, they are not marching on Flevum."

"True enough," said Valerius, "but the Governor doesn't know that. If you are wrong about the intentions of the Frisii, Gallus will give you a good kick in the arse, but if you send your message and no reinforcements arrive, it's most likely we will all die. I believe it best to err on the side of caution, don't you?"

"I think I like your message better," said Florus, grinning weakly.

"Outstanding. Now, what boats are at your disposal? If we send Gallus an urgent plea for help, we must ensure that the dispatch gets there. The Frisii, in all probability, will attempt to blockade the river."

"Thankfully, our largest craft, Rome's Glory, is at the quay; at least, it was yesterday evening. It is a ship with a crew of twenty. It's quite large for a riverboat—one mainsail and twenty oarsmen. We can supplement the crew with a few of our troops. I know what the Frisii have in terms of boats, and they are not capable of intercepting a ship the size of Rome's Glory. If we sent lesser vessels, I wouldn't be as confident. In fact, all the remaining ships in the quay are small. Rome's Glory is our only option."

"How quickly can you have Rome's Glory underway?" Valerius inquired. "I have a feeling the situation here is going to escalate shortly. The Frisii may already have boats in the water to halt us from sending reinforcements."

Florus shrugged. "Hard to say. You know how those navy types can be. They take forever to get under sail. Maybe we can take a quick walk down there and convince them that now would be a good time. What about the civilians? Should we have them board the remaining boats and send them on their way?"

"Too risky," replied Valerius. "I believe the civilians in the town will have a better chance of survival here. Let's get going to the quay."

A short while later, Valerius and Florus, accompanied by a dozen legionnaires, approached the dock. The men all carried javelins with them. Rome's Glory was leashed to the quay, the ropes gently being pulled by the river current. As Florus had assured, it was a big vessel. Valerius estimated the size of the ship to be at least ninety feet, and it had a tall wooden mast capable of holding a large sail. The vessel would need it as it would be sailing upriver against a strong current. "Tribune Florus, who is the master of this fine vessel?"

"That would be Captain Basilius. He is an experienced naval officer. I think we can count on him to deliver our message to the Governor."

The two officers walked to the boarding plank, leaving the accompanying legionnaires to rest in the shade. A large figure with chiseled features rose from his position amidships and strode toward Valerius and Florus. There was a look of uneasiness on his countenance. "It's not every day that the commander of the fortress and a dozen legionnaires approach my boat. What in Hades is going on?"

"Captain Basilius," said Florus. "This is Tribune Valerius Maximus. There have been rumors that the Frisii intend to revolt. The tribune was tasked by the Emperor and Governor Gallus to venture into the land of the Frisii and discern their intentions. He got his answer last night. He had to flee from their village twenty miles from here. As we speak, large numbers of the Frisii are marshaling their forces and marching on Flevum."

The captain stared back at the two officers, trying to comprehend what had just been told to him. "What would you have me do?"

Florus produced the wax tablet. "Take this message to the Governor. It is an urgent plea for reinforcements. The entire Fifth Legion is stationed at Noviomagus and we need them here. I have brought with me a dozen legionnaires to augment your crew. If the Frisii try to blockade the river, run them over. You must deliver this. Our survival depends on it."

Captain Basilius turned about and bellowed to the loitering crew. "Make ready to sail." He then turned back to the two tribunes. "We should be ready to get underway shortly." He started to head back up the plank and Florus waved for his legionnaires to board the ship.

Valerius called out, "Oh, Captain, one more thing."

Basilius halted and turned around. "Yes?"

"If you are asked, you saw masses of Frisii off in the distance making preparations to attack the fort. We can't have the Governor thinking that this was a false alarm or a wild rumor. They are coming and they are coming in force. Believe me on this."

The captain nodded. "Aye, I understand what you're saying. I will make sure your message, both written and verbal, is delivered."

⁂

Later that morning, Valerius, Marcellus, Florus, and Centurion Glaucus—the acting senior centurion—walked along the ramparts, examining their state of readiness for the defense of Flevum. The legionnaires of the fort had been extremely busy in your absence. It appeared that much progress had been made. Placed at precise intervals, bundles of spears rested against the wooden wall atop the earthen rampart. In addition, piles of stone from the river had been hauled up to the wall. The group arrived at the first ballista. Resting on the ground was a stack of bolts—ammunition for the ballista. "What supply of bolts do we have for the ballista?" Marcellus inquired.

Florus nodded to Glaucus to reply. "We have about ninety bolts per functioning ballista. As we speak, the armorers are fashioning more of them. However, it is an arduous and time-consuming process to shape the wooden spears and attach them to the iron shafts. I don't believe we will be able to make many more before the Frisii arrive."

"And how many of the ballistae are in working order?"

Florus frowned. "About seven out of ten are functioning. My centurions informed me that it is doubtful if we can repair those that are not working properly."

"I suppose that will have to do," said Marcellus. "I don't mean to lecture you, but the ballistae are critical to the defense of this fortress. Not only do they kill the enemy at a great distance, but the tremendous sound of the artillery firing often causes foes to duck and stop. It strikes terror into their hearts. It is an awful noise to hear if you are on the receiving end of these bolts."

Centurion Glaucus offered a tight-lipped smile. "I would agree with you on that. It is a fearsome sound that echoes above the din of battle."

The group moved down the rampart and came to the first disabled ballista. It had been moved back and away from its firing position in the crenulated slot in the wooden palisade. "If I might make a suggestion," said Marcellus, "why don't you position three of the slingers in this space to make up for the loss of the artillery piece? Slingers are more effective when they grouped together."

Tribune Florus nodded. "Good idea. I will talk to the officer in charge of the slingers, Optio Barius, and have him reposition his men so that there will be slingers concentrated where we have a non-functioning ballista."

They continued walking along the rampart. Florus gestured toward the opposite wall of the fortress. "We have conducted drill upon drill over the last several days so that each man knows where he is supposed to be stationed along the rampart in the event of an attack even in pitch darkness. In addition, we have a mobile reserve force that will be situated in the compound below to move as needed if there is a breach."

Marcellus studied the walls and contemplated the plain bordering three of the sides; the fourth was protected by the river. "The Frisii do not have siege equipment. I sense that they will attack in waves and count on their overwhelming numbers. They will bring ladders to scale the ditches and ramparts. Nothing fancy about it. A direct assault."

There was a tense silence among the four officers. Valerius peered at the front gate—the one closest to the civilian collection of dwellings, inns, taverns, and shops. He noted a steady stream of people being ushered by legionnaires through the gates and into the citadel. "Perhaps they could assist us in the defense of the fortress—at least some of them. Some could support the medical personnel and others could help carry weapons and supplies up to the walls."

"They will be put to good use," said Glaucus. "The request to enter the fort wasn't optional. My men are in town to see that the order is enforced."

"Oh, that reminds me," said Florus. "After you departed, a ship arrived carrying those people you've been searching for."

Valerius gave him a puzzled look. "What people am I searching for?"

"You know, the J&L distributors. I didn't get to spend much time with them as I was busy with the preparations to improve our defenses. They informed me that they are seeking new markets for their wine. I told them that we had happily sampled their product just the other night, courtesy of two of our officers who were out on a mission. They are probably in the fort as we speak."

"I wish I could have met them under different circumstances. Bad timing. I really would've liked to trade their wine in the German territory. Perhaps Marcellus, Hereca, and I can meet them and chat for a bit after we finish this circuit of the walls. What do you say, Marcellus?"

"Indeed, it would be a pleasure to finally meet them and make contact. I am saying this both as a satisfied customer and trader."

Florus grinned. "I will set up a meeting in the headquarters as soon as we finish here. You can find Hereca and meet us there." They continued the inspection, reviewing the defensive walls of the fortress. As of yet, the Frisii had not appeared upon the horizon.

▲

Later, Hereca, Marcellus, and Valerius entered the principia. The guard was expecting them and directed them down the corridor. They passed through a pair of double doors into a spacious room. Florus was conversing with a middle-aged man and woman. The male was tall and appeared to be fit, with short dark hair. He could be considered handsome despite his slightly crooked nose. The woman, who had her back partially turned to them, had long cascading locks of brown hair set aglow by the sunlight. Despite appearing middle aged, she carried herself well as though she was much younger. The couple turned at the sound of the approaching trio.

Valerius finally laid eyes on the distributors of the wine he so admired. The couple turned to fully face the trio.

CHAPTER XIV

REUNION

A brief silence engulfed the room. Suddenly, the woman from J&L imports let out a shriek and flew into Valerius's arms, embracing him in a mighty hug. Hereca gaped at the display of affection, not knowing what to think. The woman quickly separated from him, then opened her arms toward the centurion and warmly hugged him. "Centurion Marcellus, how are you?"

The woman's companion hurried over and shook Valerius's hand. "Tribune, we meet again. It seems our fates are intertwined."

Valerius grinned. "I can't believe this. We've been searching high and low for the identity of the J&L distributors, and all along, it was our friends from many years ago. Of course, I should have guessed it! J&L—Julia and Lucius! Forgive my manners. Hereca, these are my dear friends and former comrades-in-arms, Julia and Lucius. They are from Gaul. The two of them escaped the Teutoburg disaster with Marcellus and me. Julia and Lucius, this is my wife, Hereca."

Julia beamed. "Nice to meet you, Hereca." She turned back to Valerius and Marcellus. "Oh, this is like a dream come true. I think about the two of you all the time, wondering how you've been doing. We lost contact many years ago. I hope all is well?"

"We are fine, but all is not well here in Flevum. Not to alarm you, but we are in a rather grave situation here, and you are smack in the middle of it." Valerius told them of their mission as dictated by Tiberius and what they had encountered in the Frisii village. "We strongly believe the Frisii are going to attack Flevum. That is why all the civilians in town have been moved to the fortress."

Lucius frowned. "We have already heard those disquieting rumors. But before we arrived, we were told that the Frisii were amicable neighbors to Gaul and allies of Rome and, thus, they would be good trading partners. That is why we ventured here in search of new markets for our wine."

"I know. We were under the same impression. It was of no fault of your own that you believed the reports about the Frisii's harmony with Rome, but there has been an unforeseen change," said Valerius. "We expect an attack on Flevum imminently. I would have told you to leave, but I'm not sure that option is open to you. From what I understand, there are only small ships docked at the quay. It's likely that the Frisii, who have a large supply of small boats, may already be blockading the river." He looked toward Florus for confirmation.

"We have no reports about the Frisii yet, but in good conscience, I would be reluctant on having anyone attempt to navigate the river at this point," said Florus.

Julia spoke, her voice quivering. "What are we to do?"

"Like it or not, the grim reality is that you are stuck here. In all probability, the Frisii will lay siege to Flevum. The good news is that we've sent a dispatch to Governor Gallus at Noviomagus, where the Fifth Legion is stationed. In a matter of days, we can expect reinforcements, but until then, we will have to fight it out with the Frisii."

"How can we help?" Lucius asked.

Valerius gestured toward Florus. "The tribune is the commander of this garrison. He and his staff are looking at ways in which the civilians can help in the defense of the fortress."

"I know it has been many years since my service in the legions," said Lucius, "but I still remember how to use a sword and spear. I volunteer my services."

"Thank you. We could use all the manpower we can get," said Florus. "I was thinking we could utilize your mercenaries, Valerius, plus those civilians who have experience in fighting as part of the mobile relief force. That would leave more of my men to guard the walls. How does that sound? You may not be needed at all, but if there is a breach, you would be required to plug it."

"That would be fine," said Lucius.

"And me?" Julia inquired.

Hereca sauntered up to her and put her arm around her in a comforting gesture. "We will help Tribune Florus figure out what the women's roles might be. Isn't that right, Tribune?"

Florus grinned. "I appreciate your assistance. I know we could use your help with the sick and injured."

⏶

Julia and Hereca sat on a wooden bench outside the *valetudiarium* (the hospital). "I am curious," said Hereca. "You were with my husband and Marcellus during the Teutoburg? Valerius doesn't talk much about it. But I know some of the story. You were but a handful of survivors, yes?"

Julia gave her a warm smile. "Valerius and Marcellus saved my life and that of my husband, Lucius. Not only did we survive the battlefield, but the Germans chased us for many days on our way back to the Rhenus. My father was the chief veterinarian for the legions and he died in that bloody forest. I owe my life and those of my three children to Marcellus and Valerius."

"You have three children?" Hereca inquired.

"Yes, twin boys—Petroculus, named after my father, and Cassius, named after Lucius's friend who perished in the battle. My daughter is named Aquilonia, after Lucius's mother. You have children?"

"Yes, four—two boys, Aulus and Calvus, and two girls, Juliana and Paulina."

There was an awkward silence between the two women. Julia hesitated and then spoke, "I don't mean to pry, but when I knew your husband, he was betrothed to a Roman woman named Calpurnia. I believe he intended to return to Rome and marry her. I know that was a long time ago but…"

"Yes, it was a long time ago. Much has transpired over the years. I will give you the condensed version. It is a sad tale. After Valerius was married to Calpurnia, he was ordered to the German frontier to serve the legions in a reprisal campaign against the German tribes who participated in the Teutoburg battle. While stationed in Germania, his wife died in childbirth back in Rome. Of course, this is all before I knew him. During one of the ensuing battles against the Germans, Valerius was captured by members of my tribe, the Dolgubni. He survived captivity and later rescued me when a neighboring tribe, the Cherusci, raided my village. My father, who was the chieftain, was killed."

"How awful. So you lost all of your friends and family?"

"Yes, the two of us made our way back to Roman territory. Valerius retired from the legions and then we, along with Marcellus and a former sea captain, started a trading company on the Rhenus. We never looked back. That was fifteen years ago. But all of this is connected to our current predicament. There is a common thread."

"How so?"

"Valerius was a close advisor to Germanicus Caesar, who was the commander of the Roman forces during the invasion of Germania. He was highly decorated for his service to the legions. He is known to Tiberius Caesar, although perhaps not in a favorable way. Tiberius received a report about a possible rebellion by the Frisii. The Emperor knew of Valerius's expertise in German military affairs and that he is a knowledgeable trader in German territory who speaks fluent German. Although he doesn't admire Valerius, Tiberius enlisted his help to investigate the rumors of a possible rebellion."

Julia gasped. "I had no idea Valerius traveled in such high circles. He was only a new tribune when I had met him."

"Believe me, he would rather not, as you say, "travel" in such high circles. He was perfectly content overseeing our thriving business. That is how he came to know of your wine. A limited quantity became available along the Rhenus. He raves about it."

Julia beamed. "I must admit that our wine is superb. I'm not bragging, but it is really good stuff. Several people from this region have expressed an interest in our wine. That is why Lucius and I decided to visit Germania and expand our wine distribution. Now look at what has happened. We are in peril once again."

"Julia, listen to me. There is much I have not told you regarding the politics of things here in Germania. We believe the new Governor is responsible for this revolt. The Governor dispatched a force of bandits to kill us as we were interfering with his plans. We sent the ruffians packing. But fear not, Julia, my husband and Marcellus are excellent military men. They have taken a leadership role in the defense of this fortress. One thing I have learned about my husband is that he should not be underestimated. He has survived against incredible odds with the Germans and the leadership in Rome where lesser men would have failed. The Frisii will have a difficult time attempting to take this citadel."

Julia nodded. "I know. Marcellus and Valerius saved us from certain death. I have complete faith in their abilities."

Lucius had assembled with a collection of other men in the shadow of the ramparts. He had been fitted with a chain-mail cuirass, bronze helmet, rectangular Roman shield, and a gladius—the short Roman stabbing sword with which he was well acquainted. He shuddered slightly. He'd never thought that he would be holding a sword and shield again—it had been many years. There were about sixty men gathered about him. They comprised the relief force that would act in case there was a breach in the walls of the fortress. The sixty men were a combination of the mercenaries that Valerius had recruited for his venture into the Frisian lands, some civilians from the town, and a collection of legionnaires who had been on medical leave or imprisoned for various infractions of military discipline.

An extremely large, imposing figure with a shaved head approached him. "You are Lucius, correct?" Not waiting for an answer, he continued. "Tribune Valerius told me to keep an eye out for you in the event we experience hostilities, although he mentioned that you were one Hades of a legionnaire in your past. Oh, by the way, everyone calls me Ox."

Lucius nodded. "From the size of you, I would welcome you by my side. It has been many years since I carried the sword and shield of the legions, but it is not something one can forget."

Ox nodded sagely. "I can believe that. Once a soldier, always a soldier, right?"

"Yes, something like that."

Another figure approached the pair. "My name is Rufus Placidus, recently retired optio. Tribune Valerius suggested Ox and I team up with you, but from what I hear, you are a renowned fighter who survived the Teutoburg. Maybe it's you who will be protecting us."

Lucius chuckled. "Perhaps. It would be an honor to fight alongside you both. I know from experience that it's always good to be flanked by accomplished fighters."

"Not to worry, Lucius. Between Ox and me, you will be protected."

Their conversation was interrupted by a legionnaire, heavily muscled and short in stature, who advanced toward the ragtag collection of men. He spoke with an air of authority. "Listen up. I am Optio Severus and have been placed in command of this relief force. I need six ranks of ten men each facing me. Legionnaires in the front ranks. Make it quick."

The men sought their places in the ranks. The legionnaires, numbering approximately thirty, filled the first three ranks of the rectangular formation. Lucius was crammed between Ox and Rufus in the fourth rank, directly behind the last rank of the legionnaires. He was anxious about the potential combat but felt relieved with the two men, who seemed to be formidable fighters, by his side.

Optio Severus surveyed the formation. Satisfied, he spoke, "Alright, remember your places. This is how I want you to arrange yourselves. Our purpose is to plug any gap in the defenses of this fortress. If the Frisii break through, we will attack with force. If we require a wider front, I will issue commands for the second and third ranks to join the first ranks. The fourth, fifth and sixth ranks will be in reserve."

After a brief pause, Severus continued. "There is a chance we will not be needed. That would be a good thing. However, if we are called upon, our reserve force is the last thing standing between victory and annihilation. Try to remember this if we get into the fighting. We will reconvene in one hour and do the battle drill. Now, go get some food in your bellies. We have much work to do. Dismissed."

Hereca and Julia were sitting on a wooden bench in the courtyard of the headquarters, animatedly chatting away. They did not see Marcellus and Valerius approach. "Ah, I see you two have found much to talk about," teased Valerius.

"We have," said Julia. "Hereca was telling me about how you two met. Certainly not a classic romance."

"That is true," chuckled Valerius. "I believe the first words she spoke to me were something to the effect that she would enjoy killing me."

"My husband, sometimes, I still think that way," intoned Hereca. Everyone laughed at her wit.

"Marcellus and I have been assisting Tribune Florus with the final preparations for the defense of Flevum. The good news is that the Frisii have not yet assaulted Flevum, although my gut tells me that they are not far from here. But every hour that goes by brings us that much closer to when the Fifth Legion arrives. I believe the presence of five thousand legionnaires armed to the teeth will be enough of a deterrent for them to cease their hostilities and to send them packing. Marcellus, what say you?"

"I agree. The Frisii are smart enough not to take on a standing legion in battle on open ground. They know what happened to those German tribes that had done so in the past. I'm pleased with the progress that has been made in the fort's defenses. If only the ballistae were fully functional and we had more ammunition," he said wistfully.

"Hereca and I will be here," informed Julia, "assisting the fort's medical staff."

Valerius stared at his wife. "Did you hear what she said, Hereca? Your place is here assisting the wounded. Julia, I trust you to ensure that my wife doesn't decide to go up on the battlements and throw spears at the enemy. She was a warrior princess back in the day, but this is different. She will have no weapons or armor. It will be as dangerous as Hades up there. Can you promise me you will make sure she stays here?"

"Hereca has a mind of her own, but I will attempt to persuade her not to go up on the walls. Besides, I need a companion to assist me here."

"Mark that, Hereca. You are needed at the hospital. Please don't join me on the ramparts," pleaded Valerius.

Hereca sulked. "All right husband. But I will be armed. I want a few spears in the event I need to defend myself."

"You shall have your spears," replied Valerius.

⋏

Eadric, the Frisian chief, stood before the various heads of the clans. They were several miles away from the walls of Flevum, having traveled there from Eadric's village. The chieftains had gathered in a wooded glade sheltered from the midday sun. Although it was a peaceful environment, their deliberations would not be. Eadric was pleased that so many of the clans had agreed to participate in this revolt. He gazed at the many familiar faces—there was no hesitation whatsoever etched upon their countenances. They were eager for battle and committed to the revolt, and why not? Their survival depended upon it. To pay the levies demanded by the Romans would be an end to their way of life.

The murmured conversation ended abruptly as Eadric stepped forward. "I thank you all for joining me in this action against the Romans. I must clarify this isn't my uprising—it is all of ours. This is what we had collectively decided on. And we are almost ready to attack Flevum."

Many in the audience grinned in anticipation of the assault. Eadric continued, "As we discussed, the objective is to eliminate the fortress of Flevum from our territory. Once we have done that, our forces will sweep west toward the Rhenus, eliminating all Roman outposts and settlements. The new border of our territory will be the Rhenus. After we are finished, we will be independent of Rome and her tax collectors. At no point will we dare cross the Rhenus and invade Roman territory. To do so would be to invite severe retaliation and we have all seen the results of that with the other German tribes to our southeast."

A man named Gunwald stood. "If all goes according to plan, we can probably defeat those fortresses along the Rhenus. Some of the citadels are not well defended by the Romans since they believe we are at peace with them. We can reap much bounty from our conquests."

His remarks were greeted with thunderous cheers.

Eadric raised his arms to quell the enthusiastic audience. "That is not what we discussed in our deliberations. If we do as you suggest, we will be taunting Rome, and I have no desire to invoke their anger any more than necessary. Rome may retaliate as it is for our actions, but I am hoping that they decide to maintain their border as the Rhenus as they do for all of the other German territories. We are the only land where they have pushed to the northeast beyond the Rhenus, primarily because of the ease of transportation along the Vecht and our long-standing peace treaty with Rome. From what I've learned of the Romans over these many years, if we push beyond the Rhenus, we will be perceived as invading their lands, and they will certainly respond with extreme force. That would not be a desirable outcome."

There was more muttered conversation. "Are we agreed upon the limit of our invasion? Speak now before we get started." Eadric waited for a little while and then spoke again. "All in favor of a limited invasion that ends at the Rhenus, please stand."

Almost all the men rose. A few were undecided, but eventually, they rose as well. Eadric proffered a wide grin. "Good. We are in agreement. Now, for more news. I have been told that one of the largest Roman ships sailed upriver to the Rhenus. The boat was too large for our forces to intercept. My guess is that the legionnaires of Flevum may have learned of our intentions and requested reinforcements from the Governor. We must take Flevum before they send their Fifth Legion at Noviomagus. Our spies have informed us that Flevum is ill-equipped and unprepared for a full-scale assault. We should prevail. However, if the Romans send their legions to reinforce Flevum before we have taken the stronghold, we will break off the attack immediately. We must not openly confront the Roman forces in battle for the advantage rests heavily with them."

A chieftain in the back spoke up. "But what of our plan to expel the Romans from our lands and drive them all the way to the Rhenus?"

Eadric pondered the question for a moment. "Then we will settle for only half of the loaf of bread. We will have sent our message that we are not paying their tax levies and that we are no longer their allies," Eadric answered. "Any more questions?" His query was greeted with silence. "Then, let's move to our positions and prepare to attack."

CHAPTER XV

THE BATTLE: DAY I

Marcellus, Florus, and Valerius stood on the rampart near the front gate, which was located on one of the wider sides of the rectangular fortress. They looked out to the east at the plain beyond. The sight that greeted them was ominous: thousands of Frisii were assembling in the distance, preparing to assault them from three sides. The western side of the fortress, protected by the river, was the only side they could not broach.

Valerius turned toward Marcellus. "You have seen this more often than I have; how many do you estimate?"

Marcellus scratched his head. "I don't know, certainly more than us."

"Thanks for that astute observation, Marcellus," he said dryly.

Florus spluttered with laughter.

Valerius looked at Florus. "See what I had to deal with as a young tribune? You should be thankful you have more obliging centurions on your staff."

"You asked me a question, I gave you an answer," quipped Marcellus. "What? Do you think I'm one of those Greek mathematicians you keep talking about? But if you want me to give you a number, I will say maybe fifteen thousand. What do you think, Tribune Florus?"

Florus shrugged. "I have no experience in guessing the numbers of the enemy. It is difficult to ascertain because I don't know how many men there are behind the front ranks. However, if you had to push me to give a number, I would say well over fifteen thousand. My speculation is not based on what I observe from the walls but what I know of the Frisii. Assuming that all the clans are on board with this assault, I would put the sum as closer to twenty-five thousand based on what is documented in the tax rolls."

Valerius frowned. "That is worse than I thought. I would agree with you that the Frisii are most likely united on this revolt. The new tax burden imposed by our illustrious Governor is probably so onerous that it gave them no other option." He gave Marcellus a mocking look. "I should have asked Tribune Florus first about the numbers."

"Oh, by the way, I forgot to mention that I added another dimension to our defense of Flevum while you were away," said Florus.

"And what might that be?" asked Marcellus.

"Caltrops. We found a whole load of them in the storage area. They were not even rusty; the points on them were sharp as ever. Cut my finger on the first one that I picked up. Nasty buggers they are."

Caltrops were forged iron weapons about the size of a fist with four-pronged spikes. They were often sown in the earth so that when the enemy approached and stepped on the spikes, their feet would be impaled, they would be incapacitated, and they would thus be put out of the fight.

"We were searching for stocks of iron rods to fashion more iron heads for the bolts for our ballistae when we discovered crates filled with caltrops. In any event, we have sown the caltrops in the most likely approaches, including the ditches. I wouldn't want to step on any of them. The points will go right through marching boots," he finished, his expression smug.

"By Jupiter's holy arse," exclaimed Marcellus, "we have another Julius Caesar in our midst!"

Valerius could not help but grin. "Tribune Florus, that is fucking outstanding. It may not be enough to deter the large Frisian force outside our walls, but I wouldn't want to be in their boots out there. It will give them something to think about once they start their attack. You are a credit to the legions."

Florus preened in the sudden adulation.

Valerius gestured along the ramparts. "I believe now would be a good time for a final tour of the walls. I sense that the Frisii will commence their assault within the hour."

The three men began walking. The walls were crammed with men, anxiety etched on their faces. They fiddled with their helmets, adjusted chin straps, or absently tightened their cuirasses while staring at the gathering beyond the walls. Most had never faced armed conflict before. The three officers approached the first of the bolt throwers. The three-man crew, the *ballistarii*, flashed satisfied grins as the three officers approached. A large bundle of long bolts was stacked by the ballista ready to be fired.

Marcellus stood behind the wood and iron machine and sighted out toward the plains. It was at near maximum elevation, which meant that the range of the lethal bolt would be over four hundred yards. He addressed the crew. "Are you ready to fire this?"

One of the men stepped forward. "We are. We have it ranged. See that lone crooked tree out there? When the Frisii reach that tree, that will be our signal to fire the first bolt. The way they are assembled, we can't miss. We'll probably take out two men with each shot."

Marcellus nodded. "Excellent. Remember, keep a steady volume of fire. This is an intimidating weapon. It will strike fear in the hearts of the enemy." The three officers moved on.

They passed the first of the disabled ballistae. In its place stood three slingers with pouches containing lead shots strung diagonally across their torsos. These men were auxiliaries from the eastern edge of the empire. They jabbered in a foreign tongue, seemingly unperturbed about the pending battle.

Satisfied, the three officers continued their tour of the rampart when Centurion Glaucus greeted them. "Sirs, a good day for a fight, is it not?"

"It is," uttered Marcellus. "Is your century prepared?"

"They are. My men are a bit nervous as most haven't experienced combat. They are a tad apprehensive, but they will do their duty. We have an ample supply of spears plus piles of rocks to throw at the Frisii when they reach the walls. As you can see, we have these poles with forked ends which will be used to push away any ladders that are leaned against the ramparts. Our primary focus is to not allow the ladders to get in position for them to climb up on the ramparts. As long as the Frisii remain on that side of the wall, we will be fine."

"Centurion Glaucus has some familiarity with sieges," said Florus. "Isn't that right, Centurion?"

"That I have. I was stationed along the Danubius in a small outpost. The bloody Germans attacked us just for the sake of attacking. We certainly held no strategic ground. Anyway, we were heavily outnumbered, but they never got over the walls. We punished them severely before they reached the ramparts and wouldn't allow them to scale the parapets. It was a good day for the legions. We sent them packing and hardly suffered any casualties. I told my men about my experience, hoping to instill some confidence in them."

"Let's hope we can replicate that experience," said Marcellus.

The three officers strolled among Glaucus's men. The legionnaires tried to appear self-assured but could not quite pull it off. Facial tics, the wringing of hands, nervous coughs, and the shifting glances to the plain beyond gave them away. Marcellus stepped among the legionnaires. "You know, I remember when I was just a novice legionnaire and my mates and I were stationed in Syria. We were all young. None of us had combat experience. Anyway, to make a long story short, my unit was escorting a convoy across the desert. We were attacked one night by bandits who attempted to loot our caravan, and so, we formed a shield wall under the direction of our centurion. As I remember it, I don't believe there was a dry leg among us, if you get my meaning."

The men chuckled in unison at Marcellus's story. He continued, "Now, I know many of you are nervous about the upcoming siege. Hades, I'll admit that I'm scared, and I have been doing this for a long time, perhaps before most of you were born. But if I had to give you a piece of advice, it would be this: remember your training and listen to your officers. That will get you through this. We survived that night in Syria because we were well-disciplined and our centurion understood a thing or two about fighting. We sent those bandits fleeing for their lives. Slaughtered most of them. Now, I remember another time in Germania…"

Valerius smiled. Marcellus had the legionnaires totally relaxed and even laughing as he continued with his tales. He had no idea if what the centurion said was true, but it didn't matter. He had transformed the group from a bunch of frightened men to a confident fighting force.

* * *

Hudec was the leader of his *comitatus* and had more than a hundred men under his command. He was a large man with an imposing physique: a typical German warrior. He led from the front and by example. As he stood among his men, staring at the walls of Flevum, he had no qualms about what he was about to do. The Frisii clans had no choice but to attack their erstwhile Roman allies. There was no dissent among his posse: to a man, they felt the same. His men were aware of the harsh retribution the Roman legions had inflicted on other rebellious tribes who had attacked Rome in the past, but it didn't matter. They had no recourse.

Hudec turned to face his men. "Gather about me," he shouted. He watched as the men moved closer. "We will begin our attack shortly. Those of you carrying the ladders, make sure you keep up."

On the ground nearby were ten ladders to be carried by two men each. The crudely assembled wooden apparatuses were bulky and heavy. The comitatus could only move as fast as the men who were tasked with carrying the ladders. They were critical to their success and served two purposes. First, they would be used to navigate the Roman trenches. Once that obstacle was overcome, they would scale the walls.

"Remember what we discussed: we stay together. Our sector is midway between the river and where the front and side walls meet. That is the direction in which we focus our assault. If I should fall, Agilulf will take my place as the leader. Are we clear on that?"

The warriors were silent. Many shifted about in nervous anticipation. Hudec scanned their faces. He knew he would lose good men today, but it could not be helped. They must attack Flevum if they were to survive as a people. He knew his men were poorly armed in contrast to the Roman legionnaires manning the fort. Most of his posse were armed with wooden spears that had iron heads. A few had swords. They wore no armor except for the occasional leather jerkin. In contrast, the Romans on the walls had the feared ballistae plus the deadly slingers with their lead shots. Once they scaled the walls, they would have to fight the legionnaires, who were protected by suits of iron and armed with javelins and lethal stabbing swords. His men would need to rapidly get on top of the Roman ramparts and gain numerical superiority. Then, they could close in on and overwhelm their enemy.

Hudec grinned at his men. "Take heart, Tiwal will be with us today. We do this for our survival and families. Get ready. The time is almost here."

After a short wait, the entire Frisian force facing the Roman citadel began a loud chanting that rose to a crescendo. As one, the massive throng began moving toward Flevum. Hudec shouted above the roar, "Here we go!" His men surged forward. They were about six hundred yards away from the ramparts. Their pace picked up as the men hurried forward, although there was no need as they were still beyond the range of the feared ballistae. Once they were within range, it would be imperative to move as swiftly as possible. Hudec kept a wary eye on his men, making sure they stayed together. They moved forward steadily.

About four hundred yards from the fortress, Hudec heard the lethal twangs signaling the launch of the ballistae. Leading the men in a wedge-shaped formation, he urged them to pick up speed. He heard the first terrible screams as the bolts from the ballistae found their targets among the Frisian ranks. He kept his eyes straight ahead, focusing on the sector designated to his men by Eadric. Other clans rushed forward, now ahead of his men. He paid them no heed—he would lead his men at his pace. More screams echoed among the Frisii as the bolts found their marks.

One of his men, about ten paces to his right, let out an anguished scream. He was propelled backward and slammed to the earth by the force of a bolt now impaling his torso. Some of his men stopped and gaped in horror at the fate that had befallen their comrade. Suddenly, a man to the left was shot. The bolt pierced his chest, killing him instantly. Hudec quickly positioned himself among his men. He shouted over the chanting and the shrieks of the dying. "Don't stop. Move. We must hurry. To the walls!"

His men had no sooner rushed forward when the next calamity struck. Several screamed and collapsed to the ground, the pointed caltrops embedded in their feet. Hudec looked on, stunned at this new deterrent. He had no idea that this horror had awaited his men. He had to quickly get his wits about him. His men depended upon him. Above the fray, he heard the deadly twangs of the ballista continuing. "Move. Move. We cannot stop now. We will all die if we stay here. Onward."

His comitatus advanced and soon, the double line of ditches was in sight. This was the vulnerable Roman sector where the third trench had not been constructed. He glanced toward the sides, checking to ensure that his men were in formation. He knew he had lost men to the bolts and caltrops, but they had to keep going. By now, he had started to huff. He had been sprinting for the last several hundred yards and it was taking a toll. "Bring the ladders forward!" he roared.

The ladders were flung down the trench. As they waited to descend, a whining sound reverberated in the air. Men began to fall as the lethal lead shots from the slingers struck. They had no armor to protect them from the fusillade. Warriors tumbled lifeless into the ditch. "Hurry, into the trench!" He watched as his warriors descended the ladder only to encounter more caltrops at the bottom of the trench. When the last of his assemblage had climbed down, he did as well. He was pleased that the other ladders were already propped against the far wall of the trench and that his men were ascending instead of cowering in the protection offered by the deep ditch.

* * *

Marcellus and Valerius stood on the ramparts near the front gate, their gaze directed at the Frisii off in the distance. Even from afar, they could hear the chanting of the warriors. The rumble of voices rose to a mighty shout. In unison, the enemy advanced toward the walls.

From along the river where the civilian settlement was located, wisps of black, greasy smoke wafted into the air. Valerius pointed at the plumes of smoke. "They have torched the town."

"What a shame," said Marcellus. "It was a nice place, much better than the hovels at Noviomagus. Thank Jupiter and Mars we evacuated the civilians."

Valerius glanced toward the nearest crew of the ballista. They stood calmly, waiting for the enemy to get within range. The Frisii got closer by the second. The leader of the crew hunched over the sighting mechanism one more time. Satisfied, he then released the trigger mechanism. With a tremendous twang, the bolt streaked over the parapets. The other ballistae fired shortly thereafter. Even from this distance, Valerius could observe the terrible carnage inflicted by the bolts. The crew wasted no time loading another bolt and hurriedly cranking the torsion ropes. There was another loud twang as the second bolt from the ballista flew toward the foes.

The two officers watched the Frisii hit their next obstacle in their long gauntlet to reach the fort. Men crumpled to the earth as the caltrops pierced their feet. Seeing their comrades fall victim to the iron spikes in the ground, many Frisii hesitated, unsure about whether to proceed—that was a mistake. The ballista continued firing, occasionally impaling two men with the same bolt. The leaders of the Frisii herded their men forward, and they approached the first ditch. The men crowded the ladders, waiting to descend into the ditches. This resulted in even more staggering casualties from the whirring lead shots.

The auxiliaries along the wall twirled their slings and released their deadly lead shots toward the clustered Frisii, breaking arms, legs, and skulls. It was hard to miss when the enemy was closely packed. The terrifying crash of bolts filled the air along with the whistle of a hail of lead bullets. Marcellus turned toward Valerius and shouted above the chaos. "I'm glad I'm behind these walls and not out there. This is just plain butchery." Valerius nodded.

Valerius and Marcellus readied their bows as the Frisii were now within range. The pair unleashed a steady stream of arrows at the charging foes immediately in front of them. They could not miss as the Germans were closely packed.

The Frisii reached the second ditch, now even closer to the walls. The legionnaires along the ramparts gripped their spears tighter in anticipation. The Frisii would quickly be within range. A few wayward spears were flung from the walls by nervous legionnaires. "Hold throwing the pila!" screamed several centurions. Lead shots and bolts continued to rain down on the unfortunate Germans.

The German warriors staggered out of the final ditch that protected the wide front of the fortress. All along the walls, the command was issued. "Prepare to throw the pila." The men pulled their arms back, anticipating the final order. "RELEASE."

The air was filled with javelins. Many found their mark, unleashing their lethal toll. More men screamed as they were pierced by the iron heads of the pila. The Frisii lurched onward, finally reaching the base of the wall. The first ladders thudded against the ramparts.

* * *

Hudec's men advanced with grim determination, ignoring their terrible losses. They reached the second and last ditch before the ramparts on the right side of Flevum. The warriors quickly navigated the ditch and ascended the ladders; however, they were greeted by a barrage of spears that shot down even more men. Their progress was stymied by a fierce hail of javelins and lead shots. Hudec waved them forward. "Almost there," he screamed. The men surged forward. The ladders were planted in the ground and then flung against the earthen walls.

"Up! Up!" Hudec cried. The first two men had started to ascend the ladder nearest to him. With a grunt, the first man toppled over, impaled by a javelin. The man behind the first also fell, a spear jutting out of his throat. The defenders of the fort leaned over the wooden palisade with a wooden pole and shoved the ladder away from the walls. Two legionnaires on top of the rampart watched in fascination as the ladder slowly fell away from the wall. This was a tragic mistake: they'd exposed too much of themselves to the Germans below. Several Frisii quickly hurled spears at the two figures, impaling both. The two legionnaires disappeared from view.

Hudec's warriors managed to raise all ten of their ladders against the wall. Men climbed upward. More fell as spears and stones rained down on them, but others bravely took their place. The Frisii swarmed up the ladders. As the leading figures reached the top, they were stabbed by the legionnaires and thrown back over the walls.

Marcellus and Valerius put away their bows and quivers, drawing their swords. It was time for combat at close quarters. The Frisii planted their ladders against the wall and began climbing. Marcellus stared in grim fascination and shook his head. The Frisii were getting slaughtered but kept coming. Glancing to either side, he observed frantic legionnaires throwing spears and launching heavy stones at the assailants below. Other Romans stood ready with their gladii drawn, ready to skewer those who made it to the top. When the first of the Frisii reached the top of the palisades, the unfortunates were brutally dispatched and tossed back over the side. Several Frisii managed to make a stand on the ramparts. A group of legionnaires quickly rushed over and, after a brief skirmish, stabbed the Germans before they could make any headway.

▲

Lucius stood in the shade of the grain storage building with the others from the relief force. He could hear the familiar screams of the wounded and dying. Glancing at the rampart visible to him, he saw only Roman legionnaires, no Germans.

He hoped Julia was not worrying about him. Last night, he had assured her that they would be fine. Like the other civilians, they had been assigned an empty barrack. Although it had been crowded and lacked privacy, they'd had a bed and a roof over their heads. "Remember," Lucius had said, "we have suffered much worse." Julia had offered a tight smile but it failed to conceal her fretful disposition.

"What about our children?" she had moaned. "Who will take care of them if anything happens to us?"

"Nothing is going to happen to us. I firmly believe we will survive this. Am I concerned? Yes, but I have faith that Valerius and Marcellus will save this fortress. The Teutoburg was far bleaker, yet here we are. Try to stay positive."

Julia and Lucius had embraced each other for a long time, shocked to find themselves in these circumstances once again. Marcellus and Valerius had reassured them both that the defenses of Flevum were considerable, but it did not diminish the severity of their situation. Marcellus had calmly explained that it was perilous but he expected the legions to prevail. "We have two things going for us," he had said. "First, the Frisii have no siege equipment, and second—and most importantly—the Fifth Legion, nearly five thousand men, will be coming to relieve the siege. All we have to do is hang on until the reinforcement arrives."

Lucius now shifted about uncomfortably, his trepidation mounting. Several of the civilians in the ranks began retching. He still had trouble reconciling himself with his legionary attire of armor, sword, and shield. The weight of the equipment was strange, yet dissonantly familiar. It had been a long time since he'd served and that too under extremely trying circumstances but here he was. His reverie was interrupted by the sudden command. "Draw swords."

Lucius grasped the handle of his gladius from the sheath on his right side. It slid out with a menacing *tzing*. He quickly slid his arm through the straps on his rectangular shield, which was rectangular and curved to defend his sides. From shoulders to knees, it would guard his body. Ox and Rufus had responded to the command with similar actions. Rufus gazed at Lucius. "Don't worry, Lucius. We will get you through this."

Lucius looked toward Severus, their optio, at the front of the relief force. The officer was conferring with one of the messengers, who was animatedly pointing toward a section of the northeast wall.

Severus looked toward his men and bellowed. "Move to your assigned places. We may be needed." He waited as the men moved into their designated spots. Satisfied that they were ready, he bellowed his next command, "At double-time, forward…move!"

Lucius jogged along with the others, his stomach churning. They were in a compact rectangular formation. He was located almost in the middle and could see little outside the mass of men. The formation of men advanced down two narrow avenues before reaching the northeast quadrant. The order was given to halt and then deploy on a wide front. The men spread out as they had drilled earlier.

Lucius looked up at the ramparts directly to his front. He saw the bodies of several legionnaires slumped upon the palisade amid piles of dead Germans. There were a few outnumbered Germans still fighting, but as he watched, they were quickly dispatched by the Romans manning the walls. There was no sign of a breach. Severus darted up the ramp leading to the palisade and conferred with the centurion in charge. He saw the optio nod and then return down the ramp.

"We are not needed here for the present. They have things under control. We will stay at this location until further notice. You may stand down."

Lucius heaved a sigh of relief. He saw the others do the same. Perhaps they would not be needed today.

* * *

Hudec watched in dismay as his men continued to be slaughtered without making any appreciable headway in penetrating Flevum's

196

defenses. He tried not to think of all the new widows there would be in the village tonight. He frowned as another of his men fell at his feet, his torso pierced by a lance. More of his men began climbing up the ladders. To his left, he saw one of his ladders slowly topple from the battlements with men still clinging to it. Some jumped off before it rammed into the earth. Others screamed in pain, suffering broken limbs from the steep fall.

Hudec swore under his breath. *Damn these Romans*, he thought. He had known it would be a tough battle, but this was far worse than he had anticipated. From his limited vantage point, he could not see much progress from the other Frisian clans. It was a dark day all around. His thoughts were interrupted by blaring horns—the signal for retreat. He shouted for his men to fall back. He stood apart from the others at the base of the wall, waving his sword. Men began to rapidly retreat from the stronghold. The terrible death toll had been for naught.

CHAPTER XVI

REINFORCEMENTS

Governor Gallus, General Cethegus Labeo, and Cornelius Quadratus sat around a small table in a conference room of the principia. Off to the side sat Tigranus. Captain Basilius, the captain dispatched from Flevum, stood before them. Gallus, a bewildered expression on his face, looked at Basilius. "You're sure the Frisii were attacking?"

Basilius snorted in derision, remembering the words of the tribune about convincing the Governor about the imminent attack on Flevum. "Governor," he said patiently, "those Frisii were not surrounding the fortress as part of a religious festival, and it was not a small number either. There were thousands upon thousands of them." He decided to spin a convincing argument. "They were chanting belligerent war cries and raising their spears in the air."

Gallus sat there stunned. Finally, he spoke. "How could they do this after all these years of being allies to Rome? The effrontery of those ungrateful barbarians!" His own words seemed to incite him. "I will have those bastards' heads on spikes for this!" He turned toward Basilius. "You are dismissed. We will take it from here," said Gallus icily.

The naval officer turned and exited out of the Governor's chambers, no doubt dejected that he would not hear the subsequent discussions.

Once Basilius had exited, Labeo spoke. "Sir, we must act swiftly and decisively on this matter if we are to save Flevum." "With your permission, I can begin preparations immediately."

Gallus thought about the matter for a few moments. "Of course, you are correct, General. We must thwart the siege at Flevum and minimize the scope of this attack. I want to downplay the severity of this insurgence to the Emperor. I will communicate to Rome that it is only a minor rebellion by some dissident factions of the Frisii. Now, how rapidly can you get your legion there?"

"I have been contemplating this question. The problem is there are not enough ships here to transport my entire legion plus stores and equipment to Flevum. If we begin immediately, I can have four of my ten cohorts or a little less than two thousand men under sail on the river by late tomorrow. They would arrive there in a little less than forty-eight hours from now. Over the coming week, I could have the entire legion, horses, weapons, and stores ready for a march against the Frisii."

Gallus wrung his hands nervously. "And what about Flevum? Will it be able to withstand an assault by the Frisii until your troops get there?"

"Hard to say, sir," uttered Labeo. "I don't know the strength of the Frisian forces. We only have a young tribune in charge of the defenses, but the walls are quite sturdy, and the Frisii, I'm sure, do not possess siege equipment."

Gallus glowered at Labeo. "That's not much of an answer."

Labeo shrugged. "There are too many—"

Gallus interrupted, "Enough equivocating. I want four cohorts underway as quickly as possible. Get your men on the move."

Labeo started to rise from his seat.

"Wait, General Labeo. After you rescue Flevum and transport the remainder of your legions and supplies, you are to wage a punitive campaign against the Frisii. I want their lands savaged and their people enslaved. We must make an example of them or the other tribes might get the same idea. Is the Fifth up to the task?"

"Yes, absolutely, Governor."

Gallus countenance took on a vulpine expression. "Furthermore, when you invade the land of the Frisii, take that annoying tribune and his centurion with you, assuming they are still alive. Better yet, his entire mercenary force should be conscripted into your army. I want them at the front—the tip of the spear." His voice rose in anger. "Since my quaestor and son could not eliminate them," he glared at Quadratus and Tigranus for effect, "you will have to find a way for them to die nobly in combat. I cannot have either of them survive to relate any of this information about the Frisii to Tiberius. We will craft the story that gets delivered to Rome. Only we must communicate with Tiberius."

"Yes, Governor Gallus. I will see to it. Am I dismissed?"

"Yes, but make sure no dispatches are sent by that tribune to the Emperor. To reiterate, we alone will manage the flow of information. Just tell that damnable tribune that all correspondences are to come through my offices. Understood?"

"Yes, sir. Is there anything else?"

Gallus waved an arm, dismissing his military commander.

The Governor waited until everyone had departed. He then looked toward Tigranus and Quadratus, picked up a scroll that was sitting on the table, and tapped it on the wood. "I just received this dispatch from Sejanus this morning. It appears he has identified the person who betrayed us. The official responsible for routing dispatches at the port of Valkenberg, Quintus Sorvinius, a retired centurion, was the one who sent Tiberius a warning of a possible Frisian rebellion sometime this spring. He deliberately bypassed Sejanus and had the message delivered to the Emperor. Sorvinius must be eliminated. As I said, it is vital that we control all communications with Rome."

Quadratus stirred. "Governor Gallus, I can arrange for him to have an unfortunate accident. I'm sure the port has its share of cutthroats and undesirables. It can be attributed to them. Still, he is an officer appointed by Tiberius."

Gallus shrugged. "I understand there is certain risk involved, but we cannot afford to have this Sorvinius fellow in a position to muck things up. Do what you must to have him disposed of. Are we clear?"

"Yes, sir. I will see to it immediately."

⚊

An officer's council was convened in Flevum in the late afternoon following the attack. The twelve centurions of the two cohorts, Tribune Florus, Marcellus, and Valerius were in attendance in the principia. Florus nodded to Glaucus. "Centurion, please give us a status report of the state of readiness."

Glaucus stepped to the front of the assembled officers. He offered a brief smile. "Well, the good news is that our losses from the attack were minimal. My latest tally shows only twenty-five were killed and another fifty wounded. Perhaps half of those wounded can resume their duties in the defense of the walls. The Frisii, on the other hand, suffered huge losses. The problem is that they have a lot of replacements, but we really caused damage to them today. I wouldn't want to trade places with them. We have survived day one relatively unscathed, but there are other issues."

"I take it from your tone and lack of enthusiasm that there is some not so good news we have yet to hear," stated Marcellus.

Glaucus nervously cleared his throat. "Unfortunately, yes. Much of the damage inflicted on the Frisii was the direct result of the ballistae, the shots from our slingers, and the rocks and spears that we rained down on them from the walls. We used up a substantial portion of our ammunition for the ballistae. Most of the bolt throwers are down to thirty or fewer bolts. The same goes for the lead shots. Our supplies of javelins are down to about a third of the original number. As we speak, I have men outside the walls searching for bolts, shots, and spears. But as you know, once the bolts and pila hit a solid surface, the iron shank bends, rendering it useless. I'm sure we can recover some, and our armorers are busy fashioning additional weapons day and night, but it won't be enough."

Florus looked shaken. "What you are saying, Glaucus, is that we have enough to maybe repel one more assault. After that, it will be down to swords only."

"Yes, sir, I think that about sums it up."

"Any chance the Frisii have given up after their losses today and retreated to their villages?" quipped one of the centurions.

All eyes were directed at Valerius and Marcellus. Valerius turned to Marcellus. "Why don't you answer that?"

"From my experience, that would be a highly unlikely scenario. Their objective is to eliminate Flevum, a Roman fortress in their territory. I sense that the Frisian leaders still believe they can take down this citadel. Once they do that, they will eliminate any Roman outposts from here to the Rhenus. Their objective is most likely to establish the Rhenus as the border for their lands and cut all ties with Rome."

Valerius stepped forward. "We must hold out for a few days until the Fifth Legion makes its appearance. Once those reinforcements arrive, I believe the Frisii will abandon the siege, but until then, we must vigorously defend this fortress."

"Is there anything else we can do to bolster the defenses?" asked Florus.

Marcellus slowly shook his head. "Unless you can conjure up a few thousand spears and bolts over the next day, I think not."

* * *

At twilight, Eadric stood in front of the various chieftains, who numbered approximately forty. A small fire crackled behind him, silhouetting his figure in the darkness. His face was heavy with sorrow. He surveyed the men before him. Their expressions were somber; a few were angry. "I must apologize to you. I had no idea the Roman resistance would be this fierce. I am painfully aware of the losses we incurred. Our spies had informed us that the Roman defenses were weak and their men careless and unkempt. This was supposed to be an easy victory. Perhaps they got wind of our assault. I know many of you are discouraged, but we must learn from our mistakes."

Before he continued, one of the chieftains jumped to his feet. "What would you propose we do differently? My clan cannot afford to sustain losses like we did today."

Eadric rubbed his jaw in thought. "A fair question and one you all are probably asking. I have been thinking about this and conferred with several of you about a change in strategy. This is what I propose. First, we will attack at dawn. Our forces will advance as close as possible in the darkness, just before the first Roman trench. In doing this, we limit the amount of time we are exposed to their bolt throwers. Next, and this is most critical, I would suggest that we concentrate our forces on the sector where there are only two ditches. This is where the Romans are most vulnerable. We will continue to attack the entire fortress but only with a token force where the Romans have three ditches. I would welcome any other ideas. Please speak up—I'm all ears."

There was murmured discussion among the chieftains. Eadric waited for a while, but no one else stood up to speak. Finally, Eadric held up his arms for silence. "Hearing no other suggestions and no dissent to my plan, are you in agreement with what I propose? Are you still willing to attack Flevum tomorrow? Please stand to show your support." In unison, the men rose.

Eadric beamed triumphantly. "Good. There is much to be done before dawn. We must assign each tribe a sector and overpower the zone where the Romans are at their weakest. My friends, once Flevum is defeated, we will drive the Romans back to the Rhenus and out of our territory for good."

CHAPTER XVII

THE BATTLE: DAY II

Valerius was bedded down in the principia and in a deep slumber. He vaguely felt a hand shaking him in the darkness. He tried to ignore the hand and the annoying voice, but it was persistent. "Sir, you've got to get up. Sir, the Frisii are on the move." A light flickered in the dark.

Valerius sat upright, attempting to rub the exhaustion from his face, his vision blurry. "What's going on?"

A legionnaire holding a small oil lamp stood in front of him. Hereca slept next to him, unaware of the messenger's presence. "The garrison is being alerted," informed the man. "You need to get to the ramparts right away. I have already awakened Centurion Marcellus. You must hurry."

Valerius dismissed the man with a wave of his hand. He then lit a small oil lamp and struggled into his armor, lifting it over his head. He attempted to lace up the leather thongs but fumbled about in the dark, cursing his clumsiness. He walked over to the still sleeping Hereca and began shaking her. "Hereca, get up."

She sat up in bed. "It's still dark outside," she slurred.

"I know, but the Frisii are preparing to attack. The fortress is on full alert. I must go. Be careful, my darling, and stay off the ramparts as I asked you to do." He kissed her briefly and walked out the door.

Marcellus was outside waiting for him. "Let's go to the main gate. We will be able to judge what the Frisii are up to if we can see the front and both sides of the fortress. They walked across the courtyard of the principia, which was illuminated by several strategically placed torches, and past the workshops of the armorer. An eerie red glow suffused the interior of the dwellings, spilling out on to the streets. The armorers had been busy all night, painstakingly fashioning spears and bolts for the defense of the walls. Pounding and grinding noises emanated from the workshops. The pair quickly hurried toward the rampart over the main gate.

They strode up the ramp to the top of the wall where the main entrance to the citadel was located. It was flanked on either side by two towering wooden battlements rising another ten feet above the wall. A few torches illuminated portions of the walls and the interior of the citadel. Many legionnaires were already in position. Tribune Florus, who had placed himself up in one of the wooden towers with several lookouts, was training his eyes beyond the walls on to the plain below. A gibbous moon broke through scudding clouds shifting from the north and finally provided a bit more visibility.

"What's going on out there, Tribune Florus?" Valerius shouted out to him.

"My lookouts have been hearing noises for the past few hours. When the moon shines through, you can discern masses of men moving toward our walls. I believe they will attack at dawn."

Valerius glanced at the position of the stars. It would be less than an hour before the sun rose. He gazed back out beyond the walls. He couldn't see the Frisii yet, but he sensed they were out there, advancing toward Flevum. "They learn quickly. The Frisii hope to limit the casualties from the bolts. They will be closer to the fortress when they begin their attack this time. And once they are close to the walls, the ballistae won't be able to shoot down at that angle."

Florus gazed out in the darkness from his elevated perch. "The men are getting into position. The alert has been called. The walls should be fully manned shortly."

Marcellus had been silent throughout the brief exchange. "Why should we let them dictate their strategy to us?" he said angrily. "Get those ballistae cranked up," he bellowed. "They are within range. Let's give them a proper greeting."

The ballista crew looked up at Tribune Florus for guidance.

"Fire at will," he said.

The crew of the nearest ballista cranked the lever, the noise of the ratchet echoing ominously in the darkness. The leader of the crew positioned the machine at an estimate of where the enemy might be and fired—*twang*.

A moment later, a scream was heard from beyond the walls. Marcellus turned to Florus. "Tribune, my advice would be to get the bolt throwers in operation. Have them fire blindly. It will strike terror into the hearts of the enemy."

Florus descended from the tower and gathered his messengers about him in the darkness. "Have the ballista crew begin firing. Understood?" The men nodded and took off to issue the order.

Before long, the deadly twanging resounded in the night. Screams echoed in the blackness. The clouds hiding the moon gradually dissipated, bathing the plain and ditches beyond the wall in silvery light. The Frisii were rapidly closing in, and the slingers needed no urging. The air was soon filled with the whirring of slings and the whistling of the lead shots. In semidarkness, the first wave of Frisii swarmed into the ditches. The Romans had not yet realized that the Frisii had concentrated their forces in the northeast quadrant. The dawn began to break. Before long, ladders thudded against the walls.

The legionnaires in the northeast sector began furiously throwing spears at the teeming mass of the Frisii. Many of the German warriors fell near the base of the wall but more took their place. The hail of spears and shots could not stem the tide of the advance—there were too many of the Frisii. More ladders thumped against the walls. Men climbed toward the ramparts, only to be struck with stones and spears. They screamed as they toppled off the ladders, but more surged up the walls.

▲

Marcellus, Valerius, and Florus stood near the main gate as the sky lightened. It did not take long to comprehend the strategy of the Frisii. They realized that the Germans had concentrated their forces where their defenses were weakest. The assaults upon the other sectors were being carried out only by a token force. Marcellus was the first to see the ruse. "Tribune Florus, we must shift our forces. You must send all available reinforcements to the northeast sector immediately. We are in peril of having the wall overrun."

The tribune was flustered. He had not anticipated the problem and did not know what to do. He stood there, his face blank. "Get help," he replied weakly. Marcellus faced Valerius. "We must get the centurions to give up some of their men. Let's go now. I will go right, you to the left."

Valerius nodded and took off as fast as he could along the ramparts in the dim morning light, his armor clinking and clanking. He reached the first centurion, whose name he thought was Nolius. The officer was coolly directing the fire of his slingers. A pile of dead Germans lay at the base of the wall and a few ladders were thrust upon the ramparts, but the overall sector was bereft of any substantial German force. Breathless from the short dash in his heavy armor, Valerius led the centurion away from his men. "Centurion Nolius, you must give me some of your men, the northeast sector is in danger of being overrun. The Frisii have concentrated their attack at that point. There is no time for hesitation. No arguments. Give me half your men now or we will all most surely perish."

To his credit, the centurion quickly rounded up about half of his men, including slingers. The men assembled around Valerius. "You are urgently needed in the northeast sector. That area is about to be overrun by a mass of Germans. Just get over there as quickly as possible and drive them back off the walls. I am going to the next zone to get more men to join you. GO!"

Valerius watched briefly as the men exited down the ramparts and then charged diagonally across, toward the northeast. Satisfied that they knew their duty, he ran along the ramparts to the next centurion.

⚊

Centurion Glaucus stood on the northeast ramparts directing his men. He had been placed at this location as it was deemed to be the most vulnerable, and he was the most experienced officer. He was worried. The Frisii were beginning to gain the upper hand. Oh, they were killing Germans by the score alright. But the problem was that there were too many of them for his men to repel. Slowly but inexorably, the Germans were getting men over the wall and fighting hand-to-hand with his legionnaires. His heavily armored men dispatched many of the enemies with sword and shield, but his slingers were not as fortunate. They wore no armor and were undersized. Pitted against the much larger Germans, they stood little chance. He had attempted to move them away from the influx of the Frisii, but he had been too late. Now, most lay slain along the walls. He had dispatched messengers to request reinforcements from other areas of the wall and the reserve force as well. He looked about anxiously, hoping to see the arrival of reinforcements. As he turned his gaze back to the fighting at hand, he just barely deflected a spear with his shield. He said a quick prayer to the gods for sparing him and charged into the fray with a roar.

▲

Lucius stood in the shade of the building along with the other sixty odd members of the relief force. He could hear the fighting, just like he had the previous day, but something was different. It was the noise level. It was more strident today. The yells and screams were coming from within the walls, not outside them. He glanced over at Rufus. The former optio had picked up on it too. His attention was directed toward the northeast wall. He stared intently in that direction.

Ox, standing next to Lucius and Rufus, realized there was something amiss. Both Lucius and Rufus knew something he did not. "What's going on? You both look perplexed and I'm guessing it isn't good."

Rufus, without turning his head from the direction he was gazing at, spoke, "It's different from yesterday. The sounds of battle are louder and are now resonating from within the fortress, not outside. I believe the defenses of the fortress are in peril."

Lucius nodded. "I believe you are right. The screams are coming from within these walls."

The three men watched as a messenger, whose blood was pouring out from wounds to his leg and chest, staggered up to the optio. He pointed toward the northeast and then collapsed on one knee.

Optio Severus wasted no time. "All right, relief force, it seems our services are urgently required," bellowed Severus. "We need to move quickly. Follow me."

Lucius jogged in the formation down the wide avenue to the north wall. To his left was Ox and to his right, Rufus. He felt comforted at having these combatants with him. Gripping his shield in his left and his gladius in his right, he vividly remembered doing the same thing seventeen years ago. Here he was again, fighting for his survival and that of his wife. The sixty men arrived at the northeast wall.

Lucius looked up to the top of the twelve-foot wall. Men were engaged in hand-to-hand combat. Swords flashed and spears were thrust. There were a lot of Germans up there.

Severus pointed with his sword. "Change of plan. We are not sticking together. This entire sector is in trouble. I want the first two ranks to go up this ramp and assist the defenders. I am taking the rest of you to other ramps in this sector to reinforce the men on the wall. We can't let them get into the interior of the fortress. Now go!" The first two ranks charged up the wooden ramp to the walls.

Lucius stood shoulder-to-shoulder on the ramparts with Ox and Rufus. It was pure chaos all around. Men grunted and screamed as they fought for control over the wall. The three of them, standing abreast, took up the entire width of the seven-foot rampart. They advanced and met the first cluster of Germans who were engaged with the legionnaires manning the walls. They plowed into the backs of the Germans with their shields, knocking them over. The triumphant legionnaires ruthlessly dispatched the Frisii. They then nodded in thanks. "Help us knock the ladders off the walls," shouted a battered legionnaire with blood dripping down the side of his face. "Here, use this." He handed the men a forked pole which could be used to topple the ladder without being exposed to spears from below.

Lucius reluctantly returned his sword to its sheath, feeling uneasy about having no weapon in his hand, and grabbed the pole. To his right, he observed the top half of a German climbing onto the palisade from below. Ox snarled and smashed into the man with his shield, sending him tumbling below. Lucius thrust the forked pole at the wooden ladder protruding above the palisade and heaved with all his strength. The ladder shifted sideways but would not fall as there were too many men on it.

Ox grabbed the wooden pole from Lucius. "Let me do this." He grunted and using the extraordinary strength in his arms and legs, gave a tremendous thrust. The ladder tumbled sideways and they heard screams from the men who had been climbing up on it. Ox smirked. "I believe this is a task for which I'm well suited."

The three men moved farther along the wall and encountered the next cluster of enemies. They immediately plunged into the melee. The force of their charge knocked the Germans off balance, and in a matter of moments, they had slain the Germans. Lucius and Rufus protected Ox's back as he pushed another ladder off the wall with the pole. Triumphant, the three moved to the next group of Germans.

There was a cluster of Frisii, perhaps as many as ten, crowding the rampart. Several dead Romans lay at their feet. They had established a position, battling the legionnaires to a standstill. More Germans were swarming up the ladders from below to reinforce their comrades. Lucius squared off with a snarling figure. Just as he had been drilled many years ago, he thrust hard with his shield. The foe agilely leaped back, avoiding the blow. Then suddenly, the German thrust forward with his spear. Lucius narrowly blocked the lunge with his sword, all the while pushing forward again with his shield. The man edged back but misjudged how much room he had. He teetered on one leg, his other dangling in space, and then tumbled off the rampart into the fortress below landing in a heap.

Before Lucius could recover, another German emerged from the pack. He roared and thrust his spear at Lucius's face. The point grazed his neck, leaving a raw red streak. Before the Frisian could strike again, Lucius stabbed upward with his gladius into the throat of the enemy, slashing open a huge wound. Blood spurted out, hitting Lucius in the face. The foe dropped his spear, grasped his neck with both hands, and toppled over.

Ox charged forward. A Frisian with a spear stood squarely in his path. Ox, using the wooden pole as an armament, thrust with his make-shift weapon, knocking the hapless German off the rampart to the ground below. The trio advanced shoulder-to-shoulder, seeking the next group of Germans. Spying a struggling mass of men, they charged forward.

The number of Frisii on the ramparts began to dwindle as more reinforcements arrived. The legionnaires slowly took control and struck the Germans. The surrounded Frisii, now outnumbered, quickly perished under the swords of the Romans.

⋏

Valerius, having dispatched several bunches of legionnaires to the beleaguered northeast quadrant, raced toward the troubled sector with a final wave of reinforcements behind him. He led his band of men to cut diagonally across the courtyard and move down a wide avenue before arriving at the besieged portion of the wall. Looking up at the ramparts, he saw that the legionnaires were still holding the wall but barely. The initial wave of reinforcements that he had sent had temporarily stemmed the tide. The batch of legionnaires surged up the ramp and on to the walls, seeking to dislodge the stubborn German forces. The influx of men gave the Romans a slight edge. The tide began to turn in their favor.

Valerius was now joined by Marcellus, and they found themselves with a group of harried legionnaires on the ramparts. The small group of five was being pressured on both sides by Frisian warriors and they were holding the Germans back with their rectangular shields.

Valerius and Marcellus stood side by side, their swords aimed menacingly in front of them. Two Germans materialized. Valerius slashed with his sword with incredible speed, wounding the arm of one of the Germans. The man hastily retreated, cradling his now useless appendage. Marcellus got close to his opponent and using his bulk and considerable strength, knocked the man off the ramparts. He fell with a resounding thud. The Germans who had been besieging them were overwhelmed with the arrival of more Romans and fled in panic from the battlements.

The small force of Romans with Marcellus and Valerius charged into the next group of Frisii, who were preoccupied with other legionnaires on the wall. Attacked from two directions, the Germans were quickly slain. As the Romans advanced farther along the battlements, ready for battle, they were faced with the blood-drenched apparitions of Lucius, Ox, and Rufus. The men smiled at each other.

Echoing in the distance, they heard the German trumpets sounding the retreat. The enemy quickly disappeared from the walls. But their retreat was not marked by the deadly racket of the ballistae and the whirring of the slingers. All the Romans' ammunition had been expended.

It was nearing dusk. The officers had assembled once again in the principia, now short of three centurions who had perished in the day's battle. A few others sported bloody bandages wrapped around their arms or legs. The smell in the enclosed room was slightly unpleasant—a combination of sweat, blood, dirt, and smoke. Tribune Florus looked toward Centurion Glaucus. "Are you ready to make a report?"

▲

Glaucus strode to the front of the room. "The following is the status of the garrison after today's battle. Our stores of bolts and lead shots are now exhausted. Perhaps a few bolts can be manufactured by the armorers between now and tomorrow, but not many. We are attempting to scavenge as many as possible from outside the fort; the same with lead shots. But the Germans have become wise to our foraging; they have ambushed our retrieval forces. We can only salvage weapons at the base of the walls. The surviving slingers—for many have perished—are gathering smooth, fist-sized stones from the river as their new ammunition. Our supplies of javelins have been depleted, same for the same piles of stones. Again, we are trying to salvage what we can."

He paused as one of his men handed him a wax tablet. He squinted as he read it. "Now, for our casualties. As a result of the assault today, we lost 220 men and another 140 men were wounded.

The hospital and its staff are overwhelmed as there is no place to put the injured. I don't have a final report as to how many of the injured might return to duty."

Florus appeared stunned. "I had no idea our losses were that severe." He looked beseechingly at Valerius. "What can we do?"

Valerius moved to the front of the room. He noted the solemn faces staring back at him. "We must not give up. We fight."

"What about surrendering?" one of the centurions quipped.

Valerius shook his head. "Surrender is not an option. It is not a concept the Germans recognize. They would butcher every single one of us. Believe me, I know a bit about how they think. Centurion Marcellus will back me up on this. No surrender. Tomorrow we must fight hard once again. Listen to me. Hopefully, the fleet of the Fifth Legion will be here by then. Who knows, they could be here in an hour."

The men smiled at the prospect of a relief force. Valerius continued. "I don't know what the German chieftains are thinking now, but they have got to be discouraged. Their forces have suffered tremendous losses. We've have made some serious damage. Furthermore, they might think that the Fifth Legion will arrive soon and then all of their efforts would be for naught. The Frisii have never fought the Romans before. Do you think they'd want to endure more punishment?"

"Is there a chance they might withdraw?" asked Florus hopefully.

Valerius pondered the question. "They could but I think not." The hope in the room deflated with Valerius's remark. "But," he continued, "one must ask how much enthusiasm the Frisii have left. They made their best attempts with little success. Perhaps they don't have the mettle for another full effort. I hope they do not realize our weakness: depleted ammunition and our loss of men. We must resist, buy time, and hope the Fifth arrives soon. My advice is to rest and prepare for tomorrow. We are not dead men yet."

* * *

Once more, Eadric stood before his confederates. It had been another tough day for the Frisii. They had lost a significant number of men today. Gazing at the assembled group, Eadric counted fewer faces than yesterday. Some chieftains exhibited bloody bandages wrapped around various parts of their bodies. It was almost twilight and a fire glowed amidst them, illuminating the tired faces of the Frisian chieftains. Eadric sighed. It was not a pretty sight.

"I know many of you are discouraged by today's events. We almost had them, but they were able to rally their troops and throw us off the battlements. These Romans are a tough bunch of bastards, especially when they dictate the terms of battle, but we must overcome them. Several of you have told me that we have weakened the Romans. They are almost out of their fearsome bolts, lead shots, and spears. They are ready to fall. I observed the Romans scavenging in the battlefield outside the walls for expended bolts and spears. That is why we grabbed many of their discarded spears in our retreat. We have deployed archers so that the Romans do not venture too far from their walls. Some have already paid a very steep price."

There was silence among the Frisians. Eadric shifted about uncomfortably, wondering if he had lost his following. Had they given up?

The chieftain of a large clan, Chlodar, stood. "What if the Roman legion from the Rhenus shows up tomorrow? What are we to do?"

Eadric frowned. "If they arrive, we must retreat; but until they do so, I have every intention of burning Flevum to the ground and eradicating its presence from our land."

217

One of the minor Frisian chieftains stood. "My name is Fridumar, for those of you who don't know me. I am the chieftain of a small clan far to the north. My men will attack with me tomorrow morning. In fact, they are looking forward to it. I hope you feel the same way." Thus concluding his terse remarks, he sat down.

Fridumar's remarks roused the rest of the group. Others rose to their feet, shouting their support for the attack the next day. "Yes, burn it to the ground! It is an affront to our nation!" cried another. The men began chanting. "Burn it! Burn it!"

A wide smile spread across Eadric's face. He shouted above the din. "Good. I'm glad you have not lost your passion. Flevum will fall tomorrow."

More joined the chant. "Burn it! Burn it!"

"We attack at dawn," roared Eadric above the chanting.

* * *

Lucius and Valerius, their armor and faces splashed with blood, walked toward the medical building to visit Hereca and Julia. The hostilities had ceased long ago, however, some exhausted men had remained on top of the battlements just in case the Frisii decided upon another attack. The sun was edging toward the horizon. As the two men approached the hospital, they witnessed a chaotic scene. Piles of dead men were stacked to the side of the dwelling. In the front and off to the sides, men lay on the open ground as the hospital was filled beyond capacity.

Valerius stopped, staring at the scene before him. "By Mithras's arse, look at this place. It is a charnel house." No sooner had he spoken when the two wives emerged from the building, their clothes stippled with blood. Hereca spied the two men and, dragging Julia along, ran toward them. The couples embraced.

Julia broke away from her husband, her voice full of concern. "You're hurt," she said, gently touching the raw streak on Lucius's neck.

"Nothing to worry about," said Lucius. "It's not even bleeding; does smart a bit though. Julia, how are you holding up? You look exhausted."

Hereca answered for her. "Your wife is a natural healer. She has been a great comfort to the wounded and dying despite the overwhelming numbers." She directed her gaze at Valerius. "Perhaps you could speak with Tribune Florus to get us more help here. Look at this." She gestured with her arm. "Believe me, you don't want to venture inside. That is where the more seriously injured are housed."

Valerius surveyed the surrounding area once more. "I will speak to Florus. Perhaps some of the lightly wounded can assist you." He noticed several other women from the town who were assisting the men lying on the ground. "Thank you both for helping. It has been a rather difficult day, to say the least."

"Any word on the Fifth Legion?" Hereca asked hopefully.

"No, but they could arrive at any moment. It takes a bit of time to mobilize an entire legion and transport it to a distant location."

"It will be soon though?" inquired Julia.

"Julia," said Valerius firmly, "I cannot predict when they will be here, but I believe they are on their way. I'm confident of that. This is the most honest answer I can give you."

Julia hung her head dejectedly. "I understand. My husband and I must survive this so we can return to our children."

"I know," said Valerius. "Hereca and I share your sentiments." He continued in a confident tone, hoping she would be reassured. "We will continue to repel the Frisii and the Fifth Legion will arrive, I'm sure of it."

Hereca beamed at her husband. She knew that he did not feel very buoyant about their chances, but he did not want Julia to know what he was really thinking.

Lucius discerned the situation. Thankful for his words, he echoed Valerius's false confidence. "Julia, by tomorrow, this will just be a bad dream. We will certainly be rescued. Can they spare you from your duties at the hospital? I'm starved and we could get something to eat."

Julia offered a radiant smile. "As a matter of fact, the physician dismissed Hereca and me. He told us to get some food in our stomachs. He seemed a bit cranky."

"Come on then. We are going to the officer's mess. Marcellus is probably already there. He can entertain us with his tales."

CHAPTER XVIII

THE BATTLE: DAY III

H udec huddled with his men in the darkness. He was appalled at the extent of their losses thus far. They were down by at least fifty men, most of whom were dead. He maintained a tight-lipped expression but beneath it, he was mourning the men, who were almost like kin. He knew all their families. It would be a difficult return journey to their village. Yesterday, his men had been on the parapet when the recall was sounded. They were close to over-whelming the defenders, but then, they were driven back. He gritted his teeth. *Today will be the day. The Roman fortress of Flevum will fall.*

A sliver of dawn appeared in the east and torches began flashing. That was the signal. "Up!" he roared to his men. They charged toward the Roman fortress, covering ground quickly. Hudec, running hard in front of his men, listened expectantly for the ominous thuds of the Roman ballistae. Oddly, he heard only a few of their menacing echoes. Were the Romans still sleeping? "Faster!" he bellowed. They descended the first of the ditches, climbed out, and moved on to the second ditch. Amazingly, none of his men had fallen yet. They slowed down as they confronted the second trench. He heard several cries as the deadly noise of hissing lead shots filled the air, but his warriors continued advancing. Ladders were slammed against the wall and men began ascending. Rocks and spears rained down on his warriors. To his left, he saw a ladder slowly topple over. The men who were clutching onto the ladder crashed into the earth, moaning in pain.

* * *

Valerius stood on the parapet in the northeast sector, Marcellus beside him. He was sure the attack would follow yesterday's pattern. The Frisii would assault the weakest section of the defense with maximum force. In the dim light, that appeared to be exactly what they were doing. The screams of the wounded and dying shattered the silent dawn. Looking to his left and right, he observed legionnaires desperately heaving their last stock of spears and stones, while others used the long-forked wooden poles to dislodge the ladders thrust upon the wall.

Valerius drew his long sword. The day would be won or lost with swords and hand-to-hand fighting on the battlements. He prepared to meet the German foes as they ascended the walls. More reinforcements had been shifted to defend this part of the fortress, leaving other areas woefully short of protectors. He hoped the Germans would not spot this flaw.

Lucius stood with Ox and Rufus, waiting for the word to move toward any breach in the defenses. It was barely light and he could not see much, but already, the din of the battle could be heard. He sensed that the Germans were replicating the previous day's tactics. He looked about to see that his relief force was lesser in number than yesterday, but all things considered, they had escaped yesterday's carnage relatively unscathed. His thoughts then shifted to Julia. He hoped she would be safe. If the Frisii got over the walls and into the interior, the hospital area was unprotected. It only had stretcher bearers plus a few wounded men who were assisting the hospital staff. Every other available man was on the walls, except for his small force. Around him, the clamor of battle grew louder.

This morning, they had been positioned closer to the northeast sector as this was the place where they expected the Germans' main assault. He looked to his new-found friends, Ox and Rufus. He was lucky to have them at his side as both were fierce fighters. Yesterday, they had disposed of the attacking Germans with brutal efficiency. He had later asked Ox where he had learned to fight and had been surprised when Ox told him that he had had no formal training; he'd just picked things up here and there. In addition to his intimidating bulk and ferocity, he was as quick as a striking snake. Rufus, on the other hand, was not particularly big or quick, but he was experienced. He knew exactly how to deploy his shield to unbalance his opponent and then thrust with his sword. He was the quintessential Roman legionnaire in his style of combat. The legions had lost a good man when he retired from their service.

Lucius's musings about his companions was interrupted as a breathless messenger ran up to Severus and animatedly pointed to the north wall. Severus did not hesitate. "Follow me. Same place as yesterday." The pack of legionnaires and civilian mercenaries followed.

▲

Valerius and Marcellus charged toward a group of Frisii who had established a fighting position on the rampart. The Germans were engaged with several legionnaires who were barely holding their own. Valerius slashed with his long sword, wounding a man's leg. His opponent dropped his spear and limped away. Beside him, Marcellus swatted aside a sword and thrust with his short stabbing sword. Barreling forward, he knocked a man down and finished him with a hard thrust of his gladius. He then picked up a discarded shield and fitted it through the grip on his left arm. He charged into the pack, knocking several Frisii off balance. The desperate legionnaires who were engaged with the Germans took advantage of their distracted foe and skewered the Germans. The Romans now had a slight edge in their small space on the wall, and the remaining Germans were eventually eliminated. The Roman force of four legionnaires plus Marcellus and Valerius advanced to the next troubled spot.

They came to the aid of another beleaguered cluster of legionnaires who were engaged with a swelling force of Germans. They slammed into the Germans, knocking several of them off the rampart. They briefly held the advantage but more Germans joined the fray, the fighting taking place at close quarters on the seven-foot-wide rampart. The heavily armored Romans thrust with their shields and then stabbed with their swords. Valerius, who was without a shield, parried a spear thrust, but as he did, another spear hit him in the chest. Luckily for him, the iron point did not penetrate and deflected off his chest armor. Marcellus immediately responded, dispatching the man who had attacked Valerius with a stab to the throat. The German pocket collapsed.

In the brief respite, Marcellus yelled above the fray. "Are you all right?"

Valerius grimaced in pain and rubbed the spot of impact. "I'm going to have a very painful bruise. But the gods are looking out for me."

"As always," said Marcellus. "Let's get some more of these Germans." The group waded into the next mass of Frisii.

They engaged more Germans on the narrow rampart. The mass of men struggled, shifting about in the cramped space. Valerius was positioned on the outside of the melee, squaring off against a hulking Frisian. The man stabbed his spear in a lightning thrust, and Valerius barely avoided the deadly iron point. His evasive move put him on the edge of the rampart. Before he could center himself, his German adversary slammed into him. Valerius felt himself soar off the wall into the interior of the fort. He braced himself for the impact and the sound of breaking bones, but a pile of bodies broke his fall. The air was knocked from his lungs. Slowly and groggily, he attempted to move his arms and legs. All his limbs responded—he was shaken but everything worked. As the world came into focus again, he heard his name being called. Looking up, he saw a concerned Marcellus leaning from the wall.

"Are you alright, Tribune?"

Dazed, Valerius crawled to his hands and knees. "Never better," he croaked. He tried to rise but could not. After several more attempts, he shakily made his way over to the ramp leading back up to the wall. He waved Marcellus away, indicating that he was okay. He rested briefly and then made his way up and back into the fray.

* * *

Lucius and his companions, led by Severus, charged up the ramp. The optio divided his force, sending one group to the left and the other to the right. The mass of reinforcements savagely surged at the Germans. They raced forward and hit pockets of Frisii men. Lucius, in the center, flanked by Ox and Rufus, thrust his shield forward at a stocky German—it had no effect. Instead, Lucius was thrown off balance as a result of the contact. He staggered backward. The Frisian snarled and thrust his spear forward. Shifting his shield to his left, Lucius blocked the lunge. The German closed in, knowing he had the advantage of size, and Lucius was forced back even closer to the edge of the rampart. The menacing figure now towered over him. But unexpectedly, his assailant dropped his spear and crumpled to the floor, revealing a towering figure panting behind him with a bloody sword in his hand.

"You okay Lucius?" Ox asked.

"I am now, thanks to you. He almost had me."

"C'mon, we are needed farther down this rampart."

The three men advanced along the battlements shoulder-to-shoulder. Up ahead, it appeared that the situation was beginning to stabilize. The inflow of Germans had ceased, although a lot of Frisii had ascended the wall. The three men rammed their shields into the next group of enemies.

▲

Hudec and his men had finally reached the parapet on the far northeast corner of the fortress. Looking about, he observed that he had lost a few more of his men. Now was the time to exploit the advantage that presented itself. They did not seek battle with the Roman defenders on the walls. The previous night, Eadric had requested that his comitatus exit the rampart upon ascending the walls and immediately begin laying waste to the interior of the fort and its occupants. This would serve to distract the Roman defenders.

Hudec waved his spear, gesturing for his men to follow him. They surged down the ramp and into the interior of the Flevum. A few Romans rushed to ward off the Germans, but the Frisii greatly outnumbered them. The collection of Roman legionnaires was surrounded and ruthlessly dispatched. Hudec halted his men and looked about, unsure of where to go; he had never been in a Roman fort before. He directed his gaze toward the center, where the tallest buildings were concentrated, and decided that it was where they would go to kill and burn.

* * *

Lucius stood with about twenty others from the relief force on the battlements. They had expelled most of the Frisians in their sector, although, judging by the din of battle, this was not the case in other areas. Their leader, Severus, had died in the struggle. Some sections of the parapet were barely under the control of the Romans, and more Frisii continued to ascend the walls.

Tribune Florus materialized in front of them, his armor splattered with blood. "Follow me. There are Frisii within the fortress. We must eliminate them before they slay the civilians and the wounded."

Lucius's stomach churned—*Julia could be in mortal danger; I must rescue her.* The weary relief force charged down the ramp. Florus directed the force to a major avenue running east to west. The pack of men moved quickly along the street, and about a hundred yards ahead, they could hear screams. "Faster!" cried Florus. The men picked up their pace, their faces now masks of grim determination.

⚜

Julia and Hereca knelt beside a wounded legionnaire with a bloody hole in his stomach. He was supine on the hard ground outside the hospital, waiting his turn to be cared for—if he lasted that long. The young man grimaced in pain while the two women held a wad of clothing against the punctured flesh to stem the bleeding. Their faces would be the last thing he gazed upon in this world. Most of the other legionnaires they tended were just as bad—gruesome wounds with no hope for recovery. The one before this had sustained a puncture wound to his skull and his brains had leaked out. Another had had a sword slash across the throat. No matter what they tried, the bleeding could not be stopped. The young man died quickly, choking on his own blood.

Suddenly they could hear the sounds of piercing screams then the guttural shouts of Germans. Both women looked up to see a pack of Frisii rushed into the area and slaughtering the injured legionnaires and women caretakers. Their spears jabbed savagely, stabbing the helpless wounded multiple times. Julia screamed at the sight of the marauding Frisii. Hereca snarled.

Abandoning the wounded, Hereca grabbed Julia's hand and dragged her along. "Come with me," she said urgently. They hurried closer to the hospital. Resting against the wall were three German spears that Hereca had salvaged the previous day. She grabbed one and tested its heft, preparing to throw it at the encroaching group of Frisii.

At the same time, a band of legionnaires led by Tribune Florus charged around the corner and smashed into the mass of Germans. Although heavily outnumbered, the legionnaires surprised the Germans and temporarily stemmed their advance toward the hospital.

Lucius quickly glanced around and saw Hereca and Julia retreat to the building and away from the enemy. He charged into the mass of Germans with Ox and Rufus beside him. They thrust their shields forward and stabbed with their swords. Lucius remembered the mantra his drill instructor had often repeated—thrust with the shield, then stab. Thrust and stab. Do not slash. Stab. Lucius pushed forward, leading with his shield, his short sword poised to kill. Men fell as the savage combat continued.

Rufus was engaged with a tough-looking German who knew his business with the spear. He danced away from Rufus's advances and then darted in with his weapon. He opened a nasty gash on the former optio's right arm, causing him to drop his sword. The German then flashed an evil grin as he moved in for the kill. However, Lucius charged to the rescue, blindsiding him with his shield and then stabbing him square in the neck. The man collapsed. Rufus nodded his thanks and weakly picked up his fallen sword.

Three of Hudec's men, who were engaged with the Roman reinforcements, broke free and circled around toward the hospital. Spying the approaching men, Hereca winged her first spear. The warrior she had targeted was not wearing any armor. He was impaled in the torso and collapsed to his knees. The two surviving Germans stopped at the sight of their comrade pierced with the spear. This was a serious mistake. Hereca quickly retrieved a second spear. Hereca heaved a second spear and struck another figure in the shoulder. He stopped and doubled over, the spear jutting from his body. The surviving man hurried back to his comrades.

Observing the carnage Hereca had wreaked, a solitary warrior slid around the mass of fighting men and broke free. He rushed at her, unseen, from her flank. Julia, who was cowering in the shadow of the hospital, saw the man charging toward her friend with murderous intent. She looked about her and spied a discarded sword from one of the wounded lying in the dirt. Without hesitating, she grasped the handle of the gladius, which was thickly coated with blood, and ran to intercept the lone Frisian. As the German raced by her, intent on slaying Hereca, Julia slashed wildly at the warrior. The sharpened blade of the gladius bit deep into his neck, opening a ghastly wound. The man collapsed, blood fountaining from his neck. He shuddered once and then was still.

Hereca spied the dead German and then looked toward Julia, who was standing with a dripping sword in her hand. She nodded in thanks and gestured for her to move closer to her.

⁂

Hudec stepped back from the fight, attempting to direct his men so that they could overcome this smaller force of Romans. His men were too close together and would be more effective if they spread out and flanked the legionnaires. He began shouting above the bedlam, gesturing with his arm the direction in which he wanted his men to go. He grabbed three of his men and shoved them to the left. "Attack from there," he commanded.

Hereca seized her last spear and looked about for a target. *I have to be careful not to hit a legionnaire*, she thought. Suddenly, she saw her opportunity. An imposing warrior, no doubt the leader of this rabble, was shouting orders to his men. She remembered how she had missed the leader of the bandits who had ambushed them on their way to meet the Frisian chieftain mere days earlier. *This time will be different*, she vowed. Hereca hefted the javelin and threw the spear with all her strength. It flew straight and true, striking the chieftain in the center of his chest. He fell to the ground, blood flowing from the wound. The rest of the Germans looked about in panic and then began scurrying back to the ramparts.

No sooner had the small group of leaderless Germans run to the battlements, when the horns of the Frisii sounded. As the Germans disengaged from the legionnaires and fled, the Romans on the rampart pointed downriver and cheered. The flotilla containing the first half of the Fifth Legion rounded the bend in the river.

▲

Lucius rushed over to Julia and embraced her. They were safe. Tribune Florus walked over to the hospital, blood trickling down his face. He stood stunned at the carnage around him but was thankful for the sudden rescue by the Fifth Legion. Many of the wounded waiting for triage had been slain by the Frisii and the bodies of dead Germans, killed by the relief force, were strewn about. His trance was broken as Marcellus and Valerius hurried over. Relieved that her husband was still alive, Hereca rushed over and embraced her husband. The small group stood silently amidst the dead. After a few moments, Valerius spoke to Tribune Florus. "Good job. We live to fight another day. I didn't think we could hold them much longer till the Fifth showed up. As commander of Flevum, perhaps it might be wise for you to meet General Labeo and thank him for arriving in such a timely fashion. Just a suggestion."

Florus scoffed. "I would be surprised if the arsehole remembers my name. You know—out of sight, out of mind. I guess I should greet him. I will need to have Centurion Glaucus provide me with an up-to-date count of our losses. From what I can gather, they are pretty severe." He gestured with his hand. "Just look at this. It's a wonder we've survived at all! Another hour and we would have been overcome. I wonder what his orders will be."

"Obviously, the garrison needs to be replenished and the defenses improved," said Marcellus. "At least, that's what I would do if I were the legate."

Valerius pondered the matter. "I would say you're correct, Marcellus. I'm not sure what the Frisii's next moves are. Will they abandon any future assaults on Flevum? Their losses must be significant. Will they be satisfied with the statement they have made? I think one can safely surmise that they will not pay their taxes to Rome. If I were them, I would retreat from the fortress of Flevum into the interior and away from the long reach of the legions."

"That would be my take as well," said Marcellus. "But you never know with these Germans. You can't take them for granted. I wonder what General Labeo thinks. I guess we will find out."

CHAPTER XIX
THE FIFTH ARRIVES

Marcellus, Valerius, Centurion Glaucus, and Tribune Florus arrived at the river gate, which had been flung wide open to welcome the saviors from the Fifth Legion. The first two centuries, the vanguard, formed a corridor for the legate to make his triumphant entrance. Each legionnaire held his shield—decorated with the figure of a golden elephant on a scarlet background—at chest level. Exiting from the ship tied up at the quay, Labeo and his senior staff, their polished breastplates sparkling in the sun, followed the eagle standard-bearer, strutting through the gate and into the fortress.

As dictated by protocol, Florus, his armor and grimy face splattered with blood, stepped ahead of the other three officers to greet Labeo. "Welcome to Flevum, sir. Tribune Florus, commanding officer. Your arrival was most propitious. It was a tough fight, but the men prevailed."

The legate looked at the three officers behind Florus, scowling as he noted the presence of Valerius and Marcellus. "The garrison is still standing, I presume?"

"Yes, sir," replied Florus proudly, "although the town outside the walls has been burnt to the ground. It was close with the fortress. We were nearly overrun, but thanks to your timely arrival, we have persevered."

Valerius grinned inwardly. Damn, this Florus was getting to be a good officer. In the blink of an eye, he had given full credit to the legate for saving Flevum. Not bad. Not bad at all. Then there was Labeo. He had not even inquired about the losses of the legionnaires within the stronghold. Valerius let out a small sigh. There were leaders and there were men in leadership positions. Labeo was obviously the latter.

The legate glared at Florus. "All right, Tribune. I have brought half of the Fifth Legion. The other half will be transported when these boats from our fleet return to Noviomagus. I am now in command of all the forces in Flevum. We will need to begin preparation for a campaign against the Frisii."

Valerius was alarmed. What was Labeo thinking? Had he heard correctly that Labeo intended to pursue the Frisii into the interior? He had one legion. Surely he was not thinking of invasion. Valerius himself had been down that road twice and was extremely fortunate to be alive.

"Sir," said Florus, "I am afraid the troops assigned to Flevum will be of little assistance. We suffered a great number of casualties over the last three days. Our numbers are—"

"Later, Tribune. Better yet, write me a report. I can review it tonight. Now, why don't you lead me to my quarters? I will need accommodations and for my staff as well. As for provisions, our ships are fully laden with food stores. I will schedule time with you and your staff tomorrow."

Valerius watched Florus walk with Labeo and his staff toward the headquarters. A chill ran down his spine. What in Hades was this fool thinking of doing? He had better understand that the Frisii were much more than peaceful traders.

Valerius turned toward Marcellus, who was watching the retreating figures. The centurion had a glint in his eyes.

"Don't say anything, Tribune. I know exactly what you are thinking—'Shit, not again!'"

▲

The next day, Marcellus, Valerius, Florus, and Centurion Glaucus walked to the headquarters to meet with General Labeo and his senior staff. Valerius prepared himself for this. Deep down, he knew it was going to be more of a confrontation than a meeting. Labeo's imperious manner and his mention of a punitive raid against the Frisii were sure indicators that there was going to be a clash of viewpoints. It was clear that Labeo believed the Frisii were not a tough adversary. He wondered what the General knew of fighting Germans, if anything at all. This would not bode well for the Fifth Legion either. Pursuing the Germans in their territory was a dangerous endeavor.

As the group strode to the meeting room, there was no disguising Tribune Florus's foul mood.

"Who pissed on your parade this morning?" Valerius inquired.

"Rephrase the question," Florus replied. "The correct inquiry would be who didn't piss on my parade."

The others smirked at his response.

"Go ahead and laugh," replied Florus. "All of General Labeo's staff, including his tribunes, treat me like a servant. I received no recognition for the defense of Flevum, I have been ousted from my quarters and my office, and I have been talked down to by every officer in the Fifth. I had written Labeo his precious report on our dead and wounded, which he'd requested yesterday afternoon. I would have liked to shove it up his arse sideways."

Valerius chuckled. "Tribune Florus, you are becoming a seasoned tribune and are expressing a sentiment shared by many junior officers."

Florus grinned in reply.

The four officers arrived at the designated hour in the early afternoon and were ushered into the spacious room. Labeo was seated in a chair with two of his senior staff seated to his left. To his right was another staff member and next to him was the scowling figure of Tigranus. Valerius had not seen him the previous day. He must have disembarked later with the tribunes.

Labeo began to speak in a pompous tone. "Welcome. Let me introduce to you my senior staff. This is my adjutant, General Lollious Urbicus, my quartermaster, General Publius Terrentius, and my second in command, General Aemillius Pallus. Some of you have met the Governor's son, Tigranus. He is here in an advisory capacity."

Tribune Florus, as the commanding officer of Flevum, introduced Valerius, Marcellus, and Glaucus. He paused briefly and then continued. "General Labeo, I thought I might give you an updated status report of the fortress and the troop strength."

General Labeo waved his arm dismissively. "We can do that later. I read your report from last night. What is important is that I provide you with an overview of my plan and what role you will play. The Governor has given me explicit orders to pursue the rebellious Frisii and make an example of them. Insurrection will not be tolerated in the empire—that is the statement we must make. Therefore, over the next week, we will bring in the rest of the Fifth plus all the necessary provisions to conduct a campaign in the land of the Frisii. Once we are at full strength and adequately supplied, I will commence operations."

"Sir, and what is our role in this? You are aware that we suffered significant casualties as a result of the siege—"

"Enough about your losses, Tribune. That is only a minor concern. Now, as for the role I envision for you as officers, I want the four of you to help lead my legions against the enemy. You will be the tip of the spear. I am doing this because you are familiar with the landscape and tactics of the Frisii. In addition, I want to levy the fort's defenders plus all capable civilians for the fight against the Frisii to bolster our forces."

Valerius fumed, clearly displeased with the legate's pronouncement. "General Labeo, you cannot subject these civilians to the military standards of the legions. They are not trained, and many are not fit. That is unheard of."

Labeo glared at Valerius, walked over to him and stood merely inches away from his face. "You listen to me, Tribune. I can do it and I will. I have the authority of Governor Gallus to do as I see fit. He commanded me to punish the Frisii for their insubordination and that is precisely what I am going to do. Now, the last time I looked at Roman law, the Governor of a province has unlimited power to adopt laws and enforce regulations as he deems appropriate for the good of the province. Furthermore, I am a legate and you are a tribune. That makes me your commanding officer."

"But, sir," said Florus, "no one is questioning your authority. Tribune Maximus was only noting that these men are not trained legionnaires, and yet, you want them to be the lead element in a search for the Frisii. My legionnaires are battered and wounded. I'm not sure how effective they will be."

"Don't but me, Tribune," roared Labeo. "My decision is made. These men will be sworn in as legionnaires and take part in the campaign. I intend to bolster my forces with as many men in this garrison as you can provide, including the civilians. I know they are not trained soldiers, but I was informed last night in your brief report that they served you in the defense of the fortress, didn't they? As for your legionnaires at Flevum, they will have a week to recover. That should be enough. Now, my word is final, and I will brook no dissent."

Valerius stepped forward. He needed to rescue Florus and see if he could infuse a modicum of reason into the General's plan. "Of course, we will serve you as best as we can, General Labeo. I believe Tribune Florus was only attempting to inform you of the status of his forces and not to be argumentative. I understand your orders. My main concern is that you have an adequate force to pursue a campaign against a far superior number of the Frisii. From my experience, fighting the Germans on their terrain is a risky proposition. I have seen this firsthand and wish not to repeat the experience. Centurion Marcellus and I have limited knowledge of the land beyond these walls—only for fifteen or twenty miles. After that, it is a completely unknown terrain."

Labeo glared. "Enough, Tribune Maximus. You will follow my orders explicitly or I will have you in chains. We are going to pursue the Frisii and make an example of them. As for the Frisian territory, you will be pleased to know that I have hired German scouts to assist the legion in its quest. We will find the Frisii and destroy them. Do you understand?"

"Yes, sir. I was only apprising you of the possible risks to the Fifth Legion during this campaign."

Tigranus leered, obviously enjoying the verbal slap Valerius had received from Labeo. Valerius had been put in his place. "My father asked me to keep a special eye on you. He doesn't trust you."

Valerius turned his steely gaze toward Tigranus. After a long pause, he spoke. "I understand. By the way, what happened to your neck? That looks nasty. You should have a medicus look at that."

Tigranus's face reddened. He touched the raw cut on his neck. "A hunting accident, nothing more. I will be fine."

A mocking grin flashed across Valerius's face.

The four officers departed from the headquarters, their expressions dour. When they were well out of hearing range of anyone associated with Labeo, Marcellus spoke up. "I have a question."

Everyone looked at him expectantly. "How many generals does it take to run a legion? Jupiter's arse, they have four of them!"

"Yes," added Valerius, "and not one of them has the faintest fucking idea what they should be doing."

Despite the adverse circumstances, the group chortled in unison at the absurdity of it all.

CHAPTER XX

PREPARING FOR THE CAMPAIGN

Later that day, Valerius approached Lucius and Julia, who were seated at a wooden table in the courtyard. Valerius needed to tell them the bad news before they heard it from another source. He had asked Marcellus if he wanted to join them, but the centurion stated that he was not good at this sort of thing and wouldn't be of much assistance. Julia and Lucius were munching on bread and cheese, enjoying the warm weather and bright sunshine. They both looked up from their repast as Valerius approached. Julia smiled. "Come join us. We have lots of food. Lucius and I were just discussing arrangements for our departure. I assume it is safe now?"

Valerius offered a tight-lipped smile. "I'm afraid this is not a social visit. To answer your question, yes, I believe it is safe to depart Flevum, but the legate has other ideas. He has issued an edict that all fit males are to be conscripted into his legion to conduct offensive operations against the Frisii. This would include Lucius."

Julia gasped. "How can that be? By whose authority can he do this?"

"I asked the same question and was less than politely rebuked," said Valerius. "His rationale is that the Governor has broad powers within his province, and he is the Governor's right arm so he can do whatever he desires. What is more, I believe Governor Gallus is doing this as a way to get back at me. He intensely dislikes me because I was appointed by the Emperor to investigate the Frisii. Unfortunately, this whole unsavory stew may be traced back to the Governor and his tax trickeries. I would venture to guess that he doesn't want Tiberius to find out that the tax matter is the direct cause of this revolt. Thus, here we are. If it's any consolation, after I finish speaking to you, I must tell my surviving mercenary force, including Ox and Rufus, that they are now the property of the Fifth Legion."

Lucius contemplated what Valerius had told him. He grasped Julia's hand. "Will it be dangerous?"

Valerius pondered the question for a few moments, trying to choose the right words. He decided that he should be candid and state the hard facts. "I will not mince words. This will be a precarious undertaking. Labeo foolishly believes that the Frisii will cower at his presence when he invades their lands. I have tried to dissuade him of the folly of doing this, but he does not want to listen to what I have to say. The Frisii are a desperate and angry people. They will not surrender, and I believe they will meet Labeo's forces with ferocity. Lucius, you have seen what these Frisii are capable of first-hand. They will not shrink from the Fifth Legion. They will attempt to eradicate any Romans in their territory."

Julia was outraged; her eyes blazed. "I will give this general a piece of my mind. Has he forgotten what happened in the Teutoburg Forest to Varus and his legions?"

"I tried that line with him, Julia," said Valerius. "He doesn't want to hear it. He has his marching orders from Gallus. Furthermore, this is his chance for glory and to make a name for himself. But we will be heavily outnumbered in the Frisian terrain. This is not a good combination. Marcellus and I know a thing or two about fighting Germans so we will attempt to curtail his aggressiveness."

Not appeased, Julia stalked off in anger. Valerius and Lucius exchanged knowing glances. "I believe Julia is embracing some of Hereca's less desirable qualities," said Valerius.

* * *

Valerius and Marcellus stood before the band of mercenaries, which was now down to nine from the original fifteen. They were gathered in the shade of one of the fort's granaries. "Let me get right to the heart of the matter," said Valerius. "I have been informed by General Labeo, the legate of the Fifth Legion, that all of you are to be sworn in as legionnaires to supplement his forces. While I believe he requires as much manpower as possible, the addition of nine men does not make a whole lot of difference. I believe the real reason for your recruitment is retribution for surviving that attack by that band of cutthroats in the land of the Frisii. He intends to place us at the front of his forces."

A large swarthy man by the name of Petrus grunted in disapproval. "I was one among those wounded in that skirmish with the miscreants; then, I defended the walls of Flevum and lost my comrade, Juvicius, in the process. I was proud to serve with you but to be thrust into danger again is asking a lot. What if I refuse?"

Marcellus stepped forward. "That would not be a wise choice, Petrus. I understand what you are saying and this is unfair but that is the nature of our current circumstances. To answer your question, Labeo would have you executed, and it would be a public one so that he can demonstrate that he has total control over everyone here. Listen, Petrus, I know this is not to your liking. I would feel the same way if I were in your boots. Valerius and I will see to it that you are all compensated in addition to your legionary pay, which I can attest will not be much."

Petrus kicked the dirt in disgust. "Shit," he muttered. "None of us are going to get out of here alive." He stalked away from the group. Nobody attempted to stop him.

▲

Over the next several days, Flevum was a beehive of activity. More transports, filled with legionnaires, arrived. The ships unloaded their cargo and then turned around and went back to Noviomagus for more. Several ships carrying horses and oxen tethered to posts on the railing docked as well. Blinders had been placed over the eyes of the beasts to keep them calm. Other ships arrived carrying foodstuff, bundles of spears, and fodder for the animals. The procession of ships never stopped. Huge caches of cargo were unloaded on the dock at the back of the fort at Flevum.

Marcellus and Valerius stood by the quay, watching. It was clear that the Fifth Legion would be well equipped and stocked with the necessary food provisions and equipment for the pending invasion. Valerius turned to his former centurion. "I had forgotten how much baggage and supplies come with each legion. Labeo will be fully provisioned for the offensive. The problem is that he does not have enough manpower. You saw how many Frisii we faced. We put a substantial dent in their population, but still, they heavily outnumber us and we will be in their terrain. I don't like this."

Marcellus continued staring in fascination at the disembarkation process. "You forgot one other thing."

"What's that?"

"Our esteemed commander, General Labeo, is not exactly an incarnation of Julius Caesar. Oh, he knows how to have a legion prepared and provisioned, I'll grant you that, but he has no idea of the ferocity and cunning these Germans are capable of. Furthermore, he doesn't want to listen to us. He thinks of us as nothing but a couple of merchants."

"Marcellus, but that is precisely what we are. Look at us. Both of us are traders, dealers, or whatever you want to call us. He hasn't seen what we did in our past service. I guess we can't blame him. His opinion of us has been colored by Gallus."

"Tribune, what are we to do?"

Valerius pondered the question for a moment. "Here is what I'm hoping we can accomplish. We tread carefully around Labeo, obey his commands, but urge caution in his pursuit of the Frisii. Once we engage the Germans, I trust that it will not be the full commitment of the legion and we can tactically retreat from the onslaught. That should give him a taste of what the Frisii are capable of and he will understand that the Fifth is in a vulnerable position. But if he goes all in on engagement and we get surrounded, those Greek mathematicians' odds I mentioned are going to be sky high."

The next day, Valerius and Hereca gathered with Lucius and Julia in the accommodations that Tribune Florus had arranged for the two women. Julia and Hereca would be staying behind while their two men marched with Labeo's legion against the Frisii. As far as lodging went, it was not much, but it would have to do. It consisted of two small bedrooms and a central chamber that was sparsely furnished. While a legionary fortress was not the most desirable place for two women to stay, there was no alternative as the town outside the walls had been destroyed. Valerius did not fear for their safety in the legionary camp. The saga of the two women in the defense of the hospital grew by leaps and bounds every day. The embellished story had Julia and Hereca single-handedly stopping the German horde from attacking the hospital. As a result, the two women had been given a goddess-like status by the grateful legionnaires of the fort, especially the surviving wounded who would stay behind at Flevum.

Valerius spoke. "The legion is almost fully equipped and supplied. I expect we will be underway shortly. General Labeo is anxious to spread the glory of Rome."

"My husband," said Hereca, "your cynicism is thinly veiled."

"Unfortunately, my attempts to convince him otherwise have been unsuccessful. I'm not sure whether it is Gallus's orders or Labeo's ego that is the driving force of this campaign. In any event, if he is not careful, he is going to find a sharp German spear up his arse."

Julia frowned. "Is there nothing you can do to convince him otherwise? I don't want my children to lose their father."

"Julia, I will do everything I can to protect Lucius once we are underway. I am going to try one more time to talk some sense into Labeo. I need him to look at me as an asset who can give him advice. Right now, that is not the case. Gallus has poisoned him against me. I'm an adversary whom he views as an impediment to his plans."

Valerius was about to continue when a pair of legionnaires appeared. The taller one spoke. "Tribune Valerius, General Labeo would like to speak with you now. He asked that we accompany you to his headquarters."

Valerius looked at both Hereca and Julia and shrugged. "Perhaps the gods have intervened on our behalf."

"Let us hope so," said Julia.

Valerius nodded at the two legionnaires. They exited the room with Valerius between them.

Valerius and his escorts entered the headquarters. The outer room was full of officers and other personnel waiting to see the General. He recognized Labeo's clerk, who organized the General's calendar and affairs. The man looked harried. Valerius strode up to where he was seated: a table overflowing with documents. "Tribune Valerius here to see General Labeo upon his request."

The man looked up from his paperwork. He gestured with his arm. "Have a seat, Tribune. There is a long line ahead of you. You will be called into his chambers when he is ready for you."

Valerius nodded in thanks and occupied a wooden bench on the far side of the room. He gazed at the men gathered about in the waiting area, all of them eager to meet with their commander. Most were young tribunes. Several officers gathered in groups exchanged witty quips followed by quick bouts of laughter. *I wonder if they will be as cheery when the German spears come flying at them. They'll probably soil their pants.*

He continued to observe a few of the officers as they moved back and forth across the room with self-important strides. He wondered if any of them had been involved in combat against the Germans. Probably not. Most of them looked too young. *The defense of the empire depends on these peacocks?* He realized that he was probably being a bit too harsh on these young men. He had once been like them. Hopefully, their introduction to the world of violence would not be as harsh as his had been back in the Teutoburg Forest.

Several of the men glanced his way, wondering who the middle-aged tribune was. They clustered together, whispered to each other, and then peered back at him, looking ill-disposed toward him. Rumor must have been that he was *persona non grata* with Labeo and one to be avoided.

Valerius sat and waited. Other officers were called to enter—some individually, others in groups. He thought about what he might say to Labeo but found none that were satisfactory or appealing or which could assuage the General's feelings toward him. He had to come up with a narrative that the General might embrace. His very survival and perhaps that of the Fifth Legion depended on what he could do to convince Labeo that they needed to enter Frisian lands with extreme caution.

It was now late in the afternoon; the sun's rays slanted through the wide windows of the waiting room. Valerius fumed. He was certain he had been deliberately put at the bottom of the list of people waiting to see the legate. At last, a figure exited the General's chambers and whispered in the clerk's ear. In turn, the secretary cleared his throat. "Tribune Valerius, General Labeo will see you now."

Valerius rose stiffly from the wooden bench and entered the erstwhile headquarters of Tribune Florus. Labeo stood in the center of the room, facing him. Off to the side, a scribe sat at a table, ready to record the conversation.

"Tribune Valerius, we meet again," said the General, his expression neutral.

Valerius was relieved that his reception was not hostile. Perhaps there was hope after all. "Yes, General Labeo. Please let me know how I can be of service to the Fifth Legion."

Labeo held his gaze, waiting to see if Valerius had anything else to add. After a period of silence, the General continued. "Very well, Tribune. I am going to attach three centuries from the garrison at Flevum plus your contingent of mercenaries and civilians to my first cohort. This will give added strength to the 'tip of the spear' as my legion carries out a campaign against the Frisii. I am placing you in command of the Flevum detachment above Tribune Florus as you are the more experienced officer. Your forces in support of the first cohort should be able to punch through whatever resistance we might encounter. I will appoint my second-in-command, General Aemillius Pallus, to oversee the first cohort and your attached forces."

"Very well, sir." He had been about to address the tactics for the Germans but thought better of it. It would accomplish nothing.

Labeo gazed at Valerius. "Is that all? You have nothing more to add?"

Valerius returned the stare. "No, sir. I believe I have already made my feelings known. I would only stress again that, from my humble experiences in dealing with these Germans, it is prudent to be cautious. They are a cunning and brutal enemy and are not to be underestimated."

Labeo's face was suffused with crimson. "And you think I don't know that?"

Valerius remained silent for a while. If Labeo understood the concept, he would not go about invading the Frisian homeland with one legion, powerful as it may be. It was a foolhardy endeavor that would lead to disaster. But he merely replied, "Yes, of course, sir."

Labeo struggled to control himself. The deliberate silence had been pure insolence and infuriated him even more. He responded in a biting tone. "I expect you to conduct yourself like the military officer you are. You and your men plus those from Flevum will obey my orders without delay. Understood?"

"Yes, sir."

"You are dismissed," he said frostily.

Valerius turned about and departed, mentally shrugging off the bellicose dialogue. He had had far worse conversations during his military career, including in his recent meeting with Tiberius. He hurried to meet with Tribune Florus and explain the new command structure.

He found Florus in deep conversation with Centurion Glaucus.

"Centurion, would you mind if I spoke in private with Tribune Florus? I am sure he can catch up with you later."

"Of course, sir. We were just about finished anyway."

After Glaucus departed, Valerius began. "I just finished meeting with General Labeo. He informed me that I am to oversee the Flevum detachment. I did not seek this responsibility, and I dared not argue with him."

Florus looked relieved. "Thank Jupiter and Mars for that. I am not disappointed if that's what you wanted to know. I guess certain officers might have been offended that an outsider was placed over them, but this is not the case with me. I recognize my limitations and lack of experience with respect to leading legionnaires on a march into hostile territory. I am, in fact, thankful that this heavy responsibility has not been foisted upon me and I'm grateful to be able to defer to your veteran wisdom."

"Listen," said Valerius. "There is a role for you. I will depend heavily upon you to help lead the troops. You certainly proved your mettle during the siege. You have the makings of a good officer."

"Thank you. I hope I survive this to serve Rome in the future."

The next evening, Valerius, along with the other senior staff and cohort commanders, was invited to the final briefing at the headquarters before the march out in the morning. The men were assembled in the colonnaded courtyard of the headquarters. He stood next to Tribune Florus. "Have you ever witnessed one of these spectacles?" Valerius asked.

"No, I have not. What exactly is the purpose of these things?"

"Just wait and see. It is a pompous display of ego and bravado. A bit of high theater here on the German frontier."

As he said this, Labeo came strutting out onto a recently constructed stage along with his senior staff. They were dressed in their finest armor, which had been polished to a mirror finish and gleamed in the twilight. The audience was immediately called to attention by the adjutant.

Labeo stood in the center of the stage, while his staff took their seats to the right. He stared at his officers in silence for a few moments and then began. "Please be seated." He waited for the officers to take their seats. "As you are aware, the Frisii have broken their long-standing pact of friendship with Rome and recently attacked the fortress here at Flevum. They failed. Governor Gallus is outraged by this insubordination, this craven revolt. He has tasked us, the mighty Fifth Legion, to seek retribution against the Frisii."

His bevy of subordinate generals rose and applauded wildly. The other officers in attendance did the same out of politeness.

After the cheering had ended and the officers returned to their seats, Labeo began to pace back and forth on the stage, pausing to heighten the effect of his words. "Our mission is to destroy the enemy, forcing them to seek peace and proper terms with Rome, and that is precisely what we are going to do."

With that, Labeo's senior staff again leaped to their feet again and clapped effusively. The others in the audience followed their example.

Once the applause had subsided, Labeo continued. "We will begin to march out at dawn tomorrow. General Pallus, please come up here and explain our tactical march to our officers."

Pallus rose from his seat, approached the center of the stage, and began, "The first cohort plus several attached centuries from Flevum will lead the way tomorrow. I will be situated with the first cohort for command and control purposes. The rest of the cohorts will follow in numerical order followed by the baggage trains."

As Pallus droned on, Valerius nudged Marcellus. "How is he going to maintain security for the baggage trains? They will be unprotected in the rear."

Pallus finished his brief presentation and exited the stage. Labeo returned to the front. "Next will be General Lollious Urbicus, our quartermaster."

Urbicus rose and faced the congregated officers. "We anticipate this campaign to go on for no longer than two weeks. We have stocked rations and fodder for the animals for only that long, so we will not be unnecessarily burdened. Furthermore, since we assembled quickly, there was no time to procure the complement of mules required to carry the legion's tents. Therefore, the men will be sleeping out in the open. We believe the inconvenience will be minor given the time anticipated for the crusade against the Frisii. After all, the weather should be temperate at this time of year. The absence of the mules will considerably shorten the length of the legionary column while on the march, making it less cumbersome for the legion to advance into Frisian territory. We intend this to be a mobile force that may strike quickly when the opportunity presents itself." With that, he exited the podium.

Labeo swaggered to the front and center. "Our enemies are estimated to have around ten thousand men. Their first village is about twenty miles from here. We should easily reach it on the second day. Upon arrival, we will attack the village and slaughter all the inhabitants to let them know what our intentions are. If their warriors decide to fight then and there, all the better. We must punish the Frisii and set an example for all to bear witness. Rome will not tolerate insurrection or rebellion from its friends and allies. You have all been briefed on your assignments. Be prepared to carry out those duties beginning tomorrow morning." He clenched his right fist for all to see. "We will crush these rebellious Frisii into dust."

The senior staff again leaped to their feet and cheered as Labeo exited the stage. Florus looked at Valerius and shrugged. "From my experience with these Frisii, they will not be easily crushed."

Valerius chuckled. "I believe that is the essence of the matter. If applause could slay the Frisii, they would be dead ten times over."

The briefing continued with exaggerated bravado. The following day, the Fifth would begin their invasion and meet their destiny.

CHAPTER XXI
INVASION OF THE FRISII

Early the next morning, while it was still dark outside, Valerius held Hereca in a tight embrace in the courtyard of Flevum. She buried her face in his military cloak, not saying a word. He knew she was troubled. For that matter, so was he, but he could not afford to be distracted. If he was to survive this upcoming campaign, he needed to be entirely focused and bring all his knowledge and experience to bear.

Hereca continued to hold her husband in a tight embrace. At last, she tilted her head up. "You must survive this, my husband. Promise me you will come back to me and our children."

Valerius offered a tight-lipped smile. "I have every intention of returning to my life with you. I don't care what it takes; Marcellus and I will find a way to survive."

Hereca returned the smile. "And Lucius as well. You must bring him back to Julia."

253

"And Lucius as well. Rufus and Ox will be alongside him. The three men have bonded well. We will all be back. I will tell Lucius you'll look after Julia until we return." With that, he broke away from his wife and departed. The Fifth was marshaling outside the walls, about a mile away on the wide plain. It was time.

Valerius stood huddled with Marcellus and Tribune Florus amidst the morning mist. The men under Valerius's command—the Flevum force, as they were now known—mingled in loose formation directly behind approximately five hundred men of the first cohort. There was a slight chill in the air and the mist obscured visibility. Summer was almost over, and it was now early autumn. The walls of Flevum had already disappeared from view; not even the towering turrets of the main gate were visible.

Valerius looked at his feet, which were already wet from the morning dew. "I can tell we are on a campaign. My feet are already soaked and chilled."

Marcellus snorted. "Tribune, you should know by now—a legionnaire's feet are never dry, except perhaps, if you're stationed in Syria."

Valerius was about to reply when he saw Labeo and his staff approach on horseback. The General halted about fifty paces away and raised his arm over his head and brought it sharply down. The cornua, the large brass horns of the legions, which were configured like the letter "G" and were about three feet long, blasted the signal to begin the march out. The heavy notes of the trumpets broke the stillness of the morning air.

Up ahead of the first cohort, three *turmae* of cavalry, squadrons of approximately thirty men each, began trotting forward and off to the flanks to ensure security for the marching column. This was the standard operating procedure. The main purpose of the Roman cavalry was to act as a screening force and provide an early warning if hostile forces were near.

In anticipation of the command to proceed, the legionnaires had hefted the marching poles to which their gear was attached. Grunts could be heard throughout the Flevum force. Valerius heard commands issued to his front as officers began shouting their orders. "First cohort, make ready to depart."

Marcellus smiled at Glaucus. "Lead them out, Centurion."

"Legionnaires of Flevum," bellowed Glaucus, "Forward, march."

Later that morning, the entire legion and baggage train were spread out along the dirt road—the same one that Valerius and Marcellus had traversed to meet with Eadric. The trail was now being churned to a muddy froth as thousands of marching boots pounded the earth. The Fifth Legion had been marching for about three hours when word came to halt for a break.

Valerius, Marcellus, and Florus stood apart from the Flevum force. They the observed the collection of legionnaires, civilians and mercenaries collapse upon the ground and guzzle water from their goat-skin containers. The weather was good, even a bit on the warm side with the brightening sky, but regardless of the heat or cold, the burden of their heavy gear ground down even the strongest of men. The weight of their armor, weapons—sword, dagger, and two pila—plus their other equipment and personal gear and rations was crushing. The legion would be lucky to make ten miles today with the slow moving baggage trains.

Florus turned toward Marcellus and Valerius. "What will we encounter when we reach the first village?"

"Most likely nothing," said Marcellus. "In all probability, the Frisii will have fled."

255

Florus looked bewildered. "Don't they care about their village? After all, it's their home."

Marcellus plucked a long stem of grass and chewed the moist end of it, pondering the question. "They do but not enough to die for it. A few buildings and late crops are not worth defending. The Frisii will select the location and time of the battle, and I will guarantee you the terrain will not favor us. Now, if our esteemed General could understand this concept, we would all be better off and more secure."

"What Marcellus is saying is that one should be alert, but it is unlikely that the Frisii will attack at this stage of our campaign," quipped Valerius. "They will wait until we are tired and too far away to be reinforced."

"Truth be told, I would rather be back at Flevum and not here. I'm more than a tad nervous," said Florus.

"Take heart," said Marcellus. "You can tell your grandchildren that you fought the Frisii on behalf of Rome and survived. We will all see our way through this. Look at me. I have been in far worse circumstances over the course of my military career, and I'm still here."

* * *

Later that evening, Lucius sat around a campfire with his companions, Ox and Rufus along with a few others. They had consumed their marching rations of porridge, biscuits, and *posca*—sour wine. He absently rubbed his shoulders, which ached from carrying his belongings and other gear. He flicked wood chips into the blaze, mesmerized by the amber glow. "My arse is dragging, and we've only covered about ten miles on even terrain and under pleasant weather conditions. This is just the beginning. It was hard when I was a young lad. It's harder now."

Ox moaned in empathy. "The weight we carry would buckle the legs of a mule. I don't know how the smaller guys manage."

"Quit complaining," said Rufus. "I voluntarily retired from this shit for this very reason, and here I am back in it. I know life isn't fair, but now the gods are rubbing my nose in it. Where are the gods when I need them?"

Lucius scoffed. "Look at me: I joined the legions involuntarily. I was released from my obligation involuntarily, and here I am, back involuntarily. If there are any gods, they are playing a cruel trick on me. In addition to all of that, we have no tents. If it rains, we are really in for some shit. I'll bet General Labeo has a nice, comfortable tent."

Centurion Glaucus entered the circle of light cast by the fire and sat down. "How's it going? Actually, on second thought, perhaps it's better if I didn't ask." Not waiting for an answer, he continued. "I know you're tired, sore, and don't want to be here. Me too."

He paused, staring at the flickering fire. "Listen up. I spoke with Tribune Valerius and Centurion Marcellus. They told me we are a little more than eight miles from the Frisii village they visited not too long ago. They said that they didn't expect to encounter any Frisii. I agree with their assessment, but still, I would be on alert tomorrow. You never know. Try and get some sleep. We will move out at dawn. Let's hope the weather is as favorable. Oh, and especially that there's no fucking rain." He rose and departed.

⚜

The next day, the legion trekked more grueling miles from early in the afternoon till evening. General Labeo sat tall on his horse, his eyes focused ahead on the dirt trail, anxiously waiting for word that his scouts had come across the Frisii. He positioned his command group of officers and bodyguards behind the second cohort, ready to spring forward in the event of enemy contact.

"Rider approaching," shouted one of his staff.

A decurion, part of the cavalry scouts, urged forward a large brown horse with a splotch of white on its forehead. He pulled up about six paces away from Labeo. "Sir, there's a large Frisian village about a mile ahead, but we didn't encounter any occupants. It appears to be abandoned."

Labeo pondered the rider's words. A vulpine expression crossed his countenance. "It might be one of their traps. They are attempting to deceive us and lure us into an ambush. Well, not today and not this legion." He turned to one of his tribunes. "Have the cornua signal enemy contact." He nodded to the decurion. "Go to my second-in-command, General Aemillius Pallus. He is just up ahead with the first cohort. Have him deploy his forces into battle lines."

Labeo then turned toward his officers. "We will move forward to the first cohort shortly. Time to teach these Frisii a lesson."

Valerius, Marcellus, and Florus stood with General Pallus, his aides, and Centurion Marcus Flavius—senior centurion of the first cohort and the first spear of the Fifth. When the spears would begin to fly, Flavius would provide the necessary leadership. Several mounted men from the cavalry turma were nearby, and a bevy of bodyguards encircled Pallus. The cohort was positioned in an open field outside the main village. The remains of harvested grain crunched underfoot. In proximity were several long, wooden storage buildings that were empty as well.

General Pallus looked slowly to his left and right. "Gentlemen, we have orders to deploy our forces and approach the settlement. Therefore, form the first three centuries to my right, and the fourth, fifth, and sixth to my left. I want the centuries three ranks deep for our assault. We will sweep through the village on line." He gazed at Valerius. "Tribune, I want your forces held in reserve. We will shift your men as needed."

After Pallus finished speaking, there was an awkward silence. Pallus looked to his senior centurion, Marcus Flavius. "Any questions, Centurion Flavius?"

Marcus Flavius was a grizzled veteran with many scars upon his face. There was a reason he was the senior centurion for the first cohort. This man knew his way around the legions and was one of the few officers with combat experience. He was of medium height and had a stocky build—none of it fat. The man was a warrior through and through.

Flavius responded, "Well, sir, I don't see what all the fuss is about. The cavalry has reported that the village is abandoned. I know it is always prudent to be cautious, but this appears to be a waste of time."

Pallus frowned. "Centurion, I know what the cavalry reported to us, but General Labeo wants us to deploy and so we will deploy. Do you wish to speak to General Labeo and convey your thoughts? I'm sure he would welcome your opinion," he said tersely.

Flavius responded, "Yes, sir. We will assault in short order." He was about to turn away when Labeo and his retinue thundered into the clearing. "General Pallus, I thought you were ordered to attack the village."

"Yes, sir," said Pallus. "We were about to position the first cohort for the assault. I was just conferring with my officers to ensure we were all clear on our responsibilities. We will array in triple ranks, three centuries to the left and three to the right. The attached centuries from Flevum will be a mobile reserve force."

Valerius glanced up at the retinue of senior officers with Labeo and saw Tigranus among them. He was attired in a fancy muscle cuirass with a long sword and no helmet. The two exchanged loathing glances.

Labeo glared at his second-in-command, letting Pallus know he was not happy with the delay. "My staff shall observe the first cohort's tactical maneuver. Please proceed."

The first cohort smartly positioned itself to move into the heart of the village. The five hundred men grounded their gear and advanced through the scattered trees and brush. As they approached the large collection of dwellings, the legionnaires moved like a wave, swords and shields in hand, sweeping through the settlement.

Everything was silent. The bewildered legionnaires advanced through the empty village. Not even a bird call was heard. They entered the settlement and checked every hut and building. They were all empty.

CHAPTER XXII

THE BADUHENNA WOOD

After burning down the abandoned Frisian village, the legion advanced north for about a mile on the dirt path and established a fortified encampment in a wide field that, at one time, had been cultivated. The troops were pleased as it was easy digging—no tree roots or rocky landscape. Once the earthen walls had been erected and the protective ditches dug, the legion settled in for the night.

Shortly before dusk, General Labeo called an officers' meeting to discuss the plans for the next day. He stood before his senior officers in the dwindling sunlight and began, "It appears that the Frisii have fled. Obviously, they want no part of the Fifth Legion." He offered a forced chuckle. "Well, they shall not get off that easily. Tomorrow, we will again march out at dawn in a northeasterly direction along the dirt path. I was told by our German scouts that there are many villages on the other side of these woods and meadows to our front. This piece of land is called…" He stopped and looked inquiringly at

261

his assembled senior staff. There was a mumbled reply. His face lit up in recognition. "Ah, yes, that's it. This place is called the Baduhenna Wood, and it is supposedly sacred to the Frisii. It comprises forests and meadows. Once we traverse this wood, the villages adjacent to it are ours for the taking. Maybe even a bit of plunder for the men."

He strutted back and forth with his hands clasped behind his back. He eyed his officers. "Sooner or later, the Frisii will have to come out and fight. When they do, we will show no mercy. Remember, if they had succeeded in breaching the walls of Flevum, they would have massacred every living soul within that fortress. I say again, no mercy for the Frisii. See to your duties. You are dismissed."

▲

As Marcellus and Valerius were walking away from the officers' meeting, Marcellus stopped abruptly and turned toward Valerius. But before he spoke, the centurion looked about to see if anyone was within listening range. "I was just thinking, it might be prudent for both of us to visit the first cohort commander, Marcus Flavius. From the looks of him, he's nobody's fool. I would bet you he isn't buying what Labeo is selling. He appears to be a tough, seasoned officer. Perhaps we could discuss with him our thoughts about the perils of this expedition. We might have an ally."

Valerius pondered Marcellus's remarks for a bit. "I like the idea. Makes sense. My concern is that General Pallus has been put in charge of the first cohort, including our attached forces, and Flavius has been displaced as the commander, which I'm sure he is not happy about."

"You bet your arse he's not happy about it, although I'm sure he hasn't said anything. But the point is when the spears fly and swords clash, it will be Flavius at the front and not Pallus. Flavius may take orders from General Pallus, but he will be the one with the troops and conducting the offensive operations."

"When do you want to visit him?"

"Later this evening," said Marcellus. "Right now, he is probably ensuring that everyone is settled in for the night and prepared to go at dawn tomorrow. This will need to be a discreet conversation about tactics and what to do when the Frisii attack. If he is not of our mindset and is an ally of Labeo, we could face serious charges."

"Let's pay the senior centurion a visit tonight. I hope you are right about his attitude."

That night, when most of the camp was bedded down, Valerius and Marcellus were escorted by a guard into the campaign tent of Marcus Flavius. He was seated at a small table littered with documents. A small cup of wine rested on the table. Another soldier was also in the tent. The centurion proffered a weary smile. "Ah, Tribune Valerius and Centurion Marcellus, to what do I owe this unexpected pleasure?"

"Just thought we might become better acquainted," responded Marcellus. "Who knows what we might face tomorrow or the next day."

Flavius picked up on Marcellus's tone. "Of course." He addressed his aide, who was standing to his left. "Optio Nomidius, would you mind if I spoke to my guests in private?"

The optio nodded. "Yes, Centurion. I was just about to leave. I need to speak with Centurion Dolabella of the second cohort about the coordination of our march tomorrow. Will you need me anymore this evening, Centurion?"

"No, I think not. Thank you for your hard work. See you in the morning."

Flavius waited until the tent flaps had closed. "Let me get you some wine." He poured two glasses, handed them to the officers, and gestured to the two empty seats in front of his table. Without preamble, he asked, "What's on your mind?"

"I'm sure you know by now that Tribune Valerius and I are not held in high esteem by General Labeo," said Marcellus.

"That would be an understatement. He detests both of you. I'm not sure how you fit in with this campaign. I have heard rumors, but I'm not sure what to believe."

Valerius spoke. "Let me clarify that for you, Centurion Flavius. Marcellus and I are merchants. We have a profitable business trading with the tribes on the Rhenus. So, what in Hades are we doing here, you might ask. To make a long story short, the Emperor reinstated our old military ranks and commanded that we assist Governor Gallus and his military staff with any potential problems with the Frisii. The Governor does not welcome our help, thus our less than amicable reception by General Labeo."

"And what military experience do you have?" Flavius inquired.

"For a start, Marcellus and I are the only surviving officers of the Teutoburg disaster. Furthermore, we assisted Germanicus Caesar in his retribution campaign fifteen years ago. Marcellus spent over twenty years with the legions in Germania. In short Centurion Flavius, we know the Germans and how to fight them."

"Impressive," said Flavius. "We could use experienced officers in this campaign. The lack of veterans among both the junior and senior officer ranks is a bit unsettling."

"Indeed. Let me speak bluntly," responded Valerius. "Marcellus and I believe we are marching into a disaster, a trap. The Frisii are fierce warriors. You should have seen the way they stormed Flevum, and there were several of them. They almost had us before the Fifth showed up. It appears Governor Gallus and General Labeo have no appreciation for the Frisii as a serious enemy. In my opinion, it would be a huge mistake to underestimate them. I cannot emphasize the gravity of our situation enough."

Flavius stared back at the two officers. "You have my attention. What is it you want me to do?"

Marcellus and Valerius exchanged knowing glances and Marcellus then spoke, "We believe General Labeo is being reckless in his approach to this campaign. To be specific, he is pitting this legion, one lacking in experience, against the entire Frisian nation on their terrain. It is a recipe for disaster."

Flavius frowned. "You certainly are not circumspect. Your words border on sedition. You are putting me in a difficult position. I cannot disobey orders from Generals Labeo or Pallus."

Valerius replied, "No one is asking that you defy any orders, but you must realize that our survival may depend on your actions. What I'm suggesting is that whatever commands are issued, you must proceed with caution. The Frisii will fight, perhaps as early as tomorrow. When they do, you can expect some sort of ruse. Their leaders are smart and ruthless men. They adapted their siege tactics and came within a whisker of taking Flevum. Our attached forces will be with you tomorrow. We stand ready to assist the first cohort, but we need to think before we act. Beware of a trap. In my opinion, the Frisii will not engage in straight-up battle with the Fifth Legion unless they have an advantage."

Flavius sipped his wine, staring off into space. "The danger posed by this campaign is not lost on me. I have experience fighting with the legions. I was stationed on the Danubius, and those tribes were always rebelling against Rome. Lots of fighting with a tough adversary. That region remains unsettled, much as we would like to believe that the territory is at peace. I do not believe we will ever have full control over those people." He looked toward the tent's opening to ensure that no one was outside listening. "But I digress. Back to our thorny problem here in the land of the Frisii. To be blunt, Generals Labeo and Pallus are clueless. Neither has any experience fighting rebellious Germans. We must be allies in this endeavor. I would like to reach old age and retire one day."

Marcellus grinned in acknowledgment. "Centurion Flavius, do not hesitate to deploy our forces in support of your own. We will back you and obey your commands. When this is all over, I will buy you all the wine you can drink." He raised his cup to Flavius. "Here's to tomorrow."

CHAPTER XXIII

THE CONFLICT BEGINS

E adric stood in front of the other Frisian chieftains, who perhaps numbered thirty. Much to his relief, none of the clans had abandoned the cause despite the dreadful losses they had incurred in the siege of Flevum. Over eighteen thousand warriors were still ready to fight and defend their homeland. A fire burned in front of the assembly, casting shadows in the night. Eadric began. "The Romans are pursuing us. They are about to enter the Baduhenna Wood and are seeking us out. Tomorrow, they will find us."

A mighty roar arose from the gathered chieftains. Eadric held up his arms for silence. When all was quiet, he spoke. "This is my plan. Tomorrow, we will present our forces, or I should say, some of them, for battle against the Romans. I don't want them to discover our true numbers. I want them to believe that many have abandoned the cause. Now, listen carefully. We will assemble on terrain that provides an escape path for us. I don't want to have our full force engage with the Romans—that would be a blunder. Their heavy armor and formations would destroy us. Instead, we do this—we fight, put up a resistance, and then melt back into the forest where they cannot pursue us."

He could see disappointment etched upon the faces of many. "I know you are thinking this is no way to defeat the Romans. You might ask why we are doing this. I will tell you why: I want the Romans drawn deeper into the Baduhenna Wood. I want them to be reckless and overconfident and to think that they can destroy our forces because we are not that many in number and flee at their presence. Not tomorrow, but the day after, we will spring the trap. It will be like this." Eadric talked long into the night and the tribal chieftains eagerly listened to his every word.

▲

The next morning, the cornua blared as the Fifth Legion advanced into the Baduhenna Wood. The men of the Fifth concentrated on putting one leg in front of the other. This would get them that much closer to their destination at the end of the day. After three hours of marching, the order was given to halt and take a break. They had come across two small villages, both abandoned. The Fifth did not deploy and the collection of dwellings was spared from burning, probably because they were judged to be insignificant.

Lucius and his friends collapsed in a heap. Up and down the column, other legionnaires mirrored their actions. They were positioned in a wide field that was now devoid of crops. Rays of sunlight slanted down from a pristine sky filled with puffy white clouds. Lucius removed his helmet and poured some of the contents of his goatskin canteen over his head. Ox gasped and drained most of his water.

Lucius chuckled. "Don't like being a legionnaire, Ox? Back when I was a lad of eighteen and entered the legions, I was just as miserable as I am now. Maybe Rufus would add his two *sesterces*."

Wiping the sweat from his face with a rag, Rufus flashed a knowing grin. "Aye, a forced march will kick even the strongest man's arse. That's one of the reasons I retired. I told Tribune Valerius the same thing when he recruited me. The legions take a lot out of a man. I felt like I was getting too old for it. Even when I was on garrison duty, I knew my next assignment could be with a legion out in the hinterlands. But here I am right back where I started. I'm just concentrating on putting one leg in front of the other and ignoring the pain."

"I've had many jobs in my life, none of them too pleasant— laborer, bricklayer, bodyguard, quarry worker," said Ox. "They pale in comparison to this. I thought I would see men drop out of the march and collapse. Not one. These legionnaires are tough sons of bitches."

"The reason no one has dropped out," said Rufus, "is that they are terrified of the consequences. Their centurion would shove his vine staff up their arses."

"I did get that impression," said Ox.

"Everyone up," bellowed Centurion Glaucus. There was a collective groan as the men rose from the dirt. It was time to march.

⚔

Florus, Glaucus, Valerius, and Marcellus walked together on the dirt path. It had been a hard march. Glaucus sipped water from his goatskin container and then wiped his mouth with his arm. "What do you think, Tribune? Are we in danger?"

"If I'm reading the situation correctly, we are not—at least, not yet," said Valerius. "I sense that the Frisii want us drawn deeper into their territory. Furthermore, when and if they attack, it will be later in the day when the men are weary from marching. That is not to say we shouldn't be vigilant, but my reading is that we are safe for now."

"I concur," said Marcellus. "The tribune is correct. It is too early in the campaign for them to attack. My questions are how they will come at us and what surprises they will have in store for us. How we react to their strategy is critical. If they challenge us to battle in open terrain, watch out. It will be a trap of some sort or the other."

"Might they attack today?" Florus queried.

Marcellus shrugged and looked inquiringly at Valerius.

"Who knows? Marcellus and I had a frank discussion with Centurion Flavius. I like him. He is an experienced officer and knows his stuff. Has a good head on his shoulders. The man has fought tough tribes along the Danubius frontier. That is why he is in command of the first cohort. He is wary of the Frisii and does not underestimate them. Take heart. We will unite with his forces and fight our way out of whatever the Frisii throw at us."

By early afternoon, the legion had advanced several more miles. A decurion riding his horse thundered down to the command group. The surrounding bodyguards of the senior staff let the rider through. "General Labeo, the Frisii have been sighted at the end of a long narrow meadow about two miles ahead. Estimates are between six and eight thousand warriors."

Labeo grinned. "I knew they would stand and battle against us. Their pride will not let the legions destroy their villages." He smacked his fist into his open palm. "At last, we have them. Decurion, lead us to them. I will reconnoiter up ahead and then decide how to deploy my forces."

* * *

Valerius and Marcellus advanced with their detachment of Flevum forces over an open field toward a small knoll, where the Frisii awaited. The meadow had obviously been cultivated and used for grazing. The ground cover was a combination of tall grass and low shrubs. To the rear of the hillock was a heavily wooded area. They were now about two hundred yards away from the mass of warriors. Labeo had positioned the Fifth so that cohorts one through six were abreast of one another on line, three ranks deep. Each rank was in open formation, meaning that there was enough width between men to throw their pila. Cohorts seven through ten remained behind, acting as a reserve force.

The three centuries of men from Flevum, the recruited mercenaries, and the conscripted civilians were in the middle of the first cohort. Valerius had positioned himself with the third rank so that he could observe the ebb and flow of combat and adjust his forces as necessary. The armor of the legionnaires clinked and jangled as the men advanced. Each legionnaire gripped his shield with his left arm while in his right, he held a single pilum. The green grass was flattened and bruised as the legionnaires' boots struck the earth.

When they were about one hundred paces away, the Frisii began shouting and waving their spears. Unruffled, the Fifth continued its advance. The ranks of legionnaires edged closed to the knoll. The men gripped their pila tighter, anticipating the enemy to heave their spears when they were in range.

At about fifty paces, the Germans heaved their light spears in volleys, showering the Roman legionnaires with javelins.

"SHIELDS UP!" bellowed the centurions and optios. The men angled their shields to deflect the arcing missiles. Most of the spears rattled harmlessly off the sturdy shields and armor of the men, but some found their mark. Men collapsed with projectiles jutting from their bodies. There was a slight hesitation in the advance of the cohorts as they stopped to repel the deadly spears and step around their wounded comrades, but they continued forward relentlessly.

Despite the loss of some of the men, the ranks quickly reformed. When they approached within about twenty-five paces, commands were issued. "First rank, release pila." The second and then the third ranks marched forward and released their spears. The Roman javelin was much heavier than its German counterpart. Its range was more limited, but its penetrating power was deadlier. Thousands of javelins were heaved in waves at the ill-fated Frisii, who had no defense for the front-loaded spears. Their small oval hide shields were no match for the weighted javelins. Men crumpled to the ground in scores.

The command for close ranks was shouted. The gap between the men was narrowed so that they were almost shoulder to shoulder. Up and down the line, the command to draw swords was shouted. The six cohorts then charged into the ranks of the Frisii, barreling their way forward with the bosses on their shields. Despite the carnage reaped by the pila, the Frisii held their ranks and surged back against the Roman soldiers. The air was filled with the screams of men and the clash of shields. The troops were initially evenly matched, but the Roman forces began to slowly gain the upper hand and push the Frisii back.

▲

Lucius charged into the Germans at the crest of the hill. There was a shallow ditch there and the spoil had been used to build an elevated position for the Frisian warriors. But this was hardly a deterrent to the Roman forces. Lucius's shield was locked with that of Ox and Rufus on either side. The Roman lines presented a wall of shields out of which protruded their deadly stabbing swords.

Lucius easily navigated the ditch and thrust his shield slightly upward into the massed ranks of the Frisii. He experienced a moment of dread as a spear point glanced off his chest armor. Recovering quickly, he propelled his shield forward and then stabbed with his sword. His weapon struck flesh and he heard a brief scream. Making sure he was aligned with Ox and Rufus, he pushed forward. There was resistance, but the German lines edged backward slightly. He kept advancing, thrusting, and stabbing. After a while, he felt a familiar fatigue growing in his arms. The line advanced farther.

The centurion blew his bone whistle. Relieved, Lucius stepped back as another legionnaire from the second ranks took his place. He rested his right arm, lowering his sword. To his amazement, the German line began to retreat at a slow, measured pace. He looked toward Ox and Rufus who grinned widely. It appeared that the fighting was almost over. Their century had advanced about fifty paces when the order was issued to halt in place.

▲

Valerius watched the battle unfold. He frowned as he spied several crumpled figures among the ranks of his men. He looked to his left and right to ensure that his men were interspersed with the ranks of the first cohort and that there was no breach in the lines. There wasn't. Valerius and Marcellus moved forward with their men as the Germans wilted under the charge of the armored legionnaires. Shields smashed forward and deadly swords stabbed repeatedly into human flesh. The Frisii buckled under the thunderous charge. He then heard wild cheering and observed the Frisii gradually melting back into the forest behind the hilltop. It was not a panicky retreat but a slow, methodical process. At no time did the Frisii show their backs to the Romans.

The centurions in the front ranks bellowed for the men to hold at the edge of the wood. It would not be prudent to break ranks and charge haphazardly into the thick forest. Thus, the battle was abruptly over, the area littered with dead and dying Frisii.

▲

The legion, as was customary, built a fortified camp in the center of the meadow late that afternoon. The camp was quickly laid out in a rectangular fashion, earthen walls were constructed, and ditches were dug. Ordinarily, the men would have pitched their tents, but as the mules were not with the marching column, the tents had been left behind. In the fading twilight, Valerius and Marcellus sat with Florus and ate their evening rations of porridge and sour wine supplemented by cheese and hard biscuits. Valerius was dusting the crumbs off his hands when a messenger appeared before him. "Tribune Valerius Maximus, General Labeo requests your presence immediately."

Valerius shot Marcellus a weary glance. "I wonder what in Hades he wants of me now. I hope to be back shortly," he announced. He followed the messenger to the headquarters area of the encampment and announced himself to the commander of the guard, who in turn, entered General Labeo's command tent. He returned shortly thereafter. "The General will see you now."

Valerius brushed aside the tent flaps and walked past the two legionnaires guarding the entrance of the command tent. The spacious interior was illuminated with glowing lamps. Seated at a long wooden table was Labeo. Joining him were several tribunes and Generals Urbicus, Terentius, and Pallus. Also in attendance was Tigranus. They were feasting on roasted meats, fresh fruit, and vegetables. The aroma of the rich food wafted through the confines of the tent and cups of red wine sat by their plates.

Labeo looked up. "Ah, Tribune Valerius Maximus, my expert on German tactics," he said in a condescending tone. "Well, the Frisii were no match for the legions today, were they?"

Valerius knew he was being baited and decided it was futile to respond with any words of caution about the cunning ways of the Germans. He paused to form a coherent response.

"Well, out with it, Tribune. Admit you were wrong about these Germans. They are not a worthy foe for the legions, are they?" Several of the senior officers smirked at Labeo's mocking banter.

Valerius chose a tactful response. "Sir, the Fifth Legion won a great victory over the Frisii today. They were no match for the legions. Congratulations to you and your staff."

But Labeo was not finished. "Oh, come now. You can do better than that. Are you not going to take this opportunity to warn me again about the Frisii and their mighty warriors? Are you not disappointed that your Frisii did not give us a stiffer battle?"

"No, sir. I am thankful that the legions won such an easy victory with such small losses today. I hope we route the Frisii and teach them a painful lesson."

Labeo was disappointed that he could not draw Valerius into the conversation, which only made him angrier. His voice rose. "Some German expert you are. How could you get it so wrong with your years of experience? You know what I think? I believe your so-called knowledge was based more on luck and that time has passed you by. After all, you have been a merchant for too many years." He made a show for his audience, reveling in Valerius's humiliation. "Now, you listen to me, Tribune. I don't want to hear from you or see your face for the rest of the campaign. I shall make a full report to Governor

Gallus as to your conduct, which frankly, leaves a lot to be desired. You are an impediment to the Fifth Legion. Understood?"

"Yes, sir. Will that be all?"

The agitated Labeo bit out a response. "Yes, now get out of my sight."

Valerius exited the tent amid derisive laughter.

He ventured back to where the Flevum forces were located. Spying Marcellus, he waved for him to join him. He strode away swiftly and Marcellus had to hurry to keep pace.

"Are we in a race or are you prepping me for tomorrow's march?" Marcellus inquired.

Valerius was silent, and if anything, increased his pace. Marcellus had to run to catch up.

"What gives?"

"As you are aware, I was summoned to Labeo's headquarters. That flaming arsehole is going to get us all killed."

"I assumed your meeting did not go well, but how do you really feel?"

Valerius halted and sighed. "He made a great show of disparaging me in front of his senior staff, who, I might add, are a bunch of sniveling, arse-kissing know-nothings. We must speak with Centurion Flavius and convince him that there is a real threat here that is not typified by what we saw today from the Frisii. We need to warn him."

The two men were ushered into Flavius's headquarters once more. Flavius dismissed his two aides with a nod and sternly eyed the two officers. "Somehow, I don't think this is a social visit, and I'm not going to like what you have to tell me."

"That would be an understatement," said Valerius. "I was just summoned to Labeo's tent, where he mocked me in front of his officers. I don't care about that as much as his attitude. He thinks it is going to be an easy triumph tomorrow or the next day. I would pose these questions. First, what happened to that ferocious fighting spirit that the Frisii demonstrated in the siege at Flevum? It certainly wasn't evident today. In fact, their behavior was almost cowardly. Second, where are the rest of the Frisii? Their numbers today were perhaps a third of the force that assaulted Flevum."

Flavius threw up his hands. "I don't know. Perhaps the other Frisii were disgusted with the results and deserted."

"Yes, and I'm going to sprout wings out of my arse and fly home." Marcellus rolled his eyes.

"Centurion Flavius, I firmly believe that today's performance, and that's what it was—a performance—was but a giant ruse. The Frisii want to suck us in, overconfident and relaxed. Then, they will strike," said Valerius.

Flavius exhaled noisily. "I believe you are on to something. In my years of fighting the tribes along the Danubius, I have never seen a foe retreat so readily. I would hardly characterize it as stiff resistance or a fierce contest. In any event, it was highly suspicious. I take it our esteemed commander bought this deception?"

"He did. As we speak, he is crowing to his subordinates about teaching the Frisii a lesson they will never forget. It is you, Centurion Flavius, who must bring order and caution to our campaign. I don't mean to put the burden on your shoulders, but you are by far the most experienced officer of the Fifth."

Flavius mulled over his words. "I will do what I can without being insubordinate. But I can only do so much. My centurions of the first cohort will listen to me. I also will confer with the centurion leaders of the other cohorts and urge caution and restraint in the pursuit of the Frisii. They know I'm an experienced commander who has seen a lot of combat."

"Thank you, Centurion. I know we are asking much from you, but as you can surmise, our survival may depend upon it. See you in the morning." Valerius and Marcellus exited the tent.

▲

Later that evening, General Labeo sat at his table with Tigranus standing by his side. Flickering oil lamps cast dappled shadows across the command tent. It was nearing midnight and all the other aides and staff had been dismissed. Facing the two men was a legionnaire attired in the typical armor and outfit of the legions, standing in attention. Labeo glared hard at the figure. "Report, Legionnaire Felix. What do you have for me?"

Felix was an ordinary legionnaire in appearance, with nothing unusual or remarkable about him, which was why Labeo employed him as a spy. He informed on his fellow legionnaires and officers, especially those who were critical of Labeo. "Sir, earlier this evening, I observed Centurion Marcellus Veronus and Tribune Valerius Maximus enter the tent of Centurion Marcus Flavius. They remained there for some time."

Labeo cursed. "Those meddlesome whoresons!" He angrily slammed his fist on the table. "Continue with your report, Legionnaire Felix."

"Sir, I ventured close to the tent and could hear them speaking in hushed tones. But when I got closer, one of Flavius's guards chased me away."

"You could not discern the subject of their conversation?"

"No, sir, but they were speaking in muted voices. Clearly, they didn't want to be overheard."

Labeo scowled. "Very well, Felix. Continue to observe Flavius and the other two. Report back to me if you hear or see anything. You are dismissed."

"Yes, sir." The legionnaire did an about-face and retreated from the tent.

Labeo rubbed his jaw in thought. "Flavius is one of my most experienced officers. Now, I have those two merchants—and that is what they are, merchants, not Roman officers—corrupting his thinking."

"My father wanted those two troublemakers and their forces placed at the front of the legions so that they might be killed in combat with the Germans," said Tigranus. "That would solve our difficulties."

"The problem is, Tigranus, that given the level of resistance we have encountered from the Frisii, they may not be a reliable solution to our dilemma," sighed Labeo.

"Then have them murdered!" exclaimed Tigranus. "I'm sure you can find men who will do the deed without question or remorse."

"Much as I would like to pursue that course of action, it is not a sensible alternative—not in the legionary camp. It would be too suspicious. If word reached the Emperor that his chosen emissaries were murdered by legionary forces, then I would be dog meat. There are many eyes and ears within a Roman camp. I fear that word would get back to Rome. No, killing them outright, while it offers a desirable outcome, has the risk of severe consequences. I'm currently thinking of diminishing their role in our triumph over the Frisii. That way, they will have no standing. I am going to place the first cohort in reserve along with that mutinous filth, Marcus Flavius. They will receive no glory in our conquest. When this is all over, I am going to send Flavius to the remotest outpost in the empire, to take charge of a collection of stinking auxiliary forces. Serves the prick right."

"I would rather see them all dead, especially that Tribune Maximus," said Tigranus. "I know my father wants them killed."

Labeo sighed in frustration. "I understand your passion for their demise, but it is not a practical alternative. Perhaps when all of this is over and done with and they are no longer under the protection of the Emperor, your father can facilitate their deaths. Until then, I shall have them relegated to the rear echelons."

CHAPTER XXIV

ENSNAREMENT

The next morning, the Fifth advanced another five miles northward, following the dirt track that served as one of the main Frisian roads. At mid-afternoon, the Frisii were sighted massed on a hilltop; the crest was replete with a breastwork of earth and a ditch in front of it. The summit was at the far end of a long, sloping meadow, which featured cleared fields and thick woods bordering both flanks. The cavalry reported that the estimated number of Frisii on the summit were substantial, many more than had showed themselves the day before.

Valerius, Marcellus, Florus, and Glaucus gathered with their men, the Flevum force, who numbered about three hundred, in the shade of an oak grove. Only Flavius had been invited to the council of war convened by Labeo. Valerius knew it was a deliberate slight, but his feelings were his least concern right now. Was this the trap the Frisii were planning to spring on the Fifth Legion? It could be. The high sloping terrain and the breastwork fortifications on top would make it far more difficult to dislodge the Frisii than the day before. In his experience, the Germans rarely established a fortified position, although Arminius had deployed this stratagem against Varus on the final day in the Teutoburg. The strength of the German forces was their mobility. They were not bogged down by heavy armor and baggage trains. The legions, he surmised, would eventually overcome the physical obstacles thrown up by the Frisii. He assumed the Frisii probably knew this, so what did they hope to achieve? They were not protecting anything of value, so why this location? Looking up to study the terrain from afar, he tried to put himself in the position of the Germans. What would he do in their place?

Like a lightning bolt, it hit him. They would hide many of their forces in the woods. Once the Fifth threw itself at the breastwork, pinned in place, the Germans would envelop the cohorts of the Fifth. They would attack out of the woods on one or both sides of the meadow and then, eventually, encircle the Romans from the rear.

Before he could voice his thoughts to the others, he spied Marcus Flavius returning from the officers' conference. He walked disconsolately toward them, a scowl darkening his face. "I am going to assemble all the centurions and optios of the first and second cohort to explain our role in this battle. The legion will attack the Frisii earthworks in short order, but the first and second cohorts have been placed in reserve under my command."

Valerius was flummoxed. Why would Labeo put his most seasoned officer and his best fighting cohort in the rear? "Marcus, I believe Labeo knows you have consulted with us. He is punishing you because of us. What other explanation could there be? I'm sorry I've put you in this position."

"I deliberated on the matter and came to the same conclusion on the way back here. Labeo told me he wanted some of the other cohorts to share the glory in our upcoming victory. He thought I would buy that horseshit," scoffed Flavius.

"Listen, Marcus, I believe the Frisii are setting a trap for the Fifth Legion. Those earthworks are there to fix the Roman forces in place. Then, they will attack out of the forests on either side, enveloping our forces. It is a deception. Your cohort must ensure the Frisii don't get behind us."

"There is no strategic reason for them to defend this ground. I would wager that their flight from their position yesterday was a ruse so our commander would be overconfident," said Marcellus.

Marcus Flavius thought about their words for a while. "Shit," he sighed, "I believe I agree with you. This could go very badly for us. Come on, let's meet with the officers of the two cohorts. We will need to be extra vigilant."

Marcus Flavius stood before the twenty officers of the first and second cohorts. He had been a busy man these past few hours. He had quietly met with each of the centurion leaders of the other eight cohorts, some individually and others in groups, cautioning them of a potential trap and advising caution. He knew the officers trusted his judgment and listened to him. Now, he was speaking with the officers of the reserve cohorts. "Listen up. The first and second cohorts have been designated as reserves in the assault against the Frisii. Those are our orders and we will follow them. Now, this is important. The German forces may be setting a trap for us. They might attack from our flanks and rear. We must not get too close to the lead units. General Labeo is attacking on a wide front using the third through seventh cohorts with the eighth through tenth behind them. We will be in reserve. Be alert for commands to defend our flanks and rear. Above all, do not get sucked up in the atmosphere of a quick victory and overrunning the Frisii fortifications. We must remain alert."

The assembled officers nodded in agreement.

"Any questions?" Flavius asked. There was silence. "Good. Wait for my commands to move. You are dismissed."

▲

Lucius stood with Ox, Rufus, and the other recruited mercenaries. They had discarded their forked marching poles and assorted gear and would go into battle with a single pilum plus sword and shield.

Rufus stared wistfully at the distant hilltop and the earthen ramparts. "I hope this battle ends this campaign. I retired from the legions six months ago, yet here I am in the armor of a legionnaire and equipped with the sword and shield. I retired because I sensed I was getting too old for this shit. It is a hard and dangerous life. Make no mistake about it."

"No one twisted your arm to sign up with the tribune and centurion," quipped Ox. "This is of your own making."

"Thanks for the sympathetic ear, Ox, but two things. First, I didn't sign up to be with the Fifth Legion. That wasn't part of the deal. Second, had I known how little my legionnaire's pension would sustain me, I probably would have stuck to my job. I needed the coin, same as you."

"Quit your grumbling, Rufus. What about poor Lucius here? Talk about a raw deal. This is the second time he has been unwillingly conscripted into the service of Rome, and he has a wife and family. Right, Lucius?"

Lucius finished nibbling on a hard biscuit. After dusting the crumbs off his hands, he spoke, "This is not the business trip I had planned with my wife to sell our wine to new markets, but it isn't the Teutoburg Forest either. So far, this has been tame stuff. I have every intention of surviving this campaign and returning to my home and family in Gaul. The gods spared me in the Teutoburg disaster for a reason, and I'm sure it wasn't to perish in another stinking German forest. This campaign needs to end."

"Well said, Lucius," voiced Ox.

All heads turned as Valerius approached the group of mercenaries. "As you are aware by now, we are to be held in reserve today. That is a good thing. We are concerned this is a ploy engineered by the Frisii. They might come at us from the flanks and rear. Our forces are to approach with caution and not get too close to the assaulting cohorts. Be on guard. Listen up for commands."

▲

Like a giant wave, the Fifth Legion marched through the meadow and up the hill in good order. The lines were dressed and formations intact. The air was cool and clean; the unit standards rippled in the gentle breeze. The centuries of the third through seventh cohorts deployed into ranks three deep. At the summit, the Germans raised a mighty shout, waving their spears and beating them against their shields. The ranks of the legions did not respond. They advanced in silence, seemingly unperturbed. Their armor creaked and clanked. The ranks marched forward at a steady pace.

From his position in the rear, Valerius watched the eight cohorts of the legion—almost four thousand men—trudge the length of the meadow toward the summit. The first and second cohorts were about four hundred paces behind the main body of the legion along with the baggage trains. The Flevum force was stationed in the middle, between the first and second cohorts. Glancing to his left and right, he was relieved to see that Marcus Flavius had positioned the cohorts such that they were in a curved formation, protecting the flanks from an attack. Still, he felt trepidation. The German leaders probably knew they could not withstand a frontal assault from the heavy infantry of the legions. The Frisii, he was certain, had other plans.

▲

Eadric stood with his fellow chieftains behind the thick earth wall his warriors had been preparing even before the lopsided defeat the Frisii had incurred the day before. The wall was topped with sharpened sticks as thick as a man's wrist, which were embedded deeply into the dirt at about waist height. He knew the Romans would take the bait and attack his fortified position. It was just their nature. Their desire to punish the Frisii for their revolt and their deep-seated sense of superiority dictated the Roman strategy. If he had his way today, that feeling of supremacy would be turned against them, and they would be destroyed. Eadric was confident of his planned ensnarement, yet he remained anxious. He knew and understood what a formidable fighting force the Roman legions were. Many things could go wrong with his plan, including his forces being swept from this summit.

Eadric watched in part fascination, part dread as the solid wall of shields and clanking armor approached the Frisian fortifications. The Germans shouted insults and banged their shields. As the noise reached a crescendo, his signaling horns blew. A shower of javelins descended on the approaching legionnaires. Most bounced off the shields and armor of the iron ensconced Romans, but some found their mark. A second wave and then a third wave of javelins rained down upon the legionnaires, wounding and killing even more; yet, the Romans still approached, undeterred.

At a range of about twenty-five paces, the Romans unleashed their own heavily weighted spears, which were capable of piercing any shield or armor the Germans possessed. The Frisii had been instructed to duck and hide behind their fortification when the Roman javelins were released. Waves of legionnaires marched forward and threw their pila. While the warriors in front of the fortifications were protected, the rear ranks of the Frisii were not. Many succumbed to the heavy front-loaded javelins that pierced flesh. The groans and cries of the wounded and dying emanated from the Frisian rear.

The Romans then drew their swords and charged. Their momentum was blunted by the steep dirt wall and timber barricade. The Germans had the benefit of an elevated position and used it to their advantage, thrusting downward with their spears at the advancing Romans. It was a killing ground for both sides. The Frisii held their ranks; if a warrior fell on the front ranks, he was quickly replaced by another. They were also stacked four to five men deep so that any opening in the ranks at the top of the wall was quickly sealed. The Roman assault was stopped. They charged again, and yet again, but to no avail.

* * *

Quintus Pius, decurion of the fourth turma of the Fifth Legion, sat astride his horse, watching and making sure that all thirty of his men remained within shouting distance of each other. The riders painstakingly maneuvered their mounts through the heavy forest on the left flank of the legion, which was now advancing up the wide meadow. Another turma scouted the right flank. They were the screening force ensuring that the flanks of the legion were secure. Ordinarily, this duty was delegated to three or more turma, but given the density of the woods, the commander of the cavalry, Centurion

Satorius, had decreed that only one turma would be utilized for each flank.

Decurion Pius halted his mount. His men were, by his reck-oning, about two hundred paces from the edge of the open meadow. Through the trees, he could distinctly hear the harsh sounds of battle. Pius rose in his saddle and brushed aside an offending sapling so that he could have a clearer view of the woodland. The sapling sprung back, lashing him across the face. "Mithras's fat arse," he swore, "I can't see a bloody thing in these woods."

One of his riders stifled a chuckle at the decurion's swearing. Pius gave him a prickly look. "It's not funny, Bartelus. How are we supposed to scout the flanks through this thick shit? It's impossible."

But Bartelus would never get a chance to answer. There was a slight disturbance in the air, and in the next moment, a lance pierced through Bartelus's throat. Shocked at the sudden attack, Pius, a seasoned veteran who had spent many years in the saddle, hesitated only briefly before bellowing a command to his riders. "Back to the meadow!"

Those were his last words. Several lances penetrated the thin armor worn by the cavalry. The remaining riders were swarmed by hundreds of Frisian warriors, who had been concealed in the forest. The Romans were dragged from their horses and ruthlessly dispatched. In a matter of minutes, the entire turma was brutally killed by the Germans. As the last of the Roman cavalry were slain, a vast horde of Germans materialized from the trees to join their brethren who had eliminated the Roman cavalry. As one, they stormed through the wood toward the Roman left flank in the meadow.

▲

General Labeo sat astride his mount and viewed the carnage taking place to his front. He and his staff were situated between five cohorts in the front and three cohorts behind them. This positioning enabled him to see the battle's developments so that he could adjust the deployment of his forces as needed. He and the other officers were surrounded by a cordon of bodyguards. The uproar before him was a combination of screams and the clash of weapons. He frowned, annoyed. Not only had his heavy infantry force of five cohorts not yet penetrated the earthen fortifications, but they appeared to be taking significant casualties. "Why have we not overtaken the Frisian redoubt?" he said to no one in particular. He turned to his second-in-command, General Pallus. "I want the other three cohorts brought forward from their secondary position to reinforce the attack. The fresh cohorts can have a go at the Frisii. This should tip the balance. Bring them forward, now."

Valerius stood with his fellow officers, Marcellus, Florus, and Flavius, at the base of the sloping hill. They gawked as the three cohorts behind the five cohorts began marching forward. Flavius was quick to react. He grabbed one of his messengers. "Tell Centurion Crispus of the second cohort that he is to ignore the cohorts' deployment to our front and is not to advance. He must stand fast. Now go." With that, he strode in front of the first cohort and began bellowing above the din to the front. "We are not to move. Our position is here. We are the reserve. We protect the baggage trains and the rear."

Valerius stood there transfixed at the battle before him, wondering what would happen next. From this distance, it appeared that the legions were having a tough time dislodging the Frisii from the hilltop. Suddenly, from the woods on both flanks, screaming hordes of Germans materialized. The eight cohorts near the summit were now in danger of being surrounded.

General Labeo gaped at the events unfolding before him. Where had all these Germans come from? How was this possible? His horse reared in fright as his cordon of bodyguards was assaulted by waves of Germans. His command group was now isolated at the rear of the eight attacking cohorts. He stared in horror as his trusted adjutant, Lollious Urbicus, toppled from his saddle, his throat pierced by a lance.

Labeo glanced about anxiously. "Sound the recall immediately!" he shouted. "We must retreat."

The commanders of the eighth, ninth, and tenth cohorts, directly behind the first five cohorts, displayed remarkable judgment. The three centurion's leaders did not lose their heads and recognized the extreme peril of the situation. Marcus Flavius's discussions with them about the dangers that might arise today had been well received. Thank Jupiter and Mars they had listened to him when he had spoken to them last night and trusted his judgment. Without waiting for orders from Labeo or his staff, they began to fall back from the five cohorts in front toward the surrounded command group while, at the same time, maintaining contact with the third through the seventh cohorts. All the while, the Frisii savagely attacked from every direction.

Much to the relief of the cohorts assaulting the breastworks, the command for the fall back resonated through the ranks. The cornua blew their mournful tones, signaling the legion to retreat. They slowly began to disengage from the Frisii on the summit, leaving hundreds of dead and dying comrades on the redoubt. Broken shields, lances, and helmets littered the path of the retreating Romans.

Eadric, from his position at the height of the summit, grinned wolfishly. His ambush had worked to perfection. He had used the aggressive tactics of the legions to his advantage, but he was not finished with them—not even close. Repulsing the Roman forces was not the end of his strategy. He was intent on making a large dent in the Fifth Legion, perhaps even destroying their entire force. As planned, his men began streaming out of the sally gates of the fortifications and pressing the legions as they withdrew.

Hounded from all sides, the eight cohorts began their ragged retreat down the sloping meadow toward the reserve force under Flavius and the baggage trains. The Roman legions were a force of heavy infantry who were best utilized when in attack mode and on the offensive, not while retreating. The sheer numbers of the Germans overwhelmed the Roman lines in places, resulting in the annihilation of entire isolated centuries. The resulting struggle was not without cost to the Frisii, however. The heavy armor of the legions still proved to be a huge advantage in individual combat. Many of the attacking Frisii were slain upon the Roman shield wall.

Centurion Marcus Flavius, in the rear with the reserve forces, observed the carnage being inflicted on the Fifth. Despite his attempt to display a calm countenance, his face flashed with rage. He turned to Marcellus, Valerius, Florus, and Centurion Glaucus. "Help me get things organized here. This is what I want to do. The Frisian forces are surrounding the retreating cohorts. They hope to block their retreat by placing their forces between the eight cohorts and us. We must not let that happen. We are going to advance in a squared formation and meet up with the main body of the army, thus squashing the Frisii in between. We will be one force again and use our shield walls to slay the enemy. Understood?"

Valerius nodded. "I will request Marcellus to inform the second cohort of your intentions. Tribune Florus and Centurion Glaucus can see to our Flevum force and get them to man a sector of the box," said Valerius. "What about the baggage trains? They will be unprotected."

Flavius grimaced. "Can't be helped. We must ensure the survival of the legion."

Back up on the slope, the measured retreat of the eight cohorts lacked cohesion as waves of Germans savagely attacked the front, flanks, and rear of the retreating legion. Shield walls were penetrated and gaps appeared in the Roman lines. The meadow became a swirling vortex of destruction as hundreds perished on both sides.

Eadric sent wedge-shaped formations of Frisii out of the forest aimed directly at the command group. This is where he concentrated his assault. The wave of Frisii crashed into the personal bodyguard of the command staff. At first, the resistance was stiff and many of the German warriors fell to the swords of the legionnaires assigned to protect Labeo, but eventually, their sheer numbers overwhelmed the guards and they were slaughtered.

Labeo, surrounded by Frisian warriors, slashed left and right with his long sword. A warrior leaped on to his horse, knocking the General to the ground. Labeo rose unsteadily to his feet and stared into the faces of his executioners. Two Germans together stabbed Labeo in the throat, ending his life.

Nearby, with their instruments strewn upon the ground, all of the horn players lay dead—they had been easy pickings for the savage German assault. But what the Frisii had been unable to seize was the eagle standard. Junius Mallius, the *aquilifer* or eagle standard-bearer, had immediately recognized that things were going south. While he was not directly assigned a place in the formation, he generally stayed close to the command group. Upon seeing the wave of Germans streaming out of the forest from both flanks, he had quickly rushed to the safety of the center of the eighth cohort, which was directly behind the main assault group of the third through seventh cohorts.

It had not been an act of cowardice but far from it: Junius understood that if the eagle fell into enemy hands, the legion would be doomed. His task was to ensure that the eagle did not fall. He now raised the eagle standard high so everyone could see it.

Tigranus urged his horse down the slope of the meadow, a wild panic evident on his face. He had never envisioned such a thing happening. The legion was in danger of being destroyed. He had seen Labeo fall, and he was now without protection as all the bodyguards were dead. The smart play would have been to move forward toward the relative safety of the eight cohorts in front as they were much closer. Instead, he pressed his horse toward the rear, his sword dangling from his right hand. He spied an opening in the melee of men toward the safety of the distant reserve force. Heaving a sigh of relief, he whipped his horse with the flat side of his blade. His mount surged forward, trampling several Frisii. Onward he sped. He had almost reached his destination, but in an instant, his triumphant smirk was wiped away. He felt an incredibly heavy pain in his back. He looked down in horror and saw the tip of a spear protruding from his chest. He vomited gouts of blood. In a few moments, the horse made it back to the reserve cohorts; Tigranus did not.

The first and second cohorts advanced from their position in the rear. About three hundred yards separated the embattled retreating cohorts from Marcus Flavius's forces. The two cohorts were deployed in a squared formation, the ranks three men deep. The mass of legionnaires closed quickly with the Frisii attacking the eight cohorts, and they savagely tore into the Germans, trapping them between the two Roman forces. The battle raged late into the afternoon.

* * *

Lucius was exhausted, his armor and face covered in blood and his sword hanging limply at his side. He was too weak to hold the weapon any higher. He was now in the third rank of the Flevum centuries. He had already rotated into the front ranks three times. The reserve forces had advanced, battling the enemy that had sought to surround the eight cohorts of the Fifth. Now at the back, out of harm's way, his breath came in ragged gasps. On either side of him, Ox and Rufus hung their heads low in weariness. Soon, the signaling whistle would blow again, and they would move up to the second rank. If they were lucky, no one in the front rank would fall and they could rest in the middle rank until they moved forward to the front where the killing and dying was taking place. The din was overwhelming. The screams of men and the clash of weapons resonated in the air. Soon, the shrill whistle blew. Lucius tightened the grip on his rectangular shield and raised his sword to the waist level. The three men edged forward as the front rank melted back to the rear.

Valerius stood by Marcellus, observing the evolution of the battle. He was amazed that the Fifth had survived. The reserve cohorts had savaged the Germans, caught between two forces. However, the Roman forces were not without losses. The initial encirclement had wreaked havoc on the eight cohorts. The legion had lost many men, including from what he could determine, the entire senior command group. As for the Frisii, many were being slaughtered between the reserve forces and the retreating cohorts. The problem was that there were a lot more Frisii than Romans. He glanced anxiously toward where he had last seen Lucius. He thought he recognized his tall form amid the ranks of the Flevum centuries. *Good, he is still alive.*

The ranks of the reserve forces surged forward, closing the gap between the withdrawing cohorts and the first and second cohorts and trapping the Frisii between the two forces. A large cluster of Frisii attacked the reserve forces, their lines swelling. Unexpectedly, Valerius and Marcellus found themselves face to face with two adversaries. The Germans led with their spears, jabbing at them quickly. Valerius parried the thrust with his sword, knocking the spear aside. Before he could take advantage of this situation, another legionnaire stepped between the two men and knocked the Frisian over. The Roman then stabbed the German, silencing him. Marcellus was busy with his opponent when two legionnaires came to his aid, killing the Frisian. More Roman reinforcements arrived in the area. The sally of the Germans against the reserve cohorts was savagely eliminated.

▲

The shrill whistle sounded once more. Lucius gritted his teeth and advanced to the front ranks. He immediately engaged the German battling the legionnaire he was to replace. He pushed with his legs, leading with his shield. His adversary attempted to stab over the top of Lucius's shield, but he had no space to do so. Lucius jabbed low with his gladius, puncturing the man's right leg. The man screamed in pain and twisted away from the fray. Another took his place. He was a large youth, almost as big as Lucius but clearly inexperienced. With a mighty shout, Lucius smashed his shield into the small, round wooden shield of his opponent. The youth was knocked backward. Lucius was ready to follow through with a deadly thrust to end his life when the German horns blared the recall. The young Frisian scurried away, crawling on his hands and knees.

CHAPTER XXV

PARLAY

The officers of the shattered legion had assembled in the center of the Roman fortified encampment. Marcus Flavius, now the Roman supreme commander, had decided to relocate the Roman forces to the base of the hill in the meadow and dig the standard marching camp there. The exhausted soldiers did not complain. They excavated the earth as if their life depended upon it because it did. They dug ditches and used the spoil to build ramparts. Before dusk had settled over the area, the camp was completely encircled by the ditch and rampart. The Frisii had refrained from attacking, knowing they had the Fifth surrounded and at their mercy.

Centurion Crispus of the second cohort, Marcus Flavius's second-in-command, delivered his report of the legion's status. "The Fifth lost all of its senior officers today, including General Labeo and his lieutenant generals, and all of the tribunes of the Fifth except for Tribunes Florus and Maximus, who are appended staff. The total of our losses is still being tabulated. Several units have been commingled, and their centurions are dead. As best as I can discern, we are at less than fifty percent strength, probably closer to forty percent."

Marcus Flavius looked to Centurion Crispus. "Enemy losses?"

"Hard to say, Marcus, but once we recovered from the shock of the initial ambush, we slaughtered them. We really damaged them with our shield wall."

The anxious faces of the surviving officers turned to Centurion Flavius for direction. "I won't pretend to be the next Julius Caesar. What alternatives are available to us? We obviously can't stay here. We have a long way to go before we reach Flevum. What are we to do? Suggestions, gentlemen?"

There was a period of silence. Valerius stepped forward. "I have a plan. We should negotiate with them."

Muffled laughter and snorts of derision were heard. The men knew that the Germans never negotiated on the battlefield. Marcus Flavius gazed at Valerius. "And what are you going to do, ride out and talk to them?"

"Precisely. That is exactly what I propose. Look, there is a good chance I may get killed out there, but Eadric, who is their leader, may listen to me. I know from a tactical perspective that our odds are for shit. There are just too many Frisii out there for us to make it back to Flevum alive, but we have something to trade. We have a negotiating position."

Marcus Flavius gave Valerius a curious look. "Tell us what you will propose."

"Simple," replied Valerius. "They allow us to depart and return to Flevum peacefully. In exchange, the Frisii will benefit as follows: First, they will not incur more staggering losses of men. I sense that they are not fighting for glory or honor; they are fighting for the survival of their people as a result of the soaring tax burden imposed by Gallus. Next, I will propose that the legion return to Noviomagus and abandon Flevum. No more Roman forts in their lands. We probably cannot hold the fortress anyway, but that is for you to consider, Centurion Flavius. Last and most important, I will be Eadric's ally in that I intend to inform the Emperor exactly what transpired here over the last month. Perhaps Tiberius can be persuaded to hold off on any retaliation. Of course, that would be impossible if the Frisii were to wipe out the Fifth and take possession of the eagle standard. I cannot promise anything to this Eadric other than my best efforts to halt any vengeful response from Rome."

There was a stunned silence among the officers. "You think you can pull this off?" Flavius asked.

"I can certainly try. Do you have any other ideas?"

Marcus Flavius shrugged.

"Do I have your promise that we will abandon Flevum?" Valerius inquired.

Flavius grunted. "Yes. You do. As you noted, there is no way we could hold that fortress anyway. If the Governor decides to retake it, good for him, but he has no forces available to him now."

"Then I would like to formally request your permission, Centurion Flavius, as acting commander of the Fifth, to negotiate with the Frisii on behalf of Rome," said Valerius.

"It's not like we have a lot of options now. Go out and negotiate. Do you want me to come along with you?" Flavius inquired.

"No. I think the message will be better received if it is just me. Besides, you are too valuable to the Fifth if things go sideways out there, whereas I am not."

Valerius exited the *castrum* on horseback. The ponderous wooden makeshift barrier that served as a gate for the fortified camp was slowly swung open by two legionnaires. It was early evening but already, darkness was descending. To indicate his intentions of seeking dialogue, he waved a burning torch, which he held aloft. The beacon would be noticeable to anyone observing the Roman camp. About three hundred paces from the encampment, he halted.

A lone German warrior rode out to meet him. He pulled his horse up about twenty feet away from Valerius. He was silent and had a large scowl on his face. Valerius spoke in German. "I wish to discuss matters with a chieftain named Eadric. My name is Tribune Valerius Maximus. He knows me."

Without a word, the rider turned about and departed. Valerius waited, still astride his horse. The torch he held sparked and fizzled. He did not dare dismount in the event he needed to make a hasty retreat. After a short wait, a single rider approached. As the figure edged closer, Valerius recognized Eadric. The German halted about six feet away from the tribune, his expression blank.

"I see you are wearing your true colors tonight. Odd dress for a trader, no? Tell me why I should confer with you about anything. You are a deceptive man like most Romans. I should kill you now. It will be one less Roman to deal with tomorrow."

Valerius scoffed, "You could try, Eadric, but it would be you who would be slain, and that would be a pity. Now enough bravado. I have come out here in good faith to have an honest discussion with you. Will you not indulge me at least for a short while?"

Eadric replied, "How magnanimous of you. You have come out to talk now that you are in a hopeless position. Are you ready to face death tomorrow, Tribune?"

Valerius was silent for a moment, organizing his thoughts. "We should talk for a bit, Eadric. It could benefit both of us." Without waiting for an answer, Valerius dismounted and drove the pointed end of the torch into the ground.

Eadric sighed and dismounted as well. He approached Valerius till they were three paces apart. "Speak your piece."

"Very well. Just so you know, I really am a trader among the German people." Before Eadric could interrupt, Valerius held up his hand. "Let me finish, then you will understand what has transpired since early spring. As I was saying, along with my wife and several others, I have been a trader of goods in the German territory for over fifteen years—a successful and highly profitable one at that. Early this spring when the buds were just beginning to burst, I received a strange summons from Emperor Tiberius. I was to report to Rome immediately along with my colleague who you met back in your village, Marcellus, a retired centurion. I say strange since I am not a confidant of Tiberius, and I have not laid eyes on him for over fifteen years. When we arrived in Rome weeks later, we met with the Emperor. He said that he had solid intelligence that the Frisii were planning to revolt. My orders directly from him were to meet with Governor Gallus and arrange a discussion with your clan using my cover as a trader to determine your intentions. If there were hostilities, I was to assist Governor Gallus in any military campaign against you. Marcellus and I are experienced officers when it comes to fighting German tribes. Thus, Tiberius reinstated our previous ranks even though we had forfeited them many years ago. Now, I have a question for you that I think I know the answer to, but I will ask you anyway for confirmation. The Frisii have always been staunch allies of Rome. Why the insurrection?"

300

"The Frisii were comfortable with their relationship with Rome," Eadric began, "until this new Governor came into power. He nearly doubled our taxes. To pay them, we would have to sell our children into servitude. We had no choice. I hope you can understand our desperation. We pleaded with the Governor and his staff on several occasions, but our entreaties were rebuffed and not so politely, I might add. Now, I have a question for you. Who attacked you on the way to my village last month? I don't buy that story you told me about rival traders."

"I had heard there was a tax dispute but had no idea of the magnitude of the problem. This explains a lot, including, to answer your question, the attack on my group on the way to your village. The men who assaulted my trade delegation were hired by Governor Gallus to get rid of me. He did not want me meddling in his affairs or to know about his excessive tax levies. He didn't want word to get back to Tiberius on this matter."

Eadric stared at Valerius, contemplating his words. Finally, he spoke. "What do you propose?"

"Very simple. I want safe passage back to Flevum with what remains of the Fifth Legion."

Eadric scoffed, "You are in no position to negotiate."

"No, from a tactical perspective, I am not. But what I propose might be of great benefit to the Frisii."

"How?"

"When you attack tomorrow, we will slay many thousands more of the Frisii, and you will have many more widows to comfort. Don't argue with this point because you know it is true. Many will die at the swords of our shield wall. Next, assuming you are victorious, which is by no means certain, you will capture the sacred eagle standard of the

Fifth. Just so you understand, Eadric, I participated in Germanicus Caesar's reprisal campaign against the German tribes who perpetuated the ambush in the Teutoburg Forest. The objectives of the legions were to destroy the tribes responsible and recapture the eagle. It was a sickening slaughter of men, women, and children. Even the farm animals were slain. Is this what you wish for the Frisii? If you crush the Fifth Legion and take the eagle, you are inviting dire consequences."

"So what? Rome will probably retaliate anyway. We will be prepared for the invasion."

"Perhaps not, Eadric, and this is where I come in. Like it or not, I am your ally here. I will send a personal message to Emperor Tiberius informing him of the events that led to this conflict. Don't forget that the Emperor tasked me to be his envoy with the Frisii. He was unaware of the crushing tax burden that precipitated this revolt. In fact, he still does not know. I will describe Governor Gallus's conduct. He is not an honorable man. He is a despicable individual and solely responsible for this huge loss of lives. It will be my mission to see that he is replaced and punished to the full extent under Roman law. Next, Rome will abandon Flevum. Its continued survival would serve no useful purpose. In the end, you will have achieved what you desired—a separation from Rome without the devastating consequences of retaliation."

Eadric glowered at Valerius, contemplating his proposal. "How do I know you aren't just weaving a web of deceit with your words?"

"You don't. That is the risk you must take. Consider what I have told you about Gallus's duplicity in the attack upon my trade delegation. Do you have any other explanation for that? Furthermore, having me as an ally will focus Tiberius's attention on who exactly is responsible for this debacle."

"You should know, Roman, that we sent several delegations to meet with Gallus and his cronies to let him know that the tax burden would cripple my people. They mocked us. The Frisii had no other recourse than to break off relations with Rome and attack. Then, after we fled from Flevum when your reinforcements arrived, your legions foolishly pursued us into our territory. Frankly, you all deserve to die."

"Yes, well, I tried to persuade the late General Labeo of the futility of invading Frisian lands. He did not accept my advice and threatened to throw me in chains. The man was an inexperienced fool about military matters."

"Your commander is dead?"

"Yes, and we are all better off for it. He was a close ally of Gallus."

"You can get word to your Emperor about all of this?"

"As I said, I can document all of this and make sure it gets into Tiberius's hands. Then, it will be his decision. I can tell you that when I met with him in the spring, he was adamant that he wanted no more warfare with the Germans along the Rhenus border and beyond. The lands have been at peace for almost fifteen years. I have said my piece. Your thoughts?"

Eadric took a deep breath. "I will discuss your proposal with my chieftains. We must come to an agreement. When you begin your retreat tomorrow morning, you will have your answer." The man began to leave but then halted. He turned around. "One more thing, Roman. Assuming the Frisii let you walk, don't ever show your face in Frisian territory again."

"Acknowledged." Valerius mounted his horse, picked up the torch, and rode back to the Roman lines.

Valerius entered the gate and advanced toward where he knew the gathered officers awaited him. Anxious faces greeted him. "You are still in one piece and leaking from no holes?" Centurion Flavius quipped.

Marcellus helped him off his horse. "By Jupiter's arse, you have the biggest pair of stones for a tribune. I can't believe you are alive."

"Thanks for the vote of confidence," said Valerius drily. Before he was bombarded with questions, he addressed the group. "The long and short of it is this: I met with Eadric, their chieftain, and he was wary of me and my proposal. He does not have a lot of trust for any Roman, but he didn't say no. He communicated that this was something he needed to discuss with his fellow chieftains and that they would have to reach a consensus. We will have our answer when we march out tomorrow morning."

Marcus Flavius grunted. "Have any gut feel as to which way he was leaning?"

Valerius shook his head. "Difficult to say. On one hand, I believe he saw the wisdom of my logic, that is, Rome would be sure to retaliate if he were successful in destroying the Fifth and capturing the eagle. He knows of our reputation. He confirmed what I believed all along—that their revolt was triggered by an excessive tax burden that would cripple his people and force them into servitude. Their campaign was not based on seeking glory. I think this weighs in our favor. On the other hand, he doesn't trust me or any Roman for that matter. Furthermore, this might be a difficult sell to his warriors after all they have sacrificed. We have killed a lot of them. They want their revenge and rewards for their sacrifice. That about sums it up."

* * *

On the outskirts of the Roman camp, the German chieftains met in a wooded glade. A single large fire illuminated the faces of those gathered. Eadric stood before the overlords and began, "I received an interesting proposition this evening from a Roman tribune. I will put forth the terms as bluntly as possible. In exchange for letting the remainder of the Fifth Legion retreat to Flevum and then Noviomagus, they will abandon their fortress at Flevum. In addition, this tribune will petition their Emperor, Tiberius, not to retaliate against the Frisii for their revolt."

There was a great stirring and whispered conversations among the chieftains. Finally, a man stood up. He was one of the older leaders and went by the name of Andebert. "It seems to me that this is a shallow proposition. They don't have much of a negotiating position. All we have from them are promises. They say they will abandon Flevum and speak favorably of us to their Emperor. So what? In the end, they could reoccupy Flevum and make war on the Frisii with more of their legions."

One of the younger leaders, Cuthberht, rose to his feet and moved front and center. He was one of the more passionate men who had a strong desire to spill Roman blood. He had also been one of the strong advocates for crossing the Rhenus once Flevum had fallen and laying waste to the Roman settlement on the other side of the river. "This is nonsense. What a ludicrous proposition. I say we attack at dawn tomorrow and slay them all. That was our objective. Let us finish the job."

Many of the chieftains stood and shouted their approval. There was raucous cheering and whistling in favor of Cuthberht's proposal. Eadric raised his arms for silence. After the clamor had subsided, he spoke. "I believe we all understand your position, Cuthberht. In fact, those were my initial thoughts when the Roman made his proposition, but he elaborated as to why we should consider his offer. He said that the Emperor was unaware of why we have revolted and did not know of the new taxes. In fact, it was the tribune's mission to find out what was happening and report back. He is a trader of goods with the German tribes to the southeast of us on the Rhenus. I am inclined to believe the man. Now, he also stated that if we destroy the Fifth Legion and capture their eagle, it is certain that Rome will retaliate. The tribune said that he would act as our advocate if we refrained from attacking the Fifth on their retreat. He reminded me that if we choose battle tomorrow, there will be many more Frisian dead."

Another chieftain, named Dagrun, moved to the front. He was one of the elders who had long witnessed Roman–Frisii affairs. "Eadric, you are saying we should accept the Roman's proposal?"

"No, Dagrun. All I'm saying is that we need to consider all the aspects of what the Roman has said. It is not entirely without logic. His proposal has merit and should not be dismissed out of hand. It is for all of us to decide what the correct course of action is. Let us get it right and agree."

Cuthberht was enraged. "How can we even be considering this? It makes no sense. To me, the choice is clear. We must kill all the Romans and capture the booty. It will reflect highly on us." There was more cheering but not nearly as loud as when he had spoken previously.

Dagrun continued, "Cuthberht, let me remind you that our objective is not to earn glory and capture booty. Our purpose is to drive the Romans from our land so that we can live in peace as a people and ensure our survival without selling ourselves into slavery because of the tax burden." Others jumped forward, shouting their thoughts. The discussion continued long into the night.

The remnants of the Fifth Legion broke camp and cautiously marched out at the crack of dawn. As far as mornings went, this one was on the chilly side. Fog shrouded the landscape and dew dripped from the high grass and bushes. The Fifth was led out by the first cohort, which was at close to full strength, having been in reserve the previous day. Depleted cohorts had been combined to consolidate their forces. The Fifth was organized in a compact column so that they could defend against an attack from their flanks, front, or rear. All of the officers' tents had been abandoned. The space they had occupied in the carts was allotted to carry the severely wounded, who were piled on the floor of the carts. The vulnerable wagons were situated in the middle of the column for maximum protection. Each man walking in the column had his shield up and his sword drawn.

Valerius marched alongside Marcellus at the head of their auxiliary force, which was situated directly behind the first cohort. The sounds of the legion on the move resonated in the early dawn air. Armor clanked and jingled along with the thump of marching boots striking the earth. A few bird calls echoed eerily in the mist.

Valerius peered into the surrounding foliage for signs of an attack. He saw nothing but that was hardly a relief. It would be premature to feel safe at this point. He glanced at the forest beyond, searching for the Frisii, but the enveloping fog obscured visibility beyond thirty paces. "Let's hope it stays this calm," he said to Marcellus.

The centurion grunted. "We shall see. I don't trust them, but I fervently hope you were convincing in your arguments. I want to go home to my family."

The marching column of legionnaires plodded several miles down the dirt path, which was still muddied from their passage the previous day. The fog began to dissipate, offering some visibility. The scouts rounded a bend in the road. Off to the left was a slight ridge cleared of timber. The surviving cavalry trotted along the flanks, their heads rotating about, searching for any sign of threat. Suddenly the fog shifted and they saw German warriors standing silhouetted against the sky on the ridge, observing the serpentine Roman formation on the winding road. The legionnaires gripped their shields tighter, if that were possible, as all eyes were directed to the threat on their left flank. To a man, they all expected the Frisii to come charging down the slope and slam into the Roman ranks. However, the column moved forward without attack, and they advanced several more miles without incident.

Marcus Flavius sauntered toward Valerius and Marcellus from the head of the column. "I don't know how you did it, Tribune Maximus, but by Jupiter's arse, it appears they bought what you were selling. If they were going to attack, surely it would have been where that ridge shadowed our flank. I never thought we would see Flevum or Noviomagus again. No wonder you are a successful trader."

"Frankly, Centurion, I wasn't convinced that they were going to agree to my terms. I'm sure there was a serious debate about what we proposed. Assuming things remain peaceful, our next task will be dealing with the Governor and the Emperor. That might prove more difficult than the Frisii. We will need to discuss a coordinated strategy on how to proceed."

Flavius nodded. "Agreed, but let's get out of here first."

Engaged in intense conversation, Valerius and Marcellus marched apart from the others. "When we get back to Flevum, we must be careful to survive the Governor's wrath. He will stop at nothing to silence us," said Valerius. "We must find a way to communicate directly with Tiberius. We can't go through the Governor and have him distort our message to the Emperor. We must get our message directly to Tiberius without Sejanus getting his grubby hands on it."

Marcellus pursed his lips in deliberation. "I believe I may have a solution. A former colleague of mine, Quintus Sorvinius, is posted at Valkenberg. He directs all imperial correspondence and dispatches. If anyone can get a letter to Tiberius, it's him. He was a terrific centurion. Good man. Served with him many years in Germania. I meant to look him up when we were in Valkenberg this spring on our way to Rome, but there was no time. While we're at it, he can ensure that Lucius and Julia board a good ship back to Gaul. Quintus is a capable man of considerable influence."

"Sounds like a solution to our problems. Thank the gods you still have your contacts. I will not share our plan with Centurion Marcus Flavius. The less he knows, the better. We will simply tell him that we are leaving. No doubt Gallus will want to know where we are."

CHAPTER XXVI
RETURN TO FLEVUM

The walls of Flevum were in sight. The battered legion plodded their way toward the main gates. Centurion Flavius had sent word ahead by way of his cavalry informing them that they were returning and that they should be prepared to receive the wounded. A crowd had gathered outside the walls to welcome the survivors.

Julia and Hereca stood side-by-side holding hands—for they were now the best of friends—hoping to catch a glimpse of their husbands among the survivors. Both women broke into huge grins as they recognized Valerius and Lucius. They rushed forward and embraced their men, oblivious to their blood-spattered armor. Valerius hugged his wife and then broke free. "Forgive me for the brief reunion. I will catch up with you later, but for now, I must confer with Centurion Flavius on urgent matters. Much needs to be decided over the next several hours. I believe we are at high risk of facing the Governor's ire. Please assist Marcellus and see that our surviving mercenaries are well compensated for their services. I will join you later. Sorry, I cannot be with you; time is of the essence."

Soon after, Valerius was in a hushed conversation with Marcus Flavius in the headquarters within the fortress. "When are you departing for Noviomagus?" Valerius asked.

"First thing tomorrow morning. I will be on the lead ship. I believe it is my duty to inform Gallus of the defeat of the Fifth, the loss of his son, and the death of the legate, General Labeo. I will let him know we are abandoning Flevum as part of our agreement with the Frisii. There are probably not enough ships to transport the surviving legionnaires so I will arrange more transports to Flevum when I arrive at Noviomagus. We will need to dismantle all of the artillery pieces and take them with us. Tribune Florus can oversee that task. I'm sure the Frisii will be observing our actions from a distance."

"You will have to face great wrath, Marcus. Gallus will blame you for the death of his son and the defeat of the legion. Furthermore, you have usurped his authority by agreeing to abandon Flevum. He will want to throw you in chains."

"Agreed, but I had thought much about this on our march from the land of the Frisii. I will not meet with him by myself. I intend to have my staff and bodyguards with me. They are steadfast followers. The survivors of the Fifth Legion will remain loyal to me and not to that sorry-ass excuse for a Governor. They know who is responsible for the death of their friends and comrades."

"Centurion Flavius, that's fucking brilliant. You truly know how to take control of a bad situation. Now, listen to me; Gallus will want to know where I am. You will tell him you don't know because I am not going to inform you of my movements. You have no responsibility for me. Technically, I am not part of the Fifth. Let him know that I wandered off to parts unknown. I'm sure he does not want me communicating with Tiberius. He will send his correspondence via Sejanus and let him spin the information."

"If I might ask without going into detail, how are you going to proceed, Tribune?"

"I must find a way to get a dispatch through directly to Tiberius. He needs to know exactly what occurred over the past weeks. I will be blunt with my assessment of Gallus, his avaricious tax plan, and his even dumber decision to invade the land of the Frisii. I will not defend the actions of the Frisii, but I will state that they had no other options and were backed into a corner. I told Eadric, the Frisian leader, I would do this on his behalf."

"A good strategy, Tribune. I hope you are successful for all our sakes." He paused, then smiled. "You know, I wish I had served with you and Marcellus. You are an outstanding officer. I'm still amazed that you negotiated our way out of a dire situation."

"Thank you for the compliment, Centurion. Right back at you. I wish I had served with you as well. Marcellus had you pegged right away as a savvy centurion who didn't suffer fools. Thank the gods the Fifth had you as their first spear."

"Let us hope we achieve positive results over the next several weeks. I hope our paths cross again. Now, as we discussed, you need to disappear."

"Before I go, Centurion, I must ask a favor of you, which could be disadvantageous to your career."

Flavius snorted. "And what might that be? My career is already in the shitter."

My family—my children and parents—plus Marcellus's wife and daughter need to be put under the protection of the legions at Oppidum Ubiorum. The legate, Gaius Labenius, is a friend of mine. If I write a message to him describing our plight, I know he will comply with my wishes. I would not put it past the Governor to wreak violence on our families in retribution. He is a vile man who has no scruples. My father knows of his reputation and warned me about him. I need you, Centurion Flavius, to have a military courier deliver my message to the legate. Are you willing to take this risk?"

"Not a problem, sir. I will not have the blood of innocent civilians on my hands. Besides, the legions are indebted to you for what you did in the land of the Frisii. As soon as you have composed your message, let me know, and I will have it delivered."

▲

Early the next morning, Marcellus, Valerius, Hereca, Julia, Lucius, Rufus, and Ox boarded a modestly sized boat from Flevum to Valkenberg on the Rhenus. Valerius had decided to continue the employ of Rufus and Ox as additional protection against whatever forces the Governor might send after them. The other surviving mercenaries, seven of them, had departed wealthy men. Wishing not to be disturbed, Valerius sat at the stern of the ship by himself. Furrowing his brow in concentration, he began crafting his dispatch to Tiberius on all that had transpired in Germania since he had been commanded to resolve the issues on the German frontier.

He omitted nothing. He wrote of his baleful reception by Gallus, noting his suspicions that all was not well in the land of the Frisii, and then, his arrival at Flevum and the poor state of the fortress's defenses. He wrote of their journey into the interior and the subsequent ambush that included the Governor's son, Tigranus, among the assailants. He penned his experience of the deep distrust exhibited by the Frisian chief, Eadric, of anything Roman and their escape. Next was the heroic defense of Flevum under Tribune Florus despite the overwhelming numbers of Frisii in the assault. He recounted the subsequent rescue by the Fifth Legion and the utter foolishness of the late General Labeo in attacking the Frisii in their own territory, despite the objections of Valerius and Marcellus. Last, he narrated the crushing defeat of the Fifth, how he had negotiated a peaceful withdrawal, and the outstanding leadership of Marcus Flavius.

He stopped writing and thought hard. The next part was the thorniest. He needed to convey to Tiberius that the Frisians were backed into a corner as a result of the imposed tax burden and had no choice but to revolt. He had to do this without seeming to side with the Frisii or appearing to be offering advice to the Emperor. Both would be received poorly and put him in the way of Tiberius's wrath.

He heaved a sigh and began once again. *While speaking with the Frisian leader, Eadric, he claimed that they had no alternative but to revolt against Rome if his people were to survive. I am inclined to believe him. He said they attempted to negotiate with Governor Gallus and his staff but to no avail. In summary, there was a huge loss of life on both sides over a tax matter. Eadric allowed the Fifth to escape almost certain destruction. In exchange, I promised that Rome would abandon Flevum. I did this because there was no way we could hold that fortress given our losses. This would ensure that the Frisian lands would be free of Roman rule. I had pledged to Eadric that I would inform you, the Emperor of the Roman empire, what had happened here. As much as he distrusts Rome, he thought you might understand what occurred here and why. He did this in the hope you might show clemency for his people, although of this I made no assurances.*

Valerius penned a few more pleasantries, asked what additional service he might provide to the Emperor, and then signed his name.

He gazed out over the river. Now, he had to find a way to get this dispatch directly into Tiberius's hands. He hoped that Marcellus's fellow centurion at Valkenberg would prove useful.

⚑

The next day, Centurion Marcus Flavius, accompanied by his staff and bodyguard—about twenty men—marched boldly into the Governor's residence at Noviomagus. He sent no advance notice of his arrival from Flevum. Once he entered the gates of the fortress, he dispatched a messenger to the Governor's headquarters stating he wished an immediate audience with him as he had urgent news. He marched directly there.

Once inside the administrative office, Flavius and his men advanced brazenly to the doors of the Governor's inner sanctum. The nervous guards, noting the imposing retinue, admitted the crowd of legionnaires.

Gallus sat in his curule chair flanked by his quaestor, Cornelius Quadratus. He stared incredulously at the mass of men approaching. "Who are you? Where is General Labeo? Where is my son? Why have you brought so many men in here? This is outrageous!" he spluttered.

"I am Centurion Marcus Flavius, the first spear of the Fifth Legion. By default, I am now the commanding officer. Sir, there was a terrible setback in the Frisian territory. I am sorry to inform you that General Labeo and all his senior officers were killed in a clash with the Frisii. I regret that I must notify you that your son, Tigranus, also perished. If it's any consolation, he died bravely. My deepest sympathies."

Gallus was shocked at the news, his face pallid and his expression disconsolate. Anger abruptly replaced his mournful expression. "You

315

needed to bring an army of men with you into my inner sanctuary to tell me this news? It is disrespectful and rude."

"Sorry, sir. My men have accompanied me everywhere since the invasion of the Frisian lands began. We were on a tactical footing all the while these past few weeks. I have never had the responsibility of addressing a Governor before; hence, please forgive my manners." Flavius struggled to keep his face expressionless. He did not want the Governor to see through his ruse and intended to keep himself well protected, for he viewed Gallus as a dangerous and unstable person. He would not give the Governor an opportunity to dispose of him.

Gallus silently fumed. Regaining his composure, he asked, "What happened?"

"I will speak plainly Governor Gallus. We were ambushed by the Frisii. We lost sixty percent of the legion. We would have been destroyed if not for the bargaining skills of Tribune Valerius Maximus. He was able to negotiate a safe passage for the remnants of the legion back to Flevum. He attempted to warn General Labeo of the dangers of advancing into Frisian territory with an untested legion, but Labeo dismissed his entreaties as cowardly. I will prepare a full written report for you once I leave here."

Gallus's face reddened in fury. "Do you believe General Labeo's deployment was reckless? And where is Tribune Maximus? I don't see him here."

Flavius hesitated while he sought the appropriate words. He could not demean Labeo as he was the Governor's General, but he needed to say something. "Sir, I would have engaged the Frisii differently. Who knows if the ultimate outcome would have changed? As to Tribune Maximus, he departed when we returned to Flevum."

"He should be here. Where did he go? Why is he not with you?"

"Sir, I was unaware that he was to come back here. My impression was that he was acting on your behalf to uncover the intentions of the Frisii. I had no orders suggesting that he be brought back here. He was not part of the Fifth Legion as far as I was aware. I only knew that General Labeo had temporarily attached him to the Fifth."

Gallus glowered at Flavius. "Please explain to me how you survived and how all my senior officers, tribunes, and my son were slaughtered."

"Certainly, sir. General Labeo and eight cohorts advanced upon a fortified knoll in a place called the Baduhenna Woods. The first and second cohorts were under my command and were held in reserve and guarded the baggage trains. The eight cohorts attacked the crest of the hill. Huge numbers of Frisii attacked the flanks of the eight cohorts from out of the woods, enveloping our ranks. The Fifth was outflanked and outfoxed. The entire command staff, including your son, was slain. Then, my two cohorts advanced to rescue the survivors of the Fifth. It was a desperate battle. We managed to consolidate our forces—less than half our original strength. That night, we established a fortified camp at the base of the meadow. That was when Tribune Valerius negotiated our survival."

"I see," said Gallus coldly. "You are dismissed, Centurion Flavius, and please give me your written report as soon as possible. Oh, and don't you ever bring your guards into my chambers."

Flavius just nodded but did not reply. He did an about face and exited with his men.

CHAPTER XXVII

VALKENBERG

Valerius and Marcellus—now wearing civilian clothes—strode through the gates of Valkenberg. They had secured lodgings in the bustling town outside the fortress before entering. The purpose of their visit was to seek out Centurion Quintus Sorvinius, Marcellus's friend from the legions. They desired that Sorvinius, who held a critical post concerning imperial dispatches, aid them in their efforts to get Valerius's letter directly into the hands of Tiberius. They also hoped that Sorvinius would assist Julia and Lucius in getting safe passage on a reputable vessel back to Gaul as he would be familiar with the ships departing to Gallia and beyond.

Once inside the gates, Marcellus asked a legionnaire where the office of Quintus Sorvinius was located. The man gave him an odd look and pointed it out. "Go down this main avenue and you'll find it on the corner of the second street, on the left."

"Thanks," said Marcellus. The pair ventured onward. They reached the intersection of the main street and the second intersecting street. "This must be it," said Marcellus, pointing to a nondescript wooden building with a red tile roof. The two men entered. A clerk sat in the vestibule, busy copying a set of documents. He looked up at the two men. "May I be of assistance?"

"Certainly," said Marcellus. "We are here to see Quintus Sorvinius."

The man's face paled. He rose and scurried to the entrance of a separate office with a large wooden door. He rapped on the panel and entered without waiting for a response, closing the door behind him.

Marcellus and Valerius exchanged puzzled glances. They could hear muffled conversation in the inner sanctum where the man had disappeared. Finally, the clerk emerged along with another figure dressed in a fine tunic. He was tall with a slightly crooked nose and dark features. The man approached Valerius and Marcellus.

"May I help you?" he asked in an imperious tone.

"Yes," said Marcellus, "I am here to see Quintus Sorvinius. He is an old colleague of mine."

The man nervously cleared his throat. "I'm afraid to bring you bad news, but Quintus Sorvinius is no longer with us. He died."

"And how did he die?" Marcellus inquired.

"He was murdered several weeks ago in town, most likely set upon by thieving rogues. My name is Castor Ulvinius, his replacement appointed by Governor Gallus. Perhaps I can assist you? What business do you have with the late Quintus?"

"What? How did this happen? Marcellus asked.. He and I were former comrades in the legions. I was in Valkenberg, and so I thought I'd look him up and buy him a glass of wine."

"What brings you to Valkenberg anyway?" He continued staring at the two visitors, no doubt suspicious of Marcellus's response. Few visitors came to Valkenberg unless they needed a ship or to send dispatches to Rome. He pressed on, "Are you sure I cannot help you with anything?"

Marcellus adopted a wistful expression. "No, I was looking forward to seeing Quintus after all these years, that is all. We will be on our way."

The pair exited the building. When they were some distance away, Valerius spoke. "I'm sorry about your friend. What are we to do now? We must get this dispatch to Tiberius. Our survival may depend upon it."

"I don't know, Tribune. We must come up with an alternative plan. I find it suspicious that he was murdered."

The pair continued walking. "I've been thinking, Marcellus. What if we have Julia and Lucius take the dispatch with them into Gaul? I don't trust the postal service here. Too many prying eyes, especially that slimy character, Castor Ulvinius, whom we just met. Furthermore, if you recall, Lady Agrippina had offered her assistance. Why don't we take her up on that? I will have the document addressed to her. Assuming we can get it into her hands, she can have it delivered to Tiberius. She lives in the imperial palace—she can find a way."

Marcellus halted abruptly. "That is a fucking brilliant plan, Tribune. Do you think Agrippina will receive it unopened and unread?"

"I hope so. It will not be part of any official correspondence. It may be that her personal letters are being monitored by Sejanus, but that is the risk we'll have to take. Alternatively, we could attempt to deliver the document in person, but I fear we might not reach the imperial palace alive given the Sejanus factor. No doubt, Gallus has already corresponded with Sejanus warning him of the danger we pose. Therefore, I believe having Julia and Lucius mail the document to Agrippina is the best and most logical choice. Now, let's get down to the docks and see what we can find in the way of transport for Lucius and Julia. We need to get them on a ship sailing to Gaul with no questions asked. The less they are noticed, the better. No trail should link them to us."

The two men ventured down to the quay to see what ships might be available. Sea birds squawked and soared about the wharf. The men walked insouciantly along the bustling wooden dock, inspecting the various ships and casually inquiring when they were sailing and where they were headed. The ships were all headed south; there were no major ports north of Valkenberg. The two noted an abundance of customs officers accompanied by stern-faced legionnaires patrolling the waterfront; they ensured that the Emperor received his levy for any trades and examined manifests and passenger lists. The two men moved on but halted suddenly and stared ahead at the ship anchored in front of them, which was pulling gently at her lines in the slight swell. Its boxy shape was familiar.

"I'll be dyed seven shades of shit. Fate intervenes for us once more," said Marcellus. "This is either a pure coincidence or Goddess Fortuna indeed smiles upon us. There is our solution."

Moored at the wharf was Captain Artimus's ship—Neptune's Blessing—the same ship the two men had boarded that spring to sail to Rome.

Valerius grinned. "I believe we need to have a reunion with Captain Artimus. I'm sure he'll be glad to accommodate our request to carry two passengers to a port in Gaul. He owes us a rather large favor, don't you think? Perhaps he might be a future transporter of J&L wines."

"Yes. I believe Artimus is seriously indebted to us and will be happy to see us again."

* * *

Back at Noviomagus, Gallus paced the floor, wringing his hands. Cornelius Quadratus sat in the small private room, listening to the Governor rant. "We must find that tribune and his accomplices and eliminate them. Damn the consequences! I fear he is plotting to get his version of the developments here in Germania to Tiberius. It would cast us in an extremely poor light. Furthermore, I believe he is in collusion with that Centurion Flavius."

"Governor Gallus, I agree that he must be killed, but are you not overreacting? We have our own man, Castor Ulvinius, in place in Valkenberg to scrutinize all dispatches going to the imperial palace. Quintus Sorvinius and his meddling ways are no longer a problem for us. Furthermore, in the unlikely event that a message does slip through, our friend and colleague, Sejanus, screens all official correspondence. I believe we are protected on that front. How can this Tribune Maximus possibly get word to Tiberius?"

Gallus stopped his pacing. "You are correct, Cornelius. We have formed a tight net that favors us, but I'm still concerned. This Tribune Maximus is a tough and resourceful man. We have attempted to rid ourselves of his meddling several times, yet he is still alive. If word gets to Tiberius about the scope of this disaster and our culpability, we are doomed. Sejanus will abandon us in a heartbeat. Our survival is at stake here and that includes you, Cornelius. Anyone closely associated with me is at high risk."

"Of course, Governor. I will dispatch men up and down the Rhenus to seek out and kill this irksome tribune. I am at a disadvantage since we lost Lupus in that skirmish. My other people are not nearly as proficient, although I would still judge them capable of carrying out my orders. That tribune and his confederates must be lurking somewhere. Once we find him, he will no longer be a threat to us. By the way, where is his home? That is the first place I will have my men search."

"I believe he said he was from Oppidum Ubiorum. Yes, that was the place. Send your men there."

"Yes, Governor."

"Thank you, Cornelius. I know I can depend on you. Now, I must draft my correspondence to Sejanus and explain to him what happened. I will designate it as extremely urgent, so it gets there swiftly. The revolt is over; so, we must convey that to him. Report back to me your progress with hunting down the tribune and his friends."

▲

The group of seven huddled together in a small tavern outside the fortress of Valkenberg, cups of wine dotting their table. The place had a few tables, most unoccupied. Marcellus spoke, "Our plans have hit an unexpected snag. My friend, Quintus Sorvinius, who I had counted on to help us, has been murdered. It could have been pure chance but the more likely scenario is that Gallus was involved. We need an alternative plan. The tribune will explain what he thinks we need to do."

"Yes, here it is. I sense that even as we speak, we are probably being hunted by men friendly to the Governor. We will surreptitiously deposit Lucius and Julia on a ship to Gaul. The captain and his vessel are known to us. I will entrust Julia and Lucius with the information about the events concerning the Frisii. It will be addressed to Agrippina, Germanicus's widow. Lucius and Julia, you must mail this once you reach Gaul on your journey back home. Do not use the military couriers. It must appear like an ordinary civilian correspondence."

Julia smiled. "I can do this. My father used to keep up correspondence with a few people in Rome. I can drop this off in one of several towns in Gaul without raising any suspicions."

"Good," said Valerius. "It could be that despite our efforts, Sejanus will get his hands on this before Tiberius and our efforts will be for naught, but that is the risk we must take. I believe we are all in extreme danger. Our survival depends on getting this dispatch to Agrippina and then, Tiberius."

"Tell me about our ship to Gaul," Julia inquired.

Marcellus beamed. "It so happens that a transport is sailing tomorrow morning. We can get you aboard without anyone knowing. The captain of the vessel, Captain Artimus, owes the tribune and me a rather large favor. We saved them from some unpleasant business with pirates last spring. You will be most welcome and safe on his ship. I suggest we all say our goodbyes tonight. The quicker you get away from here, the better. Your association with us places you in peril."

"We will feel lost without Lucius to guard," sighed Ox.

"Yes," said Rufus, "Lucius is my friend. Can we accompany then to Gaul?" he asked half-jokingly.

"Unfortunately, you and Rufus will be needed here," said Valerius. "I sense that the Governor will come after us hard. We need to leave this port as soon as we see them safely aboard and their ship sails."

The next morning, Valerius, Hereca, Marcellus, Rufus, and Ox sat in the main room of the inn they were staying in, enjoying their breakfast. The conversation was melancholic as their friends, Julia and Lucius, had just set sail at dawn on Neptune's Blessing.

"We must plot our next course of action," said Valerius, "and we must do it now."

"Where do we go?" Marcellus asked. "Word will be out on us up and down the river."

Valerius directed his gaze at his wife. "Hereca, if we sail east, upriver, forty miles or more, I was thinking we might cross over to the German side and shelter there. Do you think you could arrange for one of the tribes to take us in for a while? I don't believe the Governor's reach extends to the German territory on the other side of the Rhenus. What do you think?"

Hereca paused. "Not in the land of the Frisii, I hope."

"No, definitely not the Frisii. I have no intention of crossing paths with Eadric again. Who has lands bordering the Frisii to the east?"

"The Amsivarii. Yes, we could have trade discussions with the Amsivarii. No doubt they will be on their guard after the events with the Frisii, but I believe we will be welcome there. From there, we could travel east to other tribes. How long will we have to stay in German lands?"

"Thinking out loud, we must allow at least three weeks for the dispatch to reach Tiberius. Assuming he gets the documents, perhaps another three weeks before Gallus is replaced. Once that happens, we will be safe. By then, winter will be approaching."

Valerius turned toward Marcellus. "Your thoughts?"

"I agree with you. I believe we need to get our asses out of here and venture into German territory. Never thought I would be going into German lands to be safe. Talk about irony."

CHAPTER XXVIII

FLIGHT FROM VALKENBERG

Throwing open the door, nine armed men—their garments streaked with mud and swords dangling ominously from their belts—barged into the office of Castor Ulvinius. The clerk sitting in the vestibule stared in fright at the men. The apparent leader, a swarthy individual with a long scar streaking across the right side of his face, growled. "We need to speak with Castor Ulvinius right away. Go and get him."

Ulvinius heard the loud, gruff voice and materialized from his office. He took one look at the men and knew they were trouble. "How may I be of service?"

"Governor Gallus sent us. We are looking for two men—one middle aged, one older, and perhaps accompanied by a woman. They are probably armed. Both former military men. They may have attempted to send a dispatch to Tiberius."

Ulvinius rubbed his jaw in thought. "Yes, two men fitting that description were here just yesterday. They were looking for my predecessor, Quintus Sorvinius. The older one said they were former comrades in the legions."

"Where are they?" the swarthy leader demanded.

Ulvinius shrugged. "I have no idea. They seemed disappointed that Sorvinius was not here anymore. They departed. Not sure where they went. They had no dispatches for me if that's what you're asking me."

The leader uttered a curse. "If you see these men, have them arrested and find me. I will be in town. They are criminals, and Governor Gallus wants them apprehended and brought back to Noviomagus." He gestured to his men, and they exited.

⚔

Valerius, Marcellus, Ox, and Hereca exited the inn they had been staying in. They were going to enter the citadel, go to the quay, and seek passage upriver, where they would disembark into the German territory of the Amsivarii. It would be a forty-mile journey heading east upriver before they could safely cross into friendly German lands.

Rufus, who had volunteered to go ahead and see if he could expedite their passage upriver, came running toward them, looking anxious. He halted in front of them, panting. "There are armed men searching for you in the fortress. When I was at the wharf, I heard them inquiring. They are cut-throats with evil intent; no doubt about that."

"Gallus dispatched his minions quickly," Valerius remarked. "This obviously necessitates a change in our plans. We cannot go to the quay and must forego the luxury of boat travel from Valkenberg. Our only course of action is to journey on foot upriver and then find a passage across. There must be boatmen who ply all along the Rhenus.

But if we cross the river here or within the next forty miles, we will be back in the land of the Frisii. Marcellus, what's your take on this?"

Marcellus scowled. "Yes, that would put us in Frisian territory once more, a place I do not wish to return to. I thought I was done with them. Unfortunately, I see no other viable option. Let's get going."

They walked quickly down the street. The avenue was lined with merchant shops, taverns, and inns. Hiding in the shadow of buildings, they stopped short as the next street crossing was up ahead. Nine riders cantered across the street; none of them noticed Valerius and company, who were partially concealed to their right.

They waited in the shadows until the mounted men were out of sight and then hurried across the intersection toward the outskirts of the town. None of them noticed a furtive figure lurking in the shadows. He scurried away as the group moved on.

Plaxus, the leader of the group seeking out Valerius, stood inside the citadel, fuming. The search for Marcellus and Valerius had been fruitless. His men waited silently by, pending his orders. Anger erupted on his eyes, exacerbating the twisted expression on his face. Where were they? They had to be around somewhere. Had they boarded a ship? His inquiries at the wharf did not support that possibility. No, this Tribune Valerius and Centurion Marcellus were lurking about. He needed to find them and kill them. A hefty purse had been offered by Quadratus for their demise. He would, of course, keep most of it for himself and divide the rest among his men. He needed to find them before the other bands of mercenaries, which he knew were out there, discovered his targets and claimed the reward.

A waif, dressed in rags, his face filthy, approached Plaxus. "Excuse me, sir. I heard that you are seeking some men around town."

Plaxus sneered at him. "What's it to you? Be on your way before I wring your neck."

"I might have news of them."

The urchin cowered as Plaxus strode over and lifted him by the scruff of his neck. "You might have news?" The man pulled a thin dagger from his belt and flashed it in front of the boy's face. "Speak to me now, or I will gut you like a fish. This is not a negotiation. Understand?"

Tears streaked down the lad's face. "I'm not lying. I heard them speaking a short while ago by the shops. They said they were going to journey upriver and cross into German territory."

"How do you know it is the people I'm looking for?"

"Word gets around, sir. I heard them talking after they observed your posse on a street. One of the men was addressed as Marcellus."

Plaxus threw the boy to the street. "You better hope you are correct, or I will come back and make an example of you." He shouted to his men. "Come on to the river. We will find this group and get paid handsomely. Make haste now."

▲

The weather was cool and blustery—more so along the river. The group had been walking along the river for at least four miles, yet they had not come across any transport that might ferry them across. There was little in the way of habitation other than a few scattered farms. Most of the fields had been harvested recently, a sign that autumn was ending. Valerius anxiously peered ahead, searching for a small hamlet or village that would offer the luxury of a ferry across to the German side of the Rhenus.

"I hoped that we would've come upon a boat by now. I had no idea that the population was so sparse outside of Valkenberg. We need to cross over. Our chances are less favorable the longer we stay on this side," said Valerius.

"Aye, I agree," said Marcellus. "I know there are villages along this stretch of the river. I remember having seen them when we sailed down here. It can't be too much farther."

Their conversation was interrupted by a clatter of hoofs approaching behind them. A group of riders was closing the distance swiftly, now perhaps five hundred paces away.

Plaxus, in the lead of the pack of riders, shouted above the noise of the galloping horses for his men to pick up the pace. "There they are!"

However, Gallus's thugs made several mistakes. First, as they got to within fifty paces, Plaxus ordered the men to dismount though they had the advantage of height on horseback. Perhaps it was because they had never fought while mounted. Their second error was to assume that since they were superior in number, they had the upper hand. Third, their leader presumed that his men possessed superior fighting skills, which, as they were about to discover, was hardly the case.

Plaxus and his men, now on foot, charged at the four men and one woman, who had deployed a shield wall in a tight circle. The first men to reach the circle of combatants died swiftly upon their blades. The others took no notice and rushed headlong at the group without any organized plan—their final lethal mistake. Plaxus chose to engage Valerius one-on-one. No stranger to sword fighting, Plaxus arced his blade in a cutting stroke while, at the same time, kicking out with his right leg to unbalance his opponent. This ruse had served him well in previous scuffles.

Valerius easily parried the wild attack and calmly stepped aside, avoiding the kick. He had seen that maneuver before. At the end of his parry, he brought his sword down in a vertical stroke, cutting his assailant's leg.

Plaxus gasped as the cold steel made a deep gash through his leggings. Biting his lip, he edged backward, fear in his eyes. The smart play at this point would have been to rapidly retreat to their horses and seek help at the garrison at Vandenberg. However, he did not do so. He angrily thrust at Valerius. Again, his move was deftly parried.

Valerius knew he needed to end this and assist the others in his outnumbered group. He edged forward toward his antagonist, and in a blur, his sword pierced Plaxus and rammed through his torso, the blade exiting out his back. The man gasped in horror. Blood dribbled from his mouth and he collapsed.

Hereca was engaged with a heavy brute, who through his sheer bulk, was forcing her out of the protection of the circle. He grinned wolfishly, ready to slay the woman. But he never got the chance. Valerius's sword cut deeply through his neck. The man collapsed, bleeding out in the dirt. The tribune attacked another man from the flank, ending his life in a few moments. Ox, Rufus, and Marcellus finished off the remainder of the men quickly. None escaped.

"Anybody hurt?" Valerius asked. They looked at each other—no one responded. "Good. It appears our adversaries have provided us with transportation. Let's take the horses and get out of here. I'd guess there are more of them seeking us. This is not the last of them."

⋀

About six miles up ahead, they arrived at a small village that offered a ferry service across the river. Valerius and Hereca sold four of the horses, although they got less than the market rate for them. They then purchased fodder for the remaining horses and dried meat, grain porridge, and watered wine for themselves. Valerius jingled the surplus of coins in his hands from the sale of the horses. He walked up to Rufus and Ox. Dividing the coins into equal amounts, he handed their share to them. "Consider this additional pay on behalf of Marcellus, Hereca, and me for all your service.

Ox stared at the pile of coins in his hand. "But you have already paid us extra in addition to the agreed-upon stipend."

"You have risked your life many times in our service," said Marcellus. "By Venus's pert arse, you have earned this ten times over. It is the least we could do, and I sense that the danger is not over yet. I truly hope you get to spend this."

Ox continued staring at the pile of coins. "I have never had so much money in my life. I don't regret joining forces with you even for a moment, danger be damned."

"That goes for me too," said Rufus. "If not for you, I would still be wallowing in some tavern back in Noviomagus."

"Perhaps you both would like to stay with us in our trading company when this entire mess is over?" asked Hereca. "We need good men whom we can depend upon. Would you entertain such a thought?"

Both men nodded enthusiastically. "Of course," said Rufus. "Speaking for Ox as well as myself, we would gladly accept such an offer." He looked to Ox for affirmation.

"Yes," said Ox. "Much better than working in some shit-hole back in Noviomagus."

"I just hope it will be a bit more tranquil. I thought the legions were a dangerous place for a man to earn a living. The last month or so has been highly adventurous and makes my legionary service pale in comparison," said Rufus.

Hereca laughed. "I can't promise complete serenity, but it certainly will not be like the past weeks."

The Romans walked their horses to the ferry. Because of the horses, it took two trips for them to reach the German side. "We will head east," said Valerius, "We must journey along the river path. Hopefully, we will not attract too much attention. I reckon that in about thirty miles, we will reach the land of the Amsivarii. Until then, we are in the territory of the Frisii. Stay alert. I'm not sure what kind of reception five strangers might receive."

They rode only a few hours before twilight overtook them. Marcellus selected a small pine grove for them to set up camp. They tethered the horses and cooked a meager supper over a small fire. They had warm porridge, hard cheese, diluted wine, and dried meat—standard marching rations for the legions. They then bedded down for the night with only the pine trees for shelter.

The next day dawned chilly and overcast. The group huddled in their cloaks and ate a cold breakfast of dried meat and wine. Soon, they were back on the dirt road that paralleled the river. They set a modest pace for fear of wearing out the horses and journeyed for about two hours in the early morning light. However, rounding a bend in the road, they came upon a group of eight riders blocking their path, all armed.

"Stay here," said Valerius. "Hereca and I will ride ahead to see what their intentions are."

A man, who Valerius assumed to be the leader, urged his mount to the front of the group. He was a tall, lean figure with a short beard. He didn't introduce himself, which was not a good sign "Who are you and what are you doing in the land of the Frisii?"

Hereca responded in German. "My husband and I are traders from the other side of the river. We seek new markets for our goods."

The leader snorted. "I don't see any goods. What do you trade?"

"Everything and anything," said Valerius. "We trade with many of the tribes to the east and south. Wine, farm implements, glassware, jewelry."

"I don't believe you," said the man. "Why are you trespassing on our lands?"

Valerius tried another tactic. The last thing he wanted was another fight. This bunch looked like tough and dangerous adversaries—far more formidable than Gallus's posse. "A pity. Most of our trading partners are satisfied customers. We could pay you a fee to allow us through your lands if that is what you are after."

The leader let out a derisive chuckle. "You only offer what I could take. I desire the horses as well."

This was not going in the direction Valerius had hoped. Time to shift tactics yet again. "You could try and take them from us. You underestimate our capabilities. Others have attempted to steal from us in the past, much to their regret."

The tall man proffered a sinister grin and then, putting his fingers to his mouth, let out a sharp whistle. More riders materialized from the woods on either side of the road. The band of Romans was hopelessly surrounded and outnumbered.

"You are making a mistake," said Valerius.

He grinned wolfishly. "I don't see how." Upon some silent signal, all the Germans howled and brandished their spears at the encircled Romans.

"Stand down," said Valerius to his followers. The German thugs relieved them of all their weapons and personal possessions, including their money.

In desperation, Valerius blurted, "I know Eadric. He will vouch for me."

The leader's gleeful expression turned to alarm at this unexpected development. "How do you know Eadric? You are not one of us. By your dress and accent, you are nothing but a filthy Roman. There is no disguising it. I don't care if you say you are a trader."

"I'm the one who brokered peace with Eadric some days ago. Your survival and that of the Frisii may depend upon my endeavors. I am acting as an envoy for the Frisii with the Emperor in Rome."

"I will send a rider to Eadric asking about you. What is your name?"

"I am Valerius Maximus, former tribune in the Roman Imperial Army and now a trader among the German tribes."

"You had better hope that your words are true because, if not, you and your band will face a slow death." He shouted at his men. "Bind these Romans and take their horses. They are our prisoners and are not to be harmed until we hear from Eadric."

The captives walked for several hours, heading north and away from the river, before reaching a moderate-sized village. Their bindings were undone, and they were shoved into a small hut with daub walls. The leader, whose name Valerius had learned was Othmar, entered and glared at his captives. "Don't even think about escaping. You are well guarded. Any attempt at flight or disobedience of any kind will be met with death. I await word from Eadric. It might take a few days." He turned and departed.

Valerius huddled with Hereca and the others. He spoke in a hushed tone so he would not be overheard by those guarding the dwelling, although it was doubtful whether they understood Latin. "We are at Eadric's mercy. I doubt he likes me much, but as far as I know, the legions have departed the land of the Frisii, so that is an advantage. If Eadric rides here to find out what we are doing, I'll need to convince him that this is all related to getting word to Tiberius about the duplicity and cupidity of Governor Gallus. We shall have to wait and see."

The next several days were tedious and filled with trepidation about what decision Eadric might make. Except for visits to the communal latrine, they were confined to the small dwelling under constant guard. Their only food was small pieces of stale bread and a jug of water. Valerius needed to lighten the mood. He looked to his wife, then Marcellus and finally to his two new associates. "When we get out of here and back to the Roman side of the river, I am going to host the biggest banquet with the finest foods and wine. Note I said *when* not *if*."

His words were greeted with tremulous smiles. Nobody, not even Marcellus, was buying what he was selling. "I hope you are correct, Tribune. It is hard to see that far ahead given our confinement in this stinking hut. I hope Eadric responds in our favor soon."

The glum atmosphere, fueled further by heavy, cold rain, did not dissipate. The next day, late in the afternoon, the crude wooden door of the dwelling was flung open. Standing in the doorway was Eadric, along with Othmar. "We meet again, Roman," said Eadric. He glowered at Valerius and then shifted his gaze to the others. "I have met your wife and this former centurion of yours. Who are these two others? Trading partners?" he said sarcastically.

"They are my bodyguards."

"A trader needs bodyguards?"

"Under the present circumstances, yes."

"When we last met, I thought I had told you that I never wanted to see you in Frisian territory, yet you have violated that agreement. You don't listen well. Give me one reason why I should not turn you over to Othmar. He says he will enjoy putting you to death." He snorted, "and by the way, he thanks you for your horses."

Valerius stared at Eadric. If the man had traveled this distance, probably over forty miles, to see him, then he must have an interest in what he had to say. So far, all he had done was issue bombastic threats. "Perhaps we could have a private conversation, Eadric. Othmar can have the horses; they are not mine."

"Now you are a horse thief as well."

"We need to talk, Eadric—you and me."

"Very well, Roman. Othmar, we need a place to speak in private. Can you take us somewhere so that we can have a discussion?" The chieftain nodded in acquiescence. "Follow me, Eadric."

Valerius followed the two chieftains, ignoring the hostile stares of the villagers. These Germans, he reckoned, had probably lost many warriors in the recent battles with the Romans. Eadric and Valerius entered a small dwelling furnished with a small, crude wooden table and several chairs. "I will have someone fetch ale," said Othmar. He departed. The two men sat down facing each other.

"Speak, Roman. I'm hanging onto every word. I can't wait to hear what you have to say," he said derisively.

Valerius was about to begin when a young woman carried in a tray with a pitcher of ale and a set of mugs. Othmar followed her. "Othmar," said Eadric, "it is best if the two of us speak alone, if you don't mind."

"Of course," said a disappointed Othmar. He turned and departed.

Eadric poured two mugs of ale. He casually sipped the contents of his mug. "Begin."

"I will commence my story from when the Fifth Legion returned to Flevum. As agreed between us, the legion, under the direction of

Centurion Marcus Flavius, the acting commanding officer, departed Flevum for their base at Noviomagus. The centurion informed me that it would take about a week to fully vacate the premises. I was not aboard those ships to Noviomagus. Instead, I sailed to Valkenberg. Why Valkenberg, you might ask? My purpose was to send a dispatch to the Emperor describing the actions of the Fifth against the Frisii and the agreement the two of us had reached. Just for your information, I left nothing out. I described the actions of Governor Gallus and how they fomented the revolt of the Frisii." Valerius paused to see if Eadric had any questions.

"I take it there is more to this account?" Eadric asked.

"Yes, there were some difficulties. The official we were counting upon to get the dispatch to Rome, and ultimately to Tiberius, was a friend of Marcellus's, my business partner and former centurion. It seems that this Roman official at Valkenberg had been murdered a few weeks ago; thus, there was no way we could be assured that the message would reach the Emperor directly. Hence, we devised an alternative plan. It involved two civilians taking the dispatch to Gaul and addressing it to a member of the imperial household who I know well. She will find a way to get the dispatch to Tiberius. We got the two civilians on board a ship, and as for those of us remaining from my retinue, we planned to sail up the Rhenus past the land of the Frisii and disembark on the German side of the river once we reached the lands of the Amsivarii. We never got that far. As we were about to leave Valkenberg, we observed armed riders seeking us. The port was being watched. We decided to venture on foot upriver and then eventually cross over and enter the land of the Amsivarii. We had only traveled about four or five miles before a group of nine men attacked us. We killed them all—that is how we got the horses. Governor

Gallus has a price on my head. No doubt the countryside is being scoured for my friends and me as we speak. Given the circumstances, we decided to scrap our original plan and cross at the first place possible, which brought us back into the lands of the Frisii."

"Do you think Tiberius will get your dispatch and replace Gallus?"

"I cannot say for certain, but I believe my plan has a good chance to succeed."

"And if he agrees with what you have written, he may not pursue the Frisii and we will be safe?"

"The Emperor will be extremely displeased with Gallus and recall him to Rome. I hope he will let the Frisii be. As for me, I may be safe from Gallus but perhaps not the Emperor. I far exceeded my authority in brokering that agreement with you. He will be highly annoyed with my actions and might recall me to Rome."

Eadric chuckled. "You are between a rock and a hard place, Tribune."

"I knew there were considerable risks when I was recalled to Rome and was tasked by Tiberius to uncover what was happening with the Frisii. I've done the best I could under the circumstances. That is why I am still your ally. Tiberius may demand to meet with me and explain my actions and the circumstances surrounding your revolt. I will repeat what I said to you back on the battlefield. Tiberius does not want another war in the German territory. The first step will be to replace Gallus. I am counting on my dispatch falling into Tiberius's hands."

Eadric sighed. "Tribune, you are a giant pain in my arse. However, given the circumstances, I will have Othmar escort you to the lands of the Amsivarii. There, you will dismount and give him your horses for all his troubles. I will have my informers be alert for any changes in the Governor's office and future military deployments. Now, I'm weary and want to return to my village and rest a while. The last month and a half have been hard on me and my people."

"There is one other matter," said Valerius.

"And what might that be?"

"Othmar and his men confiscated our purses as well as our weapons. My wife, Marcellus, and I can afford to lose our money, my two bodyguards cannot. That is all the coin they have in this world."

"Let me understand this. The money that Othmar's men confiscated, they can only keep yours? How magnanimous of you."

"You know, you are beginning to sound a lot like Gallus."

Eadric scowled. "You are pushing it, Tribune."

"Perhaps, but deep down, you know I'm right. Those two men earned every one of those coins. They deserve to keep them."

"Very well. I will have their purses returned. Anything else?"

"As a matter of fact, yes. The weapons, also."

Eadric sighed. "Of course."

Valerius proffered a smile and chuckled.

"What's so humorous, Tribune?"

"Oh, just the irony of the whole thing. I believe had we met under different circumstances, we could have established a much friendlier relationship as trading partners. I do have many friends and allies among the German tribes on this side of the river. And, by the way, I do not believe the title of tribune is appropriate anymore. I am done with that."

Eadric considered Valerius's words. "Perhaps we could have been trading partners. As for now, I will wait to see what develops along the Rhenus. For all our sakes, I hope your dispatch gets through."

CHAPTER XXIX

UNFOLDING EVENTS

A sinister figure grabbed the iron wolf-head knocker and pounded on the wooden door of Valerius's residence in Oppidum Ubiorum. Behind him was a band of armed men clad in long cloaks. "Open this door!" he shouted.

Valerius's aged servant, Claudius, timorously opened the door halfway. "How may I help you?"

The leader of the pack aggressively pushed past him. "Where is Valerius Maximus? I have urgent business with him."

"He is not here. He has been gone for many weeks."

"Where is his family?"

"The children and parents of Valerius Maximus are guests of the legate, General Labenius, at the fort," replied Claudius.

The leader scowled and turned to his men. "Search this place. Look in every room and closet for any signs of recent habitation." The pack of brutes spread out, ransacking the place, overturning furniture, and breaking precious vases.

One by one, the men returned empty-handed. The leader scowled more fiercely. "Where do Maximus's parents live?"

"They are two streets over; the first house on the right with the red door, but they are not there."

The man's rage flared. He cuffed Claudius on the side of the face, drawing blood. "I asked only where his parents' house is located. Just answer the question." With that, the men stormed out, leaving a wake of destruction in the house.

* * *

Hundreds of miles to the south in Gaul, Lucius and Julia disembarked from their ship, Neptune's Blessing. They said hurried goodbyes to Captain Artimus, thanking him for the safe passage and promising him that they would be in touch concerning future shipments of their wine. Julia tightly clutched the firmly sealed packet containing Valerius's dispatch. A cold wind blew off the sea, hastening them along. She and Lucius exited the wharf and walked into the forum of the seaport town of Lulobona. She looked about to get her bearings, and among the assorted buildings, she spied a stately wooden structure. It had two wide doors and a paved stone path to the door. It was easily the best-kept building in the town's forum; it had to be the magistrate's office. She tugged Lucius by his cape. "This way. I think that is the building we are seeking."

The couple strolled up to the door and entered the structure, finding themselves in a wide vestibule. There were two corridors leading to a labyrinth of offices. Julia spotted an official walking down the main hallway while perusing a document. "Excuse me," she called out, "could you direct me to the postal service? I have a large packet to be delivered to Rome."

The man didn't even look up from his reading. "Next corridor, second door on the right."

"Thank you," Julia replied.

She turned and faced her husband, patting his arm. "You stay here. Let me handle this alone. I will attempt to charm a bureaucrat of the postal service."

Lucius shrugged. "I will wait here."

Julia unfastened her cloak, revealing her stunning figure, and then entered a small office. A thin man wearing a bored expression sat at a wooden table littered with scrolls and other papers. Julia beamed at him. "Good afternoon. My name is Julia, and I have an important packet to be delivered in Rome. I hope you can help me," she cooed.

The thin man sat up straighter. "I will see what I can do. Let me see what you have."

He examined the packet and saw the name Agrippina Germanicus Caesar as the addressee. "You know the Lady Agrippina, Germanicus's widow?" he said in awe.

Julia smiled. "Well, not exactly. I have a friend in Germania who knows her very well. He said that it was urgent that she receive this packet. He said that he could not trust the postal service in Germania and that the service in Gaul is ten times better and more secure. That is why he entrusted this to me. Do you think you could help me? I would be grateful," she said, batting her eyelashes.

"I can assure you that the postal service in Gaul is absolutely reliable and, perhaps, the best Rome has to offer. We have packets and dispatches moving throughout the empire, and I have not heard of one complaint yet," he said proudly.

"Oh, I have come to the right place then! I would be happy to pay more to ensure its delivery. How much is it going to cost?"

The thin man licked his lips nervously. "Well, I can tell the courier that this is an essential dispatch. He will hand it over to the appropriate people. Let me see, considering the distance and the addressee, I would say five silver sesterces."

Julia knew the fee was outrageous—probably double the normal fare—but that was not her concern. She needed to get this package to Agrippina and soon. Many lives depended upon it, including that of Valerius, Hereca, and Marcellus. "That will be fine," she said. "Oh, thank you so much for assisting me!"

She reached into her purse, extracted the exact number of coins, and handed them to the official. She soon exited the building and found Lucius waiting for her. "How did it go?" he asked.

Julia smirked. "I think we can count on Agrippina getting the dispatch."

On the German side of the Rhenus, the group of Romans rode hard for most of the day, escorted by their Frisian captors. The group halted. It was late afternoon. The Romans dismounted and, as agreed, their weapons were returned to them along with the purses of Ox and Rhenus. Without a word, Othmar and his men turned about and departed.

The Romans traveled several hours up the river before coming upon a small settlement of perhaps thirty dwellings. The village chieftain, a man long past his prime, came out to greet them. As he shuffled toward them, he noted the weapons and eyed them warily.

"Let me handle this," said Hereca. "I am less threatening." She strode forward. "My name is Hereca, and that one," she said, pointing, "is my husband, Valerius. We are traders who have run afoul of a bunch of thugs that were close to the Governor's son, Tigranus. We would like to stay here for a while until things settle down on the other side of the river. We are willing to compensate you for the privilege of staying here. We will pay in coin and will not bother anyone."

"My name is Gudabert," said the chieftain. "I am familiar with this Tigranus and his men. I heard he was killed by the Frisii."

"So I have heard," said Hereca. "No loss there. But his men are still lurking about. We must avoid them at all costs. It is a blood feud."

The old man nodded in understanding, for the German tribes were infamous for their blood feuds. He contemplated the offer. "I can tell you are German, but you have a Roman husband?"

"Yes, it is a long story. He speaks German well. As I said, we are merchants. We have traded with many of the tribes in the eastern territory and count many clans as our friends. We attempted to expand our trading ventures to the west and south, but we met a bit of trouble with the Frisian revolt. It was not a good idea to venture this far west."

"What are you willing to pay?"

Hereca contemplated the question like she was thinking hard over it, although she had already decided on an amount. She would borrow the coins from Ox and Rufus. "How about three silver sesterces a week? That is my one and final offer. If that is not acceptable, we will go on to the next village."

There was no disguising the gleam in Gudabert's eyes. Roman silver coins carried a lot of weight and would help his village procure enough provisions to survive the winter. "Your offer is acceptable," he said quickly.

CHAPTER XXX

PALATINE HILL

Agrippina sat in her study, exhausted from her busy day. She had just finished receiving visitors, mostly petitioners who had some favor or other to ask of her. Dismissing her scribes and advisors, she rubbed her forehead in an effort to erase her nagging headache. She looked up as her chamberlain entered. "Yes, what is it," she asked testily.

"Sorry to bother you, Lady Agrippina. I know you are tired, but this large packet just arrived by courier from Gaul. I am not aware of anyone you are corresponding with from that province. Do you wish to wait until tomorrow to open it?"

She stared at the parcel, curious. "Give it here. I will read it."

She accepted the package and turned it over in her hands. She held one hand out for a knife, which was tendered to her by her chamberlain. On carefully slitting the strings that tied the bundle together and breaking the wax seal, she then began reading, her brow furrowed in concentration. When she was about half-finished, she glanced up from the document at her chamberlain, who looked on anxiously, not knowing what to do.

A smile creased her countenance. "You may go. This is from an old friend of mine. Nothing to be bothered about." She continued reading. *Valerius, you are magnificent; a true hero of Rome. No wonder my husband admired and trusted you. Now what to do with this document? Nobody must know about the contents of this dispatch. There are spies and informants everywhere, and I suspect my chamberlain could be one of them.* She began to think about how she would get this document delivered directly to Tiberius without Sejanus knowing about it. But she was not too worried. She had her ways.

▲

Tiberius fumed, his haggard face a deep red. He sat in one of his small audience rooms. Servants stood around the chamber, at his beck and call. "Go fetch Prefect Sejanus immediately!" he screamed at one of the slaves. The man scurried away through the large wooden doors.

After a brief period, Sejanus appeared in his usual impeccable uniform before Tiberius. "How may I be of service, sire?"

Tiberius picked up the dispatch that Valerius had penned and flung it on the tabletop, causing a resounding crash. "This is a report from Tribune Valerius Maximus. As you will remember, we recalled him to active duty to look into the Frisian problem. His account of what transpired is rather lengthy and is a very different version of events than the honey-coated piece of shit sent to us by your friend, Governor Gallus. According to the tribune's dispatch, we have lost our toehold in the land of the Frisii, including the fortress at Flevum, and the Fifth Legion was mauled when they invaded the Frisian territory to the point where they are no longer an effective fighting force."

"Perhaps the tribune is lying to cover up his own mistakes," said Sejanus.

Tiberius scowled. "Perhaps not. The tribune provides a detailed account of the events surrounding the revolt and a list of names that will corroborate his version, none of them his known acquaintances." Tiberius's voice rose vehemently. "The last thing Rome needed was another revolt in Germania, yet that is exactly what has occurred. We were at peace until your friend Gallus arrived at the scene last year. I am going to recall him to Rome immediately."

Sejanus shifted uncomfortably. He knew there was no saving Gallus now. "I agree, sire. What a disappointment he has turned out to be," he said smoothly. "It appears he has managed affairs in the German territory badly. I will ensure the dispatch for his recall is issued immediately."

"Make it so, Sejanus. Oh, and recall the quaestor, whoever that is, as well. No doubt he was part of this scheme. Now, I must meet with my advisors to decide what to do next. The tribune states that the Frisii were most likely forced into rebellion by the tax burden. Now how am I to deal with them? Do I accept this defeat or engage in a campaign of retribution against the Frisii to make an example of them?"

MANY WEEKS LATER

G overnor Gallus, now ex-governor Gallus, lay curled in a fetal position on the marble-tiled floor of his magnificent bath in his mansion in Rome. He groaned in pain, staring at the puddle of blood pooling on the floor, and gaped in horror at the sword protruding halfway into his torso. He had attempted to drive the sword through himself for a quick death but had lacked the fortitude to do so. He'd only got it halfway through. Now, it was extremely painful even to touch the hilt of the sword. He could not bring himself to finish the deed.

How had he come to this end? All his scheming and this was to be his reward? He had been given the choice of being condemned to death after a trial in the senate and or an honorable suicide. Why had that poltroon Sejanus abandoned him and not afforded him protection from the Emperor's wrath? And then there was that devious Tribune Valerius Maximus. Yes, he had to admit, he underestimated the strength and guile of the man. Gallus had always bested his rivals, but it had not been the case this time. Fury overcame his pain for a few moments, but then, his agony returned. He coughed gouts of blood, which spilled down his chin and mingled with the growing puddle of crimson. It took all night for Julius Frontinius Gallus to die.

* * *

Valerius and Hereca walked hand-in-hand toward their home in Oppidum Ubiorum. The sun shone brightly, and the winter wind blew chilly in the mid-afternoon. Word had reached the group in hiding that Governor Gallus had been recalled to Rome many weeks ago. They had crossed over the river, sailed to Noviomagus, and met with Marcus Flavius, the acting commander of the Fifth. He had assured them that all was well and that he had not received any dispatches from Rome indicating a retaliatory campaign against the Frisii. Relieved, the group had sailed upriver to Oppidum Ubiorum, letting Valerius's parents know by way of a messenger that they were on their way home.

Marcellus had just departed for his house, to reunite with his family. Ox and Rufus were off seeking rooms in the town. "I promised Julia that all of us, including the children, would visit them next spring. Julia and I have a lot in common. She and I became very close while you were away on the campaign against the Frisii. I assume you are okay with traveling to Gaul?"

"Yes, Hereca, that would be fine. I have not spent much time in Gaul, but I find it to be a pleasant place."

Hereca beamed. "Oh, I'm so looking forward to that. As for now, I can't wait to see our children again. I've missed them so much. It's been a long time."

They were almost there. From a distance, he could see the red-tiled roof of their home gleaming in the sun. It had been months since they had departed their home for Noviomagus and then into the land of the Frisii. A group of familiar faces came into view near the house. Recognizing their parents, shouts of joy punctuated the air as the four children bounded toward them. Valerius and Hereca dropped their satchels and weapons and ran toward them. There was much laughter and hugging as the family embraced once again.

Looking up from his children, Valerius saw his parents walking toward them, beaming. The two elderly parents joined the fray, welcoming their son and daughter-in-law home once again.

Eventually, everyone entered the house amid the constant chatter. The children demanded to know what they were going to do tomorrow now that everyone was home. A huge celebratory meal was prepared by the servants. The entire household feasted and laughed late into the evening. There was roasted boar, boiled greens, fresh river fish, onions, figs, olives, and wine. The children boasted of their adventures at the Roman fort. Valerius's parents grinned, thankful that their son and daughter-in-law were home again. As usual, Valerius's father, Sentius, consumed too much wine, and his wife, Vispania, was miffed at the display of drunkenness. Hereca and Valerius were elated to be back with their family once again, their mission completed. Finally, the children were put to bed late in the night and his parents departed for their own home.

"Are you coming to bed, my husband?" Hereca asked. "It's been a long time since we've been in our own bed. I am so glad to be home."

"Me too," he replied. "Just let me put my weapons and armor away. I don't want to leave them sitting in a pile in the middle of the house."

"Certainly, but hurry up," she replied. She gave him a suggestive wink to hurry him on.

Valerius wearily gathered up his weapons and armor and took them to his storage closet. Opening the door, he carefully hung his armor, sword, dagger, and bow on the appropriate hooks. Satisfied that everything was in order, he was about to close the door when he paused and reflected. He was back to being a trader and merchant again. He definitely preferred that way of life. Pondering his fate, he realized that this was the end of his time in the legions. He was certain that he would no longer need to use his weapons again. And for that, he was grateful. He shut the closet door softly and turned to his bedroom. Then again, perhaps the Goddess Fortuna had other plans.

THE END

AUTHOR'S NOTES

*R*evolt Against Rome—and its central characters, Valerius and Marcellus—is a work of fiction. Nevertheless, as in my previous novels, *Legions of the Forest, Return of the Eagles,* and *A Barbarian in Rome's Legions,* the stories are set amidst historical events of Roman antiquity. This work features the Frisian revolt against Rome in 28 AD.

I have included several historical figures in this novel, including Tiberius Caesar, the Roman Emperor; Lucius Aelius Sejanus, the ambitious Praetorian Prefect; and Agrippina, the widow of the late Germanicus Caesar. I have portrayed Prefect Sejanus as the nefarious and ruthless individual he was. Historians have noted his infamous and bloody reign of terror under Tiberius. He had fallen short of his ultimate ambition of seizing the throne and subsequently, he and his family were brutally executed.

The Frisii occupied parts of the countries of Belgium, Netherlands, and perhaps Germany. The Romans did not distinguish between the various tribes of northern Europe and referred to all of them as Germans. From a historical perspective, little has been written about the Frisian revolt. What is known is that the Fifth Legion successfully relieved a siege of the town of Flevum. Thereafter, they invaded the land of the Frisii and were savagely repulsed with significant losses in the Battle of the Baduhenna Wood.

The cause of the Frisian revolt was an excessive tax burden imposed on the German tribe by the Governor. There are mixed opinions from historians concerning the Roman governance of their provinces. In some cases, prosperity reigned, and in others, the locals revolted against the harsh Roman rule. The latter was the case with the Frisians.

It is interesting to note that Tiberius did not conduct a reprisal campaign against the Frisii and preferred to retain the status quo. This was unusual for Rome, which was famous for its fierce retribution against those who dared challenge its imperial authority. Why didn't they retaliate? Perhaps the Emperor knew the mismanagement by his governor was to blame or that the cost of a military campaign against the Frisii was not worth the benefits of bringing the rebellious Germans back under the heel of Rome.

At the time of the Frisian revolt, Rome had established a series of forts along the Rhine to secure their territory and protect the province of Gaul from Germanic invasions from across the Rhine. The forts mentioned in my work, Oppidum Ubiorum, Vetera, Noviomagus, Moguntiacum, and Valkenberg, were all Roman fortresses along the Rhine with legionary forces manning the walls. These fortresses all gradually transformed into major modern cities.

I have attempted to describe the functionality and defensive features of the Roman fortress at Flevum. The citadels were rectangular but differed in size. There were four gates, one on each side of the rectangle, with the main gate featuring wooden towers. The defenses included ditches and walls, of which some were made of earth and some of timber.

The Roman artillery pieces I have described in my work were fearsome weapons that must have struck fear in any attackers foolish enough to assault a Roman fortress. The range of these bolt throwers was estimated to be about four hundred yards. Latin authors often use the term *tormenta* (torsion engines) for artillery. Bolt throwers are often assigned the term *catapultae* and the smaller versions are referred to as *scorpios.*

The organization of the Fifth Legion was typical of that period. Each legion had ten cohorts, which, in turn, comprised six centuries with eighty men each. Each cohort numbered 480 men, and thus, the ten cohorts entailed 4,800 men. Every century was led by an officer known as a centurion. The legion was directed by a legate with the assistance of tribunes. Each legion had an attached ala (wing) of cavalry, which was further subdivided into ten turmae of thirty men each.

I noted that the first cohort of the legion was typically the leader when going into battle and for good reason. The first had the best men—the true badasses of the legion. They were the tip of the spear.

Mark Richards

ABOUT THE AUTHOR

Mark L. Richards is a graduate of Pennsylvania Military College (now Widener University) and served in the US Army as an infantry officer. He worked for over forty years in the healthcare industry. A CPA, he was employed as a chief financial officer of a large academic health center. Now retired, Richards resides in West Chester, Pennsylvania. He is married with two daughters and five grandchildren.

A lifelong historian of Roman antiquity, Richards was inspired by his favorite subject to publish in 2014 his debut novel, *Legions of the Forest*, and then its sequel, *Return of the Eagles*. The third book in the series is *Revolt Against Rome*. In addition, he published a novel in 2018 entitled *A Barbarian in Rome's Legions*, which is not part of the series. He can be contacted at legions9ad@aol.com

Printed in Great Britain
by Amazon